*From her deathbed, Sebastian's mother
had promised him . . .*

"You'll never have any trouble with women.
You're just the kind of man they will lose their
hearts over. You're big and rugged, but there's
a tenderness about you. Women will do almost
anything for a man who is gentle with them."

*And then he met the woman
who would become his wife. . . .*

Emily McKnight had an almost mystical beauty.
She was chastity personified. On the spring morning Emily stood in the vestibule of her grandfather's house and regarded Sebastian with large
dark eyes, he was immediately reminded of a
creature of the forest poised for instant flight. . . .

Sebastian stared, unblinking, then pulled his cap
from his unruly black mane of hair. . . .

And then he met the other woman. . . .

Somewhere in the Whirlwind

AMANDA YORK

PUBLISHED BY POCKET BOOKS NEW YORK

Another *Original* publication of POCKET BOOKS

POCKET BOOKS, a Simon & Schuster division of
GULF & WESTERN CORPORATION
1230 Avenue of the Americas, New York, N.Y. 10020

ISBN: 0-671-82606-9

First Pocket Books printing March, 1980

10 9 8 7 6 5 4 3 2 1

POCKET and colophon are trademarks of Simon & Schuster.

Printed in the U.S.A.

BOOK I

South Seas—

1829

--✠{ CHAPTER 1 }✠--

The captain's wife awoke to the sound of an agonized shriek, echoing through the timbers of the ship and across the windless sea. Stumbling from her bunk, she collided with her young son as a second scream died abruptly. Muffled shouts and the sound of feet scurrying across the deck told her that her worst fears for that doomed voyage were about to be realized.

"Under the bunk," she ordered. "Don't come out until I return." In the darkness she was fumbling in her husband's sea chest, searching for his pistol.

Since sailing from Manila, Louisa Balmain had warned her husband that the three brawny islanders meant trouble. The three believed the ship was bound for their own Pacific island, and as the days passed, the wild light in their leader's eyes told of impending mutiny. On a previous occasion the islanders had rampaged through the ship, swinging their sharp-bladed *bolos,* before being overpowered. The harsh punishment meted out had done nothing to dim the light of rebellion in those frantic eyes.

Outside her cabin door she came face to face with the ship's cook, shaking in his nightshirt. "They got the skipper, and both mates and the wheelsman. And I think three others," he said through chattering teeth.

"Dead?" she asked. There was no tremor in her voice, and the darkness hid the whiteness of her knuckles as she gripped the cabin door.

"The skipper was still alive."

"Muster the rest of the crew. Here is the key to the gun chest. Arm yourselves and overpower the mutineers. I'll go to the captain."

3

Captain Jonathan Balmain lay in a pool of blood, trying to reach the wheel. His wife thrust the pistol into his hand and tore her nightgown to bind up his wounds. There was no need for him to tell her the gravity of the situation. The ship lay aback to her canvas, six hundred miles from the nearest land, with no one at the helm.

"Get down, Mrs. Balmain," the captain said weakly. "Here they come again."

The crazed islander was rushing toward him, raised *bolo* glinting in the moonlight, when the captain steadied himself, took careful aim, and fired. The man pitched forward, rose to his knees, and tried to fling the knife. He was only a few feet away and for a second Louisa looked into the face of death and knew complete helplessness for the first time in her life. Then the knife slipped from the upraised hand. The man rolled over, his eyes staring unseeingly at the black canopy of the sky.

"The other two?" the captain asked, slumping backward into his wife's arms. "Where are they?"

Louisa pried the pistol from his rigid fingers. "I'll reload. Save your strength. I gave the gun chest key to a sailor. The rest of the crew will be looking for them by now." There was no need for her wounded husband to know that the key and the order had been given to the shaking old sea cook, who may have decided to let someone else deal with the mutineers while he hid himself.

"Sebastian . . ." Jonathan Balmain groaned with the effort to remain conscious. He peered through a deepening fog of oblivion about the ominously silent and deserted deck.

"The boy is safe," Louisa whispered, afraid the sound of their voices would bring the other two islanders out of hiding. She pressed the pistol back into her husband's hands.

"Old for his years . . . wise in the ways of the sea," Jonathan mumbled. "Time to get him aloft . . . big for his age. Strong as most men. Bit clumsy, yet . . . didn't want him on the yards until he learns . . . until—"

4

Above his head, Louisa closed her eyes in silent prayer. *Whatever else happens, grant that our son will survive. The sea has taken too many of our fathers and sons.*

A second later, when the shouts again shattered the stillness of the night, Louisa's prayer became a vow. *If I live, I'll find a way to get my son ashore and keep him there. I swear it.*

Minutes later two surviving sailors dragged a second islander, kicking and yelling, from the forecastle.

"The other one went below!" the sailor shouted. "He pried open the fore hatch and went down into the hold. He was wounded, sir."

"Mrs. Balmain . . . we have a cargo of very dry jute down there," the captain said. He had barely uttered the words when the orange flame leaped skyward, lighting up the bloodstained deck.

"Get Sebastian. I'll muster what's left of the crew and launch the lifeboat." The captain struggled to his feet, clutching his side. Louisa's nightgown bandage darkened rapidly. "Bring my sextant. The charts, too, if you can."

Smoke was already pouring into the cabin and Sebastian was pulling on his heaviest jersey when she returned.

"See if you can find your father's navigation tables and his charts," she said calmly. "We must abandon ship. I'll get the sextant and chronometer. We must hurry."

"Aye, Mother." Sebastian's voice was as calm as hers. "You'd best take your warm shawl," he added. She felt the soft wool slipped about her shoulders, along with a tentative pat of encouragement.

The rigging was already ablaze when they took their places in the lifeboat, Louisa helping her husband and Sebastian carrying the means of their survival. As the lifeboat was lowered, the topmasts crashed to the fiery deck and the sailors pulled hard over the darkly heaving sea to clear the flaming debris.

At the first light of dawn, Louisa began to stitch blankets together to make a sail. She avoided thinking

5

about what would happen to the few survivors if her husband died from his wounds. She had been sailing with him since Sebastian was five years old, nearly six years now. Louisa had listened when her husband gave her son navigation lessons, but in the dank early morning in their small boat, she knew that even an experienced navigator would have great difficulty taking a small boat six hundred miles across the unpredictable south Atlantic. The rest of the survivors were common seamen, with no knowledge of navigation. Half of them had been wounded when the three islanders ran amok with their knives.

Captain Balmain struggled back to consciousness long enough to plot a course for St. Helena, the only possible landfall. He wasted precious energy wondering how the islanders had retrieved the confiscated *bolos,* then lapsed into a coma.

There was a moment of panic among the surviving sailors when the skipper died late the following day, but Louisa quickly reassured them. "My husband taught my son and myself how to navigate. We have all of his charts and instruments." Her piercingly blue eyes sent a silent message to Sebastian, who had been composed and quiet since his father's body was slipped over the side. Sebastian stared at the gray surface of the sea that now entombed his father. He had seen death before in his short life, many times, but never with this accompanying pain and aching sense of loss. Despite his youth, he realized that what he was feeling must be even worse for his mother. Neither of them could openly grieve at this moment. The climate of panic gripping the survivors must be dealt with first.

"My mother is skipper now," he said, turning fearless blue eyes in her direction. "She'll tell you what to do and you'd all better listen." Squaring his shoulders and tilting his chin, he appeared oblivious to the superior strength of the full-grown men being so boldly put in their places by a boy not yet into his twelfth year.

He was tall and sturdy, his craggy features echoing rugged New England seagoing forebears. The rough-hewn face was animated by his mother's bright blue eyes and was crowned by a bristling mane of jet-black hair, giving an effect of vitality and movement, even in repose.

The sailors in the boat were well aware of their slim chance of survival. They were glad to let the calm-eyed skipper's wife and strapping young son make their decisions. The woman had an air of quiet confidence, while the boy had been the skipper's constant shadow. The lad must have learned something of navigation.

"Don't worry, Mother," Sebastian whispered, putting a well-developed arm about her shoulders. "I'll take care of you."

Louisa shrugged free of his embrace and turned her face to the wind. Under her breath she said, "We must not let them panic." Her heart was filled with pride in her son but she would never have considered expressing that pride to Sebastian. "Even if there is no work for them, we must make work to keep them busy."

Sebastian nodded. He sniffed at the air, scanned the sky, and noted the gentle swells rolling toward the boat. "Weather's going to be on our side," he whispered back.

The gestures were his father's. For a moment Louisa wished she could go back five years and send Sebastian to school ashore. Was it already too late to cleanse the sea fever from his blood? she wondered. But she knew she would not have been able to leave her only son ashore, any more than she could allow her husband to sail away without her. They were a family, and families should be together.

"Sebastian, now that we're alone in the world, we must think about living ashore. It's not too late to send you to school. You must make something of yourself."

"School!" Sebastian repeated, horrified. "I've had lessons from you and father every day of my life."

"There's much more to be learned than we've taught you. Your world has been the sea and ships. A way of life exists beyond the wharves and waterfronts of foreign ports that you know nothing about. Sebastian, you're almost grown and I must tell you the truth. We haven't any money. There may be something due your

7

father from this last voyage, but we never managed to put anything away. And they canceled his insurance years ago, after he went aground in the Caribbean. We'll talk about it later. First you'd better get the men to hoist the sail I've made and see that we're on course."

The sail she had stitched was hoisted and the able-bodied men were ordered to help the wounded, bail any water that was shipped, and take turns catching fish with the limited number of hooks aboard. Louisa saw to it that everyone was kept busy. Her voice never rose above its normal tone, but she never had to issue an order twice.

Sebastian had learned more about navigation than she realized and kept them steadfastly on course. They were fortunate; a steady wind kept them moving with little need to paddle, and there were no heavy seas. Two men died of their wounds, but the rest were in good spirits when the boat entered Jamestown harbor in St. Helena just before dusk in the final hours of the year of 1829.

Louisa Balmain was a no-nonsense New Englander who had let her heart rule her head only once. She had fallen under the spell of the handsome but unlucky Captain Jonathan Balmain.

She herself had come from a family of seafaring men, mostly whalers, and a line of women who knew with chilling certainty that the sea would claim at least half of their sons before they were far into manhood. They would be reported missing from a deepwater ship, or lose their lives while hauling lobster pots in the vicious riptides of the bay. Sometimes a schooner simply sailed away and disappeared forever. Louisa had lost her father and two brothers in a violent storm just off their own treacherous coast.

Jonathan Balmain, however, managed to stay alive while losing crews and ships to natural and man-made disasters with distressing regularity. He had run aground more ships, suffered more disabling epidemics among his crews, and sustained more crippling damage in storms, yet lived to tell the tale, more than any owner had a right to expect.

Being a proud and stubborn man, Jonathan refused to sail in any lesser capacity than master, and the ships he commanded grew steadily smaller and more decrepit as time went by. He had been fortunate that a packet owned by a Britisher put into Boston from Liverpool with a dying captain aboard. Since a speedy return was imperative, as the owner was also aboard, Jonathan had been signed on as replacement with little investigation. On the return voyage the ship was damaged by an iceberg and the Balmain hex came to light. The owner, Job McKnight, took Jonathan off the packet and gave him a small schooner that had already been written off as past its prime.

Matters improved somewhat when Louisa insisted that she and their only son would in the future sail with him. During that five-year period it had seemed that the Balmain hex had at last been overcome.

Louisa shed her tears for her dead husband in private and announced that they would not be returning to New England. A sympathetic captain had agreed to transport them to Liverpool, where the owner of the lost schooner lived.

Sebastian regarded his mother quizzically. "There was no money for us, was there? So you're going to Mr. McKnight and tell him he owes father something, for giving up his life."

Louisa looked at her son sharply. "You remember Mr. McKnight? You were only five years old when he came to see your father."

"I remember. White hair and a white beard. Cold eyes. Don't go to him, Mother. I'll work and support us."

Louisa's lips compressed into a tight line. "Your father . . . and grandfather and two of your uncles, and more of your ancestors than I care to think about . . . gave their lives to the sea. I've a different future in mind for you. And a plan to achieve it. Now we'll say no more about it."

The owner of her husband's ship was a dour old

9

man who had been widowed for nearly twenty years. There were only two concerns in his life: the speed of his ships, and the chastity of his only relative, a fragile granddaughter named Emily. Louisa had listened when Job McKnight offered her husband command of one of his ships. Faster ways to transport emigrants to the New World; better ways of rigging ships to carry cargoes; speed. Full sail at night, fast turn-around in port. Nothing else was important to Job McKnight. He did not let personal relationships interfere with his business, except to the extent of isolating his granddaughter from seagoing scum.

Louisa knew only that McKnight drove his crews hard, his ships were poorly provisioned and allowed to weather into dangerous states of disrepair, and he placed the value of his cargoes above the lives of seamen. He had a reputation as a miser who would undoubtedly leave behind vast wealth when he died, although his crews felt perhaps he might find a way to take it with him to hell.

Knowing this about Job McKnight did not deter Louisa. She sailed to Liverpool determined to marry him.

The three-story brick house in Princes Park on the outskirts of Liverpool presented an austere facade to the street, softened only by neatly trimmed privet hedges. Six immaculately scrubbed and whitewashed steps led to the front door whose leaded-glass panes gave a muted glimpse of the vestibule beyond.

Louisa and Sebastian stood in the vestibule, dripping rainwater onto a coconut-fiber mat. Louisa announced quietly that although she realized her late husband had lost his ship, she hoped there was some money due him. If not, perhaps Mr. McKnight could help her find work. She added, without visible emotion, that she and her son were destitute.

"Providence is on your side, Mrs. Balmain," Job McKnight said in his rasping voice, shrewd pale eyes taking in every detail of her bearing and handsome, rather than pretty, features. She was tall and slender, and while she did not look particularly strong, considering her years at sea, there was an air of dignity, an enduring charm of demeanor and the indelible stamp of good breeding about her. "My housekeeper died last month," he went on. "I've not yet replaced her. The woman I hire must be a suitable companion to my granddaughter, in addition to performing the other household duties. You can have the position."

Louisa's joy and relief flooded her eyes. A smile of gratitude lit up her face. Sebastian was smiling, too, and Job McKnight stroked his silky white beard and looked at them calculatingly. He had once been a handsome man, with even features and an imposing way of carrying himself, head held proudly, shoulders squared; but he had grown gaunt with age. "Your son cannot live here. I have a frail granddaughter who wouldn't be able to tolerate a rambunctious boy in the house."

The smiles faded. Like a light going out, Job thought, noting how both sets of features had been transformed by the radiance of those smiles. Louisa said, "Then I'll find a place for my son to stay."

"He can sail as cabin boy on one of my packets, if you wish. Might as well start earning his keep."

"But he's only eleven." A cold hand had closed over Louisa's heart.

"He's been at sea with you and the late captain."

"I'll go, Mother," Sebastian said. "I'd rather be at sea than live in this place. And I don't want anyone's charity."

"The boy has an impudent tongue," McKnight observed, "but a wise philosophy. It's time he was free of your apron strings, marm."

"But I could find a room for him. Send him to school . . ." Louisa began.

Job McKnight sighed impatiently. "And you could visit each other, I presume? No, madam. The offer of the position is for you and you alone. If you are not interested, there is always the workhouse. I'm offering you a home and the chance to work for your living only because your husband was one of my skippers. We won't mention all of the disasters he brought about —or the loss of the last ship due to his bungling.

11

Since it cost him his life, we'll say no more about it. I'll merely remind you that the streets of Liverpool are swarming with beggars and urchins who would kill for the opportunity I'm offering you."

Sebastian flushed angrily at the old man's harsh words about his dead father, but before he could speak his mother's hand was on his arm, restraining him. Job McKnight turned and went through the vestibule door, down a long hall, calling over his shoulder, "Good day to you if you don't want the position. If you do, come in." He walked with the aid of a walking stick but still managed to move with military precision.

"Sebastian," Louisa whispered, "I haven't enough money to take us back home. And he's right about our chances for other work. It's this or the workhouse. We'll have to accept his conditions for now, but I promise you I'll get you ashore as soon as I can."

"It's all right, Mother. I meant it about going to sea. I want to be master of my own ship one day, like my father."

Louisa gave him a stricken glance before proceeding along the hall. Sebastian followed her into a damp and gloomy parlor. Faded wallpaper bulged away from the wall behind an aspidistra plant standing morosely on a dark pedestal. Gray bloom covered the surface of a rosewood upright piano. A driving rain rattled against the windows and the small coal fire in the grate hissed as the raindrops came down the chimney.

"You may go to the kitchen and make a pot of tea," McKnight said. "Then I'll take your son down to the landing stage and put him aboard the *Merry Widow*." He seemed unaware of the irony.

"So soon?" Louisa asked faintly.

"Aye. She sails with the afternoon tide."

Sebastian met Emily McKnight briefly before departing from the austere hospitality of her grandfather. She came hesitantly down the staircase as Sebastian was being ushered through the door into the vestibule. She was a tiny, fragile child with enormous dark eyes and a mass of burnished dark hair hanging in two plaits that pulled her heart-shaped face downward with its sheer weight.

McKnight glanced at his granddaughter, then barked at Sebastian, "Shut that door! Do you want to give her pneumonia with the draft?"

Startled, Sebastian slammed the door with unnecessary force. McKnight's cold gray eyes flickered over him in reprimand. Looking back at Emily, McKnight said, "This is Mrs. Balmain, Emily. She's going to take care of you." He did not introduce Sebastian.

The boy soon found himself squeezed into a small carriage, rattling down to the rain-drenched waterfront. He watched the dismal streets slip by and hoped the packet would be sailing for an American port . . . Boston, New York . . . perhaps Philadelphia . . . it didn't matter. It was better than staying with this bad-tempered old man. Sebastian wished his mother had not chosen to come here, but he knew better than to question her.

His chest rose in several deep breaths. He was impatient. Impatient to be back at sea and headed for America. Impatient to be grown up and in charge of his own destiny. Above all, he was impatient to be rich so that his mother would not have to work for a surly old man and a little girl who looked as though she were frightened of her own shadow.

The taciturn McKnight did not tell Sebastian he was to sail on the largest ship he owned, a new five-hundred-tonner that was to be the first of the "liners." The days when packets waited to acquire cargo and a quota of passengers before they sailed were coming to an end. The demand for ships that departed on a specified date were at hand, and the *Merry Widow* would sail this day or McKnight would personally take her out of the Mersey.

She was a trim-looking, well-sparred craft. About one hundred feet from knightsheads to taffrail, Sebastian guessed, as they stepped out into the drenching rain and biting-cold salt air stinging their cheeks.

The rain stopped just before the tide turned, and

Sebastian, unceremoniously dumped on deck and left to his own devices, watched the last of the passengers stumble aboard. Sailors jumped to obey the mates' orders. Topsails were mastheaded, lines hauled in, and the *Merry Widow* slid out into the river to the chorus of cheers from passengers and spectators. Under snowy-white sail, new paint sparkling in the sunlight that pierced the cloud cover, the *Merry Widow* drove down the river. Sebastian's bright blue eyes took in every detail of the ship and every action of the seamen.

"It's not a bad life," he lied to his mother when he returned to Liverpool. "I mostly take care of the passengers and help in the galley. Eight cabins there are, and the rest in steerage 'tween decks. They all get seasick, though, no matter where they bunk."

They were sitting in the bare kitchen of the Mc-Knight house and Louisa was peeling potatoes into an iron pan atop a scrubbed wood table. Sebastian stood at the fireplace, warming his hands and sipping from a mug of hot cocoa. "Why do you have to do that kind of work?" Sebastian asked, nodding toward the potatoes.

"There are no servants. Just various cleaning women who don't live in, but come on a regular schedule. Sebastian, I'm glad to see you, but you must go back to your ship before Mr. McKnight comes home."

"But—can't I stay here while we're in port?"

The kitchen door moved slightly and they stared at it, feeling the unseen presence. A moment passed and, unable to stand the tension, Sebastian sprang forward and jerked the door wide open. Little Emily of the huge dark eyes and too-heavy hair cowered back into the hall as she looked up at the muscular boy who appeared ready to pounce on her. Her hand flew to her mouth in fright.

"What are you doing? Eavesdropping?" Sebastian demanded.

Louisa hurried to Emily's side, taking her hand and glaring at Sebastian. "It's all right, Emily. It's just my son come to visit me."

The child covered her face with her hands and began to cry soundlessly.

"What's she crying for?" Sebastian asked in amazement. "I didn't touch her."

"Hush, dear. Don't cry, please," Louisa implored, gently stroking Emily's hair.

Sebastian stared. He had never seen his mother make such an affectionate gesture, nor speak so humbly. She seemed so much older since his father died. All of the vitality seemed drained from her. Shoulders drooping wearily, she wore a bitter expression that had not been there before. It was not difficult for Sebastian to guess the reason. His father died horribly aboard a ship owned by her employer. Despite the austerity of the house, Job McKnight was a wealthy man. He grew rich on the sweat and blood of skippers and crews and never ventured into the treacherous embrace of the sea to earn the riches.

Frightened dark eyes, swimming with tears, appeared over the pale fingers. "I'm s-sorry," Emily gulped in a tiny voice. "He is so big . . . and fearsome looking . . . he startled me." She bit her lip. "Oh . . . I'm so sorry. I didn't mean to be rude. I didn't mean fearsome. I meant—strong—" The tears drowned out the rest of her words.

Sebastian looked at Emily and felt his anger subside. Not really understanding why he no longer resented the hold she evidently had over his mother, nor recognizing his own sudden protectiveness toward the child who had been the cause of their separation, he glared speechlessly. At the back of his mind was the thought that he was looking at a tiny fledgling angel, no more real or to be chastized than the pale cherubs that clung to the embossed ceiling in McKnight's damp parlor.

"You shouldn't have crept up on us like that," Sebastian said. "But I didn't mean to startle you, either."

The scene seemed to have frozen into a tableau: Emily still crying and Louisa trying to comfort her, Sebastian poised ready to spring, when the vestibule door opened and Job McKnight entered the hall. His bushy white eyebrows descended over pale eyes like a blizzard over an Arctic sea. "What is this?"

Louisa straightened up abruptly. "Emily was just startled, that's all, Mr. McKnight."

"Come here, child," McKnight said.

Emily tried to hide her face in Louisa's apron, but McKnight snapped, "Emily!" The child hesitated, then approached her grandfather with reluctant steps. He picked her up and her thin body was rigid in his arms. Over her polished hair he glared at Sebastian. "Rushed to your ma's apron strings the minute your ship docked, like a babe in arms, d'ye? Did he frighten you, princess?"

"I didn't do anything to her," Sebastian said indignantly. "She was in the hall and I opened the door suddenly, that's all."

"That's true, Mr. McKnight," Louisa said. "Emily, tell your grandfather what happened, please."

Emily was no longer crying. Her eyes were wide with fear as she stared at her grandfather. Sebastian could see that her frail body was shaking within her grandfather's arms and she made no move to put her own arms about his neck, nor bury her face against him in the manner she had clung to Louisa. Emily moved her lips, but no sound came from them.

McKnight shriveled Sebastian with his stare. "Get out of my house and stay out. And don't come running here every time you're in port." He carried Emily up the stairs.

Louisa put up a restraining hand when Sebastian stepped forward to argue. "Do as he says. Just for a little while longer. I'll know when your ship docks, and I'll come to the Pier Head to see you."

"Why do you let him treat us like this? Why do you stay with him?" Sebastian asked angrily.

Louisa's determined eyes locked with a gaze that matched her own. "Because your father lies in a cold, wet grave, and one day you are going to own all of the McKnight ships. It's the only fitting epitaph I can think of to give him."

CHAPTER 2

Louisa was always waiting at the Pier Head when Sebastian's ship docked, and a year after their first meeting with Job McKnight, she announced she had been quietly married to her employer. She did not say how or why the marriage had come about.

Sebastian was stunned. "Married him? You *married* him?" He thought of his father's laughing blue eyes and how fondly they had caressed his mother with every passing glance. Sebastian had never thought of them as separate entities while his father lived. One had always been an extension of the other.

"I knew how you would feel, so I spared you the ceremony," Louisa said, not meeting Sebastian's eyes. "We were married in a registry office while you were at sea." There was much about her marriage her son must never know.

A week before they took out the license, Job had come downstairs after his customary bedtime hour with Emily, and Louisa had pointed out that a girlchild should more properly be put to bed by a woman.

Job's white eyebrows rose obliquely. "One thing I admire about you New Englanders, marm, is your straightforwardness. Kindly, therefore, say exactly what you mean."

"There is gossip about you and your granddaughter. More than once the local shopkeepers have asked me embarrassing questions and thrown out vulgar hints. It seems some of your cleaning women have carried tales around town."

Job's expression was carefully guarded as he asked, "Of what nature?"

17

"An unnatural attachment." Louisa's gaze was unwavering, but a pulse beat rapidly in her temples and her cheeks were tinged with pink. "Your last housekeeper told everyone she was never allowed to put Emily to bed."

"The woman was an old witch who frightened Emily with stories of bogeymen and evil spirits," Job growled, but he was no longer meeting Louisa's gaze.

"I'm asked if *I* ever put the child to bed," Louisa added.

Job turned to the fireplace, shoveling coal from the copper scuttle and rearranging the embers with a brass poker. "What must I do to put paid to this vicious gossip?" he asked gruffly.

Louisa hesitated for a moment, then replied, "You could marry me."

The marriage made little difference to Sebastian's status. He was still not welcome in his stepfather's house and given no special privileges at sea. The eastward voyage took about twenty-four days, and westward usually at least forty days, so with the layovers in port, several months elapsed between visits. McKnight was obsessed with speed. He wanted his packets to beat the record held by the Black Ball Line from Liverpool to New York.

When his vessels were in port he would storm up and down the decks, berating the masters for their tardiness, their lack of competitive spirit, and, above all, the slack hand with which they handled their crews. This, he felt, had to be the only reason McKnight liners could not match the Black Ball's Atlantic crossings.

"I want every man aloft. Cooks, cabin boys, carpenters, sail-makers. The only dead weight you carry will be the passengers. Do you understand?" he bellowed, poking the air with his walking stick to punctuate his words. "From now on I'll choose your first officers myself."

The next voyage brought the first of a series of brutal first officers of McKnight's choosing. The mate's words

18

to the crew were brief. "Every man-jack of you relieve the watch at the capstan in five minutes. Any man not ready when called will carry my mark on him for the rest of the voyage. Now masthead the topsail yards and be damned to you."

"Aye, aye, sir," the crew responded.

"Starboard watch aft—port watch forward. Where are you going?" The last was addressed to Sebastian.

"Below, sir. I'm a cabin boy."

"There's no boys aboard this ship. Aloft."

Sebastian hesitated, unsure how to proceed. The first mate's hand came crashing into his cheek, sending him sprawling on the deck. "Jump to it, boy. Or you'll get a taste of the cat."

Sebastian's father had never allowed him to climb aloft. He was the skipper's son and destined to be a skipper himself. There was no need for him to learn how to reef and furl sail in practice, his father had said. The theory of it would suffice. Sebastian jumped to his feet and started toward the shrouds, his cheek stinging from the blow and his mind outraged by the unnecessary brutality.

The sun sparkled on the benign surface of the sea and a gentle breeze played with the canvas overhead. All around him the crewmen made ready to set sail, keeping one wary eye on the first mate and the other on their task.

Sebastian felt no fear, but he felt an obstinate reluctance to confess to the new first officer that he had no idea of what was expected of him.

He was about to swing up onto the shrouds when a bony-fingered hand closed about his arm. Turning, Sebastian looked into a lively pair of light brown eyes and a reassuringly crooked grin.

"If it's your first time up, lad, the chanteyman will tell you what to do. Me name's O'Toole, and when I sing me chanteys, the work goes easier."

Despite Sebastian's youth, he was taller than the slightly built chanteyman. O'Toole had carrot-colored hair and a face that appeared to have been pounded out of soft clay and then hardened in the wind.

O'Toole swung up into the rigging and motioned for Sebastian to follow. Sebastian watched, fascinated, as the sinews of the man's arms rippled like steel snakes. For all O'Toole's small stature, Sebastian could see he possessed the strength of a coiled spring.

The main royal was 130 feet above the swaying deck, but it was the usual practice to send inexperienced boys to the top of the mainmast to accustom them to the rolling of the ship and movement of the yards. Sebastian was fortunate that his first climb into the frightening world of snapping canvas and slippery yardarms was completed in calm seas with only a slight breeze. His hands cracked and bled as he wrestled with the damp canvas.

Sebastian cursed his own clumsiness as he clung with one hand to the only solid object in a world of flailing canvas and writhing rope. O'Toole grinned and watched.

"Irish" O'Toole, the wiry chanteyman, had a voice like the pealing bells of a cathedral. He had sailed on American ships and sometimes sang American chanteys. Sebastian forgot his precarious perch and recalled voyages on his father's ship when the haunting strains of "Shenandoah" filled the air.

A good chanteyman was an asset, as the singing produced teamwork and coordination. He would burst forth with "Blow the man down" to the answering chorus of the crew during the long task of mastheading the topsail yard, or make up verses to "Whiskey, Johnny." Unobtrusively, he took Sebastian under his wing.

Sebastian learned that for all his diminutive size, Irish O'Toole enjoyed a good brawl ashore, and his face was more the result of barroom fights than a trick of nature.

Two trips later, McKnight found his wife waiting for Sebastian at the Pier Head. He was promptly transferred to a small schooner picking up tramp cargoes in the southern hemisphere, and it was six years before he saw his mother again.

Irish O'Toole, luckily, was aboard the same ship.

Sometimes he took Sebastian ashore with him, although invariably he was abandoned when Irish either became belligerently drunk or enraptured of some waterfront lady of the night.

One of his lady friends cast a speculative eye over Sebastian one evening and suggested he help her take the tipsy chanteyman up to her room.

"Wouldn't want him falling down the stairs, would we?" She winked at Sebastian as Irish hiccoughed and grinned foolishly.

In her room Irish promptly collapsed onto her bed and began to snore lustily.

His lady friend moved closer to Sebastian, smiling and running her tongue over her lower lip. "My name's Gladys, and he's already paid me," she said, pressing her ample breasts against him. Her hand dropped to his blue drill trousers and she nudged him suggestively.

Sebastian felt his blood surge and he was swelling inside his bell-bottoms as her hand expertly found all of him. She knew the exact moment to stop the caresses. She stepped backward, unfastening her bodice. Her large white breasts spilled from a grimy chemise. "Come on, then," she invited softly with a little giggle. "They're for playing with."

She guided his hands to hard brown nipples and then pulled his face down to her flesh. She smelled of musk and the wet earth and the sea where it touches the land. He thought of seaweed glistening beneath the water and darting fish.

He was no longer aware of Irish, snoring contentedly on the bed, but only of the magical things she was doing to him with fingers and lips and tongue. Her skirts were gone and his manhood was between her thighs, warm and moist and ready for him.

"Go on," she urged hoarsely. "Push it in, dearie. Don't be shy."

Sebastian thrust with all his might and she sighed and wrapped her legs about him as Irish gurgled softly in his sleep beside them on the bed.

When at last they returned to Liverpool, unannounced and unexpected, Sebastian said, "To hell with McKnight. I'll go and see my mother at the house. What can he do? Keep me off his rusty old scows? I can sign on any ship I like now. I'm a sailor."

"Let's get us a room first," Irish said. They had become a pair. Not quite father and son, nor older brother and younger brother, yet more than friends. Each accepted the other exactly as he was. It seemed there had never been a time they did not either sleep in hammocks side by side, or share a seedy boarding-house room ashore.

"While ye're visiting with your mum, I'll make a couple of fast trips to Belfast or Dublin," Irish said as they walked up Paradise Street looking for lodgings. "Now, listen Ballymain, I want ye to keep your wits about you."

Whenever Irish called him "Ballymain," it meant he had better listen carefully to what was being said.

"The streets of Liverpool are crawling with crimps and sharks. Filthy scum. Flesh-peddlers living off the likes of us. Jesus, I hate them."

"I'll be careful, Irish," Sebastian promised. "And if I do get shanghaied, I'll be sure to send them after you, too." He laughed and dodged the punch Irish aimed in his direction.

"Never mind joking," Irish said darkly. "Just remember not to walk down any dark alleys by yourself. And watch what you drink and who with. You're altogether getting too cocky, boyo. Just because you're bigger than most men, you think you're safe. I keep trying to knock some sense into your thick skull, but you don't listen. You think everybody is going to fight fair, just because you do." Irish sighed deeply.

They found a boardinghouse, stowed their gear, and carefully locked the door. Irish then headed for the nearest pub, while Sebastian hired a hansom cab to take him to Princes Park.

Presenting himself at the severely unadorned brick house, Sebastian was amazed when the door was opened by an astonishingly lovely young girl. Enormous mys-

22

terious eyes regarded him shyly. A mass of soft brown hair was piled on top of her head, accentuating the beauty of her features, which seemed to glow with an inner radiance.

"Emily McKnight?" Sebastian asked in a small, awed voice.

-⊸❦ CHAPTER 3 ❧⊷-

Emily McKnight had an almost mystical beauty. Seeing her for the first time, women thought of the tragic heroines they had wept over in innocent girlhood; while men associated her ethereal presence with the madonna to be worshipped from afar, or the princess waiting for the knight's rescue. In either case, Emily was chastity personified. Yet there was a spiritual sensuality about her that some found baffling, because they were unable to define why they were mesmerized by this frail beauty.

On the spring morning Emily stood in the vestibule of her grandfather's house and regarded Sebastian with large, dark eyes, he was immediately reminded of a creature of the forest poised for instant flight. The weight of her mass of deep brown hair, as smooth and shiny as polished mahogany, caused a slight drooping of her head so that she looked up at him from beneath a fringe of silken eyelashes curling upward over languid lids.

Sebastian stared, unblinkingly, then pulled his cap from his unruly black mane of hair, conscious only of the miraculous changes that six years had wrought in McKnight's little granddaughter. "Good day to you, Miss McKnight. I am Sebastian Balmain."

Emily's dark velvet eyes disappeared under the blue-veined lids. "Yes. I remember you. Please come in." Her voice was as gentle as a summer breeze; it seemed to Sebastian that the sound of it whispered along his senses, leaving a delicate imprint, like a flower pressed within the pages of a book. He would remember her mystical eyes and her haunting voice on his next long and fearful voyage, and there would be times when the memory would be enough to temper the murderous rage he felt toward her grandfather.

On this morning, however, he followed Emily into the hall, feeling clumsy in her petite and graceful presence. He did not think about the little girl who had cried and brought down Job McKnight's wrath on his head the last time he had come to this house, so many voyages ago.

Louisa heard their voices and came from the kitchen, eyes lighting up with a mixture of joy and apprehension. Her greeting was restrained, a defensive New England greeting to hide her emotions. She wiped her hands on the voluminous white apron she wore over a dark morning dress. The apron did not conceal the thickening of her body. She moved stiffly, lethargically, and gave the impression it took every ounce of her strength and concentration to force her body to obey her numbed mind.

Sebastian gathered his mother into his arms, despite her protests, and planted a kiss on her cheek.

Louisa smiled at her son with quiet pride. "Sebastian —look at you." Almost at once a worried furrow appeared on her brow. "You shouldn't have come here. . . ."

"Oh, to hell with old Job," Sebastian said easily. "He's not dealing with a boy any longer. I'm a man now and not about to be put out of my mother's house."

"Sebastian, watch your tongue," Louisa said with a warning glance in Emily's direction.

Sebastian was immediately contrite. "I'm sorry, Miss McKnight, but your grandfather's hospitality has been grim." He grinned suddenly. "I just realized, you are my stepsister now, and I have a kiss coming."

Releasing his mother, Sebastian placed his hands about Emily's tiny waist, hoisted her up in the air, and kissed her lightly on the cheek. Emily blushed crimson and Louisa immediately began to apologize for her son. "He's too boisterous for his own good. Excuse him, Emily. His manners are the rough-hewn ways of seamen."

"Please . . ." Emily said breathlessly. "Come into the sitting room. I'll make some tea. Your mother should be resting . . . oh!" Her heavy lids descended over her eyes and she bit her lip as she realized she had unwittingly called attention to his mother's delicate condition.

Louisa was pale and thin, accentuating her obvious pregnancy. Her blue eyes lacked their former luster, and her movements were slow and clumsy. Sebastian slipped his arm about her and led her into the sitting room.

He was appalled at the ravages caused by her pregnancy. At the back of his mind hovered a slight jealousy over the thought that a woman carrying a new life within her must of necessity put that life and her own above all others. He reflected that his mother's earlier determination to find a way to keep him ashore seemed to diminish with the passage of time. She had made no protest, to Sebastian's knowledge, when he was sent to the China seas. He did not know that Job McKnight had promised Louisa that Sebastian would be brought into his shipping office, made a full partner in the McKnight Line, if and when Louisa gave birth to Job's son.

Louisa's strength had been sapped by an unbroken chain of miscarriages as she relentlessly strove to achieve her goal in spite of her distaste of her husband's lovemaking.

Above their bed was a large oil painting of Job's first wife, the lovely Emily, for whom his granddaughter had been named. Except for the difference in the style of clothing and the way the dark hair was dressed, the sadly smiling woman of the portrait might have been the present Emily. The mysterious dark eyes of Job's lost wife seemed to seek out Louisa wherever she moved. Especially when they lay together in the bed and Job's gaunt frame pressed hers to the unyielding mattress.

"There was a time . . . a few years ago when you came to see me at the Pier Head . . . that I thought perhaps—" Sebastian began as he carefully lifted his mother's feet to the footstool.

Louisa put out her hand to smooth the unruly black hair from her son's brow in an affectionate gesture that was unlike her and strangely foreboding. "I have lost several unborn children, Sebastian. But this child will come into the world strong and healthy. Now please don't embarrass me further by saying anymore about it."

Emily said, "Please excuse me. I'll go and make the tea."

They watched her move gracefully through the doorway, closing the door quietly behind her.

Louisa leaned her head against the antimacassar over the back of the chair, her eyes going thoughtfully over Sebastian, who still stared at the door through which Emily had departed.

"Where did your ship dock?" Louisa asked.

"London. I've been making my way here for the best part of three days. I've been on a schooner that never left the China seas . . . smuggling opium from India to China, then picking up cargoes of tea. And fighting off pirates both ways. I decided I'd had enough." Sebastian laughed and opened his duffel bag, spilling out an assortment of exotic souvenirs from his voyages.

Louisa blinked as scrimshaw, Oriental fans, and carved ditty boxes were dropped into her lap. One particularly delicate fan was retrieved. "This one looks like it was made for pretty little Emily." He studied his mother with a worried frown, noting the tired lines about her eyes, the limpness of formerly busy hands. "You and Emily . . . there are just the two of you and some part-time cleaning women to take care of this big house?" Without waiting for a reply he added, "That old skinflint could well afford servants. By God, I'll have a word with him. Mother, in your condition . . . and that fragile slip of a girl was never meant for heavy work."

"Job doesn't like live-in servants. He feels they spy on him. You know, he runs his shipping company almost singlehandedly. I suppose he feels I should be able to handle the house."

"You should have a woman here all the time. Mother, you don't look well. Have you seen a doctor?"

"What for? I'm just with child. Now listen to me. You can't stay here. It wouldn't be proper, with a young girl in the house. You can visit me while Mr. McKnight is at his office."

"Don't worry, I've already taken a room on Paradise Street," Sebastian said. "I'll share it with Irish O'Toole between his trips to Ireland."

Louisa's eyes drifted in the direction of the piano, standing against the damp wall and fighting its silent battle against the creeping fog of gray bloom that misted the surface of the rosewood. "Emily has grown into a lovely girl, hasn't she? And she has a sweet disposition, too. She plays the piano and sings like an angel. She's so shy, but perhaps I can persuade her to play for you."

Her tired mind struggled to cope with her hopes and fears. *If I lose this child, too, then I must assure Sebastian will still become a partner in the McKnight Line. Emily . . . Emily is the answer. No other heirs.*

"Emily is breathtaking," Sebastian agreed. "A fairy princess. I'm afraid she'll disappear in a puff of smoke if I turn around suddenly." He gave a quick grin, his eyes teasing as he added, "I'm used to earthier women."

Louisa frowned. "Don't let yourself sink to the level of a drunken, whoring sailor. A man without a wife is no man at all. And a sailor needs a wife more than most men. She will be the one to guide you, inspire you to *be* somebody. You must have a lady for a wife, Sebastian. Don't ever think you deserve less."

Sebastian nodded solemnly, humoring her.

"You'll never have any trouble with women. You're just the kind of man they will lose their hearts over. You're big and rugged, but there's a great tenderness

27

about you. Women will do almost anything for a man who is gentle with them. Your father was always so gentle with me. . . ." She stopped before the sob in her throat could break through the stony barrier she had erected long ago on the day Jonathan, her true husband, died.

Her eyes went to the rosewood piano again and she repeated her earlier thought: "I must try to get Emily to play the piano for you. Somehow when she plays and sings all the cares of the world fly away."

Several weeks and many afternoon visits went by before Emily could be persuaded to play the piano. She always accepted Louisa's invitation to remain in the sparsely furnished sitting room during her son's visits, but was obviously overwhelmed by shyness. Emily would sit quietly, hands demurely folded on her lap, answering questions in her melodiously soft voice. Occasionally, when Sebastian's stories of their voyages became amusing, the tinkle of her laughter could be heard in faint accompaniment to Sebastian's ribald guffaws.

At Louisa's gentle urging, Emily eventually sat at the piano and her delicate white fingers drifted over the keys, making the ivory look yellow by comparison. She played several old English ballads, but blushed to the roots of her hair when Louisa asked her to sing the words.

"Please—I'd rather just play. I think I'm catching a cold; my throat is a trifle sore."

"It's all right," Sebastian said. "The piano music is a treat for me. I should have brought Irish with me —he sings like a bird. He knows some American chanteys, Mother. When he sings 'Shenandoah' it would bring tears to your eyes."

The following day when Sebastian arrived, his mother quickly ushered him into the sitting room. "I've sent Emily down to the apothecary for some cough mixture. I wanted to speak to you alone and didn't want to hurt her feelings."

"What is it, Mother? Come on, sit down. You look as though you're collapsing on your feet."

She swayed, all of the color draining from her face.

Sebastian caught her, picking her up as easily as if she were a child. He placed her carefully in a chair. "You're ill. I must fetch a doctor."

"No! I don't need one. Just let me rest a minute." Her voice was firm, despite the clammy limpness of the hand that clutched his arm. "I must talk to you . . . while Emily is gone. She is a lovely girl, isn't she? Just as sweet and kind as she looks."

"You don't have to point that out," Sebastian said, puzzled. "Right now I'm more concerned about you."

Louisa lay back limply in her chair, eyes half-closed. "You must marry her. Promise me you will."

Sebastian was too surprised to do anything but listen as his mother continued. "Job has given me a home and his name . . . but his will leaves everything to Emily. When he dies she will inherit the ships, the warehouses, this house . . . everything. He never lets anyone near her—no young men. If he knew you had been coming . . ."

Her hand went surreptitiously to her side, trying to press away the pain that had plagued her for days. She had already decided not to tell Sebastian of her pact with Job. No use making her son hate his stepfather even more than he already did. But he would have to know Emily's story.

"He wants to keep her sweet and pure. He thinks she will always be the sweet young girl she is now—never grow into a lonely old maid. I've tried to talk to him, but he's blind to everything but her innocence and purity. Fearful she will be contaminated, as her mother was. You see, Job's daughter ran off with a married man. She came back just before her child was born and died giving birth. Job had lost his wife shortly before—they say she died broken-hearted over her daughter's shame. Little Emily became his whole life . . . except for his ships."

The color was slowly returning to Louisa's face, but her eyes were still glazed. She paused, catching her breath, and Sebastian waited so long for her to continue he was afraid she was dozing off to sleep. She was not. Stretching out interminably in her mind were the toil-filled years of exile she had spent with a man who treated her alternately as a servant and a whore.

Job McKnight had shown little concern for her comfort and less tenderness. Louisa was in his house on sufferance and she was never allowed to forget the fact. When Job taunted her with the fact that she had blackmailed him into marriage, Louisa gritted her teeth and told herself silently the end justified the means. The bleak years were well worth the knowledge that Sebastian would be saved from the most treacherous mistress of all. The sea.

To Louisa the sea had been a natural enemy, snatching loved ones from her family for generations. The sea would not have Sebastian. She became aware of his worried stare and picked up the thread of her story of Emily's birth.

"Emily's father was a Frenchman, named La Flair. When the baby was only a few months old, he sent word that he had been widowed and wanted to marry Emily's mother. It seemed that La Flair had a son by his wife and he wanted to make a home for the four of them—not knowing the poor girl had died in childbirth. Job sent word back that if La Flair came near Emily, he would kill him. I believe Job would kill any man who tried to take Emily away from him. Sometimes he talks in his sleep . . . he moans about Emily —calling her name with such anguish it's hard to realize he's the same harsh man you see in the daytime."

"Mother, Emily is beautiful, but I'm not sure she's beautiful enough to die for," Sebastian said with a rueful laugh. "You tell me this blood-chilling story right after suggesting I marry her."

"Emily is fascinated by you, Sebastian. You are like a great roaring whirlwind, while she is an elusive zephyr. The attraction of opposites. You are rough and clumsy and just a little uncouth—"

Sebastian threw up his hands in mock horror. "Stop! I don't know if I can stand all this flattery! I don't agree with you, either. It's not I, but life itself that is the whirlwind."

30

"Marry her secretly. Don't let Job know," Louisa said, her eyes burning with a fierce determination, despite her wasted features.

"And what do you think Emily will say about having a great roaring whirlwind for a husband?" Sebastian asked, a teasing glint in his eye.

Louisa ignored his light tone. "Emily will be fortunate to have you for a husband. There is much of your father's wayward charm in you—although he was not such a great ox as you are."

Sebastian smiled at her fondly. "You're not a demonstrative woman, Mother, but I know you've missed him. It must have been hard for you to accept a man like Job McKnight in father's place. But the world is a dismal place for a widow, isn't it? And I wasn't old enough to support you."

Louisa sighed. "With Emily's refinement and beauty . . . you can go far. Being a man of action isn't enough. Emily will add a little polish and culture to your life."

Sebastian patted her hand affectionately. "Leave it to me. If you want Emily for a daughter-in-law, by God, you shall have her. For hasn't every fancy lady from Bombay to Canton assured me of my irresistible charm?"

"You sound as if some of your Irish friend's blarney has rubbed off on you," Louisa commented.

Later, when he returned to the seedy boardinghouse on Liverpool's most misnamed thoroughfare—Paradise Street—Sebastian pondered upon his mother's matchmaking. He had been at sea long enough to know that a sailor's wife was little more than the anchor that brought a man back to a certain port, unless, like his mother, she was strong enough to accompany her husband at sea. Sebastian could not imagine the fragile Emily aboard a ship. He lost no time in telling Irish O'Toole of his mother's plan.

"Choose your own wife, lad. And don't be in too much of a hurry," Irish advised.

"I must keep Mother happy—at least until after she

has her baby." Sebastian was shaving, peering into a cracked mirror. "Oh, God—imagine a little baby with bushy white eyebrows like old Job!" He roared with laughter.

"If ye're going out, watch your step. The taverns are crawling with crimps, and I know ye want to stay here until your mum's confinement ends."

"I'll be careful. I don't want to wake up aboard a ship bound for China." Sebastian used a handful of cold water to calm his bristling hair, then rummaged in his duffel bag for a clean shirt.

Despite telling himself he was too young to think of marriage, Sebastian exercised his inborn charm relentlessly the following afternoon. He asked Emily to walk in the park with him as the flowerbeds were ablaze with daffodils and narcissus.

For a moment Emily's dark eyes were filled with fear, but Louisa said, "Just a little walk, Emily. It's time you left the house in the company of someone other than me or your grandfather."

Emily went with him, and Louisa, looking exhausted, was dozing beside the fire when the door burst open and Job McKnight stood on the threshold.

--*{ CHAPTER 4 }*--

"You're home early," Louisa stammered, struggling to her feet.

"Where's Emily? Is her cold better?"

Louisa swallowed. "She went for a little walk."

At that moment they heard Sebastian's booming laugh and the vestibule door opened.

Job's eyes turned to glass as he stared at his granddaughter. Emily's normally pale cheeks were flushed and her eyes were large and bright. Several pins had slipped from her hair and strands of the polished dark locks waved softly about her porcelain features. Supporting her with his hand under her elbow, Sebastian's black hair was also wind-blown, and a wide smile revealed strong white teeth.

Louisa realized with dismay that everything about her son appeared threatening, from the proprietary hand on Emily's arm to the hunter's teeth bared in anticipation. Sebastian's bulk filled the narrow hallway and Emily seemed tiny and shatteringly fragile beside him.

"Take your great paw off my granddaughter," Job said in a voice wrenched from a throat tight with rage.

"Grandfather . . ." Emily's joyful smile was frozen on her face and her eyes were wide with fear.

"Sir, we've been walking in the park, that's all," Sebastian said amiably.

"Go to your room, Emily," Job said. "Louisa, you'd better go with her. I'll speak to you about this later."

Sebastian's grip on Emily's arm tightened. "She isn't a child to be sent to her room. And if you have anything to say to my mother, by God, you'll say it in front of me, you old curmudgeon."

"Curmudgeon, is it? Who took your mother and her brat in off the street? And this is my thanks—my granddaughter in the company of a common sailor. You impudent wharf rat, I'll see you in hell for this."

Sebastian patted Emily on the arm reassuringly, then stepped forward, placing himself between her and her grandfather. "You might as well know it, McKnight—I intend to court your granddaughter. And if you bully my mother because of it, I swear you'll live to regret it."

Louisa had risen unsteadily to her feet, her face deathly pale. She opened her mouth to speak, raised her hand, then slid to the floor in a faint.

Emily gave a little cry and ran to the crumpled figure, dropping down on her knees to unfasten the buttons at Louisa's throat, patting the limp hand anxiously.

33

"Grandfather—please, my smelling salts—quickly."

The two men stood transfixed, staring helplessly at Louisa's body with the vulnerable bulge beneath her apron; then Job went hurrying up the stairs to Emily's room.

Coming to his senses, Sebastian said, "We must get her into bed. Emily, you go and turn back the sheets. We must get a doctor." Sebastian bent to pick up his mother, appalled at how cold and clammy her flesh felt.

Job appeared at the bedroom door clutching a bottle of smelling salts as Sebastian laid his mother down on the unyielding surface of the bed. He gave a shiver of distaste and anger as it crossed his mind that she had undoubtedly conceived the child that now plagued her body in this very bed. He shut out the picture of the gaunt old Job McKnight making carnal love to his mother. Sebastian was equally sickened at the sight of the portrait hanging over the bed. Emily's grandmother, Job's first wife.

As Sebastian straightened up and Emily pulled the sheets over Louisa, the cold voice from the door said, "Now get out of my house, Balmain. This is your doing. Your mother knew I'd rather see Emily dead than involved with a common seaman."

"I'll go after a doctor has seen to my mother," Sebastian growled. His hands trembled with the need to seize McKnight by the throat, but his mother's motionless form and Emily's pleading stare kept him from doing so.

"We'll see about that," Job said grimly. He tossed the smelling salts on the bed and turned and went thumping down the stairs.

Sebastian returned with a young and nervous physician at almost the same moment Job appeared in the company of two burly officers of the law. The "peelers" stood in the hall as Job told Sebastian, "You can either leave under your own power, or they'll use their batons on you and drag you out. I think you've done your mother enough harm in one day. If you go now, I won't bring trespassing charges against you, and

34

I'll send word to your lodgings in the morning as to your mother's health."

"Sebastian," Emily said quickly, "I'll take care of your mother. Please go now."

"Where are you staying? I'll send a message to you about your mother," Job said. Sebastian was too angry to notice the crafty gleam in the old man's eyes when he mumbled the number of the Paradise Street boardinghouse.

Sebastian placed a kiss on his mother's cold cheek and looked across the bed at Emily. "Take care of her—and we'll walk in the park again, I promise you."

The young doctor placed his black bag on the bed and opened it with shaking fingers, his eyes fixed on the wildly staring eyes of Job McKnight. When the sailor had departed, the room seemed much larger.

Sebastian and Irish went to their cramped room after a stodgy boardinghouse supper made palatable only by the flagon of ale that washed it down. Irish had caught a cold in Ireland that lingered in his chest, and he sank to the bed listlessly.

"Old sod might have let me stay until Mother came to her senses," Sebastian said. "I've a mind to go back, and Job McKnight be damned. He had no right to turn me out like a dog."

"It's because of the girl," Irish said. "You're a threat because of his granddaughter. You know what they say about sailors." His voice was slow and uneven, a great lethargy creeping through his bones.

Sebastian yawned widely. "God, I'm tired all of a sudden. And that mutton lies heavy in my belly. What . . . what the hell—I never get sleepy when I'm this angry . . . but—"

Irish's eyes met his in the second before everything blurred and he heard his own voice, as though coming from a dark and hollow cave: *"The . . . ale . . . we drank . . ."*

A minute later when the men kicked open their door, both of them were submerged in an unnatural sleep.

"Well, nah," the crimp said, "these two bully boys

35

will bring a tidy penny. 'Ave a look in their bags, 'Enry, and see if they've any money left."

"McKnight said we're to give 'em to Gunnar on the *Dancer*," Henry replied uneasily, his cosh held aloft as Sebastian groaned and stirred. "Said Gunnar would pay us the usual."

"Aye, I know," the crimp said. "Only it seems to me we should get a bit extra for a likely pair like this, delivered to order and all. Look at the shoulders on this one. Come on, let's be 'aving yer."

It took three of them to carry Sebastian, two at his head and one guiding his feet down the narrow stairs of the boardinghouse and out into a misty street.

Sebastian's arm was dangling from a hammock and the churning of his stomach was not helped by the pitching of the ship. Someone was shaking his shoulder. "Wake up, boyo," a familiar voice said. "Come on, lad, it's all hands on deck. The first mate is Erik Gunnar. He's a bucko with more blood on his dirty hands than any man at sea. So come on, now, me hearty, on your feet."

Irish pulled him from the hammock with determined strength, considering his slight build. He had a wiry stamina to show for his twenty years at sea. A second later Sebastian found himself sprawling on the deck.

"I'm sorry, lad, but you mustn't give Gunnar a reason to set about you."

Sebastian cursed as he struggled to his feet, clutching the bulkhead for support. "What ship, whither bound?"

"The *Dancer*, bound for New York. No passengers, just cargo. She's American registry—a tramp."

The first mate paced the deck, slapping a knotted rope against his calloused palm as he told the assembled crew what was expected of them. Erik Gunnar was six and a half feet tall and built like a bear, but it was perhaps his eyes that instilled more fear in fresh crews, where brawn was a prerequisite of their calling. Gunnar's eyes were sorrel-brown, but when he was angry, which was often, they glowed a fiery red. It was an illusion that had stopped more than one prospective mutineer dead in his tracks.

When Gunnar pounded his great fists and bellowed, his salt-caked beard stiff around his face, rat-brown hair bushing out beneath a filthy watch cap, even hardened sons of the sea scrambled to obey his commands. And when they returned to port, most of them marked with his blows, if they were asked to describe the bucko mate who had made their lives hell, all they would be able to say was, "Big and mean. With eyes like hot coals." And they would shiver and swear they'd never let a crimp catch them again, never set foot on the deck of another ship. They seldom noticed that in spite of the devil's eyes and unkempt beard, Erik Gunnar was an exceptionally handsome man.

"And here comes Mr. Balmain," Gunnar said, catching sight of Sebastian and Irish O'Toole. "Did we wake you, then?" he added with mock solicitude.

"Go easy there, sir," Irish said with a desperately engaging grin. "The crimp gave him enough knockout drops to kill a horse. You can see he's still staggering on his feet."

Gunnar's red stare was turned on Irish, and the knotted rope whistled through the air before it connected with his shoulder. Irish went down on one knee on the deck, his arm upraised to protect his face from the second blow.

Sebastian shook his head, clearing his senses, and stepped forward. "Why are you hitting him? He was only trying to—"

The words were cut off as the mate's rope hit Sebastian full in the mouth.

"Nobody questions Erik Gunnar. Nobody speaks to the first mate unless told to. You understand me? One more word out of you and both of you will be seized up and hung from the shrouds for a flogging you'll not forget."

Sebastian looked into the burning eyes and recognized the gleam of anticipation. Gunnar was a man who savored brutality for its own sake. Out of the corner of Sebastian's eye, he saw Irish, still crouched

37

on one knee. Sebastian clamped his mouth shut, tasting the salty blood that oozed from his split lip. No use in being the cause of the chanteyman's punishment.

Hours later when they went wearily below, Irish told him gloomily, "The skipper is one of them that blew in through the porthole," which was sailors' jargon for an officer who had not come up through the ranks, but was in command by virtue of his knowledge of navigation.

"Gunnar doesn't like you, Sebastian. I think it's because you're the only man aboard who can match him for size. He's a bully, and bullies don't like to take on men who can lick them."

"Gunnar won't get the best of us," Sebastian said. "We'll do our work better than any man aboard. In New York we'll jump ship and get on the fastest packet back to Liverpool. I'm truly worried about Mother."

Reaching New York in one piece was easier said than done. Constant grinding toil and the blows of fists, ropes, and belaying pins in the hands of Gunnar and his second and third mates were only the beginning of the sailors' woes. The young and inexperienced skipper, anxious to set a record on his first voyage as master, had a topheavy ship that staggered under the weight of her canvas. He had eyes only for the sail, the sea, and his instruments. He appeared oblivious to the fact that there was fresh blood on the deck every day of the voyage.

Three days out of Liverpool, Irish let go a wrong halyard.

When Gunnar berated him and set about him with a belaying pin, the wiry little Irishman turned with a shout of rage. Head down, he butted the first mate in the stomach. As Gunnar staggered back, winded, O'Toole went after him with flailing fists and rich Irish curses.

Sebastian was aloft and watched helplessly as the brief drama was enacted on the deck below. The second mate rushed to Gunnar's aid, and Irish fell unconscious. By the time Sebastian had slithered down the rigging,

O'Toole's limp body had been hoisted up in the shrouds by wrists and ankles.

A shipmate, a soft-spoken man by the name of Ned Hake, restrained Sebastian from rushing through the circle of angrily muttering watchers. "You'll make it worse for the chanteyman, lad," Ned warned, catching Sebastian's arm. "And these others, they'll mutter and curse, but they won't back you up. Irish attacked an officer, and that's a mutinous act in any man's language."

At the same moment, Gunnar shouted that the chanteyman was to be left hanging in the shrouds until the first mate himself ordered him cut down. Sebastian stopped his headlong dash to his friend's aid. *At least he won't get the cat,* he thought.

"Come below," Ned Hake said. "And be thankful he isn't in for a flogging."

"You sound like an educated man," Sebastian said. "You always been a sailor?"

Ned smiled grimly. "I was senior draftsman for Smith & Dimon—they've a shipyard at the foot of East Fourth Street in New York. God willing, I'll be a draftsman again. I was shanghaied. I've had my eye on you, lad. You've a good head on your shoulders. You should think of another profession for yourself."

Sebastian grinned, despite his nagging fear for Irish. "Ships and the sea are all I know. But someday I'll be a master, and maybe even an owner. I even know what kind of ship I would design." They discussed ship-building and design until they fell asleep that night.

Awakening to find Ned Hake's hand on his shoulder at dawn, Sebastian cursed himself for not standing watch over Irish when Ned told him, "Gunnar just gave the chanteyman a dozen lashes before cutting him down."

Sebastian fell from his hammock. "Oh, God, he's been sick, and he wasn't ready for a long voyage. He's got more guts than any man I know, but if he keeps running afoul of Gunnar . . ."

"He's below," Ned said. "Moaning and delirious. He's lucky to be alive. The welts on his back will scar him for life. Take water to him—clean his back with salt. That's all you can do."

"I'll take care of Irish. And Gunnar won't lay a hand on him again, I swear—"

"Listen, lad, in a day or so every man on this ship will be fighting for his life. You've a more powerful enemy than the first mate. We're carrying too much sail, and there's weather ahead. Wait till you get on deck; you can smell it."

The captain had been on deck since noon, watching the canvas, the falling glass telling him he must shorten sail soon.

At last, reluctantly, the captain ordered the mate to call all hands to double-reef the main topsail.

The seas were heavy, gray mountains that spewed angry white foam from their peaks, bursting over the bow in a torrent of icy spray. The watch was not relieved, all hands ordered to remain on deck as the fury of the gale increased.

Cursing the extra canvas the ship carried, the men scrambled aloft as Gunnar shouted orders over the shrieking wind. The helm was put "hard-up" and the ship swung off before the wind. The jib-halyards were let go and the sails hauled down. Sliding out on the boom to stow it, sailors were drenched with a ton of water each time the ship dipped into the waves.

Pitch-darkness now enveloped the struggling ship, but both watches were ordered aloft to close-reef the main topsail. The men laid along the main yard to reef the mainsail, then furl it. Jumping to the deck to haul taut the halyards, Sebastian saw to his horror that the sick and flayed Irish O'Toole was on deck, swaying as though drunk, as Gunnar ordered him forward to haul up the foresail. O'Toole had a deep, wracking cough in addition to the wounds of his back and shoulders, and the bow of the ship was plunged into the icy water each time she pitched forward.

Sebastian seized Irish by the shoulders and spun him around. "Get below!" he shouted, shaking the man's skinny frame to make him understand.

Gunnar's roar of rage drowned out the din of the gale. "Stand aside, Balmain, or you're a dead man."

"That man is sick!" Sebastian shouted back. "You'll be guilty of murder if you don't relieve him of duty." He placed himself in front of O'Toole.

Gunnar came at him over the wet and slanting deck, belaying pin held aloft and his eyes red beacons in the darkness. They grappled in the heaving, shrieking gale, sliding and crashing into one another like ponderous bears as they fought both for balance and possession of the belaying pin. Locked together, they grunted and cursed in a deadly embrace as giant hailstones pounded the deck.

The first mate went crashing down on the slippery deck, the belaying pin rolling away from him. Sebastian came down on him with a yell of triumph that died in his throat as the second and third mates rushed to Gunnar's aid. Irish O'Toole staggered forward to try to pull one of the men away, but he was quickly felled by a vicious blow to his knee. Lights exploded in Sebastian's head as the blows rained down on the back of his neck. He lost consciousness.

The storm was still raging when he blinked open his eyes and became aware of the torture in his arms. He was tied to the shrouds, arms above his head, feet dangling above the deck. With each roll of the ship, the icy seas enveloped him, bringing him back to consciousness from the merciful void to which the blow on his head had consigned him.

For O'Toole's part in the fray, he had been sent to spend the night on the topsail yard, where he clung precariously, his knee throbbing from the blow with the belaying pin, each breath he took an agony for his fluid-filled lungs.

Looking up, Sebastian saw that the gale had swept every inch of canvas from the yards. Dimly he heard Gunnar order the crew to goose-wing the main trysail and heave to until dawn.

Sebastian was left hanging from the shrouds, without food or water, for twenty-four hours. He and O'Toole were thrown below in irons while the ship was in New

York, where the young captain was taken ashore with a broken leg suffered during the storm. He was replaced by a cold-eyed shipmaster named Curt Vanders, who spent much time in conference with First Mate Gunnar before the ship sailed.

⟶ᕯ CHAPTER 5 ᕬ⟵

Emily sat in the damp parlor, her hands plucking at the folds of her skirts. Her pale, translucent fingers smoothed, pressed, and rearranged the black merino, with the grace of fluttering doves.

Her eyes moved to the space in front of the bay window. All of the furniture had been moved to make room for the coffin, but now it was gone and the empty space was strangely more disturbing. It represented, she decided, the hole that had been left in her life.

Emily would miss Louisa terribly. She had loved her step-grandmother quietly but deeply. She wished there had been a moment when she could have told Louisa this, but Louisa was a no-nonsense woman who, like Job McKnight, would have been embarrassed by any word or deed that hinted of sentimentality.

In addition to her grief, Emily was battling her terror that now Louisa was gone Job would come creeping into her room again at night. Emily remembered the time before Louisa married Job. Awakening to feel the hot fingers sliding down over her stomach, probing secret places, hurting and making her cry.

He would pick her up then, holding her and whispering that she was just having a bad dream . . . go back to sleep, little princess. She would lie back on her pillow, rigid with fear, biting her knuckles in the darkness. The mattress would shift, springs creaking, as her grandfather sat beside her.

Sometimes there would just be a long silence and the jerking of the blanket as he twitched and his breath rasped. Emily felt the movement, heard the muffled sounds, but kept her eyes tightly closed. Other times he would tell her he would tickle all the bogeymen away. He would make her laugh and forget all of the bad dreams, he said. The tickling meant hot fingers on her skin until she was gasping for breath and unable to either laugh or cry.

But the worst times of all were when he took her hand and made her touch that terrible creature he brought with him. "Your little playmate, princess," he would say. "Play with your friend." She could not see what she touched, in the inky darkness behind closed eyelids, but the pulsating hardness frightened her so much that long after he departed she would lie awake, afraid to sleep.

Louisa had come into Emily's life and ended the nightmare. But now Louisa was gone.

From upstairs came the thin wail of Louisa's as-yet unnamed son. Emily resisted the impulse to run upstairs and pick him up. An Irish girl named Mollie Flanagan, with a ferocious expression and wild eyes that melted the moment she saw the infant, had been hired as his nurse. Mollie quickly let it be known she would tolerate no interference in the nursery.

Job McKnight had looked down at the son born to him so late in life, an incredulous smile of pride transforming his gaunt features. If he felt any grief at losing his wife, it was eclipsed by the arrival of his son and heir.

During the somber days before the funeral, he had been occupied with endless interviews before deciding Mollie Flanagan met his rigid requirements. Job had completely overlooked the presence of his granddaughter. Emily was grateful for his preoccupation. She had surreptitiously brought in a locksmith to make a lock for her bedroom door.

Emily jumped as the doorbell rang. Her grandfather was at his office and Mollie was busy with the baby. Emily hoped the bell did not herald the arrival of another applicant for the position of housekeeper. A hawk-eyed matron had already been hired to begin her duties the following day. Emily shrank from telling the desperate-eyed women who came looking for work that the position had already been filled.

Opening the vestibule door hesitantly, she saw with relief that the figure outlined against the leaded-glass door was a man wearing a tall hat.

A gust of wind swept into the house as she opened the front door, and the white silk scarf wrapped about the man's throat whipped across his face as he removed his hat. His hair was straight and dark. Deep brown eyes regarded her languidly from beneath long, curling eyelashes. Full lips smiled at her from a bony but handsome face. He was of average height and slender build, but appeared taller beside the diminutive Emily.

"You are Emily McKnight," he said, his voice musically vibrant. "I would have known you anywhere."

"Sir?" she asked uncertainly, both hands holding the door.

"I am your half-brother. Cyril La Flair."

Emily's lips parted in surprise and the wind almost wrenched the door from her grip. Her visitor quickly stepped inside the vestibule, and, closing the door behind him, said, "Perhaps I could come in for a moment? I regret I am the bearer of sad tidings that even your grandfather does not have the right to keep from you."

His coat sleeve was frayed, she noticed, and the white silk scarf had yellowed with age. He was probably in his mid-twenties, but his eyes were much older.

"Of course . . . come into the parlor. Grandfather isn't home. Could I offer you a glass of sherry?"

He moved with a curiously loose-jointed gait and Emily had to tear her gaze away from his long, sinuous fingers and extremely flexible wrists as he began to unbutton his coat. There was a waxy sheen to his skin which emphasized the dark hollows of his eyes. He smiled, showing slightly pointed teeth. "Make it brandy and you have a customer. I hope you will not bring

44

your grandfather's wrath down on your head if he finds you have invivted me in?"

"Mr. La Flair . . . I'm afraid you have me at a disadvantage. Until this moment, I was unaware of your existence." Emily picked up the brandy decanter as Cyril La Flair placed his hat and coat on the settee and went to warm his hands by the fire. Such extraordinary hands, she was mesmerized by them. He kept the silk scarf wrapped about his throat.

"Your grandfather never told you how many times your father tried to see you? Never gave you any of his letters?"

"My grandfather told me only that my mother had been disgraced—betrayed by a man not free to marry her. That she died giving birth to me . . . just as poor Louisa . . ." Emily broke off, realizing that he had no idea who Louisa was.

"André La Flair was your father and mine. I suppose since you never knew him, I can simply tell you that he died last month in France. I myself had not seen him for the past few years, but I know that he wrote to your grandfather many times—he even came here to see you once. He was turned away, and always the presents he sent were returned. I'm sorry I was not able to let you know father was ill, but I only learned of his death myself after the event." The expressive long fingers closed about the brandy glass and he quickly drained it.

Emily sat down on the edge of a chair. "I'm so sorry to hear of your loss. I thought my father had died years ago . . . I didn't know . . . I wish I could have met him. What was he like?"

"A poet and a dreamer. Not very practical. But very romantic—a typical Frenchman in that respect."

"And you, Mr. La Flair—are you also a poet and dreamer?" Emily smiled shyly, feeling oddly at ease with the young man.

"Please call me Cyril—I *am* your half-brother, you know," he reminded her. "I am a pianist and composer. Somewhat unsuccessful in both endeavors, I regret to say. And I don't have the stamina for romance. My mother was English, like yours. Father seemed to have a fatal weakness for Englishwomen." He paused, glancing at the closed curtains and remembering the wreath on the front door. "Emily, I was surprised to find your house in mourning."

"My grandfather's wife died a few days ago."

"I'm sorry. Perhaps I should leave. I wouldn't want to confront your grandfather at such a time. However, I would like to get to know you, Emily, my little sister, now that we've met at last. Could we meet sometimes? I have taken rooms and will be staying in Liverpool for a time."

"Yes, of course. Perhaps we should keep our acquaintance secret? For the time being?"

Cyril picked up his coat. As he turned his back she saw that the seat of his trousers was shiny with wear. "I would say that would be most advisable. I loathe scenes, don't you?"

His eyes went to the upright piano, and on a sudden impulse, he went over to it and raised the rosewood cover. The piano was woefully out of tune, but Emily clapped her hands in delight as his graceful fingers brushed over the keys, covering an unbelievable number of notes as he found the chords he was seeking. The flexibility of his wrists was equally astonishing. The ancient piano had never made such hauntingly lovely sounds.

"Oh, how beautiful!" Emily cried. "The piano needs tuning—it's so damp in here . . . but you make it sound like a music box. What is that lovely piece?"

He turned and smiled at her, his dark eyes glowing within the shadowed hollows of their sockets. "I wrote it for the occasion. I call it 'Dream of Emily.' "

She was not embarrassed, but her heavy lids closed over her eyes to conceal the brightness of the tears that sprang inexplicably from a well of happiness. She felt, all at once, that she would never be lonely again.

Emily had timidly inquired of her grandfather if he had sent word to Sebastian that his mother was dead and had been curtly told there was no way to communicate with a ship at sea. "He'll be back in port one of these days and can see Louisa's grave then."

His eyes narrowed as he regarded her silently for a moment. "I see a lock has appeared on your door. When did you decide there would be locked doors in my house?"

Emily colored, looking at the floor. "I was so upset over Louisa's passing . . ." she stammered, not sure if she could bring herself to tell the lie she had prepared in readiness for this question. *It is necessary,* she told herself desperately. *I shall never be able to sleep again without the lock* . . . but he has taken care of me all these years and he is good to me . . . during the day . . .

". . . that I started to sleepwalk," she said, raising her eyes to meet his gaze. "I didn't want to disturb the baby, so I had a locksmith come in and make me a lock and key."

Job stared at her for a moment and then turned away silently. He went slowly up the stairs and into the nursery. Looking down at the pink perfection of the baby, Job was overwhelmed with feelings he believed he had buried long ago. Love, pride, joy. He was also aware of the nagging pinpricks of guilt that marred his happiness in his new son. Louisa had been a good woman, for all she tricked him into marriage. He wished, for the baby's sake, that he had been kinder to her. He worried that when all of his sins were balanced against too few virtues, that he would be made to pay dearly.

Then there was Emily. Growing more like her grandmother with each passing day. Would she fade and die, too? They were such fragile creatures, all of them. Better to have a son to love. A man's hopes and dreams could come true through his son. Job's gnarled fingers went gently to the curled little fist lying in the crib. Tiny fingers closed about his thumb and all at once Job wanted to weep.

Between his obsession with beating the Atlantic records of the Black Ball Line and the time he spent in the nursery with his son, Job scarcely had a spare glance for Emily. It was, therefore, relatively easy for her to keep her promise to meet Cyril.

One memorable Saturday afternoon he arrived wearing a grand, if somewhat threadbare, dress suit. Dark eyes smoldering crisply as burned sugar, he announced Emily would at last hear him play in concert. He had an engagement at a workingmen's club to entertain during their monthly "bring-your-wife" tea concert.

Emily was beside herself with excitement as she was seated at a small table, the surface of which was marred by circular stains testifying to the fact that mugs of ale rather than tea were the usual fare.

The hall was crowded with couples, the women wearing black shawls over somber-hued dresses, and the men keeping their cloth caps on their heads. They all turned to stare at Emily.

Just before the entertainment began, a ripple of excitement preceded the arrival of a powerfully built man with extraordinarily long arms and a tiny bald head set upon massive shoulders. "Lefty Boyne—the heavyweight boxer," the men whispered to their wives.

The first act came on stage a moment later: a young tenor who sang a sad ballad in a wavering falsetto. The audience occupied itself with tea and iced cakes.

Emily leaned forward eagerly as Cyril came out and sat down before the grand piano. His beautiful mobile fingers brought forth the opening arpeggios, trills, and octaves of *Concerto No. 5* by the German genius, Beethoven. Emily held her breath. Surely the audience would be astonished at the bravura opening, the bold defiance of convention.

Incredibly, there was an irritable murmuring and a noisy scraping of chairs. Someone coughed and a loud voice suggested, "Play us a song, lad. None of that toff stuff."

Cyril faltered, then went on gamely. He missed a note, then stopped as several catcalls echoed about the room. Emily leaped to her feet, eyes blazing, her hands outstretched. Before she could cry out her outrage, a quietly authorative voice silenced the muttering. "Give 'im a chance. Shut up and listen."

In the ensuing silence Emily could hear her heart beat. She threw the bald head of the heavyweight boxer a grateful glance and sank to her seat, losing herself in the spellbinding magic of the music that now filled the air, filled her heart, mind, and soul.

Slowly Cyril captivated the group of people, for whom the music was as mysterious and unintelligible as a foreign tongue. They listened raptly after a short time, not understanding the piano's message, but awed by the pianist's mastery of his instrument.

Several weeks went by and Cyril did not mention receiving any other engagements. One afternoon, with a sheepish smile, he asked for a small loan.

"I hate to ask," he said apologetically, his dark eyes sadly fixed on his hands as the sinuous fingers traced the gold rim of his china teacup. They were seated in the window of a shabbily genteel tea shop where they could be seen by passersby on the street. The elderly proprietress had personally seated them in the hope that the aristocratically beautiful young couple would attract patrons of similar quality.

"But if I don't pay my rent," Cyril went on, "I shall be without lodgings. I've a couple of jobs coming along soon—playing at weddings and copying some music. But until then—I'm afraid your Liverpool has few opportunities for a struggling concert pianist."

Emily was more embarrassed than Cyril to admit that she had no money of her own. It had simply never been necessary for her to ask for any, as all of her needs were taken care of by her grandfather. If she wished to give a gift to someone, she would embroider a handkerchief or pillow, knit mufflers and mittens, or make a pomander potpourri.

"Of course, I understand," Cyril said quickly. "I shall return to London. Who knows, perhaps someone is ready to play my music by now. I can certainly find enough piano engagements there to keep the wolf from the door."

"No—please don't leave, Cyril. Let me ask grandfather for some money." Her soft brown eyes were filled with apprehension. "I couldn't bear it if you left. You can't know what it has meant to me, being able to talk to someone who understands . . . I've never had any friends. I didn't know it was possible to share so much of one's mind with another human being. . . . Oh, no, Cyril, you can't leave me now."

His hand closed over hers on the faded tablecloth and his touch was comforting, despite the icy chill of his fingers. His hands were always cold. Emily loved the bracing touch, so cool and safe and quite unlike the hot touch of her grandfather.

"Since you came into my life, Emily, I've been inspired to write music as never before. There's no piano at my lodgings, of course, but I know it's the best I've ever written. Oh, how I wish I could play it for you," he said passionately.

They were silent, dark eyes gazing into dark eyes, Emily's pale, slim fingers entwined with the pianist's long, graceful ones. Even the air around them seemed heavy with the crushing weight of the outside world pressing in to engulf them with the details of daily existence. They yearned for a quiet place to be together to discuss music and poetry. A place where flowers and butterflies and the gentle creatures of the earth came together in sweet, warm sunlight and there was no jarring note to spoil the harmony.

"You mustn't tell your grandfather you've been meeting me," Cyril said. "I'm afraid just the mention of my name will revive all of his old hatred for our father. Don't worry, I'll manage, somehow. I shan't leave."

Emily blinked away a tear at the proud resolve in his resonantly melodic voice and went home that afternoon determined to approach her grandfather. Her terror of him was submerged in her greater fear of losing Cyril's companionship.

The days since Cyril had come into her life had slipped by like a wonderful dream that fades with the early dawn. Sometimes she would imagine they had been mysteriously cast away on a desert isle together, far from the cares of the world. She would think of fearsome hardships and terrible dangers that she would overcome bravely for his sake. She told herself this was because they were related by blood, because he was her half-brother.

Cyril was so much like her in mind and thought that it seemed incredible they had grown up so far apart. She had seen Cyril brush away a tear at the sheer beauty of a stanza of verse he brought to her. Once he had stopped as they walked through the park to clasp a small barefoot beggar boy to his chest. The child had regarded Cyril with wide-eyed amazement from an angelic, if dirt-streaked, face.

"You are beautiful," Cyril assured the child. "No matter how harsh the world seems, remember that *you* are beautiful."

Cyril had given the child a threepenny bit, which the latter cynically tested between his teeth before scampering off to join his ragged and scavenging co-horts. Cyril was never able to pass a beggar without emptying his pockets into a battered cap or tin cup. Often this meant there was no money for a visit to the tea shop, but Emily didn't mind. The strolls through the park on fine afternoons were enough.

They talked. Conversations that began the moment they met and ended reluctantly as they parted, with never enough time in between to share all of their thoughts. To Emily it seemed she had stored up every idea and observation that had ever come to her, just waiting to share them all with Cyril. It was easy to understand why her mother had run away with his father. André La Flair must have been as gentle and sensitive as Cyril, with the same keen appreciation of all that was fine and beautiful in the world.

As had become his custom, her grandfather deposited his hat on the hall stand upon arriving home and went immediately upstairs to the nursery to see his son. The christening was to take place on the following day, and a name must finally be chosen. As soon as she heard her grandfather's step on the stairs, Emily went to join him in the nursery. She was afraid of

Mollie, the nurse, and only dared visit the baby when her grandfather was home.

"Emily . . ." Job said absently as he stood looking down at the sleeping infant. Mollie sat rocking the cradle, her starched white apron creaking in cadence with the aged wood.

" 'Even', sir—'even', Miss," Mollie whispered in an exaggerated display of concern that the slightest sound would awaken her charge.

Job said, "I shall name him for my father, even though he resembles his mother more than us. What do you think of that, Emily? Mark McKnight." Job stroked his white beard as he rolled the name around his tongue.

"Yes, Grandfather. Mark is a fine-sounding name. He's a beautiful child, Grandfather. He will have Louisa's bright blue eyes, don't you think? And your fair skin. Grandfather—could I speak with you for a moment?"

The pale old eyes were withdrawn reluctantly from the sleeping baby. "Downstairs, then. Mollie will be after us if we awaken him. You know what a screaming little tyrant he is." The last was added with an indulgent smile, as Job was convinced his son's future strength was indicated by his present sturdy lungs, which emitted ear-splitting yells if the infant's needs were not immediately met.

Downstairs the pinched-faced housekeeper, Mrs. Turner, was setting the table in the dining room. They went into the parlor, where the fire was reduced to a faint glow beneath a mountain of ash. Job stirred the embers and shoveled coal from the brass scuttle.

"You shouldn't let the fire burn so low, Emily," he childed. "We must keep the house warmer now that there's an infant."

"Yes, Grandfather. I'm sorry. I haven't been in here all afternoon."

"Oh? And where were you?" he glanced at her sharply.

"I . . . went for a walk . . . just across the street to the park."

"You know I don't like you to go out alone, Emily. You can take the air from the back garden. This is a seaport, and the scum of the earth sails up the Mersey."

"Yes, Grandfather. Grandfather, I was wondering if it would be possible for me to have a small allowance. I'm quite grownup now, and I was thinking . . . I know nothing of money matters." Emily felt a flush come to her cheeks as he stared at her in surprise and went on quickly: "Oh, you've always been generous to me, but I worry that I know so little of managing my own affairs. If I could perhaps buy my own clothes and personal items?"

"One of the new women been putting these ideas in your head? Mrs. Turner? I was afraid she might be a little busybody . . ."

"Oh, no, Grandfather."

He gazed into the fire, which was flickering to life. "I suppose it was Louisa's passing on. It made you realize that I shall be next, and you'll be all alone. I've thought about that, Emily, and seen to it that you'll always be provided for. Of course, you understand that now I have a son, he will be my sole heir. But there'll be an annual annuity for you, so never fear you'll be dependent on anyone else. You'll be wealthy in your own right. Still, perhaps you're right. You should learn the value of a shilling while I'm still here to see you don't spend your money foolishly. I shall give you an allowance. Ten shillings a month to start off, that should be ample. But you'll buy your own clothes, remember."

Emily smiled, dark eyes bright with joy. She could hardly wait to tell Cyril of their good fortune. The fact that she had just been informed that she was no longer the heir to McKnight Shipping was quite immaterial to her.

Several days later, the housekeeper knocked on Job's study door as he went over his books late one evening. Emily had retired for the night.

"Come in. Yes, Mrs. Turner, what is it?" Job asked impatiently. She was an unattractive little runt

53

of a woman, but a worker, and she came both highly recommended and cheap.

Mrs. Turner's thin lips were pursed, her small eyes darted about on either side of the bony bridge of her nose, and wisps of iron-gray hair escaped from her mob cap like tendrils of fog. "It's about your granddaughter, Mr. McKnight, sir. I feel it's my duty . . . and high time I told you what's going on. Don't like young people sneaking about behind their elders' backs, I don't."

Job regarded her coldly from beneath bushy white eyebrows. "What are you trying to tell me, woman?"

"Miss Emily sneaks across to the park and meets a young man . . . almost every afternoon while you're at your office. Seems to me that a respectable young chap would come and ask your leave to court her."

There was a long pause. Job's gnarled fingers closed around a sheet of parchment in front of him and slowly crumpled it. "Very well, Mrs. Turner. My granddaughter was perhaps aware of her own wickedness when she brought in the locksmith. She was silently pleading with us to lock her away from temptation. Go now and lock her in her room. Her food will be taken up to her. Tomorrow afternoon you will accompany me to the park and point out the young man she has been sneaking out to see."

Standing on his desk was a silver-framed miniature of Emily. Reaching for it, he placed it face downward. There were no pictures in the house of his dead daughter, but now he realized that Emily was just like her mother, in every way. His fist clenched about his quill until it snapped and he stared unseeingly at the open ledgers on his desk.

-•€ CHAPTER 6 }€•-

The stowaway was not discovered until New York was two days behind the *Dancer*.

Sebastian and the chanteyman were back in the forecastle. O'Toole's face was gray and he coughed and wheezed, but his spirit was indomitable. "I'll be singing ye a chantey one of these foin days, boyo," he croaked.

"Too bad we didn't get to jump ship in New York."

"What? And lose our flamin' pay? Not bloody likely! We must stick it out. We've stops to make at Charleston and New Orleans before we'll be paid."

The shouts of excitement reached them then and a sailor's head appeared around the bulkhead, yelling excitedly, "A stowaway—a woman! Young and good-looking, too!"

She was on deck, surrounded by crewmen, awaiting the arrival of an officer. The men were taking the opportunity to feast their eyes on luscious female flesh. Her dress was damp and clung so excitingly to an extravagantly curved body that no one noticed she reeked of bilge-water. Bright green eyes regarded the men defiantly, and a dimpled chin was thrust in the air. A tangled mane of deep auburn hair fell about her shoulders, the creamy skin of which was exposed by numerous holes in her filthy dress. She stood, arms akimbo, bare feet planted firmly on the heaving deck, her sensuously full lips pressed together. Her face was pert rather than beautiful, and every line of her body expressed her complete disdain for her captors and their snickering remarks.

"Shut up, all of you," Sebastian said, pushing through

55

the group. "Are you hungry?" he asked her. And without waiting for an answer, he turned to the nearest man and said, "Go and fetch her something from the galley instead of standing there gaping." The sailor blinked, but obeyed. Sebastian towered over every man present.

"Seaman Sebastian Balmain, at your service, ma'am," he said with a respectful bow. "You must excuse my shipmates; they mean you no harm."

The shamrock-colored eyes met his haughtily, but she answered in a surprisingly cultured voice: "Garnet is my name. Garnet Wade. And I am hungry."

"Garnet . . . a pretty name for a pretty lass," Sebastian said.

"Stand aside, Balmain." Erik Gunnar's voice silenced everybody on deck.

The girl whirled around and, seeing Gunnar, she turned white, her eyes as large as saucers as she stared at him.

Standing close to her, Sebastian was aware of her breasts rising and falling rapidly, and only he heard the name that sprang to her lips like a sob as she stared at Gunnar. "Tom . . . ?" Then she blinked and wiped her knuckles across her brow as though awakening from a confused dream.

The first mate made a slow circle around the girl, his red stare devouring her greedily. "Where did you find her?" he asked no one in particular.

"In the foreward hold—in one of the boxes. Reckon some longshoreman slipped her aboard in New York," a voice answered.

"This is the skipper's business, Mr. Gunnar," Sebastian said.

Gunnar did not have time to comment as he made the mistake at that moment of reaching to touch the girl. There was a sudden glimpse of a shapely leg and then a flash of steel as she withdrew the stiletto from the sheath fastened to her thigh by two satin garters. She sprang backward, brandishing the knife, turning to slice the air behind her to discourage anyone from

56

approaching her from the rear. "Keep your hands off me," she warned.

Gunnar roared with laughter and sprang at her, catching her wrist the second before the knife connected with his flesh. He spun her around and picked her up, holding her against him, her feet kicking furiously in the air. The stiletto clattered to the deck.

"She's got more spirit than this whole scurvy crew," Gunnar said, then let out an oath as she bent and sank her teeth into his hand.

"Let her go, Mr. Gunnar," Sebastian said. "There's no reason to manhandle her."

"That's twice you've opened your mouth now, Balmain—" Gunnar did not finish what he was about to say, as the captain appeared on deck and the circle of men fell back to allow him to pass.

Captain Curt Vanders was young, a powerfully built blond Adonis only slightly less muscular than the other two giants aboard the ship, Gunnar and Sebastian. The last glimpse Sebastian had of the green-eyed stowaway was her one anguished glance in his direction as Gunnar carried her, still struggling and kicking, in the direction of the captain's cabin. Sebastian was haunted by the combined desperation and defiance in that one glance for the rest of the nightmare voyage.

Gunnar was back on deck within minutes, his face ruddy with anger, and the second and third mates at his sides. Before Sebastian realized what they were about to do, they had seized his arms and Gunnar had jammed a marlinspike against his throat. "You opened your mouth to the first mate, whoreson. Now you're going to learn to keep it shut."

Sebastian struggled and fought them, until three crewmen were ordered to assist the mates. He was stripped to the waist, a strap fastened around him, and he was hoisted, upside down, to the mizzen stay. When they cut him down, his face was black.

Irish O'Toole pleaded with Gunnar that he was killing one of his best hands, and for his pains the little Irishman had a heavy capstan bar lashed to his back and he was forced to pace the deck, staggering beneath its weight, his injured knee wobbling alarmingly.

"I'll teach you bilge rats to question an officer," Gunnar roared. "Cap'n Vanders is in command now, not that milksop we had before. And you whoresons have no rights except the rights the skipper and I give you. You're cattle and you're here to follow my orders. If I say jump overboard, by God, you'll do it."

Sebastian lay on deck, the blood slowly ebbing from his head and his senses returning. He pulled himself up on his knees as Irish, still bent beneath the weight of the capstan bar, lurched past on his tour of the deck. Even as the red mist cleared from Sebastian's eyes, he saw Gunnar raise his knotted rope to club the Irishman as he went by. O'Toole's knee twisted grotesquely and he crashed to the deck.

Sebastian was on his feet, growling with rage. His hands locked about Gunnar's throat and the red eyes bulged. "Order them to remove the bar and carry him below, or, by God, you're a dead man."

Gunnar's tongue was protruding between his lips and he was rolling his eyes and making a gurgling sound as Captain Vanders' voice cracked across the deck. "Seize up that man if you don't want to see a pistol ball in his back."

Brawny arms went around Sebastian and he was jerked away from Gunnar to face the captain's cocked pistol.

"Mutiny, is it? Do you know the penalty for striking an officer?"

Sebastian glared at him. "No court will convict me of mutiny when I tell them I saved a man's life—that man, Captain, who lies on your deck spitting blood. And if you kill us both, there'll be someone on this ship to testify against you." He jerked his head in the direction of the angry group of sailors who watched, murmuring among themselves. Encouraged by his defiance, Ned Hake went to O'Toole and began to unfasten the capstan bar. Irish was pale as death, but managed a grateful grin as he was hauled to his feet.

Gunnar paced the deck angrily, the knotted rope swinging ominously, as he waited for the captain to speak.

"You risk your neck for the sake of this shriveled-up little excuse for a man? Sailor, you're a bigger fool than you look," the captain said.

Irish O'Toole drew himself up to his full height and said quietly, "I'm as much a man as anyone aboard, Cap'n. But I've done nothing to warrant this kind of punishment, and neither has Ballymain."

The captain swung the pistol and the barrel caught O'Toole full in the face. He fell to the deck, blood running from his nose.

Struggling in the grasp of the men holding him, Sebastian could do nothing but shout his futile curses.

"Captain—" Gunnar said, his eyes going to the saloon door. Captain Vanders turned to see the stowaway watching them.

"Throw them both in irons and keep them on bread and water until I decide what's to be done with them," the captain said. He went quickly to usher the woman back into his cabin.

"You're dismissed, Mr. Gunnar," Vanders said as the first mate followed him into his cabin.

Gunnar closed the door, his eyes fixed on the red-haired stowaway. "What about Balmain? That's a decision that can't wait. It was mutiny. And what about the girl? Are you going to put back into port? If so, I need your orders now."

"Please . . ." the girl broke in. "Don't charge that man with mutiny. I believe it's all my fault—I caused the fuss on deck."

Vanders raised a blond eyebrow and his thin lips curled into a smile. "Where are you from, my dear? And, more importantly, where are you bound?"

The green eyes met his defiantly. "I hope to reach New Orleans. I have a friend there."

"But no money for passage, I take it?"

"They told me this ship is bound for New Orleans and is under the command of a skipper and a mate who aren't above transporting contraband cargo. Including the human variety."

Vanders and Gunnar exchanged glances and Gunnar laughed aloud. "So much for all the secrecy about the cargo we're picking up in New Orleans, Skipper."

"Shut up, Mr. Gunnar," Vanders said.

"If you'll take me to New Orleans—and if you'll not press mutiny charges against that sailor—I swear I'll keep my mouth shut about the slave cargo."

"From the look of you, you're running away from something. You in trouble with the law?" Vanders asked.

"My only trouble is no money and no job. And a woman who wanted me out of town." The green eyes flashed again.

"You've got to admire her spirit, Skipper. I'll be more than willing to share my cabin with her," Gunnar said, his red-brown eyes slipping down her body again.

"Get out of here, Gunnar. Keep those two in irons until after we leave Charleston. This whole crew has to be replaced before we pick up the cargo in New Orleans, anyway."

Gunnar paused, one hand on the cabin door. "What about her?"

Surprisingly, the girl said, "I'll share the mate's cabin, if I have a choice." The expression on her face reminded Gunnar of the white-lipped recognition he had seen there when she first saw him on deck. He searched his memory, but knew if he had ever met her before he would have remembered.

"You'll stay here," the captain said.

The moment the door closed on the first mate, Vanders' hand snaked out and caught the ragged material of her dress, ripping it from shoulder to waist. "Get out of those rags," he said. "Then we'll scrub you so clean you'll squeak."

Her eyes remained veiled during the next hour. Cat's eyes narrowed and cat's claws bared when he tried to wash her. There was warm salt water and soap all over the deck. They struggled in the confined space

60

and she bit and kicked and clawed until at last he trapped her squirming, wet body against the bulkhead.

"A very good performance," Vanders said, breathing heavily. "But now you'll cooperate or I'll throw you to the sharks. No timid little virgin ever stowed away aboard a tramp like this, so let's see your true colors. You've probably been whoring as long as I've been sailing."

She was breathing rapidly, also, her full pink-tipped breasts rising against his wet shirt. She glared at him and tried to free her arms, which were pinned to her sides. When he leaned forward to smother her mouth with his, she bit his lip.

He spat out his rage in a stream of curses and his hand closed over her breast, squeezing until she moaned and turned pale. "All right . . ." she gasped out at last. "Don't hurt me—"

He released her, jerking his head toward his bunk before starting to unbutton his trousers. She collapsed weakly onto the bunk, watching him warily. The moment his shirt was up over his face, she leaped for the door and jerked it open. He was after her in a second, dragging her back and slamming her down on the bunk. Her arms were above her head, pinned by his forearm, and his other hand was forcing her thighs apart. He thrust himself inside her, than let his weight fall heavily to pin her down.

"Now, you little hell-cat," he said grimly. He probed and twisted and thrust, forcing himself deeper and deeper, as she squirmed and gasped in pain.

Her eyes watched him like glittering daggers, all her hatred and rage contained in their green depths. When he reached a shuddering climax, she caught him off guard and managed to fling him from the swaying bunk.

He staggered to his feet, catching her by the hair as she tugged at the cabin door. "We're not finished yet . . . there's a few other tricks you'll perform, lady. You'll work your passage aboard my ship."

She managed to get the door open the second before

he flung her to the deck and Erik Gunnar stepped through the opening. "Let her up, Skipper," he said.

"Damn you—how dare you—" Vanders was white with rage, the hand tangled in the girl's hair shaking her head violently.

Gunnar rèached out and his hand closed over the captain's, his eyes glowing red. "Without me, you won't get this tub to the Gulf—nor your illegal cargo back to the Carolinas. So stow it. You, girl—wrap a blanket around yourself and come with me."

The captain let her go and she pulled a blanket from the bunk to cover her nakedness. She followed Gunnar along the narrow passageway to his cabin, an even smaller one than the captain's, but a safe haven for her bruised flesh.

"I'll get you something to eat," he said gruffly. "And find a shirt and bell-bottoms for you to wear until we put into Charleston. Then I'll get you a dress."

"Thank you," she said weakly. "Someday . . . I must tell you how much you look like someone I used to know . . ."

"We've stopped moving," Sebastian whispered to Irish in the darkness 'tween decks. "We must have reached Charleston."

"Aye, and still alive to tell the tale," Irish wheezed back at him through the gloom.

They did not know how long they had been below decks. Food was thrown to them at undetermined intervals, and Sebastian suspected that Gunnar sometimes had the moldy bread and filthy water delivered in the middle of the night to confuse them.

"And you're resting your bad knee," Sebastian observed, shifting his weight to his other side with a clanking of chains.

Irish was overcome with a paroxysm of coughing. Gasping for breath, he could make no reply.

"That girl . . . Garnet—" Sebastian mused. "She saved us from a hanging for sure, popping up on deck like that. Wonder why she chose to stow away on this tub. You'd have thought she'd have picked something better."

"Maybe she weren't stowing away," Irish croaked. "Maybe some tar brought her aboard for his pleasure and didn't get her ashore in time."

"You think she's a waterfront doxie, then, Irish?"

"What else, boyo?"

"I don't know. Maybe a servant girl. Or even a lady, down on her luck. She sounded like a lady." And carried herself proudly, like a princess, Sebastian thought, remembering the tilted chin and defiant green eyes. "You know, what they call an impoverished gentlewoman in England."

Irish snorted derisively, then groaned as pain shot through his inflamed lungs. "She's no lady, that one. That was all woman. That body was sending its own sweet message to every man on deck. Sweet Jesus, did you ever see breasts like those? And her little round hips seemed to be moving even when she was standing still. She's had it more times than you've had your Sunday dinner, boyo."

If anyone else but Irish had said that, Sebastian thought, I'd have laid him flat on his back. Not since the first time he saw the grown-up Emily McKnight had a woman made such an impression on him. He could still picture the stowaway in his mind. Every curve of the white body that seemed gilded with a glow so warm he knew her flesh would melt and yield to the touch. Her provocative smile, the wicked dimples, and the full, sensuous lips. But Irish was right; she couldn't be a lady. Sebastian felt deep regret as he told himself this. A man could never marry such a woman.

As though echoing his thoughts, Irish added softly, "I pity the man who gets entangled with the red-haired stowaway, Ballymain. He'll never dare take his eyes off her for a minute. If he does, she'll be romping with his best friend."

The movement of the ship told them they were again in the open sea. When the hatch was opened, bright sunlight blinded them. They reeled drunkenly as they were freed from their chains and prodded to their feet.

Gunnar's fiery eyes watched them as they stumbled on deck. He was tossing a belaying pin from one hand to the other. "Aloft," he ordered. "Both of you."

Sebastian watched Irish closely, fearful his wasted frame would slip from the yards, but the little Irishman gamely handled his share of the canvas, despite his weakened condition.

The sunlight caught a gleam of bronze at the stern of the ship. Sebastian saw the stowaway, Garnet, watching the wake foam away. Her auburn hair blew about her face and her head was thrown back on her shoulders in sensual appreciation of the sunshine. Sebastian almost let go of the yard as the breeze outlined her body beneath the thin material of her dress. A new dress—bright green and very becoming, although of a gaudy shade not usually worn by ladies. As that thought crossed his mind, Sebastian reminded himself again that she was not a lady. He and Irish had clearly established that fact.

The mates were no longer on deck. The ship moved briskly before a fresh breeze. Sebastian strolled back to the stern.

She turned as he approached and he was struck immediately by the endless depth of the green eyes that seemed to reflect all the turbulence of the sea. "Mr. Sebastian Balmain," she said softly, and there was a hint of pleasure in her voice, as though she were glad to see him.

"You remembered my name, Miss Garnet," he answered with a wide grin.

"How could anyone forget such an impressive name? Or the man who goes with it?" Twin dimples had appeared on either side of her wide and generous mouth. "But I remember you most, Mr. Balmain, because you were the only man on this ship who stood up for me that first day."

"I wish you'd call me by my first name."

"Sebastian . . ." she said, emphasizing each syllable. "It sounds invincible."

He squinted at her in the sunlight. "You speak . . . use words that . . ." He stopped, wishing he had not begun to express the thought.

She pushed back a strand of auburn hair and finished for him: ". . . that don't seem to go with my appearance and circumstances."

"I reckon you must want to get to New Orleans pretty badly, to have stowed away," Sebastian said, trying to cover his clumsiness. She was a magnetically exciting woman. Standing near her, he was afraid she would notice that he had immediately become aroused by her.

"The only friend I have in the world lives there. Her name is Cassie Madigan, and she's one of the bravest women I know. She ran away from a philandering husband and three louts of sons and went into business for herself in New Orleans."

"Oh, I see," Sebastian said, relieved that the friend was a woman. "You're going to work for her?"

"Perhaps."

"Did you know the first mate before coming aboard? I heard you call him 'Tom,' though he goes by the name of Erik Gunnar now."

She flushed and turned away. "I was mistaken. He looks like someone I used to know, a long time ago."

Sebastian did not want the conversation to end. He said, "Are they treating you all right? The food isn't much at sea, is it?"

The green eyes were searching the distant horizon. "I've eaten worse. I must go. Erik doesn't like me to come on deck. I couldn't resist the urge to feel the sunshine on my face. I am an evil omen, you see. He tells me the crew is superstitious about having a woman on board. I'm supposed to bring bad luck." She made no move to leave.

"Some of the more stupid tars believe that," Sebastian said. "But my mother sailed aboard my father's ship for years, and except for his last voyage, it was the smoothest sailing my old man ever had." *Gunnar,* he thought, a sick feeling at the pit of his stomach. *She's sharing Gunnar's cabin.*

"And on the last voyage?"

"The crimps sold the mate some Kanakas and they panicked when they realized they were in the wrong ocean. My mother was mainly responsible for getting the survivors to St. Helena."

"A proud glow comes to your eyes when you speak of her."

"A strong woman. Strong and no-nonsense. She'll come though all right."

"All at once I get the impression that your mother is facing some new trial—that you're no longer speaking of your father's last voyage."

"Childbirth," he explained, and realized Garnet was the only person he had talked to about it, except for Irish, who was like family. "And she's too old for it."

Garnet's hand closed over his on the rail and she squeezed lightly. Despite the cool breeze, her fingers were warm. "She gave birth to a great lout like you, didn't she? She'll be all right."

There was, he thought, great good humor in Garnet's voice. She was undoubtedly a woman who would always look on the bright side of life, no matter how bleak the circumstances.

"Look . . ." she said suddenly. "Over there—following the ship."

He looked back at their wake. On either side of the foaming path of white water were dark triangular fins.

"Now there's something that sailors are really superstitious about," Sebastian said with a shudder. "When those evil creatures follow a ship, it's believed someone is going to die. Lord, I hate sharks."

⊶⊷ CHAPTER 7 ⊷⊶

Cyril La Flair knew at once what had happened when
he saw the tall, stoop-shouldered man with the white
beard and pink cheeks, accompanied by the ferret-like
housekeeper, walking through the park. He knew Mrs.
Turner. Although Emily herself had admitted him to
the house, he had seen the woman hovering like a
wizened bird of prey in the shadows at the end of the
hall.

Emily always insisted upon meeting Cyril in the park
and would not allow him to call for her at the house,
but he waited across the street to see her safely home
and he knew the lace curtains in the bay windows
moved surreptitiously, and small, deepset eyes watched
their comings and goings.

Cyril walked toward the sinister-looking pair, his
head held high, black overcoat flapping against his lean
frame. He found the overcoat necessary even though it
was a mild afternoon. Cyril was always cold.

As they drew nearer, Job McKnight turned to speak
to the housekeeper. She hesitated, then turned and went
back toward the iron gates of the park. The old man
stood still, leaning on his walking stick, waiting for
Cyril to reach him.

"Mr. McKnight? I am Cyril La Flair. Emily's half-
brother."

The old man glowered at him silently, misty-pale
eyes taking in every detail, from the threadbare coat
to the down-at-heel boots.

"I plead guilty to cowardice, sir," Cyril continued.
"I should have faced you like a man and asked that I
be allowed to visit my sister . . . who is my only living

relative, by the way. When I learned you had been so recently bereaved, this did not seem to be the time to probe old wounds."

"You're trying to tell me that you look on her as a sister—and you're expecting me to swallow that?" Job snapped.

"Yes. I am and I do."

"You look like the Frenchman. You're a decadent race, La Flair, but I didn't think even a Frog would stoop to incest."

A small muscle twitched in Cyril's long jaw, but his voice was level, if lacking in his normal musical resonance. "Sir, before you make any further ugly and unfounded accusations, I beg of you to remember that Emily's father was also the Frenchman, as you call him. May I inquire where Emily is? I hope she is not indisposed."

"My granddaughter is no concern of yours. You'll never see her again, I promise you." McKnight gave Cyril one last withering glance and then turned on his heel and walked away, his walking stick jabbing the gravel path.

Job McKnight wanted the image of La Flair's son out of his mind's eye with all speed. The memory of his lost first wife and daughter was painfully invoked at the sight of the almost supernaturally handsome young man. Job blinked, his teeth coming down over his lower lip to keep the anguish at bay. How he had loved them, his Emily, and their daughter, Cecily.

Had there ever really been a time when Job McKnight had been the boyishly handsome young genius of shipping circles? Acquiring a fleet of ships and a fortune before most men had even begun to make their mark had been pale glory beside Job's real accomplishment. He had persuaded the breathtakingly lovely Emily to marry him. How he had loved her! The days with her were still golden-bright in his memory.

When their cherished Cecily, symbol of all their love for one another, had disgraced them by running away with her married French tutor, Job's beloved Emily had pined away rapidly and died.

The happy young shipowner and dedicated family man died with her. He was replaced by a coldly calculating man who saw evil where formerly there had been goodness; darkness where there had been light; decay instead of renewal. Where once each day dawned bright with wonderful promise, now it marked only the passing of time to be endured. In Job's pain and grief, he wanted everyone around him to feel the misery he felt.

When Cecily returned, heavy with the Frenchman's child, Job was angry that they lived and Emily was dead. Soon his daughter, too, was dead, and there was a tiny little replica of his lost Emily in her place. There could be no other name for his granddaughter.

The arrival of the granddaughter came too late to undo the disintegration of his personality. He still paced the floor at night, his heart chained to a memory that would not let go. In the daylight hours he was a shrewd and pitiless machine, devoid of compassion or any human feelings; known as a skinflint and miser. At night he fell into a trance-like state, hovering between sleep and wakefulness, that produced tormenting images. The unfulfilled desires became more acute as his granddaughter grew more like his lost love with each passing day.

It became necessary to obliterate the image of his lost wife with brandy before he retired for the night, crawling into the cold comfort of his empty bed. Sometimes he was troubled by terrible dreams. More than once he had awakened in his granddaughter's room and did not know whether he was there because of his own nightmare or in response to hers. He dare not let himself speculate on what was real and what was only a dream, or the confusion of drunkenness.

Reaching the park gates, he glanced backward for a second. Standing behind him amid the soft green foliage was La Flair. Son of the man who had made the dream crumble into ruins.

Cyril watched the retreating figure disconsolately. Until this moment he had not faced the possibility that Emily would be snatched from his life as quickly as she had become a part of it. There was little they could do if Emily were forbidden to see him. Emily was not yet of age, and even if she had been mistress of her own destiny, Cyril doubted she would defy her grandfather.

Cyril's soul cried out in despair. The agonizing sense of loss filled his being. Yet he had been unable to define why Emily had become so important to him. His half-sister. But the blood tie was not the only thing. She was his dear and true friend. Yes, that, and much, much more. Emily had filled a space in his life that had never before been occupied.

He had always been odd man out, from back in his itinerant childhood when he attended a succession of schools that changed with his father's ability to pay their tuitions. Rarely staying long in one place and not being interested in the pursuits of other boys, he never made any close friends. He was always the "sissy" who preferred the piano to rugby, poetry to cricket, quiet meditation to rough-and-tumble play.

Cyril had lived with his mother, an English opera singer whose roles became smaller and farther from London as her youth and health faded. Occasionally, his father would come into his life for an intensive purge of fathering that left Cyril exhausted and thankful his father's paramours left him little time for a discarded wife and son.

By the time he reached manhood, Cyril was sickened by his parents' excesses. Both flitted from lover to lover with as little concern for lasting relationships as the rabbits of the field. Apparently the only woman his father had genuinely cared for had been the frail Cecily McKnight, Emily's mother. André La Flair had wrung his hands, paced the floor, and lamented the cruelty of Job McKnight in preventing him from seeing his one true love and their child. He had shown Cyril the unopened letters and returned gifts.

Cyril shivered, thrusting his hands deep into his overcoat pockets, as he walked back to his lodgings. A thin drizzle had begun to fall and the gaslights were ghostly yellow beacons above the squalid streets through which he trudged. Occasionally a carriage rolled by, sending a spray of filthy water cascading over him. The silk scarf he wore to ward off the frequent attacks of quinsy that had plagued him since childhood hung damply down his chest. Emily had told him it made him look "dashing." He smiled, remembering.

With Emily he felt like a king—powerful, wise, and invincibly masculine. He did not dwell on the fact that he would never be called upon to prove his manhood with her, since they were blood-related. Cyril had avoided thinking about sexual relationships for several years.

In his first year at a certain boarding school he had been flattered when a sixth-form student offered him the job of "fag." The older boys were allowed to have younger students run errands for them, clean up their rooms, and do other chores in return for pocket money and help with schoolwork. The "fagging" system benefitted both parties. Cyril, unfortunately, was chosen to be the fag of a muscular rugby player who had already discovered a sexual preference for his own sex.

The night Cyril found himself cornered with the door locked, the strapping rugby player's roommate in sickbay, there was little a puny fourth-former could do to protect himself. He begged to be allowed to go and burst into tears, to his even deeper humiliation. The older boy had merely laughed and unfastened his trousers to expose the largest male organ Cyril had ever seen.

When it was all over, Cyril crawled into his bed bruised, shivering, and bleeding. After lights out, he climbed out of his window on the third floor, letting himself down to the ground on knotted bedsheets.

Fortunately, his father arrived at almost the same moment Cyril presented himself at his mother's flat. His father had laughed at his initiative in running away from a school he disliked and did not ask for a reason. Cyril never told anyone what happened. After that he avoided even casual friendships with men or boys.

At seventeen, worried that the experience had turned him into a homosexual, Cyril went to a prostitute. Since he had no knowledge of the best way to select one, he went to Piccadilly Circus after dark and allowed himself to be picked up by a streetwalker.

She took him to a grimy room on a mean street near the river. An elderly crone and half a dozen children huddled around a dying fire, trying to keep warm with the aid of old newspapers. Behind a flimsy curtain was a sagging bed, covered with a stained blanket across which fat cockroaches scurried as she lit a candle.

Cyril shivered, his nostrils closing in revulsion at the stench of the room and, worse, the smell of the woman's unwashed body as she began to undress.

She was on her knees, trying to coax his reluctant organ with her lips, when one of the children's heads appeared, grinning, around the curtain. Cyril pulled up his trousers and fled, the prostitute's howl of rage following him down the cobblestoned street.

He had tried to form associations with respectable girls, but these had been even less satisfying than his acquaintances with men. The flirtations were embarrassingly superficial and neither the prospect of marriage nor a casual affair seemed worth the effort of enduring the company of vacant women with minds that had evidently begun to atrophy at birth. Until Emily.

She was so like him in every way. Her quick, creative mind. Her passionate love of music and poetry. Her discerning eye for beauty.

His visit to the dismal city of Liverpool had extended into days and weeks because he could not bear to be parted from the one human being in the world with whom he felt total communion.

Few carriages traveled the street in which his boardinghouse was situated, and pedestrians scurried for shelter as rainclouds darkened the sky and thunder rumbled up the river. He had been so wrapped up in his misery and sense of loss that he was unaware of the footsteps that had followed him all the way from the park.

The two crimps moved forward now and caught up with him, one on either side.

"No need to knock this one over the 'ead, 'Enry. Looks like he'd break too easy. Shouldn't wonder if he keeled over in fright if we say 'boo.'"

There was a nasal snicker of laughter and Cyril found his arms gripped by rough hands that propelled him forward almost at a run.

Emily had watched helplessly from her window on the second floor of the house as her grandfather and Mrs. Turner went across the street to the park. Cyril had confronted the old man so bravely, his head held proudly and his beautiful long-fingered hands gesturing so earnestly. How she wished she could have heard what was said.

Her breath caught in her throat and her heart hammered painfully against her ribs as her grandfather left and she saw the two roughly dressed men emerge from behind the trees and follow Cyril. She did not know who or what those men were, but from their shifty-eyed glances about the quiet street and the furtive way they walked close to the garden walls, heads down, she knew they were men of evil purpose.

Emily ran to her bedroom door and tugged at the brass knob futilely. "Mollie! Mollie! Please unlock my door!" she called, but there was no response.

Mrs. Turner came up the stairs and stood outside the door. "Be quiet in there. Do you want to wake the baby? Mollie just got the little tartar to sleep. I'll bring you your tea when it's ready." There followed an audible muttering about spoiled rich girls who didn't know when they were well off and who never lifted a hand to fend for themselves.

Emily went back to the window and pressed her face to the steamy glass, trying to see down the street, but the rain and gloom obscured everything but the yellow glow of the gas lamps, flaring to life one by one as the lamplighter made his rounds.

The dismal afternoon faded into early twilight and Emily thought it must surely be raining all over the earth. She would never see Cyril again, never hear his melodious laughter ring out, or feel the bracing touch of his cool hands as he enclosed her fingers. Together they had explored realms of spiritual mystery whose existence she had previously dared only to imagine. Everything had begun to make sense . . . the purpose of living. The stark ugliness of the world was there merely to open inner eyes to that sharp contrast between bleakness and all that sent the human spirit soaring. But the journey to that wondrous understanding required a partner; one could not see all aspects of beauty by oneself.

A frozen tear slipped down Emily's cheek. Cyril was not a man to come storming a castle in order to rescue the imprisoned princess. Inexplicably, Emily thought suddenly of Sebastian Balmain. He would have come and released her, if he were still in Liverpool. But he had sailed away again without even saying goodbye to his mother.

She remembered the afternoon she had walked with Sebastian in the park. He had teased her and told her outrageous stories and made her laugh, but all the time she had been painfully aware of his size and strength, and felt threatened by it. Or was it, she wondered now, his masculinity?

There was always the sexual undercurrent to everything he said to her, even when on the surface he was being perfectly proper. She remembered the angry declaration Sebastian flung at her grandfather that one day he would return to court her. Had he meant it, or was it his way of lashing out at the man who felt he was not good enough to associate with a protected granddaughter?

Louisa had from time to time spoken about her son. Once she had even told Emily, bluntly, "You will need a husband like Sebastian one day, Emily, after your grandfather is gone. You will need someone to protect you from the world, run the ships for you and see you are always sheltered from the harsh realities of life. You see, Emily, there are the dreamers of the world, and the practical ones who must take care of them. It doesn't do for two dreamers—or two practical people, for that matter—to pair up."

Emily liked Sebastian. She liked his bluff and hearty ways, his free and easy attitude, but she suspected that all of Sebastian Balmain was there on the surface, to be seen. There would be no wondrous peeling away of the layers to reveal interesting and mysterious new facets of his character and personality. There would be no brilliant ideas, flashes of uncommon wit and analysis, to look forward to for the woman who shared Sebastian's life. Protected from the world, yes, she would be that . . . but at what cost to her soul?

Cyril, Emily thought, feeling her heart would break, *oh, dear God in heaven, please protect him.*

Cyril was lying on the bottom of a boat, his face inches from the foul-smelling water seeping through sodden boards. Other inert bodies pinned him down. He squirmed sideways, trying to raise his hands from the imprisoning limbs of the drunken sailors tossed like so many sacks of refuse in the narrow boat.

He was soaking wet and felt the ominous tightening of his throat, the difficulty in swallowing, that heralded a dreaded abscess. His hands were free now and he gripped the side of the boat and raised his head cautiously to look across the dank water.

Two men were rowing the boat downriver and he could see the gaunt outlines of ships lying in the docks. He had no idea how treacherous the currents of the river were, and he was a poor swimmer, but he knew that once aboard one of those ships his fate could be worse than drowning in the murky depths of the Mersey.

He had never worried about being shanghaied, despite the waterfront boardinghouse where he was staying. He was too slightly built and delicate looking to bring a crimp's fee. No doubt Job McKnight was paying handsomely to separate Emily and the Frenchman's son.

The other unfortunate wretches in the boat were all sleeping off drunken binges, and the oarsmen seemed intent only on pulling the boat. The distance to the docks did not appear to be great, although in the darkness of a rain-filled evening it was difficult to judge. Slowly he dragged himself up on his knees, his hands still gripping the sides of the boat.

"Look out, 'Enry—the skinny one is thinking of drowning hisself," a hoarse voice said.

Cyril did not see the oar swing toward him. He turned in the direction of the voice and the next second the dripping wood crashed down on his fingers and the pain exploded in his hands, raced up his arms, and screamed through his brain. He fell backward, thrusting his hands under his arms, rocking back and forth soundlessly, the cry of agony frozen on his lips.

His hands . . . his pianist's fingers . . . so carefully exercised and protected. *Oh, God,* he thought, *have you no mercy? Better to let him hit me on the head and kill me than deprive me of my hands.*

By the time the boat stopped beside one of the ships, Cyril was shaking violently and waves of nausea were engulfing him.

A rope ladder came over the side. One of the two crimps went up the ladder and then a rope was passed down and the second crimp fastened it about the middle of one of the men. All of the shanghaied men were passed up to the deck before the crimp produced Cyril.

"Go on, now, up the ladder, if you know what's good for you."

"I can't . . . my hands . . ." Cyril gasped out. "I think the fingers are broken. . . ."

"Come on, up the ladder, or else I'll break yer 'ead," the hoarse voice said. "You'll get worse than a wrap on the knuckles before you're done."

His right hand would not close about the rope, but he had some use in his left hand. In the dim light he could see his fingernails were black and all of the knuckles swollen. Barely aware of what was happening to him in his pain and misery, he climbed the rope ladder, prodded from below with an oar.

--⊰{ CHAPTER 8 }⊱--

Erik Gunnar lay on his bunk, hands behind his head, and when Garnet entered the cabin, he growled, "I told you not to go on deck—especially not wearing that dress I bought you."

Garnet smoothed the bright green material over her hips. "It fits well. You've got a good eye for a woman's size."

He got up and went to her, pulling her into a rough embrace and bending her backward to kiss her hungrily.

When his mouth released hers, she put up her hand and smoothed his beard away from his lips. "If you'd shave it off . . ." she said. *You'd look more like him.*

"The beard makes me look older and meaner." His speech was thick with passion and he plucked impatiently at her buttons.

"Wait a minute. You'll tear it." She unfastened the bodice carefully, slipped out of the dress, and laid it on his sea chest.

He picked her up and tossed her to the bunk, crashing down on her and exploring her thighs with impatient fingers. She sighed and closed her eyes as he pushed his engorged member into her. The hard bunk bruised her back and sent a sharp pain down her leg as he slammed her down with increasing urgency.

After a few seconds, her memory conjured up another image, from long ago. Her imagination substituted someone else for Erik Gunnar. She parted her lips and moaned. Now she undulated her hips with his, ran her hands over his chest, and clasped his buttocks to bring him deeper inside her.

77

They rose and fell together, breathlessly, faster and faster, until everything soared to the exploding release from tension they both sought. When she blinked open her green eyes again and looked at him, she seemed shocked to realize who he was. But in his euphoria he did not notice.

"Stay in the cabin from now on," he mumbled just before he fell asleep. "I've enough trouble blackmailing the skipper to keep him away from you, without you tempting every hand in the fo'c'sle."

She lay beside him on the swaying bunk, eyes open and staring. For a few minutes, in the heat of passion, it was possible to forget. But afterward there was no magical ebb tide to carry her away from the sensory pleasures to the deeper, more spiritual joining of a man and a woman. Minds and memories, dreams and nightmares, hearts and souls . . . there was more to a man and woman coming together than the mere joining of flesh.

As Erik Gunnar slept contentedly beside her, Garnet thought suddenly of another man on board the ship. She visualized clear blue eyes, shining with honesty and integrity. Sebastian Balmain. She had spent only minutes with him, yet those were the words that sprang into her mind when she thought of him. Honesty and integrity. Erik mumbled in his sleep and she blinked, wondering if she had spoken aloud. Sebastian Balmain would never knowingly hurt another human being, especially not a woman. Garnet remembered the gentle protectiveness in his voice when he spoke of his mother. She wished that Sebastian had been first mate, or skipper, of the *Dancer*. She wondered, idly, if he had, if she would ever have reached her friend Cassie Madigan in New Orleans.

The weather changed abruptly and the *Dancer* battled mountainous seas. Gunnar and his mates kicked and beat the weary sailors mercilessly for the slightest hesitation in obeying an order, while the growing dissension between master and mate was taken out on the crew in conflicting orders and unnecessary deprivations.

78

Torrential rain pelted the struggling ship, and, when night fell, the gale-force winds made it impossible for a man to draw a breath on deck. Nevertheless, Gunnar and the second and third mates entered the forecastle, dumped the half-frozen men out of hammocks, and ordered them back on deck. Two men fell to their knees under blows from belaying pins. Irish O'Toole was coughing and holding his thin arms crossed before his face to avoid Gunnar's knotted rope.

"For God's sake, Mr. Gunnar, what do you want us to do?" Sebastian asked, struggling to pull his still-wet shirt over his head.

"Aloft, all of you!" Gunnar shouted. "Take in the mizzen topsail."

"How the hell—" Sebastian's words were lost under the impact of Gunnar's fist in his mouth.

"You'll lie out on the yard and pick up the sail and I'll kill the next man that questions my orders."

"Come on, lads," Irish O'Toole croaked. "Let's trim the yard and be done with it. I'll sing ye a chantey and drown out the wind." And the wiry little Irishman limped out into the icy tempest.

Sebastian never knew if Irish found the strength to sing, but between the howling fury of the wind and the great hollow roar of the waves, there were split-seconds when he was sure he heard the mellow peal of O'Toole's clear, true voice rising above the shrieking storm.

"Blow the man down, will you . . . blow the man down . . ."

Fighting for breath and wrestling with the wind-whipped canvas, Sebastian did not know if he actually heard the words or if they were inside his head, remembered from days of clear sailing when Irish sang and the crew chorused an answer and the work went smoother for it.

When it happened, it was so sudden that Sebastian did not have time to cry out. A vicious gust of wind caught them and the sail came over the yard. One moment Irish was clinging to the yard, and the next he

79

was struck by a trailing leech on the edge of the sail and swept away into the blackness of the night.

Sebastian never remembered making the descent. He hit the deck, yelling, "Man overboard! Man overboard!"

Sliding across the deck, he collided with Gunnar and seized his shoulders, shaking him frantically. "Irish fell from the yard—heave to, for God's sake. We've got to lower a boat and find him."

Gunnar struck out at him, sending him sprawling as a giant swell hit the ship and broke over the rail in a blinding deluge.

Sebastian was on his feet, running across the slanted deck, fear for the little Irishman giving him the strength and agility to stay upright in a wind that sliced through flesh and bone like the thrust of a sword. He reached the boat on the starboard quarter and was fumbling with the lines when Gunnar's fist crashed into the side of his head. "I didn't order a boat lowered!" the mate shouted above the roar of wind and sea. Sebastian shook his head, then turned, fists raised. He felt skin split beneath his knuckles, the jolt as his hands crashed into bone. He was shouting hoarsely and raining blows on Gunnar when the second and third mates came up behind him and felled him with blows to the back of his neck.

Hovering on the brink of consciousness, he found he was restrained by wrists irons, lying on deck under a sullen dawn. Two men were lashed by their wrists to the ratlines and the mates were flogging them. The sickening sound of rope cutting into bare flesh mingled with their choked-off screams as they tried to suck breath into their starving lungs between the crushing blows.

As soon as Sebastian began to stir, he was seized and hoisted by the wrists for his share of punishment. His shirt was ripped from his back and the cool air caressed his naked flesh as Gunnar shook out the cat-o'-nine-tails. Sebastian heard the peculiar whistling sound of the vicious tails the instant before they connected with his back and shoulders; then he was fighting for breath as the air was forced from his lungs, shuddering as the crushing pain blacked the light from his eyes.

Some of the blood from the open welts ran in swiftly flowing red rivulets, around his chest, over his face, trickling to the deck beneath his dangling feet.

"You're a dead man, Balmain," Gunnar grunted as he wielded the cat. "I'll teach this crew what happens to a man who strikes an officer."

Only half-conscious, trying to squeeze air into his collapsing lungs, Sebastian lost count of the blows. All he could hear was the pounding of blood in his ears and his own torturous gasping.

Irish, he thought weakly, *maybe you were a lucky little Mick, after all.* Then the world rushed away as though it were sucked into a great black hole.

He did not hear the strident female voice ringing out across the deck: "In the name of God, stop this barbarism . . ." Nor did he see Garnet fling herself between his limp body and Erik Gunnar's blazing red eyes.

Blinking open his eyes, he groaned at the carpenter's fumbling ministrations to his back. Ned Hake pressed water to his lips.

"Irish?" Sebastian asked, appalled at the effort it took to make the word come from his lips.

"Not a trace of him," Ned responded.

Tears formed at the back of Sebastian's eyes. "They . . . will pay." He groaned his agony. "The skipper and the mate—I swear it. They murdered Irish."

The effort to speak was too great; Sebastian lay still and made his plans. He knew he could not cold-bloodedly kill Gunnar and the captain. Lying in wait for them ashore, the recourse of most disgruntled sailors, would serve no real purpose. They must be brought to trial for murder. Surely the testimony of the entire crew would count for something in an American court of law.

Sebastian was still weak and his flayed back had not healed when they reached New Orleans. He was dumped ashore without his pay. When he recovered sufficiently to go looking for the *Dancer,* she had sailed on her homeward voyage. There was nothing for it but to sign on another vessel sailing for New York.

He found Ned Hake, reinstated as draftsman at the ship-builders Smith & Dimon, and Ned readily agreed to help him round up other shipmates. They waited for the *Dancer* to return to New York.

When Sebastian tried to get the City Constabulary to arrest the captain and first mate, he found the law ashore was not interested in the oft-told tales of a seaman's miserable lot.

"By God, we'll make them listen," Sebastian told Ned angrily.

"Let it rest," Ned advised. "What good will it do? You're alive and you're ashore. Nothing you do will bring the chanteyman back."

Sebastian's blue eyes flashed almost visible sparks. "And what of the other poor devils who will be flayed and tortured by fiends like Gunnar? Maybe there'll be another chanteyman . . ." His voice broke and he turned away, adding in a strangled voice, "Irish was my dearest friend, and I won't let it rest."

The strident cry of a newspaper boy on the street outside their window broke the ensuing silence. Sebastian's head turned in the direction of the sound. "That's it! I'll go to the newspapers. Tell them my story. Maybe after I get back from Liverpool they will have stirred the public up enough to do something."

"You're sailing for Liverpool?"

"On the fastest packet I can find."

But Sebastian did not sail. A McKnight packet was entering the harbor and the skipper had dismal news for young Balmain. His mother had died of childbed fever, and the old man was acting like an idiot over his new son and heir. Emily? The captain didn't know; McKnight talked of nothing but his son these days.

Sebastian was right about the power of the press.

On a day when there was a little other news, the editorial thundered:

If the Dancer came into port short of a bale of goods or a ton of cargo, the captain would be compelled to account for its loss. Will no one demand an accounting for the loss of a human life?

When the ship next put into port, the captain and first mate were surprised to be confronted by two impressively arrayed constables bearing a warrant for their arrest.

Sebastian was outraged when the court refused to hear the testimony of the abused crew. Captain Curt Vanders and Erik Gunnar were charged only with the maltreatment of Sebastian Balmain and causing the death, by negligence, of Patrick O'Toole.

The defense freely admitted that it had been necessary to punish Sebastian due to his mutinous behavior. The death of O'Toole had been an accident, it was claimed, and occurred because the man had been concealing a severe case of consumption. Weakness, due to illness, had caused him to fall to his death.

Defense counsel then paraded an impressive array of shipmasters, merchants, and insurance men as character witnesses for the captain and first mate. The captain's wife, a pale and bewildered-looking woman with three stone-faced daughters clustered about her, was brought into court. The jury was admonished that this family would be in dire straits if the testimony of a common sailor were heeded and the captain thrown in jail.

The final preposterous excuse for the brutality was that "the rashness and inconsiderateness of youthful command—the first mate being only a lad in his early twenties—must be given allowance."

Erik Gunnar appeared in court clean-shaven, his hair neatly trimmed. He was handsome, virile looking, and properly respectful to authority.

When he charged the jury, the judge did indicate that if the man O'Toole were ill, then he should not have been sent aloft in foul weather. He added that the other punishments described must be judged as cruelty and instructed the jury to consider the captain an accessory, aiding and abetting the mate. Balancing these facts, however, was the counter-claim of the mate that Balmain had struck an officer and, therefore, some form of punishment was justified.

Unfortunately, Sebastian made a poor witness. Despite the flogging he looked a picture of health: big, tanned, and clear-eyed. Just as muscular and youthful as the first mate.

The jury was about to be dismissed to consider their verdict when there was an excited stir at the rear of the courtroom. A woman entered, sweeping aside bailiffs and guards with a furled parasol. She wore a deep green velvet walking dress and a bonnet aflutter with feathers perched atop her auburn curls. Her eyes burned like green opals, but her voice was cultured and controlled.

"I want to testify," she declared in ringing tones. "I am a witness to what happened aboard the *Dancer*."

There was an uproar among the spectators as they leaped to their feet to get a better view of the startlingly pretty woman. A recess was immediately ordered.

The fact that Garnet was a stowaway diminished the effectiveness of her testimony. Defense counsel suggested that "nice women" did not stow away on tramp vessels. It was also quickly established that Garnet had been in the first mate's cabin during the storm in which the chanteyman had allegedly fallen from the yardarm. It was hinted broadly that the first mate had promised marriage, and her testimony was nothing more than the spiteful revenge of a woman scorned.

"I saw that man flogged unmercifully," Garnet told the court, looking at Sebastian. "He was unconscious and the first mate threatened to beat him to death. I also saw other members of the crew kicked and beaten repeatedly."

The jury listened. The woman was a tart, but she was an educated tart. More than one spectator wondered about her background. She was young, yet there was a worldliness and blatant sexuality about her that were at odds with that cultured accent.

An uproar broke out as the jury returned a guilty verdict. The judge, however, was lenient. The captain was sentenced to ninety days in jail and a fine of $100. Erik Gunnar, his face livid, was dragged off to serve three years for manslaughter. Once way from the scrutiny of press and spectators, however, he was quickly reassured that most of his sentence would be suspended. It had been imposed to quiet the newspapers. The malingering habits of seamen were well known, and good officers were hard to find.

Unaware Gunnar was being promised no more than a three-month jail term, the crowd spilled into the street. Sebastian jostled aside the congratulating hands of his shipmates who had been barred from testifying and found his way to Garnet's side. Wordlessly she slipped her hand through his arm and they walked together, as though it had been prearranged.

"I thought you were going to New Orleans. I looked for you there before I sailed back."

A carriage waited for her. They climbed inside and closed the window curtains on the peering crowd.

"Lucky for you I did come back," she replied. There was no point in telling him she had been tied to Erik Gunnar's bunk for the short stay in New Orleans when the ship was loaded with black slaves. The illegal cargo was smuggled ashore in Charleston, and Garnet had no choice but to return to New York.

"I wanted to testify that they are slavers, too," she told Sebastian. "But the prosecutor said we had no proof of that."

"No matter. We put him away for three years. He wouldn't have got that much for slaving," Sebastian answered. He glanced about the richly upholstered interior of the carriage. "You seem to be doing well for yourself."

"It belongs to a rich friend. Will you have supper with me?"

"Your rich friend won't mind?" He tried to keep the disappointment out of his voice. She had, after all, been servicing the first mate. He knew what kind of woman she was.

"He's out of town."

Sebastian had never seen anything as opulent as the hotel suite in which Garnet lived. His feet sank into plush carpeting, the walls were covered with brocade, and there was a separate sitting room furnished with delicate Queen Anne chairs and settees; all this in addition to a luxurious bedroom boasting a velvet-draped four-poster.

Garnet giggled as Sebastian tested the bed, then, roaring with laughter, bounced up and down on the pale pink quilt. Lace-edged pillows flew in all directions as Garnet leaped onto the bed with him and they jumped up and down, laughing and tickling one another until they were gasping and shedding tears of merriment.

"I can send down for some food," Garnet said as she got up and went to the dressing table to tidy her hair.

Sebastian looked about the room at the graceful furniture and the profusion of pink hues. "What sort of a man shares this room?" he asked curiously.

"He owns the hotel."

"Then someone might tell him you brought a common sailor up here."

She surveyed him from beneath a flutter of red-gold eyelashes, her eyes sparkling. "Oh, you don't look so common to me."

The invitation in her eyes was unmistakable. Sebastian had felt the growing bulge in his groin as they bounced together on the bed, and now the blood began to pound in his temples, too. Slowly he stood up and went over to her, slipping his arm about her waist to pull her close. Her breath smelled faintly of peppermint and he noticed for the first time that there was a sprinkling of pale gold freckles across the bridge of her tip-tilted nose.

"We'd have lost the case today without you," he said, and his voice was strangely hoarse as she pressed against him. Her breasts molded to his chest and the hard points of her nipples probed him through the silk of her bodice.

She watched from beneath half-closed eyes as he kissed her, his tongue finding her parted lips and exploring her mouth. Her hands went around his back, slid downward, over his buttocks, and then to the erection that strained against her.

"Just as I suspected, Sebastian Balmain," she murmured against his mouth. "A very uncommon sailor." Then her tongue was darting, seeking his mouth, and there was a distant echo of laughter in her fondling fingers and caressing lips.

She pulled away suddenly and pushed him backward.

"Oh, no, you don't. You won't have me fully dressed like some waterfront doxie. Off with your clothes, you great ox, and be damned quick about it."

He laughed, pulling his shirt over his head in a quick movement and finding when he emerged from the moment of darkness that her dress was already a green froth slithering to the floor about her ankles. She was fumbling with the ribbon ties of her chemise, and, a moment later, she stood before him naked.

For an instant the image of her naked in Gunnar's arms intruded upon his thoughts and he realized in dismay that his bold erection was faltering. Fortunately, at that moment she sprang toward him, pushing him down on the bed as she caught him off balance.

She came to rest on top of him, squirming to re-arrange the soft flesh of her breasts and covering his mouth with her kisses. He caught her by the hair, pulling her closer, then rolled over with her and found her thighs already parted.

Garnet sighed deeply as he entered her and arched her back to meet his thrusts, rotating her hips and alternately squeezing, then releasing him until he felt himself slipping into a climax that came too soon. She was not perturbed. She looked up at him, running a little pink tongue over her lower lip and keeping him imprisoned within the soft warmth of her thighs. "Impetuous sort, aren't you, Sebastian Balmain? We shall have to rekindle all that ardor and show you how to make it last a bit longer." Her laughter rang out again and he buried his face in her breasts and laughed, too.

They were still making love when the dawn broke, and she asked him sleepily, "What do you want out of life, Sebastian?"

"To own my own ship," he said at once, not stopping to think. "And make life tolerable for the tars who sail her. An end to the brutality they put up with now—some rights for seamen. What about you, Garnet —what do you want?"

She opened green eyes and surveyed him speculatively. "I may have found what I want," she said enigmatically, but he was only half-awake and too sated with her to ponder what she meant by that.

Drifting to the surface of a deep and contented sleep sometime later, Sebastian's arms tightened about the softly yielding body beside him. With his eyes still closed, the first image that flickered hauntingly across his mind's eye was that of a dark-eyed face of exquisite loveliness. Emily. But, of course . . . he told himself distantly as he slipped back into slumber, Emily was too pure and sweet to give herself to anyone but her husband.

—⊰ CHAPTER 9 ⊱—

Emily was sure that if it had not been for Mollie Flanagan, she would have lost her mind. The first days Emily saw only Mrs. Turner, who brought food, and water for her bath. When Emily begged to speak with her grandfather, she was told that he had no wish to see her. When she asked the ferret-like housekeeper to tell her what had become of Cyril, the woman pursed thin lips and sniffed as though overcome by noxious fumes. "We never discuss him."

"The baby—little Mark, how is he?" Emily asked, desperate to keep the woman with her, yearning for a moment's contact with another human being.

"Well enough. A handful." Mrs. Turner sniffed again and departed.

Then one afternoon when Mrs. Turner had gone to the market, there was the sound of the key in the lock. Mollie of the ferocious stare and wild eyes slipped into the room. She carried a pot of tea and teacups.

"Owd biddy is out shopping and the baby's asleep," she announced. "So you have a nice cup of tea and I'll read the tea leaves for you. Helps get through times of trial if you know something better's on the way."

While Emily sipped her tea, it transpired that Mollie blamed herself for not warning the girl of impending disaster. She had seen it in her own tea leaves.

"Don't like this house, I don't. Especially not that old woman. Ah, but the baby is a little love. I shan't ever have any of me own, but he'll be a son to me. He's going to be a very special man, my little Mark— though the lord knows he's going to live through perilous times."

Mollie chattered, her melodious brogue soothing to the ear and her presence easing Emily's loneliness. After a time, the girl produced a small flask from her apron pocket. "You don't mind if I have a little nip? Have to be careful around the old woman . . ."

Emily watched with astonishment as Mollie drained the flask and breathed a whiskey-laden sigh of satisfaction. Then the Irish girl studied the pattern of the tea leaves in Emily's cup. Her stern expression relaxed into a smile of joy. "Ah! I thought so—rescue for you. A man . . . love and happiness . . . and a child for you—ooh! Such a child! A journey over water . . . a strange place . . . but beautiful." She twirled the cup in her fingers and then stopped abruptly, catching her breath. She closed her eyes and her lips moved in what appeared to be a prayer.

"What is it? Oh, what do you see? You look so horrified!"

"Nothing . . . I must go. I'll come back tomorrow when she goes out."

Mollie never again read Emily's tea leaves. She did come back to visit, until Mrs. Turner caught her. After that, when Mrs. Turner left the house, Mollie and the baby, snug in his perambulator, accompanied her.

Emily's isolation was complete. She turned in desperation to her books after exhausting every possible avenue of escape. Her sensitive soul knew only too well why her punishment was so excessive. Her mother had returned to Job McKnight's house in the last stages of pregnancy. She had not lived long enough for him to purge himself of the anger he felt toward her. Now Emily must pay for her mother's sin, for the sin of her own birth.

She lost track of time. Each day was a repetition of the last, endlessly, like ghostly footfalls in the corridor of time. Her books became frayed from the turning and returning of pages. She painstakingly unpicked all of the embroidery on her pillowcases and created new designs. She spent hours at the window, watching the trees in the park come into leaf, the first golden daffodils, then the unfolding of the carpet of bluebells beneath the trees.

Carriages rolled up the street. Nursemaids wheeled perambulators in the park. From her window the passersby took on distorted gargoyle-like appearances, with enlarged heads and stunted legs. She was living on the rim of a glass bottle, peering over the edge at the inhabitants, seeing but never able to touch.

To save her sanity, she wrote letters to Cyril and composed poetry in her head. She had no notepaper. But the sweet, sad verses and fragments of lyric poems did not express her misery.

A spider filling a corner of her ceiling with a lace star filled an empty hour. She drew pictures in the steam on her window. In her imagination she flew up her chimney and emerged, sooty but triumphant. She tied her hair in tight little knots and then had to cut them out with her embroidery scissors.

Then one day she looked down and saw a sailor's watch cap atop a bristling mane of black hair, shoulders with muscles that strained against a salt-whitened melton cloth jacket. Sebastian! He had come back.

Emily drew back from the window, her thoughts flying like a flock of birds rising in confusion before an unexpected intruder. Her grandfather was not at home. Did Sebastian know of his mother's death? Would Mrs. Turner admit him to the house?

Sound was muffled by the thick brick walls, and she felt rather than heard Sebastian pound on the front door. Heavy footsteps took the stairs in impatient leaps, punctuated by Mrs. Turner's shrill protests. Voices argued in unison in the hall and then Sebastian said loudly, "Open the door, damn it, or I'll kick it in."

There was a fumbling with the key and then the door burst open. Emily stood motionless in the center of the room, her head inclined to one side, her hands clasped in front of her.

Sebastian, his eyes brightly blue and searching, stopped so abruptly in his headlong dash into the room that Mrs. Turner almost collided with him.

"She tells me you've been locked in here for weeks. Is it true?" A terrible anger coursed through his veins. The helplessness of the frail girl and the harshness of the punishment inflicted upon her were, he was sure, his fault. He had been too blinded with rage to hear exactly what Mrs. Turner had said about Emily's transgression. The woman had muttered something about sneaking around with a man behind her grandfather's back. Sebastian knew from his mother that he had been the only man Emily had seen away from the house. The white-bearded old swine had killed his mother and had come damned close to letting this exquisite creature pine away with loneliness. God, she looked so pale and frightened. Sebastian's blood boiled anew. "Is it true?" he asked again. "You've been locked in here and not allowed to leave this room?"

Emily nodded dumbly, more afraid of the powerfully built man facing her than of her own loneliness. In that one minute before he burst through the door, her room became a refuge and Sebastian the intrusion of the terrifying outside world.

"That old bastard," Sebastian said savagely. "Come on, start packing. I'm taking you out of here today." The where, why, and how of this decision did not strike him. He had come to see Emily and his little half-brother, to try to ease his grief over his mother by talking about it with Emily, who, he was sure, was as saddened by his mother's death as he was. This was not the time to pay court to Emily, although that he would one day do so was a foregone conclusion. Apart from the fact that it had been his mother's wish, Sebastian had kept Emily in a special place in his mind. Her unsullied beauty and purity, her grace and charm, the delicate manner that concealed an underlying intelligence and strength of character were all in sharp contrast to the brazen women of the night that a sailor usually associated with on his brief stay in port.

Behind him, Mrs. Turner was recovering from her shock at being rudely shoved aside. "I'll fetch the peelers," she cried in alarm.

Sebastian turned and looked down at her. "One more word out of you and I'll put you up there." He jerked his head in the direction of the top of Emily's wardrobe. Mrs. Turner quickly backed away as Sebastian reached up to pull a portmanteau from the top shelf.

Emily opened her chiffonier drawer with trembling fingers. She removed neatly folded handkerchiefs and gloves. There didn't seem to be anything else to do. Sebastian was completely in command of the situation. She felt swept up by his strength and decisiveness. What an attractive giant of a man he was. Was he aware, she wondered as she placed a scarf over her underwear before removing it from the drawer, of the masculine power that he exuded with every movement of his muscular arms, or flexing of those massive shoulders? She blushed to the roots of her hair as a lace-edged pair of pantelettes slipped from her shaking fingers and fell in full view of Sebastian.

"Do you have a trunk?" Sebastian asked, pretending not to notice either her embassasment or the cause of it.

"In the attic." Emily's voice cracked. She was unsure if she was catching another cold or if it was merely because those were the first words she had spoken aloud that day.

"I'll fetch it. I'm going to look in on the nursery, too, and meet my half-brother. I'll be back in a few minutes." He paused, then went to her and smoothed back a strand of dark hair from her alabaster forehead. "It's all right now, Emily. It's all over."

"Where . . . where will we go?" She managed to get the words out before he disappeared through the doorway.

He glanced back at her in surprise. "Why—we'll go and get married, of course," he said.

They found a room in a boardinghouse, away from the waterfront, on a street of slate-roofed terrace houses, each one identical to the next. Sebastian left Emily there after telling the landlord's wife they were already married, then went to make arrangements for the wedding.

It was late when he returned. He brought pork pies and cider for their supper, then tucked her into the double bed and kissed the tip of her nose. He slept in the chair by the fire and she lay awake under blankets that smelled of moth balls and listened to him snore. It was a comforting sound.

The next day they were married in the registry office and one of the clerks punctuated the ceremony with a series of sneezes. When Emily promised to love, honor, and obey the giant of a man who stood at her side, he slipped a thin gold band onto her finger and grinned ruefully when it promptly slipped off again.

It was raining, a deluge coming in almost horizontally from the river, and they were drenched to the skin by the time they returned to their room. Emily was clutching her too-large wedding ring on the inside of the palm of her glove, afraid she would lose it.

She was shivering from the cold, yet her neck felt hot as Sebastian's hand brushed it when he helped her remove her sodden cloak. "I'll soon have a fire going," he said. "Come on, out of those wet clothes quickly."

She nodded, her teeth chattering. Sebastian made a small firewood tepee over the crumpled newspaper in the grate. He balanced the lumps of coal atop the wood and set fire to the paper, which blazed brightly for a moment, then died, leaving the wood and coal sputtering and hissing reluctantly.

Emily kept her back to him and draped her dressing gown over her shoulders. With stiff and awkward fingers she peeled her wet dress from her aching body. Her undergarments were wet, too, but she felt Sebastian's eyes on her, and so she slipped her arms into her dressing gown and buttoned it. Her hair hung wetly down her back.

Sebastian went to his duffel bag and fumbled among the jerseys and socks, then, triumphantly, held up a flask. "Rum," he said. "That will warm you, Emily." He went to the cupboard and looked in vain for glasses. At last he brought two chipped cocoa mugs to the fitfully flickering fire, dragging the only chair closer so she could sit down.

"Drink some of this," he said, handing her the mug. "I'm sorry it isn't much of a wedding toast, Emily . . . and a pie from the pie shop will be the only feast we'll have. But I promise you one day we'll have a great ball and champagne to drink and you'll be warm and dry. I'll do my best to make you happy, pretty little Emily."

There were glistening drops on her eyelashes that he thought were raindrops. Her slim shoulders were still shaking. She felt so overwhelmed with gratitude and comforted by his strength and gentle protective presence that she thought her heart must burst with love for him. "Only promise me one promise . . ."

"Anything, my sweet wife."

"Never leave me alone again."

Sebastian hesitated as the full implication of this came to him. Seeing the frightened pleading in her eyes, he swallowed and said quickly, "I promise. Now drink some of that rum and I'll tuck you in bed." When the shadow of fear darkened her eyes, he added hastily, "I think you caught a chill. I'll go and borrow a hot-water bottle for the bed. When I come back I want you completely undressed and under that quilt."

He borrowed a stone jar from the landlord's wife and stayed away long enough for Emily to undress. When he returned to their room she was in bed, her hair a dark cloud on the pillow and her face so pinched and pale it seemed the lustrous fringe of eyelashes was too heavy for her delicate cheekbones.

Sebastian tucked the hot-water bottle under her feet and laid his hand on her brow. She was burning with fever.

He sat beside her all night, refilling the stone bottle, keeping the fire burning in the grate. She slept fitfully and murmured in her sleep. He couldn't tell what she said, although he was afraid she must be delirious, because once he was sure he heard her say "squirrel," and that was one animal she was not likely to encounter on the streets of Liverpool.

Sebastian had not intended to marry Emily so soon. Marriage with Emily was for later, when he had enough money to care for her properly. But he could not leave her in a locked room, a prisoner of the white-bearded old fiend who had killed his mother . . . whose last wish was that he marry Emily. Now Sebastian pondered how he could keep the promise not to leave Emily alone. If he returned to sea, the only life he had known, she would be in worse straits than when he found her.

Yet he could not imagine life ashore. He had never intended to give up the sea. He shook his head, wonderingly. Emily had been the unattainable princess—marriage to her an impossible quest. Merely to know a woman of such beauty, education, and refinement was more than most sailors could hope for . . . to claim her as wife was like Beauty marrying the Beast. Sebastian felt like a man who reaches for a star, never expecting to find it suddenly in his hand.

Cursing himself for acting on the spur of the moment, with no plan for the future, he stirred the glowing coals in the grate and told himself drowsily that Emily would be a dazzling wife for the head of a shipping line . . . beautiful, cultured, educated. With Emily beside him, there was nothing he could not do.

In his weariness he did not recognize that the words were his mother's, echoing in his memory. The seed of Louisa's wish for her son to marry Emily, stay ashore, and become a shipowner had taken root and flourished.

Sebastian had been filled with desire for his wife from the moment they stepped into their shabby room. He knew he must be patient. Emily was not a doxie versed in the ways of men and the flesh. Besides, she was frightened of her wedding night and not feeling well. Sebastian had never taken a virgin and was apprehensive about consummating his marriage. What if he hurt her? He *had* to hurt her. Deflowering was painful for a woman. It didn't seem fair to him that it began and ended with pain . . . the pain the woman must suffer to deliver the child. His mother had died from it.

No, there was no hurry to consummate his marriage. They could get used to one another first. After all, there had been no real courtship.

Emily was so beautiful, lying there in the bed. Sebastian could feel himself grow in his britches. He swallowed hard and looked away.

I'm a married man, he thought. *A husband. One day in the not too distant future I shall be a father.* He felt a sudden quickening of his senses. God, what a thing it would be to have a son!

When a cold dawn broke over the slate roofs stretching endlessly beyond their window, Emily opened her eyes and looked at him. "I'm sorry . . . I must have caught a cold." Her breath wheezed in her chest. For a moment he was reminded, frighteningly, of Irish O'Toole's long bout with the ague. Sebastian wrapped his arms about her and held her close to him.

"Emily, I'm sorry. I don't have enough money for a doctor. Dearest, I'll have to go to your grandfather."

He was surprised at her strength as she struggled to raise her hands to his face, placing her slender fingers on his cheeks. "No! Sebastian, I shall be all right. You

96

must never humble yourself to him . . . or to anyone. I could not bear it." She tried to smother a cough.

Sebastian went to remove the soot-blackened kettle from the fire to make her some tea. "We'll see how you are by tomorrow, then," he said gruffly, hating the feeling of helplessness. He took her a steaming cup of tea and sat beside her. "If the landlord's wife looks in on you, will you be all right while I look for work? I'll be back before dark, I promise. I'll not take a chance of some crimp throwing me aboard a ship."

"I'll be all right," she wheezed. "Knowing you'll be coming home to me isn't the same as being alone."

The rain was a steamy drizzle and the puddled pavements reflected a somber sky. Atop Bidston Hill a yellow flag with a black ball in the center hung limply from Cropper & Benson's flagpole, signaling the arrival of a Black Ball liner off the Bar Light, fifteen miles down the river. Each of the more prominent merchants and agents had his own flagpole, and the flags were hoisted so that preparations could be made at the Pier Head to receive the incoming ships.

Sebastian walked down Water Street toward the Pier Head. Office boys darted in and out of the shipping offices on either side of the street, dashing across rain-soaked pavement with rolled documents under their arms. The business of sending cargoes and passengers around the world required a great deal of along-shore activity.

A hand-lettered sign tacked to one door stated: OFFICE BOY WANTED—CLEAN AND INDUSTRIOUS—APPLY WITHIN. Sebastian shook the rain out of his hair, smoothed the unruly mane back from his brow as best he could, and strode purposefully through the door.

Inside the poorly heated office, clerks stood up beside their high, slanted desks; bills of lading, consular invoices, and letters ordering cargoes forward were spread out in front of them. Many of the clerks wore woolen gloves with the fingers cut out to allow them to hold their quills. The high-ceilinged room was heated by only a narrow fireplace, and a brick at one side cut the coal fire down to the barest minimum.

Sebastian approached the only man who was seated, at a small desk, away from the slanted tables. Waiting for the man to come to the end of a long column of figures in the ledger in front of him, Sebastian was uncomfortably aware that he was dripping rainwater in a spreading puddle at his feet.

The man behind the ledger eventually dragged his gaze from the heavily inked figures. He looked at Sebastian's large frame and rough clothing. "You're in the wrong office, sailor. We don't sign on crews here. We are packers and forwarding agents."

"I'm not looking for a ship," Sebastian said. "I came about the office boy's job."

Interested glances were turned in his direction and several clerks covered their smiles. The bookkeeper laughed aloud. "I'm sorry, my good man. You've got Jack Tar written all over you. We need a boy; we've no use for a man. Our clerks work for seven years as office boys before they earn the right to call themselves shipping clerks."

"I'm a little older and a lot bigger, but I want to learn the shipping business. I'm willing to start at the bottom." Sebastian spoke with quiet sincerity, despite the muffled guffaws all around the room. "I'll take the office boy's job."

The room echoed with laughter.

"Look—" Sebastian said, his color rising. "I can see you're having trouble getting those columns of figures to balance. All of these columns are supposed to equal this column's total, is that right? I'm good with figures. Let me balance it for you, to prove to you I can do anything your office boys—or your clerks—can do, with a little instruction."

"Go on, Donald," one of the clerks said. "You've been cursing that balance all morning. Let the Tar show you how to do it."

Donald stood up. The top of his balding head barely reached Sebastian's lower chest. "You can have five minutes." He tossed a sheet of paper on the desk. "Write the totals on that paper; I don't want you putting blots all over my ledger."

Sebastian ran his forefinger quickly down the columns of figures. At the bottom of each he paused to remind himself silently: *Twelve pennies in a shilling, twenty shillings in a pound*.

"I've never seen an educated sailor before," Donald said, breaking the sequence of numbers in Sebastian's head. "Where did you learn arithmetic?"

"My father was a ship's master and he taught me mathematics—it's needed for navigation," Sebastian said, starting on the next column. "I'm a bit slow with pounds sterling."

"American, are you? What's a Yank wanting to live in Liverpool for?"

"I've got a wife here."

"You'll not support her on an office boy's wages."

"Then I'll take a second job. But I want to work in a shipping office, to learn the business."

"We work from dawn to midnight, most days. You'll take a night job, will you?"

Sebastian was silent. He pointed to the column of figures marked "consular charges," then wrote a new total on the sheet of paper. "There's your error. I believe it will balance now." He stood up as the bookkeeper looked over the figures.

The other clerks crowded around to see why Donald was staring silently at his ledger. "Maybe he should have your job, Donald," one of them said, slapping Sebastian on the back in approval.

Donald said grudgingly, "You still can't support a wife on an office boy's wages. But maybe we could use you in the packing company. Think you could make crates and cases? You've got the brawn for it. I'll give you a note to the manager."

Sebastian didn't open the sealed envelope he took to the dockside warehouse where men were hammering together crates and kegs, but all the contents brought him was a rude dismissal from the manager and the advice that there were plenty of ships in need of crews.

Before darkness fell, Sebastian had balanced books and performed mathematically in several other shipping agents' offices, but was still without a job when he returned to the bleak boardinghouse. He bought some hot chestnuts from a street vendor and sniffed longingly at the appetizing aroma of stew drifting from the landlord's ground-floor flat. He hoped the landlord's wife had kept her promise to take some soup to Emily at midday.

The soup had congealed in the earthenware bowl, yellow grease floating on brackish broth. Emily's eyes fluttered open and her porcelain features lit up when she saw Sebastian.

"I'm feeling much better," she croaked. "Perhaps you could look in my valise and find one of my books for me to read while you're at work tomorrow?" She never doubted that he had found a job.

Sebastian kissed her pale cheek. *Tomorrow,* he thought, *I shall have to bring a doctor.*

Surprisingly, when the following day dawned, Emily's eyes were clear and her fever had abated. Sebastian made tea for her and toasted the last of their bread. He found a slim volume of poetry for her to read. He turned the book over in his hand before giving it to her. He had never read for pleasure and knew nothing of poetry. The books his parents took to sea were all of a utilitarian purpose: to teach navigation, mathematics, geography; any other type of reading was considered frivolous.

The sun was shining. Even Liverpool's bleak streets were touched with golden promise as he again set out to look for work. Today he would find a job, he was sure. Everyone would be more charitably inclined on such a sparkling day.

But his luck was no better than the previous day. He was a sailor, and a sailor had no business ashore. He stopped looking for work in the shipping offices and tried warehouses and shops, even boardinghouses. At the latter it was suggested that with his size and brawn there was one sure way to earn a living. Angrily, Sebastian responded that he would not crimp. The lowest scum of all were crimps and sharks, preying on their fellow seamen.

100

His money would last a week or two, no longer. Perhaps he could dodge the landlord and avoid paying the rent on Friday.

By Friday Sebastian still did not have a job, but he returned to their small room that evening to find Emily up and dressed. Her eyes were clear, and although she still had a tight, dry cough, she was obviously feeling much better. She had cleaned the room and a batch of laundry hung on a line in front of the fire. She smiled at him shyly, inclining her head in that quizzical way she had, like a gentle forest creature seeking reassurance.

Sebastian drew her into his embrace and kissed her on the lips. Her mouth was cool and she trembled in his arms.

"Ah, it's good to see you up and about, Emily," he said against her hair.

She shivered and closed her eyes as his mouth found hers again, hungrily. She knew that their marriage must be consummated before her grandfather found them.

-->{ **CHAPTER 10** }<--

Garnet tossed her auburn ringlets over her shoulder and put on her best be-damned expression as she returned her visitor's stare. The thin voice of the woman was becoming shrill with anger. ". . . and I could have you arrested for . . . for fornication."

She tottered on tiny high-heeled slippers, bristling indignantly as her darting eyes examined the contents of Garnet's boudoir. They flashed from the row of cutglass perfume bottles reflected in the gilt-framed mirror of the dressing table to the open wardrobe door, where satin, lace, bombazine, and velvet pressed together in a profusion of sensual hues.

"You realize, of course, that I am *Mrs*. Van Haig?" Her voice, shaking with rage, rose to a crescendo and her stays creaked beneath the stiff sweep of her skirts. She waved her beringed fingers perilously close to Garnet's tip-tilted nose. Her fingers were somewhat like pale radishes, Garnet reflected idly.

Garnet's long leg leisurely kicked aside her satin robe with its swansdown-trimmed train, and she moved away from her unexpected and unannounced visitor.

"I shall have you thrown into the street," Mrs. Van Haig continued, index finger pointing and lips pursed. "I shall fetch the doorman and have you thrown into the street. Oh! How dare you . . . tempt my husband . . . lure him into sin like this. How long has this been going on?" She leaned forward now, bending over Garnet, seated on the edge of the bed and looking to the girl like a hungry little bird about to peck a tasty morsel.

Garnet sighed and picked up one of her stockings. She pulled the fragile silk carefully over her foot, rolling the stocking up her leg. It never ceased to amaze her that during confrontations such as this one, and there had been others in Garnet's life, the offended party always reached the point where outrage was equally balanced with curiosity. The questions would come next—how long, how often, and always the undercurrent: *What do bad women actually do to lure husbands away from God-fearing wives?*

"How often does he come up here?" Mrs. Van Haig demanded.

"Mrs. Van Haig," Garnet said, "I'm going to get dressed now. In a second I shall remove my wrapper so that I can put on my underwear. If the sight of a naked body doesn't offend your sensibilities, then by all means stay where you are. But don't expect me to add to your titillation by describing what goes on between your husband and me in this room."

"Oh!" Mrs. Van Haig gasped in dumb fury. She

102

quickly turned her back as Garnet rose, leaving the satin wrapper a shimmering heap on the bed.

"You take just one set of clothes, do you hear? Everything else stays in this room. And one petticoat will be enough."

Garnet pulled on three fine lawn petticoats and a taffeta evening skirt under her best velvet dress. She was reaching for her beaver-trimmed coat when Mrs. Van Haig whirled around and snatched it from her hands. "Oh, no, you don't, you . . . you . . . evil . . . adulteress." She pulled a plain black shawl from the wardrobe and tossed it into Garnet's face. "And take off those rings—or I'll have the doorman remove them."

Garnet slipped the jade ring from her finger and dropped it into the middle of her satin robe. She kept the diamond twisted in front of her finger, under her thumb. "The other one is mine, and you'll have to cut off my finger to get it," she said, green eyes narrowed.

Mrs. Van Haig could see only the narrow gold band, and she sniffed disdainfully.

Garnet put on her bonnet, carefully tying the long ribbons under her chin. Unhurried, she picked up her reticule and strolled toward the door with an exaggerated hip-swiveling gait that brought the expected torrent of wrath.

"Get out of New York completely, do you hear? I'll know if you are still in town."

Garnet looked back at the small plump woman and blew her an airy kiss, then went out into the hall and walked slowly down the stairs. *Don't worry,* she thought. *I won't wait around to be robbed and beaten. I'm leaving for New Orleans, and this time I'll make it.* She reflected back on her last attempt. Stowing away on the *Dancer* months earlier had been an act of desperation. This time she would pay her passage.

Pity, though, that she could not at least have stayed in New York until Sebastian came sailing back from Liverpool. Now he would not know where to find her. *Someday,* she smiled to herself, *I'm going to reel you in, you big ox, and anchor you to me for life. Only I'll never let you know what I'm up to*. Life had taught Garnet that the way to deal with men was the same as dealing with pain . . . feign indifference.

There had been plenty of both in her short life.

After her mother died of cholera, her father, who taught all eight grades at the country school in the small Ohio town where they lived, allowed the sixteen-year-old Garnet to assist him with the student papers he brought home for correction and grading. Although she had never actually been trained to teach, when her father died a few months later she inherited his job in the one-room school.

She had been happy for a little while. Her pupils were mostly farm boys from five to fourteen who came to school when they were not needed to pitch hay or harvest the crops. Few girls attended on a regular basis. Females, it was felt, learned all they needed to know at their mothers' sides in the kitchen and nursery.

But Garnet was too flamboyantly pretty and far too outspoken and spirited for the solid country women. They tolerated her presence with a wary eye on their growing sons. When one of the boys accused her of making improper advances, it was generally agreed that they had expected something like that to happen.

Garnet tried to explain that the boy was being vindictive because she had threatened him with a failing grade if he did not turn in homework assignments. She had, in fact, stayed behind to coach him after school. The boy turned innocent eyes on the assembled tribunal and declared that Miss Wade asked him to stay after school, all right, but the kind of coaching she had in mind was spelled out in the Bible as a sin.

Losing her temper, Garnet told the boy, his parents, and the rest of her judges a few home truths that would have been better left unsaid—especially in the burst of colorful language Garnet used.

She was not exactly thrown in the stocks, or lashed to a dunking stool, but only because such practices had been discontinued. She was escorted out of town by one of the church elders who stopped the buggy in a shady hollow and put his hand on her knee. Garnet promptly punched him in the jaw, vaulted out of the buggy, and fled. Unfortunately, she hadn't had time to grab her belongings or money.

There followed a variety of positions, each one a little more demeaning than the last. Seamstress, maid, washerwoman. Always there was a fine, upstanding pillar of the community who eventually cornered her and tried to put his hand under her skirts or inside her bodice. Then his broad-hipped wife would dismiss her.

Eventually she had come to New York, sure that in this large, bustling city there would be a place for her. She chose not to think about the three thousand cholera fatalities the city had suffered in the summer of '32. There were more pleasant and exciting aspects to life in New York. The Erie Canal had been opened, the city below Canal Street had been piped for gas, the New York & Harlem Railroad was now incorporated, and horsecars transported one about the city.

She found a position as nursemaid to a family with young children, lying a little about previous experience and writing her own letter of recommendation.

Once a month she was given a Sunday off, and on June 21, 1835, she decided she would ride the horsecars and explore parts of the growing city she had not seen before. Unfortunately, she had been up most of the previous night with one of her young charges, and the motion of the stuffy car soon made her drowsy. She blinked and drifted off to sleep.

Afterward, she was never sure how she came to be in the Five Points area. She was walking along, having come to the end of the line, beginning to realize that her surroundings were taking on a distinctly shabby appearance, when she heard the shouts.

The next moment she was in the midst of a howling, shoving mob. Brickbats were flying through the air.

She was pushed aside by a roughly dressed man whose colorful curses were turning the air blue. "Look out, colleen, or you'll get clouted with a brick," he interrupted his curses to warn her. His voice was drenched in a rich County Cork brogue.

Garnet stood in front of a shattered glass window, her

green eyes widening at the sight of the brawling mob. Some men were locked together, rolling about the littered street as they punched and choked each other. Others were content to throw anything they could get their hands on at the opposing force across the street. From every window and doorway, groups of wild-eyed women shrieked and taunted and several of them joined in the fray, swinging clubs and throwing bottles.

"What is it all about?" Garnet gasped.

"The good citizens of New York don't want an Irish regiment in the National Guard," the cursing man informed her, before moving off to find more ammunition.

Looking back, Garnet saw her retreat had been cut off by throngs of people swarming down the street.

Suddenly a ripple of fear passed through the crowd and the shout went up: "Run! It's the police!"

She was part of the mad scramble as the police, mounted and on foot, waded into the crowd. She was running, stumbling, and her hair had whipped loose and was streaming out behind her. The heel of her shoe snapped and she kicked off both shoes so she would not be impeded in her dash for safety.

All around her the mob shoved and heaved, the smell of unwashed bodies assailing her nostrils, the animal sounds of fear spewing from hoarse throats. Some fell and were trampled by those who came after, their screams and the sound of police clubs cracking skulls adding to the terrifying din.

Garnet managed to work her way closer to the buildings and plunged into the first open door she came to. It was a small grocery store, its window smashed and goods scattered all over the floor.

"If you come in here," a voice said from behind a pickle barrel, "you'll be arrested for looting."

Garnet hung onto the door, gasping for breath, as a man with a shotgun under his arm stepped out of the gloom.

"Please!" she cried. "Don't shoot! I don't know what's happening . . . I don't even know where I am."

"A likely story. Barefoot and a mop of red hair.

106

You're an Irisher, and don't deny it. Now, get out of here."

She tossed her hair back over her shoulder and tried to hide her bare feet under her skirts. "A moment— please, to catch my breath."

A second voice said, "She's just a girl, Dad. Let her rest for a minute." A younger man emerged from the rear door of the shop.

He was tall, well muscled, with light brown hair and an engaging grin. A handsome Teddy bear of a young man. Garnet liked him on sight. He found her a chair among the wreckage of his father's store and told her the riot had been caused by a meeting of the O'Connell Guards. His name, he said, was Tom. His father growled something about filthy Micks and went back to his vantage point behind the pickle barrel.

Tom flashed her a look of apology for his father's rudeness and offered her a piece of salt-water taffy from a large glass jar.

"But why? I don't understand," Garnet said.

Outside the crush of humanity still surged like stampeding cattle. The police were in sight now.

"You're new here, are you?" Tom asked. "The Irish aren't too popular—being papists, and all. You mean you really aren't one of them? It's like Dad says —you look like one."

"I come from a small town in Ohio. No one there bothers much about bloodlines; we were all born there," Garnet replied. "My last name is Wade . . . I got my red hair from my mother, and her name was Downes . . ." She realized that Tom's eyes kept dropping to her bodice, and, glancing down, she saw her dress was torn. Hastily, she pulled the cloth together.

A tall-hatted policeman stuck his head around the door. "Everything all right in here?"

When the streets were cleared of everything but the brickbats and blood, Tom took her back to her place of employment. It seemed natural that he would ask and she would agree to meet him on her next afternoon off.

Cassie Madigan was the cook in the house where

Garnet worked as a nursemaid. Cassie was a plump and jovial woman, and only her tired eyes hinted of disillusionment. She had adopted a motherly attitude toward Garnet and was the first friend she had ever had. Cassie was convinced she smelled bad; no matter how many times she bathed, she could not face the world unless she was doused in strong-smelling perfume. It was, Garnet decided, her friend's only weakness.

She had been married to a tavern-keeper and had cheerfully worked behind the scenes from dawn to dark, as well as raising three sons to manhood. On her thirty-ninth birthday her husband brought a young girl to work in the tavern and told Cassie she could stay home. A week later Cassie found her husband making love to the girl behind the beer barrels in the rear room. She could stay home and suffer the humiliation, or she could leave for an uncertain future with no man to support her. Garnet admired her for making the latter decision.

From Cassie she learned that the Five Points riot flared up again several times in the following days. There was more sporadic violence until the official announcement was made that the O'Connell Guards would not be allowed to hold any further meetings.

Tom courted Garnet with both reverence and exuberance. She fell in love with him with all the passionate abandon of her fiery nature.

"Marry me, sweetheart?" he asked right after their first kiss, and before she could accept, he leaped up on to the iron railings around her employer's house. "If you don't say yes, I'll stay up here and howl at the moon," he threatened.

He was always gamboling about like an overgrown puppy, filled with boundless energy and high spirits. Garnet watched him as fondly as a mother watches a daredevil child. Tom bubbled over with fun, glorying in the sheer joy of living. There was heady excitement in merely walking down a street with him. He was always performing daring stunts to impress her, never content to walk if he could run, never able to resist the challenge of raising eyebrows with his unorthodox approach to life.

Beneath it all, however, Garnet knew he was serious and steady. He was saving for a home of their own, and besides working in his father's store, he had a second job.

Garnet could not understand why Tom, who courted disaster with wild stunts and mad dashes across traffic-filled streets, was so hesitant when it came to love-making. When he kissed her she could feel him tense and draw back as she pressed close to him, and she was puzzled. Every time she was near him she wanted to run her hands through his hair, entwine his fingers in hers, touch him . . . she felt greedy with need for him. One night she took his hand and pressed it to her breast. He fondled her for only a moment. Then he groaned and said, "Ah, Garnet, I wish we could be married right away."

"Why can't we, Tom?" she asked, her voice husky as his touch quickened her senses and a delicious tingling sensation radiated from her inner thighs.

Tom was breathing raggedly and her breast was free of her bodice, hard little nipple rearing against the warmth of his hand. He buried his face in her hair. "I've not enough money yet, sweetheart. Soon as I've enough so we can have a place of our own."

"But I don't mind living over the shop with your mother and father," she protested, melting with need for him. "And I could keep on working. Maybe your father and mother would let me work in the shop, too?"

"Ah, love, I haven't told them about us yet. I must wait until the memory of the Irish riots fades from their minds."

"But I'm not Irish. I'm American. I was born here."

"You look Irish, sweetheart. Be patient . . . just a bit longer, that's all."

"I don't want to be patient," she murmured rebelliously. She pulled him closer to her in a fierce embrace. "And neither do you. I can feel you growing against me."

109

That night he pushed her away, strong enough for both of them. She lay in her tiny room next to the nursery, wide awake all night long, her body aching with longing.

She loved him so much, wanted him, needed him. Her mother had died before she had a chance to indoctrinate her daughter with the horrors of premarital sex. Knowing that Tom was the only man in the world for her, Garnet saw no reason to deny themselves what their bodies fevered for simply because a slip of a legal document was not yet theirs.

She tried to understand Tom's feeling that he wanted to have a home of their own first. She knew it was a protective, loving feeling toward her and was grateful that he loved her so unselfishly. When her blood churned with desire for him, however, rhyme and reason were forgotten. Perversely, she made it more difficult for him to resist temptation. Leading him on with every glance and careless brushing of his body with hers, she fanned the flame to white heat. She made love to him with her eyes, promising that the reality would be more wildly fulfilling than he could imagine.

On the hot summer night on the riverbank when their caresses took them to the point of no return, Garnet was not at first aware that Tom was at last where she wanted him to be, inside her. She had dreamed of their coupling so many times, making believe that he was easing up her skirts, laying bare her breasts, touching her in the way she wanted him to touch her. When she felt the stab of pain and then the wonderful slow thrust of Tom's organ deep into the center of all her desires, for a second she was afraid she was imagining it.

"Ah, Garnet, oh, oh, sweetheart . . ." he was mumbling. She was raising her hips to meet his thrusts, swiveling her body, contracting silken muscles to hold him to her. And the reality was better than all the dreaming. It was over too soon, after a blinding explosion of delight that sent them both crashing into a star-hazed moment of oblivion. Panting, they lay beside each other with their clothes in disarray and their minds numb with the magic of fulfillment.

After that night there was no turning back. They spent every moment they could be together making love. They could think of nothing else. They tried to find out-of-the-way places and longed for the enveloping darkness to conceal them from prying eyes.

She asked him once why he never took her to see his parents. Surely they had a right to know their future daughter-in-law.

Tom looked away, agony on his normally sunny countenance. "My dad would recognize you—from the day of the riot. That's why I have to move out—make us a home of our own. And I won't be able to work for him after we're married, either, love. But I'll have my night job to tide us over. My parents, Garnet . . . they're good people, really. But I'm their only child. Perhaps in time—when we're married and we've given them grandchildren—"

Garnet took his work-roughened hands in hers and held them to her heart. "I love you, Tom, but I don't understand. I don't understand why they won't believe the truth of that day and how I came to be on your street. And I don't understand why they hate the Irish so much. I mean, just because they're Irish—how can people hate others when they don't really know them? Your parents don't know me—"

Unable to bear the pain in his eyes, Garnet sighed and gave up. After all, they were only a few months away from their goal of having enough money to get married. At least now they were enjoying all the privileges of marriage, except for a place to call their own.

Besides, she was never able to quarrel with him. Nothing was serious enough for a disagreement between them. She wanted their love to remain lighthearted and carefree forever. So they made love, whispered, and laughed together. She loved the shared intimacies of mind and body. When the fever of passion abated, she loved to curl up in the warmth of his arms, sharing their thoughts, feeling his heart beat with hers. No two people had ever been as happy as they were.

Still, she longed for marriage and a room of their own. Where they could remove all of their clothes and do all of the things she ached to do. Where she could cry out with pleasure instead of biting her tongue. Where furtive speed could be replaced by slow and sensual lingering.

"We'll have a great big enormous bed," she whispered to him as they stood under a bridge one night. "And you can chase me all over it until I catch you. And you'll come home for lunch every day . . . and some days you won't go to work at all." She giggled and slowly unbuttoned his trousers, as he unfastened her bodice. "I shall kiss every inch of you," she promised.

"I love your breasts," he murmured. "I love the way they feel in my hands . . . firm, but they mold themselves to my touch."

"I wish we could lie down," she whispered, drawing in her breath sharply as she released the object of her pursuit and cradled it in her hands.

"Pull up your skirts, sweetheart, we'll manage," he gasped.

When she told him she was carrying his child, Tom gazed down at her as though she were a goddess come to life. Then he picked her up and swung her in a wild circle as he yelled his joy to the world. Several passers-by on the dark street grinned at the enthusiastic young man and his exuberance.

Remembering suddenly that mothers-to-be should not be handled so roughly, Tom set her back on her feet with exaggerated care. "We'll be married right away, sweetheart. You stay home and rest. Take care of yourself and our child. I'll see to all the arrangements and come and fetch you when it's time to make you my bride. Ah, Garnet, darlin', how I love you."

She watched him fondly, smiling, as he stumbled down the doorsteps into the street. On the pavement he turned to look back at her, his smile wide and his eyes filled with love. He tore his cap from his head and tossed it high in the air. Then he dashed across the street, dodging carriages and a horsecar and laughing at the curses of the drivers.

"I'll be back with a marriage license, Garnet, sweetheart!" he shouted to her from the other side of the street.

When he didn't come to meet her on her next afternoon off, Garnet walked all the way to Five Points. She expected to see him coming toward her as she turned each corner. They had given up riding in horsecars in order to save money.

The day was fine and sunny and she felt well, despite the nausea of pregnancy that came each morning. Tom would have the marriage license by now, she was sure.

She came at last to his parents' grocery store, remembering as she approached the terrible day of the Irish riots. The broken window was repaired and the shades were drawn. A black-edged card on the door proclaimed: CLOSED, DUE TO BEREAVEMENT.

Garnet stood uncertainly outside. His father? Or perhaps his mother? Oh, poor Tom, to lose one of them now, amid their own happiness. Would they have to delay their wedding?

When the neighboring shopkeeper came out to sweep the sidewalk, Garnet asked him which of Tom's parents had died.

The man looked at her, uncomprehendingly, for a moment. "What are you talking about? It was neither the mister nor the missus. It was young Tom. He was killed by a horsecar—knocked down and trampled."

That December she awakened one night to find her room filled with flickering yellow light. She watched the dancing shadows on her walls for a moment until she realized the strange glow was coming from behind the thin blinds that covered her window. Shivering, she left the warmth of the bed to investigate.

She felt the shock of the cold glass as the scene beyond her window jolted her fully awake. Behind the city skyline the night sky blazed sunset-red, filled with billowing clouds of black smoke and leaping orange flames. The inferno was framed by icicles along her

113

window and the white sheen of frost gilding the roofs of nearby houses.

There was a pounding on her door. At the same instant the startled cry of the children in the adjoining room reached her. Cassie flung open her bedroom door. "The master says to get the children out at once. He's having the carriage brought around. Can you manage alone? I've got to see to the mistress and her packing."

Cassie disappeared in response to a frightened summons from down the hall. Garnet snatched up her dressing gown, feeling the familiar nausea that plagued her upon arising. No time to get into her stays while the children cried in fear. Besides, she wasn't really showing yet. She had managed to conceal her pregnancy and hoped to hold on to her job as long as possible.

The house was filled with scurrying servants, carrying valuables down the stairs. Garnet managed to get the children dressed and down to the front door.

It was a night of ice and fire. Zero-degree temperatures were freezing the limited water supply in the firemen's hoses and thirteen acres of the city were burning. The frightened horses were rearing, their hooves slipping on the icy street, while the coachman fought to hold them. All along the street people were rushing from their homes to evacuate the city. The scene was one of noisy confusion. Acrid air sent another wave of nausea through Garnet as she clutched the youngest child in her arms. The other two clung to her skirts in terror, refusing to go down the steps to the street.

"Cassie! Somebody . . . help me!" Garnet called, but her voice was lost in the din. She balanced the baby on her hip and scooped up his sister with her other arm. With one leg free of the clutching hands, she stumbled down the steps, dragging the other child.

The smoke burned her eyes and the carriage swam dizzily in front of her. She felt the knife-twist of pain in her side as she strained to lift the two children into the carriage. As she turned to pick up the third child,

114

warm blood streamed down her leg. She did not remember anymore that night.

Cassie was bending over her anxiously when she opened her eyes. "You're going to be fine, but you lost the baby, Garnet. You've been out like a lamp for two days now. I'm sorry about the child . . . and Garnet, I've had to rent this room for us, because we're both out of work."

Later Garnet learned that seven hundred buildings in the vicinity of Pearl Street and Hanover Square were destroyed, and the following morning every insurance company in the city was bankrupt. The aftermath of the catastrophe saw a huge number of failed businesses, including that of their employer. It was this that cost Cassie and Garnet their jobs.

Cassie could not find a job, and one day in desperation she said, "If only I had enough money to get to New Orleans."

"Why New Orleans?" Garnet asked. She had found a job as laundress, but often wondered how long she could keep it because of the fainting spells she suffered since the miscarriage.

"My sister lives there." Cassie colored, defensively, and told her for the first time about the sister who had married a man from New Orleans and shortly thereafter found herself widowed and penniless in a strange city. She had gone to work in a sporting house.

"I've always thought that with what I know about running a tavern . . . and what my sister knows about . . . well, you know—the two of us could have a place of our own."

Over the years the sisters had corresponded and planned, but neither ever raised enough money for Cassie's fare.

Garnet slipped the gold chain she always wore about her neck out of her dress. Tom's engagement ring had hung there since the day he died. She pawned the ring and financed Cassie's trip to New Orleans and was sorry she did not do it quickly enough, because Cassie's sister died while she was on the voyage.

Garnet's health was never again quite as robust, and she lost several jobs in quick succession. When the son of one rich household offered her money if she would sleep with him, it seemed less of a chore than rubbing calico shirts over a scrub board. One thing led to another, and soon Garnet was seeing several men. The young wife of one of them had discovered Garnet in bed with her husband, and it was the row that ensued that Garnet had decided to stow away on the *Dancer*.

The Van Haig Hotel was out of sight now and she slowed her pace, once again wondering where to go, what to do. Sebastian . . . if only they could have had more time. She had not been as attracted to anyone since Tom. She wondered if she would be able to sell the ring she hid from Mrs. Van Haig for enough to provide passage to New Orleans and Cassie. Well, there was one way to implement her resources. . . .

She set her bonnet at a jaunty angle, deepened her dimples, and headed for the nearest waterfront tavern.

The last man on earth she expected to see when she walked into the smoky atmosphere of the saloon was Erik Gunnar. The *Dancer*'s first mate whom she had so handily sent to jail rose unsteadily to his feet, staring at her.

"Hello, stowaway," he said with a sly grin. "Guess who's been sprung from the tombs? They didn't want a dirty old sailor man in their nice new jail, see."

Garnet was again aware of how much Erik Gunnar resembled Tom. Gunnar was again sprouting a beard, but it did not quite conceal the handsome face she had to remind herself was marred by a cruel expression Tom had not possessed. "You got off easy, Mr. First Mate," she said. She was conscious of a slight headache that was becoming steadily worse and the blurring of her vision that often preceded a fainting spell.

"Not as easy as I would have if you hadn't walked into the courtroom," he answered, his eyes going slowly over her body and returning to linger in the vicinity of her breasts. "That was a poor reward for all I did for you." There was genuine puzzlement in his tone.

Garnet looked at him through a mist of smoke and

disorientation. How like Tom he was. She wondered vaguely, ridiculously, if her liking for big men was a weakness in the way some women like gum drops, or pastries. Had Erik paid for his crimes at sea? She had lost track of time, but surely he hadn't served much of his sentence.

"You had it in for the little Irishman. I don't like big men picking on small ones. And I don't like being tied to a bunk and held against my will—or being part of the slave trade."

A wave of dizziness swept over her and she clutched the nearest barstool for support.

Erik Gunnar slipped his arm about her waist. "Come on, let's get you into a booth. You're unsteadier on your feet than I am." He bore her no grudge. Women were too flighty to be held responsible for their sudden whims and impulses. Besides, she had got under his skin somehow. He had not been able to put her out of his mind. If he ever ran into Balmain again, well, that was something else.

She didn't object when he sat down with her. Pale she was just now, but, God, what a fine-looking wench. He looked into her fevered green eyes and felt a wave of desire that engulfed any resentment he felt for her perfidy.

CHAPTER 11

Emily lay in bed beside Sebastian, staring into the foggy gloom of daybreak beyond the uncurtained window. Her limbs were stiff, despite the comforting warmth of her husband's body, and the soreness between her legs made her long to soak in a bathtub. She did not move, however, for fear she would awaken the sleeping giant next to her.

117

Her cheeks burned with shame as she recalled the events of the previous night.

At first she had welcomed Sebastian's caresses, his gentle kisses. He had been so afraid he would hurt her, his strong hands touched her timidly, wonderingly, as though she were a delicate piece of china. His touch was warm; it seemed to warm her all the way to the marrow of her bones. When he stroked her hair she nestled against the broad expanse of his chest contentedly, feeling secure and protected.

There was, Emily decided, as Sebastian's rope-roughened hand moved slowly from her shoulders down her back, nothing in the world as comforting as the warm and tender touch of another human being. His lips were dry and hesitant as he pressed his mouth to hers. She wrapped thin arms around his neck to hold him, feeling the soothing warmth of his body all down the length of her own slender form.

It was then she became aware of the hardness against her thigh, pressing painfully into her flesh. She tried to move backward to avoid it, without disentangling her arms from her husband's neck, but as she moved the great swelling seemed to grow and, as though with a mind of its own, seek her most intimate and secret places.

The next moment Sebastian had lifted her from her feet and laid her down on the bed. She murmured in protest as she felt his hands raise her cotton nightgown, feeling the chill air envelop her body. Her words were stopped in her throat as his mouth came down on hers again, and this time his lips were moist and his tongue was forcing its way between her teeth.

He was breathing rapidly now and his breath was hot in her throat. His tongue seemed to fill her mouth and she feebly tried to turn her head. As his rough hands closed over her small breasts, it was as though her gentle and comforting protector had suddenly been transformed into a great beast of prey, clawing and devouring.

When his mouth released her, she had only one second to gasp for breath before his lips were upon her

118

breasts, sucking the nipples into his mouth until she winced with pain. She could feel her lungs collapsing with the need for air and realized she was holding her breath. A long tortured sob escaped from her throat, sending a shudder through her body. Sebastian felt her trembling and it seemed to goad him to commit further indignities upon her shrinking flesh.

She thought suddenly of the hot fingers of her grandfather, tormenting her in the night, forcing her hand where it didn't want to go. All at once she realized what it was he had forced her to touch. The knowledge of the true nature of their shame was now combined with revulsion and fear of all men. Especially Sebastian, her husband, to whom the law gave the right to ravish at will. She was whispering his name through swollen lips, imploring him to stop, but her words were a meaningless whimper. The great swelling of his manhood was probing her thighs and he was panting and telling her of his need as his hands wrenched her legs apart.

Emily thought she was being torn in two. The pain was so intense her body seemed to freeze, yet she could feel perspiration drip from her brow to mingle with the salty tears running down her cheeks. The terrible tearing pain seemed to last endlessly until she could not endure it. She was sure she was being killed, was praying for death, when something gave way and he was forcing that enormous organ still deeper inside her. She bit her lips and her fingers clutched the bedsheets as Sebastian thrust into her.

Far away in a dark recess of her mind, a horrified whisper was pointing out that he surely was no longer aware of her identity. He seemed to be engaged in some depraved ritual that was building in intensity until he must burst into a fit of madness.

Suddenly Sebastian gave a choked cry and a great shudder shook his powerful shoulders and rippled down his broad back. The terrible pain between her thighs gradually lessened.

Clinging to him, afterward, she welcomed the proximity of his body and his soothing stroking of her hair

119

and trembling body. It was, she decided, as though a beloved creature had become temporarily insane and was now trying to make amends. Just as her grandfather had always been more patient the day after a nocturnal visit. Sebastian whispered that next time it would not hurt her so much, and she was his precious little wife, and someday he would give her the whole world.

She had sighed and pressed herself near to him, wondering fearfully how often this ugly scene would have to be repeated. No one had ever discussed the marriage bed with her, although she had acquired a rudimentary idea of the act of procreation from a medical book she found in her grandfather's library. Nowhere in the ancient volume, however, was it explained that the man's organ would grow and harden into such an instrument of torture. She had vaguely imagined that the small appendage illustrated in the diagram would somehow be held in place for a moment until the man's seed passed to the woman's womb. Was a child beginning to grow inside her now? She was warm and sleepy, drifting off to oblivion. Perhaps, she reasoned, there was something wrong with Sebastian, that it took him so long to produce the seed. Perhaps, in time . . .

Her eyes blinked open in horror. His organ was again stirring and growing against her. . . .

Lying within the embrace of her sleeping husband as the dawn came across the gray slate roofs toward their window, Emily knew she must escape from the warm bed and brave the chill of the room. She must not be at Sebastian's side when he awakened. How many times had he used her body last night? Three? Four? She had at last fallen asleep from exhaustion.

Carefully she squirmed away from his imprisoning arm, lifting the leg he had carelessly draped over her. He stirred and mumbled in his sleep, but did not awaken as she cautiously drew back the covers and slid into the shock of ice-cold air.

By the time he awoke she had managed to coax the

fire to life, pleased at the accomplishment, and was boiling water for tea. She could hardly conceal her eagerness for him to leave on his daily excursion to look for work so that she might fill the hip bath with warm water and soak her raw and tortured flesh.

That evening when he returned to her he was bearing a small bunch of daffodils, his face wreathed in smiles. "I've got a job. Start tomorrow," he announced happily.

Emily clapped her hands, accepted his flowers and his enthusiastic hug. "Where? What will you be doing?" she asked breathlessly.

"Office boy," he replied ruefully. "But he says he'll let me help out with the signing on of crews and perhaps some cargo loading. The man who owns the company is a quiet sort—Norwegian, I think. His name is Knute Kolvoord and he feels a bit out of place here. He seemed drawn to me because I'm a foreigner, too."

The days and then the weeks sped away. Sebastian ran errands about the Liverpool streets, carrying shipping documents from the shipowner and forwarding agents to masters and merchants. He made tea for the other clerks, carried out their waste paper, cleaned their inkwells, washed windows, swept out the office, built the coal fires and refueled them.

Cheerfully he shrugged off the taunts of twelve-year-old office boys employed in a similar capacity—scrawny boys whose families were delighted they were learning an important trade, and, when they arrived home before eleven o'clock at night, asked anxiously if they had been given the sack.

Knute Kolvoord owned a small fleet of cargo vessels and also ran a profitable forwarding agency for other shippers and lines. One afternoon Sebastian was sent down to the dock with one of the clerks to check the manifest and state of the cargo of a newly arrived ship. They arrived to find the dock officials in a state of agitation as the ship was anchored in the wrong place and a packet was expected at any moment.

Sebastian sized up the scene, his eye measuring the length of the small ship owned by his employer. "We can move her," he told the clerk. "Put our shoulders to her hull and move her along. I know the New York packets; there'll be enough room for the two of them if we move this one to the far end of the landing stage."

The clerk looked at the brawny office boy dubiously, but when Sebastian put his huge back against the ship's hull and shoved, the small vessel did indeed move without benefit of sail or tow line.

Back the the office, Sebastian's brawn and quick thinking were the topics of the day. Later that afternoon Knute Kolvoord sent for him.

Sebastian went into the private office of his employer, a room as austerely furnished as the main office. Kolvoord sat behind a large oak desk. He was a strapping man, a former deep-sea fisherman and whaler who had started his fleet on the proceeds of the successful salvage of a galleon. At fifty-two, his only passion was ships and the goal of owning the largest private fleet of merchant ships in the world. He was unmarried and childless.

Kolvoord's ships never shortened sail at night, as did many ships on tediously long voyages, and his captains were urged to make quick turn-arounds in port. Handsome bonuses, well-provisioned ships, and comfortable accommodations were the incentives, rather than the blustering threats with which McKnight tried to motivate his skippers.

"I hear what happen today. I'm pleased you used your head," Kolvoord said to Sebastian in his halting and carefully selected English.

"It seemed the best solution to the problem," Sebastian answered with a grin.

"How old you be, Balmain?"

"Going on twenty, sir."

"You've worked for me for a month. I think you not stay, that you make up story of wife. I think you be back at sea soon."

"I want to learn the shipping business from shore-side, sir. Someday I intend to be a shipowner myself."

Kolvoord raised an iron-gray eyebrow. "You have plan to this end?"

"I'll build my own, sir. I've been at sea most of my life, and it's always puzzled me why someone hasn't started a ship-building yard in a place where there's unlimited teak to build and where local labor can be had cheap. I've a friend who writes me—he's a draftsman for a ship-builder in New York—and from what he tells me . . . it seems to me that—" Sebastian broke off, aware that he was talking more than he intended. He had not meant to divulge quite so much of his secret plan.

"Native workmen aren't reliable. It's been tried." Kolvoord's fluency in the language seemed suddenly much improved, and it occurred to Sebastian that perhaps the hesitancy had been used to build a wall between a man who preferred to work alone and those who approached too closely.

"I know of a place where I'm sure the locals—under close supervision—could handle it."

"Sit down, Balmain," Kolvoord said. "Perhaps we shall come to some arrangement that will benefit both of us."

Sebastian pulled a chair close to the desk and leaned forward eagerly. "Burma, sir . . . Moulmein. The finest teak and all the men we need. And I've some ideas about the design of the ships, too. . . ."

Kolvoord would have dispatched him forthwith to Burma, but when Sebastian told Emily of the plan she had grown pale, and within hours, it seemed, succumbed to a severe attack of ague. Regretfully, Sebastian told his employer he would have to remain in Liverpool, but would be glad to make all the plans for the Burmese shipyard for someone else to execute. Perhaps, he added, one day Kolvoord would build a ship there for Sebastian.

The next morning Sebastian found a space had been cleared for him to stand at the high, slanted desks with the clerks, and instead of delivering shipping documents from that day forward, he prepared them.

Often he would be called into Kolvoord's office and the two of them would discuss the problems of moving

123

ships and cargoes that the landlubbers could not fathom. Sebastian learned rapidly and worked tirelessly. His wages were increased and he no longer worried about putting food on their table, but Emily's frail health took its toll in doctor's bills and medicine costs. They were not able to afford to move out of the cramped boardinghouse.

Sebastian wondered when the inevitable confrontation with Job McKnight would come. It was, he felt, nothing short of a miracle that their paths had not crossed as they went about their business. He was careful while traveling the city streets after dark, for fear of falling prey to a crimp's cosh, but after a time he began to relax. It seemed that Job McKnight had calmly accepted his granddaughter's disappearance. Was that possible? Well, no doubt the arrival of his first son had helped alleviate the loss.

Unknown to Sebastian, Job McKnight had found their boardinghouse a week after their marriage, but Emily had been too afraid to tell her husband of the incident.

She was washing Sebastian's shirts in a corrugated bowl on the table, rubbing the flannel over the scrub board, when their door opened suddenly. She caught a quick glimpse of the landlord, key in hand, withdrawing into the darkness of the landing. Then her grandfather stepped into the room. He stood, supporting himself on his walking stick, his hat still on his head, his eyes reminding her of the icicles that hung along the window frame.

She dried her hands on her apron and tried to control the trembling of her lower lip. "Grandfather . . ."

"So you're reduced to this," he said, pale eyes sweeping from the corrugated bowl, along the line of clothes hanging in front of the fire, to the double bed with its patchwork quilt. "A sailor's whore. You gave up a comfortable home and respectability to live like this. Even your slut of a mother did better for herself than this."

Far away in a misty recess of his mind, that other Emily shook her head reproachfully. Job closed his eyes for a second, hating himself for what he had become; hating his granddaughter for her unwitting part in turning him into a depraved old man. He was filled with self-loathing and a yearning to wipe out the past. To start anew for his son's sake. Unreasonably, he placed half the blame for his sins on his granddaughter's blameless shoulders. If she had not been so hauntingly like her grandmother, tempting and taunting him with her very presence . . .

Emily bit her lip. "Sebastian and I are married, Grandfather," she said, her voice shaking.

One white eyebrow went up. "Balmain? You've married him?" Perhaps this marriage, repugnant as it was, was ordained by fate. With Emily gone, perhaps he could forget his own past?

"We were married in the registry office—a week ago."

Job didn't want Emily back, but he cared enough to worry about the union of his delicate grandchild and a brawny sailor. Their worlds were too far apart to bring happiness to either of them, with or without Job's financial help. Job had shrewdly suspected that Louisa had married him only to ensure her son's future. No doubt young Balmain believed he could still claim the McKnight fortune by marrying Emily. Well, he was wrong. There was Mark now.

"Grandfather . . . you wouldn't talk to me. We would have asked your blessing."

The cold eyes regarded her bleakly. "Will you ever know what pain you've caused me, Emily? Do you not realize, girl, that Balmain is a fortune-hunter? He married you to get my ships. But he'll be sadly disappointed, believe me. I've cut you completely out of my will. And don't you come running back to me when he finds his marriage was for nothing. I took your mother back, and what did I get for my pains but a second helping of grief? No, Emily, you might as well be dead as far as I'm concerned. I'll never take you back into my house."

Job gave one last disgusted glance at the double bed in the corner of the room and then departed.

Emily sat, shaking with emotion, for several hours, her dark eyes wide, staring into the fire until it went out.

Surely it could not be true—that Sebastian had married her for her grandfather's ships and fortune? She was more afraid than she had ever been. Frantically, she searched her memory for some clue that would put her grandfather's vile supposition to rest. But recalling every word Sebastian had ever said to her was no comfort. He had never once told her he loved her. He'd promised her the moon and the stars, and told her she was beautiful. But not that he loved her or needed her.

In their bed at night he would sometimes tell her how much he wanted her. Once or twice he had made a coarse comment as he was copulating with her that had caused her blushes to deepen. But these expressions had to do with the strange madness that overcame him and had nothing to do with true love. True love, she was sure, was a union of mind and soul and spirit. She was convinced that the madness of his flesh would cease as soon as she was with child. She prayed nightly that this would soon be achieved.

Agonizing over her grandfather's accusation, Emily thought back to Sebastian's storming of the house to rescue her. Was he an opportunist who had seized the chance to whisk her away and marry her without the bother of courtship and winning her grandfather's blessing? How could he love her? Her husband did not know her. Emily was perceptive enough to realize that Sebastian was a man to whom true love would come slowly, growing by inches. His was not a temperament with the flash point of love at first sight.

Waiting for Sebastian to return, she decided not to tell him of her grandfather's visit. If she told him, then she would also have to tell him what her grandfather had said . . . and Sebastian might then, by word or glance, confirm that horrible accusation. And Emily would not be able to bear it, for despite her revulsion at the physical side of her marriage, Emily loved her husband with fierce loyalty and all the devotion of her deeply sensitive nature. For Emily the flash point had

126

come when a fearless young boy had bravely stood his ground before her grandfather . . . all those years ago. Then he sailed away as a cabin boy, head high and shoulders squared. How she had admired him for his courage, she whose fears made her shrink from the terrors of the world beyond her books and music.

Over the years Sebastian had become the symbol of strength and courage in her mind. A man who would be a loving bulwark between his wife and the world. Fed by Louisa's prompting, Emily had long ago known that one day she wanted to be Sebastian's wife.

It was only after Cyril came into her life that she began to wonder about other alternatives. The magic of her relationship with her half-brother had taken her breath away. Cyril could make the sun shine brighter merely by smiling at her. Her heart fluttered when she even thought about him. His words comforted her long after he had departed. After a wonderful, stimulating, perfect day with Cyril, Emily had once wondered what would have happened had Cyril not been her half-brother.

But he *was* her half-brother. She must never again allow herself to speculate on any other relationship. Such thoughts were wicked and forbidden.

Still, she missed Cyril desperately. Not knowing where he was or what he was doing was agony to her. Had he really been shanghaied by those dreadful-looking men that day? Or had her grandfather convinced him to go away, back to London or the Continent? Oddly, although she was so afraid of meeting the challenge of life head-on for her own sake, she would gladly have attempted to slay dragons for Cyril. Someday she would have to tell Sebastian more about her half-brother than the bare fact of his visit to inform her of their father's death. Sebastian would protect them both from her grandfather's wrath. Sebastian was so brave. He feared neither man nor beast. Yes, she loved her husband desperately.

Sebastian was learning the business of shipping. He was also forming a restrained but solid friendship with

Knute Kolvoord, who more and more sought his opinions and views on the best way to rig, stow, and provision ships. Like Sebastian, Kolvoord deplored the brutally miserable lot of the common seaman. He smiled with grim satisfaction when Sebastian told him of bringing the skipper and first mate of the *Dancer* to trial in America for the death of the chanteyman.

Kolvoord would often quietly watch Sebastian at work in the outer office, his muscular shoulders and biceps incongruously out of place. At times Kolvoord would ponder how it might have been to have a son . . . someone like young Sebastian, big, strong, openhearted, honest—yet ambitious and energetic enough to rise above the common herd.

One evening he called Sebastian into his private office.

"The first ship is ready to be launched from Moulmein. Since the idea was yours in the first place, I think it's only fair that you benefit by it."

Kolvoord reached into his desk and produced a flask and two glasses. "We shall drink a toast—to our newest ship and to the new manager of my office." He paused, his eyes glinting with anticipation as he studied the pleased expression on Sebastian's face.

"Manager . . . why, thank you, sir," Sebastian said, accepting the glass.

"And future partner, Sebastian," Kolvoord said.

"Partner?" Sebastian felt his jaw sag.

"Sebastian, sit down. I have no family. I'm not a young man, but I'm a stubborn man. I've worked hard to build my fleet of ships, and I shan't be content to sell out to some big company when I'm ready to retire. I want my ships to go on after I'm dead . . . like the family I never had, I suppose."

"Mr. Kolvoord, I hardly know what to say. I'm grateful—God, I'm more than that. But I don't know if I'm worthy."

"Sebastian, you know how I learned to swim? My father was a fisherman and one day soon after I learned to walk he took me sailing in the bay. Two miles from shore he dropped me overboard."

Sebastian grinned. "I reckon you must have learned —since you're here to tell the tale."

"I'm dropping you overboard, Sebastian. I'm sailing for Burma to see my shipyard there. You're going to run things here. Tonight we'll go over all you need to know."

During the following five hectic years, the details of that night blurred in Sebastian's memory. He remembered only that they talked far into the night and that then Sebastian walked home through deserted streets, his step light and his heart racing with excitement at the news he was bearing to Emily. By the time he reached the boardinghouse, the sky was silver all around the edges, sharpening the silhouettes of the city buildings.

As soon as he stepped inside the dark hallway of his boardinghouse, the landlord's wife appeared at her door. "That you, Mr. Balmain?" she called, her voice competing with the raucous quarreling of her brood of children as they rose for the new day.

Sebastian realized with a qualm that he had left Emily alone all night long, but when he told her the news she would understand. Their fortunes were about to change, there was no doubt of it. "Yes, it's me. I hope I didn't wake you," he called back.

The smell of frying kippers wafted out to greet him as she stepped into the hall. "I've been watching for you. They came to get your missus last night . . . I didn't think you'd been home, 'cos I was up most of the night with the youngest. Got the croup, she has."

"Emily is ill again?" Sebastian asked, his enthusiasm doused with apprehension.

"No—not your missus; it's my youngest who has the croup. It was 'er grandfather. Your wife's grandfather." She opened her door a few inches and bellowed to her children to be quiet.

"He came here?" Sebastian asked.

"Not him—a woman. Little woman with a face like a ferret."

129

"Mrs. Turner," Sebastian said. "Emily went with her?"

"Couldn't do owt else, could she? Not with him being stricken."

"Who? For God's sake, woman, tell me the whole story."

"Your missus' grandfather. Had a stroke, he did."

--◆{ CHAPTER 12 }◆--

Cyril La Flair stood on deck, watching the Liverpool docks glide by in solemn review. After so much time at sea, it seemed to him that the land was moving and the ship was stationary.

Cursed city . . . it had given him Emily and then obliterated all hope that he could ever play in the concert halls.

All around him sailors were scurrying about, preparing to dock, but the mates did not bellow for Cyril to join the activities. He watched the Pier Head drawing closer, remembering his first return to Liverpool. . . .

He had spent that first voyage in the deckhouse and galley, too desolate to consider he was at least being spared life in the forecastle. The ship's carpenter, sailmaker, and cook shared the cramped deckhouse, and Cyril had been given to the cook as a helper when it was obvious he could not climb aloft with hands swollen to twice their normal size.

Within a few days the three broken fingers on his right hand had turned black and he was suffering from a raging fever. The carpenter had forced him to drink rum until he passed out. When Cyril opened his eyes and looked at the bloodstained bandage encasing his right hand, he knew without being told that three fingers had been amputated.

The carpenter was a morose Welshman who had shipped out following some private tragedy that left him perpetually unsmiling and of the most pessimistic disposition. Dai Williams, like many of his countrymen, sang in a deep, true baritone voice, but the ships' officers quickly begged him not to lead any chanteys, because instead of inspiring the crew to a concentrated effort, Dai's sad tones had the effect of reducing everyone to listless gloom. So Dai hammered his nails, sawed his planks, and occasionally hacked off a damaged limb for some unfortunate shipmate, all with the dark cloud of despair hovering about his drooping, elongated features.

Since the cook and sail-maker were both old men and hard of hearing, they simply ignored Dai's morbid stories and equally disturbing protracted periods of silence. Cyril soon learned that no matter what the subject of conversation was, Dai could soon turn it into a melancholy discourse on the hopelessness of the human condition.

Dai took care of him during the time it took for his fever to abate, his quinsy to burst, and his hand to stop torturing him. According to Dai, Cyril would be lucky not to lose the rest of the fingers on that hand. Still, he added, in a typical Dai Williams attempt at cheerfulness, "At least the crimps will leave you alone in future. There's not much use you'll be, boy *bach*, with no hand."

Cyril learned to cook on the iron stove in the galley, using his left hand and flexible right wrist to hoist the cast-iron pots. The ship's old cook was only too pleased to teach him all he knew so that he could spend his time dozing in a warm corner of the galley.

Surprisingly, Cyril's general health improved after a few weeks at sea. The finger stumps healed and the sail-maker fashioned a canvas glove to protect his right hand. For the first time in his life, Cyril was not plagued by constant sore throats and colds. The physical labor of cooking and scrubbing pots and pans, to

131

say nothing of the brisk ocean air, improved his appetite. When his chores were done, he would walk briskly around the deck, thankful that he never suffered from seasickness, as did most of the other first voyagers.

His state of mind, however, was not matched by his physical condition. He missed Emily and he longed to have a piano near, despite the loss of his fingers. The sound of the wind in the rigging and the rhythm of the waves against the hull whispered new melodies in his ear. The aching loneliness for Emily also found expression in sharps and flats he heard only in his imagination.

The endless gray sea seemed to him symbolic of the minds of the uneducated sailors, where no original idea or illuminating thought was allowed to ruffle the flat surface of consciousness. Cyril preferred Dai Williams' bleak soliloquies, which were at least coherent, to the fragmented and mundane conversation of the sailors, whose only interests appeared to be the soaking up of rum and sexual gratification.

They sailed down the African coast, delivered a cargo of cast-iron pots and trivets, went on to the Indies and picked up a cargo of sugar before completing the last leg of the triangular voyage home.

As the ship again reached the Pier Head, Cyril remembered with what relief and eagerness he had rushed ashore on that first return. Dai Williams insisted he would accompany Cyril to the lion's den.

"At least you'll have a witness, look you, if the old devil decides to kill you," Dai offered with his customary cheerfulness. "And I can see to it that some boardinghouse runner doesn't part you from your wages. There's a puny thing you are, La Flair. A bird with a broken wing could better defend itself. You need someone to look after you."

Cyril looked into Dai's melancholy countenance and realized the Welshman was offering his friendship. *Perhaps in return for depriving me of my fingers,* Cyril thought, with a cynicism that was new to him. No! His conscience cried, outraged, it was not Dai's hacksaw that removed the fingers . . . it was the crimp's oar. "Come on, then, Dai. Perhaps it will be easier to tell Emily what happened if I have a shipmate at my side."

McKnight's housekeeper had cowered in the vestibule like a cornered rat. "You get away from here!" she whined. "Or I'll send for the police. She doesn't live here anymore, and her grandfather will have your skin if he sees you."

"What is it, Mrs. Turner?" a masculine voice called from within the house.

Cyril stiffened as footsteps came down the hall. A moment later Job McKnight's white eyebrows were knitted in a frown as he glared at the two seamen. "What are you doing here? What do you want?"

"I wish to speak with Emily," Cyril said.

"Show him your hand, boy *bach,*" Dai said. "You've surely paid with flesh and bone for a minute of his precious granddaughter's time."

"Be reasonable, sir," Cyril said. "I'm not going to leave until I've seen her."

"Then you've a long wait. She ran away with an American."

"An American . . ." Cyril repeated, as though the word conjured up a creature from the far side of the moon. "Where did they go?"

McKnight shrugged indifferently. "America, I suppose." And he slammed the door in their faces.

Cyril found a marriage had been recorded between Emily and Sebastian Balmain, whose nationality was given as American.

Although he insisted that Emily had nothing to do with his decision, he signed on again as ship's cook on a brig bound for America, using his left hand and keeping his mutilated right hand hidden in his coat pocket. Dai Williams went with him, and in Boston they decided to sail around the Horn and see for themselves the hospitable islands of the Pacific and the rich trading along the Mexican territory of California.

They were an odd pair, and for the most part were left to their own devices by both ships' officers and ordinary seamen. The cook and carpenter were not

133

men whom other sailors would choose as friends. A few minutes in the company of the carpenter tended to reduce most men to suicidal depression. There was something decidedly strange also about the cook. He was slightly built and almost cadaverous in appearance, with waxy skin and shadowed eyes. He moved in a loose-jointed way that someone said reminded him of a flitting bat. Cyril La Flair did not wear seamen's clothes, but went about the ship dressed in a black overcoat, a dingy white cravat at his throat, and it was perhaps his clothing as much as his curious gait that brought the flitting of bats to mind.

Weird, the pair of them, was the consensus of opinion, as though they sprang from a cemetery. "You ever brush against the cook, lad," old salts would tell the ship's boys, "and you'll feel the chill of the grave. No matter how many hours he spends in the galley, he's always ice-cold." And the boys would shudder and avert their eyes from the cook's right hand and its extraordinarily long, lone forefinger. . . .

The officers, however, noted that both the Welsh carpenter and the almost supernatural-looking cook attended to their duties, never got drunk, and didn't involve themselves in the brawls that flared up frequently among men confined to a small space for long periods of time.

How long has it been? Cyril asked himself, as they again sailed up the River Mersey. Four years—five? What had happened to all that time? He had never found Emily. Perhaps he would go and see McKnight again, try to get her adddress. Then he would find a piano and play some of the music that was bursting inside his head, tearing him apart in its effort to be free. And if he could not make the two remaining digits of his right hand do the work of five . . . well, perhaps he could find someone who would play his music for him. *Oh, if only that person could be Emily. . . .*

Dai didn't go with him to McKnight's house this time, and Mrs. Turner, the ferret-faced housekeeper, did not respond to the bell. Instead, a fresh-cheeked young girl wearing a black dress and white apron ushered him politely into the house when he asked for Mr. McKnight.

"The old gentleman's been ill for some time, sir," she said. "He had a stroke and he can't talk, you see. If you'll just wait in the hall, I'll fetch Mrs. Balmain."

Mrs. Balmain . . . Emily! Cyril felt weak at the prospect of seeing her again. He stood with his right hand behind his back, his left hand clutching his hat, so that when she came flying on winged feet to fling herself upon him, it was her arms that held them together.

"Cyril, Cyril . . ." she kept crying and repeating his name.

His own face was drenched with tears as she smoothed the straight black hair from his high forehead, touching his cool skin to assure herself he was indeed there in the flesh.

He kept his right hand hidden as she tugged gently to remove his hat from his other hand and pulled him into the parlor, closing the door behind them.

"Oh, you poor darling, look at you," she cried, her soft, dark eyes brimming with tears. "You're so thin and sallow looking."

Cyril smiled and supposed silently that the tanning of his skin under the tropical sun probably had faded by now to an unhealthy sallowness. Emily herself did not look as robust as she might. There were dark circles under her eyes and the skin of her pointed little face was stretched transparently over gossamer bones.

"Oh, my dearest . . . I worried so about you. Why did you not write to me?"

Cyril had maneuvered himself in front of the fire, his right hand still behind him. "I came to see you, Emily . . . years ago, but I was told you had married and gone to America. I was shanghaied, you see. Can you believe it, I've been making my way as a sea cook." His laughter rang out melodiously at the absurdity of it all, and Emily dried her eyes and smiled happily to hear the most wonderful sound in the whole world.

Cyril's eyes drifted in the direction of the rosewood

piano and Emily said, suddenly teasing, "So, you've been away at sea . . . and do you come now to see your dear sister, or to visit my pianoforte? Ah, have I lost your affection to an inanimate object?"

Cyril ignored her attempt at humor. "Tell me about Mr. Balmain," he said, fixing his dark eyes on her. "Is he good to you? Does he deserve you?"

The color came flooding up over her cheeks and blue-veined lids were lowered over her eyes. She turned quickly to open the glass-fronted cabinet containing decanters and glasses, busying herself with the gestures of hospitality.

"I told you about Louisa's son . . . Sebastian. Since grandfather had his stroke, Sebastian has taken over the running of the McKnight Line. He helps to run another line, as well, called the Knute Kolvoord Line. Grandfather had always done everything practically singlehandedly, you see . . . there was no one else to take up the reins, except my husband."

Cyril smiled and accepted the glass of brandy with his left hand. "There's really no need for you to justify your husband to me, Emily," he said gently.

"Oh, Cyril!" Emily sat down on the couch abruptly and burst into tears that were no longer caused by joy. Deep wracking sobs of anguish shook her fragile body.

Alarmed, Cyril dropped to his knees beside her and drew her into his arms. She clung to him like a frightened child and her fears came tumbling from her trembling lips as he rocked her gently back and forth. A sudden hope that her husband was the cause of her anguish was stilled with her next words.

"It's grandfather's eyes . . . he stares at us so . . . malevolently. He's completely paralyzed, you see, helpless as a baby—but his eyes—he looks at us and sees us and knows we are here . . and this terrible hatred burns in his eyes."

"But why should he hate you? Emily, surely you don't believe he blames you for his stroke?"

"Yes, yes, I think he does." Her head nodded vigorously and her heavy mass of dark hair strained at the pins and tortoiseshell combs that held it up from her slender neck. "You see, he didn't like Sebastian because he felt he was a fortune-hunter—a common sailor, without breeding or education. . . . He didn't want me to marry him and I think I b-b-broke Grandfather's heart. . . ." She was engulfed in heart-rending sobs again.

"But surely, if you feel your grandfather knows what is happening around him, he must know that your husband is keeping the McKnight Line going."

"That's just it, Cyril." She regained her composure with obvious effort. "Sebastian wants to discontinue the Atlantic packets. He says McKnight liners can't compete with the Black Ball and all the other large companies. He wants to move our ships to the east coast of America and send them trading to the west coast."

"It could be a wise move, Emily. The United States is growing rapidly and Pacific trade is proliferating. Small ships are ideal to put into the Dog Holes along the California coast . . . and there's good trading in tallow and hides for ships that take cargoes from the eastern coast of America around the Horn to the Mexican territories of Alta and Baja California."

Emily inclined her head to one side and listened carefully. "Why, Cyril . . . where did you learn all that?"

He laughed and pressed his cool lips lightly against her brow. "I spent the last couple of years in the Pacific. I only came back because I had to find you, my precious one."

She nestled against his shoulder, which was damp with her tears, and sighed contentedly. "I'm so happy you are back. There's so much we must discuss. I was afraid I'd lost you forever. . . . Tell me every one of your thoughts. We've talked enough of ships. Have you read any new poetry? I found a very old piece:

> *"The Moon amid the Lesser lights,*
> *the Stars around the lovely moon,*
> *Fade back and vanish very soon,*

137

> When, round and full, her silver face,
> Swims into sight, and lights all space."

Emily's eyes were softly luminous. "And how much music have you written . . . ? No, don't tell me. Come, you will play for me. I've kept the piano tuned ever since we moved in with Grandfather, praying for the day you would come back to me. . . ."

Emily was on her feet, dragging him toward the piano, when silently, wretchedly, he withdrew his mutilated hand from the folds of his coat. He caught her as her eyes glazed and she crumpled into his arms in a dead faint.

CHAPTER 13

The dispassionate doctor watched unseeingly as Garnet fastened her chemise. "You're a healthy young woman," he said in a slightly accusing tone. "There was no need for you to come to see me. You should look for a midwife; you don't need a doctor. You're with child."

"I know that," Garnet said, her eyes as opaque as a cat's. "I wanted to be sure I hadn't hurt the child. I had a . . . fall the other day."

"A little bruising won't damage the child," he replied icily. "The baby is safely wrapped in a tough cocoon. You must be at least five months along, aren't you? You're past the stage where you need fear a miscarriage."

She went out into the bright sunlight to await the horsecar that would take her back to the apartment she shared with two cats while her husband was at sea.

Rolling along the bustling thoroughfares, she closed

her eyes wearily, glad he would not be waiting for her when she arrived home. He had slapped her for the last time. There was the child to consider now. She must be gone before his ship reached port.

She did not feel well, despite the doctor's reassurances. She sighed. She had been dangerously ill once before, and that illness had brought about her present predicament.

Garnet was never sure whether she drank bad whiskey that night, or whether the illness was already upon her when she entered the tavern. Perhaps, she thought wryly, it was part of the curse the outraged Mrs. Van Haig had wished upon her. Garnet had been drinking and laughing one minute, and the next she was sinking into a quicksand of pain and terror, fighting for breath, swallowed up by some frightful churning mass that wanted to drain away her life.

When at last she returned from the far shores of delirium and opened her eyes to survey her surroundings, she was lying on a clean bed in a simply furnished room. A jolly faced woman was at her bedside. The woman giggled and bathed her, combed her hair, and fed her soup, all the while babbling in some strange tongue.

Garnet had begun to giggle, too. Perhaps she had died and this was . . . well, could it be heaven or hell? She giggled even harder and the woman joined in.

Later Garnet awakened from a disturbing dream of leaping flames and a nameless horror waiting for her in a cloud of smoke. As she struggled to escape the delirious sleep, she became aware of the shadowy figure beside her bed. Big . . . handsome . . . fun-loving Tom.

"Oh, Tom," she whispered gratefully. "I dreamed you were dead . . . I thought I'd lost you."

His face came and went during the twilight of her illness, but she knew he was there, taking care of her.

Once he grinned slyly. "You don't remember me yet, do you?" There was a disturbing red glint to his eyes. It must be the firelight, she decided.

"Don't tease me—I'm so drowsy," she murmured.

139

"You're so desirable, too," he said. "Hurry up and get well." His large hand slid across the sheet and up over her middle, one finger probing the soft hollow between her breasts.

She fluttered her lashes down over her eyes sleepily, but not before her body responded to his masculine message. "I think . . ." she mumbled just as she drifted back to sleep, "I'm feeling better already. . . ."

Those first days it was simply easier to defer thinking about anything. Her body shrugged off the effects of her illness and her mind drifted along on a purely physical level. She was aware of the comfort of the fire, the smooth caress of clean sheets, the smells of bubbling soup and brandy-laced coffee. Ripples of sensation when he touched her, little exploratory journeys of his fingers, and then, one evening, his lips encircled her pink areola and sucked gently on the pointed nipple. His beard was surprisingly soft against her silken flesh, and her hands went to the sides of his head and found his bush of hair just as soft.

He was not Tom. How could he be? Tom was dead. Her Samaritan was Erik Gunnar, who took care of her in her illness despite what she had done to him. "Why . . ." she said, "your beard is so soft. . . ." There was molten liquid between her legs, and her body was beginning to move sensuously in a rhythm as old as time.

"There's one part of me hard as a rock, I promise you," he said with a bellow of laughter that shook the rafters. He rose and tore off his flannel shirt, unbuttoned his blue drill trousers, and showed himself to her proudly.

Garnet ran her tongue over her lower lip and dimpled at him. Her hand darted out to caress him, but he had waited too long for this moment to be bothered with preliminaries. She found herself gasping for breath beneath his weight as he flung himself on her.

"It's a good thing I'm ready for you, you big ox," she gasped, spreading her legs so that he might drive his engorged member home.

He grunted an unintelligible reply and twisted and thrust until she timed her own writhing response to his rhythm, pushing herself upward to meet him, making a circular motion with her hips. Her senses raced away from her and she was aware only of that throbbing delight at the core of her being as, shuddering and crying aloud with pleasure, she felt her climax approach.

Gunnar strove mightily to crash over the edge with her, sweating and groaning and pressing her into the mattress with such fury that she was sure the bed must collapse. A second later he gave a great cry of triumph and one final thrust exploded in a scalding finale.

Garnet let out her breath as after-shocks went rippling through her body. Opening her eyes as the fog of her illness lifted, she allowed the full realization of who this was to wash over her. Gunnar! She mumbled her thanks that he had tended her illness, and asked that he help her get to Cassie Madigan, in New Orleans.

"You don't need any Cassie Madigan," he said. "I'll take care of you."

It surprised her when he immediately offered to marry her. "A sailor—doesn't have an anchor, unless he has a wife," he said. "I'd like to know that you'd always be waiting for me." It was a touching admission from the great bully who had terrorized an entire crew.

Still she had refused him at first. She married him when he returned from a trip to Liverpool with the news that Sebastian had married old McKnight's granddaughter and was running his shipping company. Garnet didn't know why that news hurt so much. It had never stopped hurting. She carefully mended the cracks in her carefree but brittle facade, and in time she almost came to believe herself that she had not fallen in love with Sebastian.

Her troubles with Erik began about a year later. He was away at sea much of the time, and when he was in port he was an amiable, if demanding and somewhat rough, lover. He never questioned her about her past, and Garnet, in turn, did not ask about her husband's former paramours. She was, therefore, astonished and outraged when a male acquaintance bade her a friendly hello on the street one night and Erik promptly sent the man crashing to the ground with a bone-splintering blow.

Dragging her back up to their apartment, Erik then demanded to know how many men she had been lying with while he was away at sea. He punctuated the questions with teeth-rattling slaps and vicious pinches.

She tried gamely to defend herself, but without a weapon she was no match for the rampaging giant. She was saved from broken bones by the fact that her dress was torn to ribbons and Erik's red-hot stare had gone to her naked breasts. He paused, hand raised to slap her again, but instead clasped her breast roughly, squeezing and kneading until she felt more pain than the blows to her face had brought.

Since she felt no desire, his entry into her was dry and painful. She bit her lip in agony as he seized her hips and forced her to move with him. His own pleasure seemed to be heightened by the blows and abuse he had rained on her. He took delight in driving deeply into her, crushing her with his weight.

"You little whore . . . you'll perform all the whore's tricks for me tonight!" he shouted a moment after his climax. He was on his feet, dragging her from the bed by the hair, shoving her face downward.

Garnet left him. Many times. He always found her, somehow. Perhaps she wanted him to, she thought. She was his wife. Despite her grievances, their marriage was not something she could easily dismiss.

The journey from the doctor's office back to her apartment came to an end and she alighted from the horsecar and went into the building, wrinkling her nose at the stale cabbage smells in the hall. She unlocked the door and her cats leaped from the window ledge to greet her. The ginger tom rubbed against her leg, purring, while the white Persian maintained her aristocratic distance and acknowledged her mistress' return with a faint feline smile.

This time, she told her cats silently, *I shall have to go far away, where he can't find me. I have to con-*

sider the child. There had been a third cat, a tiny black kitten she had befriended that Erik smashed to its death the minute he saw it. It was, he said, bad luck to harbor a black cat. He was obsessively superstitious.

She emptied her drawers, laying petticoats and chemises on the bed. "This time I *will* make it to New Orleans," she told the aloof white Persian. "I swear to it. I'll be with Cassie Madigan before the baby is born."

Cassie's last letter had been full of the news of her "new place" and "partner," and had concluded with the mysterious promise of more news of both to come. The letter had arrived the morning before Erik returned from the docks in a murderous rage. Garnet had no way of knowing that he had run into Curt Vanders, who had taunted him for marrying a woman who could be had for the price of a drink . . . or a dress. Garnet did not get a chance to tell her husband she was pregnant. The next day he had shipped out once again.

"I'm going to take you two down to the landlady," Garnet told her disinterested cats. "Then I'm going to buy passage to New Orleans." She bent to stroke the white Persian, thinking that felines had the right idea. They would go to anyone who gave them a saucer of milk, some food, and didn't restrict their movements.

Garnet was heavy with child by the time she found Cassie's place, a small drinking and gambling establishment on a narrow street festooned with lacey iron-trellised balconies. She was astonished at the change in Cassie. Only the overpowering aura of perfume was the same. Some of her excess weight had been pared away and she was magnificiently dressed in vivid orange satin, trimmed with glittering rhinestones. Garnet recalled that Cassie formerly had mouse-colored hair, already streaked with gray. Now she wore an elaborate profusion of golden curls, decorated by a wickedly swaying ostrich plume. Cassie was a handsome woman, now that someone had peeled away the dowdy trappings. She roared with laughter at Garnet's obvious amazement, sweeping her into an enthusiastic embrace.

"It's a wig," she whispered, with a coy wink. "And I can't breathe for fear of busting out of my corset. But my new partner was right about dressing the part. Oh, I knew all about liquor, what to order and how much . . . but he knew about the gambling and what brings the customers in. Come on, Garnet, honey, sit down. That brute of a husband of yours must have really scared you to send you traveling when you're this far along."

"Your partner? Garnet asked faintly, allowing herself to be seated in the garishly splendid saloon bar.

"Oh," said Cassie. "My partner. He's in the back room; that's where the gambling is. He's a Frenchie . . . his name is Leon."

"Cassie, will it be all right if I stay with you? Just until the baby is born?"

"As long as you like. Soon as you get your figure back, you'll bring the customers in like a magnet." Cassie beamed at her.

Garnet was aware of a prickling sensation all along her spine, and she turned slowly to see the man who leaned against the opened door behind her. Lazy amber eyes regarded her with the merest flicker of interest, while a lean body propped itself lethargically against the doorjamb. His hair was as black as Sebastian's, but it was the only feature they had in common. This man had finely chiseled bones with a minimum of flesh drawn tautly over them. A thin black moustache emphasized his long upper lip, while deeply clefted cheeks and chin added to the illusion that his face was the work of a gifted sculptor.

"Good-looking rascal, isn't he?" Cassie whispered. Then she added, in a louder voice, "Come over here, Leon, and meet my friend Garnet."

His clothes were elegant, tailored to fit the narrow hips and long legs. As he moved toward them, Garnet thought that she had never before seen a man who moved with such careless grace. His heels came together and he bowed over her outstretched hand, brushing his lips over her wrist. His amber eyes held hers fast, and she thought suddenly of sunlight shining through a glass of golden wine.

"Leon Pierre Montbeliard. *Enchante, madame.*" There was only a trace of an accent. "But Cassie, *belle amie,* this is no place for a lady who is *enceinte.* Let us take her at once to our private quarters."

Following them to the suite of rooms on the upper floor, Garnet told herself silently that she was *not* hoping that Leon and Cassie were not lovers. She certainly did not care for men who were beautiful, rather than big and handsome. No, indeed. She liked big rough men who were simple and uncomplicated, not indolent dandies who would spend as much time choosing a wardrobe as any woman. And whose thoughts, she was sure, would remain forever obscured behind those strange amber eyes.

--⊰{ **CHAPTER 14** }⊱--

Sebastian paced restlessly back and forth within the drab olive-colored office overlooking the mist-cloaked Mersey. If he had ever had any intention of remaining in Liverpool, he would have had those somber walls painted a more cheerful hue. But Sebastian had never intended to settle here. Apart from the sad memory of his mother's death in McKnight's house, Sebastian felt a growing yearning to return to sea.

He could not desert Emily, he knew. She was so sweet and gentle, so breathtakingly beautiful, that it still seemed incredible she had consented to marry him. She presided over their household with grace and patience, never complained about the long hours Sebastian worked, or the business acquaintances he brought home unexpectedly. Having an invalid, an infant, and a nanny who was occasionally too tipsy to care for the child did not dismay Emily, either. She rose quickly to Mollie Flanagan's defense when Sebastian suggested replacing her.

"Oh, no, dear. We couldn't. She is devoted to Mark. Once in a great while she has a drop of sherry . . . really, it only happens ever so seldom. I believe she gets a little homesick. I can understand that . . . I don't know how I should survive in a strange country."

Sebastian pushed aside the thought he had been harboring about asking Emily to return to America with him. "But then you have to take care of the baby as well as helping the nurse with your grandfather—oh, yes, don't deny it. I know she leaves most of the hardest work to you. They all lean on you, Emily, and tax your strength."

Chiding her for working too hard for others, he did not consciously connect this with the fact that she fell into exhausted sleep while he paced the floor coping with unfulfilled desire. He felt guilty and unworthy of a woman who gave of herself so unselfishly, despite her fragile health, and cursed his own lust before reproaching her, even in his own mind.

Home, he thought. *If only we could go home.* Of course, home had been for the most part a deep-water ship, but Sebastian believed he hungered for the land of his birth. There were times when he returned to the damp house in Princes Park and went up the stairs to Job McKnight's bedroom and spoke to the old man who now lay in the immense bed, shrunken and paralyzed, only the pale eyes glowing accusingly, silently following every movement Sebastian made.

"I've taken care of your business," Sebastian would tell him. "Your liners sail on time and you're making a fair profit on your cargoes. You'll never be a threat to the Black Ball Line or any of the other big companies, but you haven't gone under, either. And you would have, if it hadn't been for me. You played it too close to the chest . . . nobody knew what to do when you had your stroke. I walked into an office full of

146

clerks sitting around drinking tea, waiting for someone to tell them what to do. You'd never given anyone any responsibility. I've changed all that. When I leave, McKnight ships will still sail. Do you hear me, Job? Do you even know who I am?"

Sebastian stood at the bedside, looking down at the crafty eyes beneath overhanging white brows. A shiver passed through Sebastian's large frame and he resolved silently to speak to Emily again about leaving. "I'm a caretaker for your ships, that's all. I'm wasting my own life," he said aloud. "Emily feels we must stay here while you live. But you're going to live forever, you old curmudgeon. Lying there, staring at us with those eyes . . . all right, you can stop sending out the evil sparks. I'll send your nurse to you."

Halfway down the stairs Sebastian heard the shrill cries from the nursery, followed by Mollie's voice hissing out dire threats that Mark McKnight knew would never be carried out. The child was nearly five years old and ruled the entire household with an iron will. Sebastian grinned. His little half-brother was an engaging child, nothing like his father, except perhaps, for his intelligence. Mark was fearless and practical as Louisa, but there was a searching restlessness about him. He was inquisitive about everything and everyone.

Sebastian had tried to discipline the boy, but the doctor who was in daily attendance had warned him that Job became visibly agitated and his heart labored alarmingly if anyone so much as looked at his son disapprovingly. Both the doctor and Emily appealed to Sebastian not to make the child cry. Sebastian complied, more because he found Mark irresistible than for old Job's peace of mind.

It was incredible that his mother and Job could have produced such a child. Mark was almost too beautiful to be a boy. Black hair, soulful blue eyes, features so perfect they put the portraits of Gainsborough to shame.

He was also astonishingly bright for his tender years. Mark learned to walk when most babies could not yet crawl, to talk in complete sentences long before he was a year old, and now, at an age when most children were just beginning their lessons, Mark could already read and write.

Emily's doing, Sebastian thought. Mollie Flanagan doted on the child, but Emily was never too busy to answer his questions. Sebastian put aside the thought that Cyril was also exceedingly patient and spoke to Mark almost as though he were an adult.

"Tell me a story! Tell me a story!" Mark would cry. Sebastian would find himself listening with one ear to the stories Cyril related. Once he had asked Cyril casually if he did not think the bedtime stories were a little "old" for the boy.

Cyril smiled faintly. "Greek mythology is both old and new. As Mark is. Linked to both past and future. He understands the stories. He admires the courage of the heroes, the splendor of their quests. It's never too early for a child to have a glorious example to follow."

Cyril, Sebastian thought irritably, how much longer was he going to stay with them?

From the parlor came the strains of a piano duet and the soft murmur of voices. Sebastian hesitated, his eyes on the closed door. Emily had not heard him come home, engrossed as she was with her half-brother and his music.

Cyril had been staying with them for several weeks and made no mention of returning to wherever he came from, despite Sebastian's hints that he would perhaps find a market for his compositions in a more culturally fertile spot than the seaport of Liverpool.

Emily treated her half-brother as though the loss of three fingers was somewhat in the nature of Christ's crucifixion, and Sebastian resented the care and devotion she lavished on Cyril. But Sebastian worked such long hours he dared not protest while Cyril kept her company. Sebastian not only ran the McKnight Line, but he continued to manage Kolvoord's office during the shipowner's frequent trips to Burma.

On the hall table were a number of letters, and

148

Sebastian picked up the one with the American stamp first. It was bulky. Another long epistle from Ned Hake. During their long correspondence Ned had tried many times to get Sebastian to return home. He had no doubt found more ammunition in his quest to lure Sebastian back to America.

> *Sebastian,*
> *Hope you and the family are well. Expect you will have heard there may be a war with Mexico . . . more on that later. Want to tell you first about John Willis Griffiths, here at Smith & Dimon. Mr. Griffiths is creating a sensation in ship-building circles here with a revolutionary design for new merchant ships. I mention him because some of his theories are the same ones you used to write me about in the days before you became old man McKnight's flunky. The ships Griffiths proposes are knife-like, to slice through the water, with easy and graceful lines and breadth at the beam. He claims —as you did—that it doesn't matter how a ship leaves the water; it's how it enters it that counts.*
> *I've heard also there is a young Scotsman named Donald McKay who is designing what they call "clipper" ships up in Newburyport [to "clip" down the wind]. Sebastian, I really believe exciting times are coming in American ship-building. We're going to challenge the limeys and leave them behind. And you should be here, a part of it.*

Sebastian looked up, reading another unwritten message between the lines. Ned had hinted many times that Sebastian was foolish not to take advantage of McKnight's stroke and divert some of his ships to the American coastal trade, where a few cargoes would finance the purchase of a ship of their own. Ned was tired of working for someone else, but had no capital of his own. The letter continued:

> *There is talk that we are already at war with Mexico, although this has not yet been confirmed.*

149

*General Zachary Taylor has an army on the Rio
Grande and there's been a rush of men to enlist
... so many that quotas have been established lim-
iting enlistments to fifty thousand for each state.
If there is a war, ship-building will surge forward
again, as it did in 1812. Wartime profits will be
substantial. So why not come home?*

Sebastian tucked Ned's letter into his pocket and went
up the hall to the parlor. The notes of the piano faltered
and stopped as he entered the room. Cyril and Emily
sat close together on the piano stool, Cyril playing the
bass with his left hand, she the treble. Emily immediately rose and ran to greet her husband, standing on tip-
toes to kiss his cheek.

"Sebastian, dear . . . we didn't hear you come in . . ."
she began.

Sebastian wrapped his arms about her and swung her
into the air, his mouth finding her lips and bruising
them as he kissed her, thoroughly and possessively.
Bright blue eyes met Cyril's dark stare over the top of
Emily's polished hair. The gesture and the glance sent
an unsubtle message that caused Cyril's long fingers
to move down the keyboard in a cacophony that jerked
Emily's face away from Sebastian's lips. Her cheeks
were bright red and her eyes those of a wounded deer.
Sebastian sighed and put her down.

The house was just too damned full of people. It
seemed that he and Emily were never alone. The feeling
of the walls closing in returned, and with it a longing
for the space and solitude of the sea.

"You see how much I need Emily," Cyril said from
the piano. "She is my right hand. How was the mighty
world of seagoing commerce today, Sebastian?"

Sebastian went to the glass-fronted cabinet and
reached for the brandy decanter. He was always conscious of his clumsiness and lack of formal education
in Emily's presence. Since Cyril's arrival he was even
more aware of the considerable gap that separated a
man who had spent most of his life at sea from one who
had the polish only British public schools and French

universities could impart. Emily had been taught by governesses and tutors, but seemed almost as well read as Cyril.

Neither of them knew that Sebastian often sat up in the early hours of the morning, poring over the books he had previously scorned.

It had seemed enough, the lessons taught by his parents; the clerking skills he picked up in the shipping offices. Since Cyril's arrival, Sebastian had set about transforming himself from the sow's ear he believed himself to be into an imitation of a silk purse. Perhaps if he acquired more polish, Emily would not stiffen in fear when he touched her. . . .

"I have a letter from Ned," Sebastian announced. "I must return to the United States immediately. The country will soon be at war with Mexico."

Emily turned pale and clutched the arm of the nearest chair for support. Cyril turned around on the piano stool and looked at him warily.

"But I can't leave Grandfather . . ." Emily began.

"He has a nurse," Sebastian said. "A doctor comes in regularly. There are servants—Mollie to take care of Mark. Your grandfather probably doesn't know you're here, anyway."

"Oh, yes, I think he does. His eyes . . . seem so knowing." Emily's hand flew to her hair, a nervous gesture that Sebastian knew meant she was battling some secret terror. Sebastian had never been able to get her to tell him what it was.

"Why don't you see if dinner is ready?" Sebastian said quickly. "We'll talk about it later."

Emily glanced apprehensively from Sebastian to Cyril, as though afraid to leave them together, then left the room.

Cyril stared at Sebastian. The expression on Cyril's face was a mixture of both anger and pity. He did not rise from the piano stool. Sebastian grew uncomfortable as the seconds passed. *Damn it,* he thought, *I've more of a right to be here than he has . . . more of a right to tell Emily what to do.*

"If Emily were aware of what you expected of her,"

151

Cyril said slowly, "or if you would discuss with her your private hopes and fears, perhaps you would both benefit. You share so little of your mind with her."

Sebastian drained his brandy glass. "What the hell do you know about what I share with my wife? Has she been complaining to you that I don't share my thoughts?"

"Do you?"

"Damn it, don't answer a question with another question."

"You know as well as I do that Emily has never in her life found fault with another human being. No, Sebastian, she has not told me that you shut her out. But I see her trying to share with you all that she finds beautiful in the world, while you ignore her and devote all of your energies to your ships."

"And if I didn't, who would run the line?" Sebastian asked. "Would you like the job?"

"I am not capable of assuming your responsibilities. I merely feel that no matter how busy you are, you should try to give your wife some of your life. You have just informed her that your country is going to war and you will be returning home. You haven't told her what your plans are after you get there, nor what will become of her. She has a right to know these things."

"And how do you know what my wife and I discuss in the privacy of our bedroom, my friend? Do you think we only talk to each other in front of you?" Sebastian's face was flushed and his fists were clenched. He was well aware that something was missing in his marriage. He blamed it on all of the added responsibilities that had fallen on both Emily and himself since Job's stroke. He also blamed it partly on Cyril's presence.

There were times when Sebastian had been on the point of telling Emily how lovely she looked in the candlelight of the dinner table, or of confessing to her that he felt landlocked and longed for a brief time on the high seas. But always Cyril was there, sitting across the table and talking to Emily in a way Sebastian knew he would never be able to.

Cyril had risen and was moving toward the door. The dark eyes in their shadowed sockets regarded Sebastian with the flicker of a raw emotion that was unmistakably pain. "Of course not, Sebastian. How can I possibly know what you discuss in the privacy of your bedroom? Forgive me, I was only trying to help. My only desire is my sister's happiness."

"Your *sister*, yes," Sebastian said, emphasizing the word as though to reassure himself.

Cyril loathed Sebastian with a quiet but steady passion. He could scarcely bear to look upon the huge raw-boned man who used the delicate body of his beloved Emily as a receptacle for his lust. The man clearly had no appreciation for Emily's sensitivity, for her fine, quick mind, and creative thoughts.

They did not seek to consciously shut Sebastian out of their conversations, but whenever their after-dinner talk drifted to music or literature, Sebastian's vivid blue eyes would glaze slightly and he would yawn in that ill-mannered way that made Cyril flinch for Emily's feelings.

Once Sebastian emitted a distinct belch when Cyril started to quote a poem Emily mentioned. Cyril himself had been to sea and was well aware of the uncouth ways of seamen, but that Emily should be subjected to such *gaucherie* was intolerable to him, particularly as he was powerless to protect her from it.

Emily had spoken quickly in an attempt to cover her husband's churlishness. "Cyril was about to quote the poem I mentioned, dear," she said a trifle breathlessly. "It just seemed to fit in with what we were saying . . . Cyril was speaking of the beautiful Pacific islands, and I remembered 'Farewell to Bithynia' . . . Sebastian, dear, the first verse, especially:

"A balmy warmth comes wafted o'er the seas,
The savage howl of wintry tempests drear
In the sweet whispers of the western breeze
Has died away; the spring, the spring is here!"

153

The night Sebastian announced he must return to America, Cyril thought about Emily quoting "Farewell to Bithynia." Oddly, for once Cyril was on Sebastian's side. *The sweet whispers of the western breeze,* he thought silently.

"Emily, if the Americans push their western frontier all the way to the coast, you must persuade your husband to take you there someday. I sailed between the Sandwich Isles and the California coast . . . the Pacific appealed to me more than anywhere else I've seen—especially the Sandwich Isles, with their warm tradewinds. I'm sure that, like me, you would find your health much improved in that gentle climate."

Sebastian glowered across the table at him and drained another glass of brandy, ignoring his soup. "The shipyards are on the east coast. That's where we will go. My friend Ned Hake thinks we could start our own shipping company and make a go of it." Sebastian paused, then added, "I reckon I've earned the right to borrow enough from McKnight Shipping to get started. I shall speak with the bank in the morning, Emily. I will probably need your signature."

As Job McKnight's only adult relative, Emily had been given the power to act on her grandfather's behalf while he was incapacitated. She gave a stricken and hopeless glance in Cyril's direction and her hand crept up to the long corkscrew curl that fell in front of her ear. It was clear from Sebastian's eyes, which had darkend to navy-blue, that this time his mind was made up.

Later, when they retired to their room, Emily lingered at her dressing table, trying to untangle the knot she had tied in her hair. Sebastian lay on the bed, watching and waiting.

"Dear . . ." Emily said, furiously picking at her tangled hair.

"Yes?" The hard light was still in his eyes.

"About Cyril . . ."

"What about him? He can stay here until he decides what he wants to do, of course. I think your grandfather owes him that much."

That was not what Emily wanted to ask. But, unfortunately, it precluded her suggesting that perhaps Cyril should accompany them to America and try his luck there.

"Come to bed, Emily. The fire's burning low and you'll catch a chill sitting there."

"I'm sorry, dear. I try not to catch so many colds." *And I'm sorry I haven't conceived your child.* But that thought was too painful to express aloud. How she had longed to give her husband a son. She would gladly have given up her own life to express her love for Sebastian in the only way she believed he would understand.

"Dammit, woman, don't apologize to me. It isn't your fault your health's frail. It's a lifetime of living in this damp mausoleum." Sebastian was angry without knowing why he was angry. Beneath the sheet his hands were clenched into fists. He had to restrain the urge to leap from the bed and sweep her into his arms.

There were times Sebastian thought that she must surely be a dream . . . that he had merely imagined this lovely creature was his flesh and blood wife. Even when he held her in his arms, he was afraid she might suddenly vanish, leaving only the memory of her beauty.

He tried to speak reassuringly. "Emily, your grandfather will be well cared for after we leave. Don't fret about him. In God's name, Emily, have you forgotten what he did to you? Locking you up in this very room? For all that time? Did it ever occur to you that it's a fitting punishment for his mind to be locked in that shell of a body?"

She gasped, her dark eyes glancing about fearfully, as though she expected some avenging god to strike Sebastian down, or, worse, her grandfather to materialize in the room with them. She was torn between wanting to follow her husband to the ends of the earth and her duty to her grandfather. Being intensely loyal, it did not occur to her that her grandfather had forfeited the right to her devotion by his treatment of her.

"It's time we lived our own lives, Emily," Sebastian said, "and got out of the shadow of his. I know you feel guilty—though God knows you shouldn't—about his

155

stroke. And don't think I haven't known why you shrink from my lovemaking. It's because he's in the next room, isn't it?" *Talk to her,* Cyril had said. Sebastian cast about for the right words to tell her of his feelings.

Emily hung her head in dismay, unable to speak because the truth was so much worse than what he knew. Silently she went to the bed, into his embrace.

The great rough hands went down her back, up over the suddenly taut stomach muscles, fondling the small, well-shaped breasts. His lips sought her mouth. His manhood swelled and grew against her thigh. "Emily, ah, Emily, sweet wife," he whispered. His hands easily spanned her waist as he turned her onto her back. "You're such a little thing," he said huskily. "Tiny little rib cage . . . sometimes I'm afraid I'll break you in two. But, oh, God, I want you so fiercely. All though dinner I could hardly sit still for wanting you." He kissed her breasts, pushed her thighs apart, and kneeled between them. His member was fully erect, but Emily did not see it because her eyes were tightly closed.

He pushed against her, tentatively. The entry was closed to him. He looked down at the whiteness of her skin, the soft sweep of dark hair spread over the pillow, the smaller triangle of pubic hair. He could feel his own passion running away from the restraints he always tried to impose. He bent to kiss her nipples again, allowed his mouth to drift lightly downward, tasting her sweetness. His blood was pounding, every nerve alive, his body filled with throbbing need.

She did not move. *This is the way it's supposed to be; she's a good woman, not some waterfront doxie,* he told himself desperately as he tried to find some response with his lips, his tongue, his fingers. He managed to insert just the tip of his organ and felt the tremor pass through his wife's body. *She wants to respond to me,* he thought excitedly, *but she's afraid I'll think less of her.* He tried to push farther into her soft warmth, and, in doing so, could not stop his own climax. It had been too long since the last time. Emily always left the bed immediately to go and wash and put on a clean nightgown. Sebastian often wished she would remain in his arms. *Perhaps if I talked to her,* he thought. When she tried to free herself from his embrace, he said quickly, "Emily . . . about our going back to America. You see, there's just too much competition for the Atlantic trade. Your grandfather's ships aren't large enough or fast enough anymore. But I believe we'd do well trading in American coastal waters. But it's not only that; America is my home. That's where I want to settle. I feel particularly bad being away now that the country is going to war."

"Of course, Sebastian. You must do what you believe is right, and, of course, I shall go with you." She was scarcely aware of what she was saying, wanting only to escape before his now flaccid member aroused itself for another assault upon her flesh. Often she tarried in her dressing room until Sebastian fell asleep. She brushed her hair, changed her nightgown, washed her hands. She was, however, careful not to wash away his seed. "Whither thou goest, I will go. Thy people shall be my people," she added softly, squirming free of the weight of his arm.

He made no attempt to hide his sigh of relief. In a moment of magnanimity, he added, "If you'd prefer, I could go first and find a place for us to live—then come back for you."

Emily agreed too readily to this arrangement. Later Sebastian wished he had insisted that her half-brother move out before he sailed for New York. Sebastian told himself that such pettiness was unworthy, since the two of them shared only a love of music and were, after all, blood-related. If he had not been secretly jealous of Emily's attachment to Cyril and afraid to give shape and form to that jealousy, he would have seen more clearly how it was influencing all of their lives. The more Sebastian resented Cyril, the more he withdrew into his shell. Unreasonably, Sebastian felt that Emily could have made more of an effort to understand the problems of his life if she chose to do so. After all, she had no trouble sympathizing with Cyril. That Cyril was in turn sensitive to Emily's feelings was something Sebastian, in his unacknowledged jealously, chose to ignore.

A man's wife should be *for* him all the way, to the exclusion of all others. Wasn't that what the marriage contract said . . . forsaking all others?

A month later Sebastian stood on the deck of a McKnight packet as she pulled away from the Pier Head and waved good-bye to Emily and Cyril, their identical dark eyes fixed on the departing ship. Sebastian felt a heart-tugging pang of regret and an unexpected sense of foreboding which he tried to overcome by making a nuisance of himself in the captain's chart room. After all, he would return shortly for Emily; they would not be parted for long.

He could not know that they would be parted for the duration of the Mexican war.

Within a week of setting foot on American soil, Sebastian was overwhelmed by a rush of patriotism and a desire to make up in some way for his long absence from his native country. It was typical of him, upon learning that the merchant navy was paying high wages and shipowners were becoming rich, that instead of pushing forward with his own plans, he enlisted in the navy. The Navy Department announced there was a critical shortage of sailors to man the Gulf and Pacific squadrons, despite the surplus of enlistees for the army.

Three of the McKnight ships were diverted to the American coastal trade and Ned Hake agreed to run the newly formed Balmain Shipping Company. Sebastian sailed off to blockade Mexican ports.

--=⚞ CHAPTER 15 ⚟=--

Late in the year Garnet's baby was born, eight pounds of the most exquisite baby girl the midwife, Cassie, or Leon had ever seen, they assured the happy mother. Garnet looked down at the silken hint of red-gold hair on the baby's pulsating little head and named her daughter Cerise.

Within two months, Cassie laced Garnet's waist back to its former twenty inches and she began to circulate in the saloon, drinking with the customers, sitting in on their card games "for luck." A freewoman of color, named Fern, was hired to care for Cerise.

Amber eyes watched Garnet lazily, but the air crackled every time she and Leon were in the same room.

She was surprised to learn that he was not a footloose drifter or soldier of fortune, nor even a pirate, but was the owner of a large plantation a day's journey from New Orleans. He was also married, with children. He had apparently met Cassie during an altercation over cheating at another gambling house and expressed the wish that a gentleman could be assured of an honest game. Cassie had suggested that owning his own place might be the answer, offering to use her small capital and vast knowledge in the endeavor.

"Do you sleep with him?" Garnet asked her.

Cassie gave a sigh of regret. "No, honey. He has a Creole mistress—beautiful young thing named Delphine. And his wife is a pure-blooded French aristocrat. We just have a business relationship, that's all. He sometimes stays over in our private rooms, but only to sleep. Delphine has a small house in town."

Garnet could hardly stand to look at Leon, for fear he would read her feelings in her eyes. She grew warm whenever he was near and found herself squirming in her seat, her nerves tingling. Surreptitiously, she would glance beneath lowered eyelashes at his trim hips and long, lean legs, always encased in perfectly fitted, skin-tight breeches.

When he returned to his plantation, Garnet dragged listlessly through the days with little interest in anything but her baby. She flared to life when he returned and contrived to be alone with him, following if she saw him go upstairs to the private rooms and then pretending she hadn't known he was there. She had never been so dazzled by a man and was unaware that part of the magic spell was caused by the birth of her child and resulting changes in her own body.

One evening she found they were running short of dice and, finding the new ones were kept on the top shelf of the tiny storeroom, asked Leon to help her get them down. "They're up there," Garnet said, feeling him standing close behind her in the confined space. Her heart had skipped, then raced. She did not dare look over her shoulder at him.

She felt his warm breath on the nape of her neck, then the lightest touch of his lips. A tremor passed through her as his hands clasped her waist. He turned her around to face him.

The amber eyes glowed like polished glass as Leon looked down at her. She caught her breath at the physical jolt the closeness of his lean, hard body gave her.

"Chérie . . ." he murmured lazily. "It is inevitable, is it not? Shall we continue with the pretense? Or shall I tell you that you are the most exciting woman I have ever known? My blood races and my loins ache with need for you. I want you more than I have ever wanted any woman." His lips teased hers, nibbling, then pulling away.

Her hands went to his hair, fingernails scraping his scalp as she pulled his face close. There had never been such a kiss. It was the blending of two white-hot comets in the far reaches of the universe. She felt it in every

160

inch of her body, and her mind shut out everything else. There was nothing else in the world except this moment, this man. Her hands clawed at his back, their bodies straining with the need to meld into one. She was shaking as his lips traveled down her neck and he bent her backward over his arm to kiss her breast. She felt the warmth of his lips through the thin silk.

He straightened up and kissed her lightly on the tip of her nose. "Go upstairs to Cassie's room. I shall follow."

Garnet stumbled upstairs, tiptoeing past her own room, where Cerise slept. It was as though all of her senses had deserted her, except for the sense of touch. Tiny prickling nerves in her fingertips, in the secret places between her thighs, and in her nipples were aflame with desire. She had known passion before, but never anything like this.

Fumbling with the lamp beside the bed, she heard the door open and Leon came across the dark room to take her in his arms. "We don't need the light, *chérie,*" he whispered, his hands helping her with her gown.

His body was like a finely tuned instrument: lean, taut, supple. The experience of exploring, tasting, joining, was the mutual expression of equals. At no time did she feel subjugated to superior male strength, nor bound by coy female restraint. There were profound moments of the deepest sensual satisfaction, and there were outbursts of relaxing humor. Their lovemaking was the purest tribute to the senses she had ever known, perhaps because they met on that level and no other. He had no interest in her past, her future, her mind, or her spirit.

They existed in a dim, twilighted world of breathless sensual pleasure, always finding new ways to delight one another. Garnet would sometimes undress slowly in front of him, moving her body and arms in provocative dancing gestures to draw attention to her charms; discarding her chemise and bending forward so that her breasts spoke their own message. Gradually her lace-edged pantalettes would be wriggled to her ankles, revealing long, slender legs.

He would come to her, sinking to his knees to clasp

161

her sweet, musky warmth to his lips, slipping his tongue into the soft, moist down and making small sounds of pleasure.

Some days it would be she who would feast her eyes on the beauty of his body, the taut skin of a light tan color, the glorious symmetry of his manhood, rising to seek the warm caress of her lips and tongue, her breasts, her innermost places.

He would smile lazily, amber eyes languid despite the fever that throbbed and pulsated in her hands as she tenderly stroked and teased and played with him. Then she would move, unhurried, to the bed, and lie down. Her thighs would part and they would be curiously defenseless until his burning eyes moved to her breasts, with pert nipples and soft shadow between them, and sometimes he would begin by placing his organ there, in that silken hollow.

There were so many ways to lie, to turn, to savor the sensation of warm skin and moist, secret caresses. But best of all was the sweet, wonderful thrust of his manhood deep inside her, stabbing and filling her undulating body in frenzied harmony as they reached the peak of their desire.

After a few weeks he rented a house for Garnet, her baby, and Fern. Cassie helped her pack.

Cassie said, "I hope this doesn't mean I shan't be seeing you as often." She was encased in a lavender vapor.

"Of course not."

"Has he mentioned Delphine?" Cassie avoided Garnet's eyes as she asked the question.

Garnet had tried to forget about Leon's former mistress. That Delphine was a former mistress, Garnet was absolutely sure. She doubted Leon had enough energy left to make love to his wife, let alone a mistress, after he left her own demanding arms.

"Be careful, honey," Cassie said. "She's a hot-tempered little gypsy."

A week after she moved into her own house, Leon returned to his plantation. His overseer was complaining about problems that were arising due to Leon's constant absence. The next afternoon Fern answered the doorbell and was rudely pushed aside by a diminutive olive-skinned woman with a lovely heart-shaped face and a luxurious mass of black curls.

"Where is she?" she demanded, eyes going wildly about the hall and living room beyond.

Fern's dignified black countenance clearly expressed her disdain. "Miz Garnet is not receivin'," she said in her liquid Louisiana drawl.

"Who is it, Fern?" Garnet called from her bedroom. She came out onto the landing and looked down the stairs. Delphine . . . it must be she. Garnet went down the stairs toward her visitor. It would, she thought wryly, be a new experience to have a confrontation with an irate mistress . . . Garnet was accustomed to dealing only with wives.

Delphine's eyes went over Garnet maliciously. "They told me you were a showy-looking woman. Not a beauty —just . . . ah, what is the word?" she asked herself, exasperated.

"Flamboyant, perhaps?" Garnet suggested. "Arresting? Sensual?" She laughed softly. "Let me give you a piece of advice, Delphine. Never try to hold on to a man when he's through with you. All you'll accomplish is the loss of your pride. Believe me, it's better to let him go regretting you than pitying you."

"Shut up!" Delphine screamed. "I did not come to listen to you talk. I came to tell you I shall kill you if you take Leon away from me."

"Come on, now. You must know that no man on earth is worth dying for . . ." Garnet did not raise her voice. "Especially since he doesn't belong to either of us—but to his wife."

"There are ways—things I can do . . . I can go to a conjure woman. You . . . you . . ." Delphine lost control and lunged for Garnet's throat.

Taken unaware, Garnet staggered backward, trying to disentangle sharp-nailed fingers.

Almost instantly, Fern stepped forward, her strong arms going about the middle of her mistress' attacker. She easily lifted Delphine and flung her backward through the open front door.

163

Delphine picked herself up and glared murderously at Garnet. "You've been warned—" she gasped in the instant before Fern closed the door.

Leon had not returned from the plantation, and Garnet was lonely. She decided to go and visit Cassie. The streets were swarming with navy uniforms, for the war was now being carried into Mexico itself. Four coastal brigs were being outfitted as bomb vessels. The word among the sailors was that all were intended for the bombardment of the fortress at Veracruz.

Garnet saw the group of naval officers strolling along the narrow street, ogling the pretty mulattoes and quadroons who called to them from wrought-iron balconies. Despite the sameness of the uniforms, she recognized Sebastian instantly.

People were thronging the streets and she called his name while being swept in the opposite direction. He turned his head, squinting bright blue eyes to find her in the crowd. He pushed through the sea of people, laughing delightedly as he caught up with her and swung her into a sheltering doorway.

"Garnet! I don't believe it . . . after all these years! My God, you're lovelier than ever."

Smiling up at him, she touched the uniform buttons and raised a quizzical eyebrow. "Navy, Sebastian? Wouldn't you have made more money in the merchant marine?" She was actually thinking that he was a splendid sight in his gold-braided blue. Even standing still, the power and strength of his body was evident. When he moved, the muscles of shoulders and back drew the navy-blue cloth taut and it was easy to imagine the symmetry of tanned bare flesh beneath. Invincible, Garnet thought. The word had always personified Sebastian in her mind.

He had lost the clumsiness of youth and, for a large man, moved with extraordinary grace. There was also a new confidence about his speech and manner that Garnet did not dwell upon, for fear he had acquired it from the woman he married.

Sebastian wrapped his arm protectively about her

waist as he drew her out into the street again. "Come and have dinner with me and tell me everything you've been up to."

They ate gumbo and drank wine and talked until the small hours of the morning. Garnet didn't think about Leon until Sebastian asked about the current man in her life.

She smiled her slow seductive smile, green eyes sparkling. "You know there'll always be one, don't you? That's what I like about you, Sebastian. You don't imagine a woman will pine away for you. Or expect her to live by a different set of standards from a man. I was afraid when you said you'd been living in England that you'd have changed into one of those moralists I hear are taking over since Victoria became queen."

Sebastian grinned. "They've always been with us. It's just that now they're becoming popular again. The pendulum swings constantly. I reckon after all the excesses of England's last royal family, they were bound to get a prude on the throne this time. But Garnet, you still haven't told me if you have a protector—more important, if he's going to come after me with a shotgun for keeping you out so late."

He spoke lightly, twisting his wineglass between his fingers. He felt as though he were holding his breath, awaiting her reply, despite the grin that seemed to have frozen on his face. He had difficulty keeping his eyes from straying to the perfection of her body. The gentle curve of her shoulders, the swelling breasts that accentuated a tiny waist. *I'm a married man*, he told himself sternly, *but, oh, God, when she looks at me in that promising, tempting way, I'd have to be a saint not to respond.*

"His name is Leon and he's a planter," Garnet said at last. "I share his bed, but nothing else. He has a wife and family." Later she would realize that she had not told Sebastian of her marriage to Erik Gunnar and would wonder if the omission was deliberate. There had been a time when she wanted to hurt Sebastian, as he had hurt her. But the woman who had married Erik

165

partly to spite Sebastian now shrank from telling him the sordid details of her impulsive marriage.

Sebastian's hand slid across the table and closed over hers. "So have I . . . a wife, at least. But I haven't seen her for a long time. I've resisted temptation until now . . . but, oh, God, Garnet, seeing you again is like showing a starving man food."

He believed in the sanctity of marriage and had always been faithful to Emily, even when it became evident that she cringed from the physical side of their marriage. But Emily was on the other side of the world, and a war had to be fought. Sebastian had seen men die and knew only too well how fragile a hold on life he had. If enemy cannon didn't get him, there was a good chance the sea itself would. Sailors had a reputation for having a girl in every port that was well deserved. And justified, some said.

Sebastian battled his conscience as his arms ached to embrace Garnet and his body throbbed with desire for her. He tried to conjure up the image of Emily and her purity and beauty. He desperately forced his mind to think of his ship, the sea, the war. Anything to dull the growing need for Garnet. Oh, God, how he wanted her; even as he sought to obliterate his desire with other visions, his manhood stirred again. Emily was a distant dream that lost substance and reality as their absence from one another lengthened. Garnet was a warm-blooded woman and she was here, real and ready to melt into his arms.

"I know a place where we can be alone," Garnet said softly, her eyes liquid with longing.

She took him back to Cassie's place, each minute in his company reminding her how easy it would be to love this man completely. It was as though the intervening years had been no more than fleeting hours. They were comfortable with one another, happy to be together. Making love seemed the most natural expression of their feelings.

For Garnet, when Sebastian wrapped his muscular arms about her and his powerful hands fondled her breasts and his lips drew her flesh into the warm abyss of his mouth, she felt not only the wildest, deepest joy, but also a profound sense of being totally protected.

"Sebastian, you've improved with age, like good wine," she murmured contentedly. "You're no longer a boy in that magnificent man's body. You have a sure and deft touch that is sending me slowly, exquisitely, out of my mind."

He picked her up, cradling her to his broad chest, and laid her on the bed, looking down at her. His bright blue eyes filled with the wonder of a man glimpsing paradise. Garnet's hands and lips found his body eagerly and he lost himself in her kisses, drowning in sweet warm flesh and silken hair. When he entered her, she arched her back and thrust her hips upward to meet him, crying out her delight, seeking each exquisite sensation with unashamed pleasure, lingering on the brink of completion until a spasm passed through Sebastian's body and she gripped his back and tumbled with him through star-filled eternity. Afterward, he held her and laughed and joked and talked to her. With Leon she always felt like a pampered whore, sharing only the pleasures of the flesh, never sharing any other part of herself, or him. Sebastian made her feel like a friend, as well as lover. Perhaps, Garnet reflected with a pang of sadness, that was how it would be to be a wife to a man like Sebastian.

"Do you remember Ned Hake—he was aboard the *Dancer*—a quiet-spoken man? Well, he's running the Balmain Shipping Company while I'm in the service. When I get out I'm going to be a shipowner, Garnet, just like I told you I would. We're using three of McKnight's small schooners, and as soon as we make enough, we'll buy our own ship." He drew her back into his arms, eyes and hands appreciating every inch of her.

"I was in the Pacific," he went on. "I'd like to go back there someday. The California coast is breathtaking and the climate is mild. Emily's health might be improved there."

Garnet flinched at the reference to his wife. She said

quickly, "You're sure we're going to follow our 'manifest destiny' all the way to the coast, then?"

"No doubt about it. The Mexicans have never really settled the territory. When we do, the possibilities for fast ships around the Horn will be endless. Ned is in touch with a man named Donald McKay who is building a special kind of ship called a clipper. If we can raise enough capital to buy one, the profit on one cargo trip to California would pay for it."

Garnet smiled at the boyish eagerness in his eyes and wondered silently if the shadowy Emily appreciated him. His wife had managed to keep him ashore with her for a long time. She must be a remarkable woman, for Garnet knew that Sebastian was a true sailor and could not be happy away from the sea for long. He had only a few days in New Orleans, and Garnet spent all of his shore leave with him.

Afterward, Garnet knew she should have read the danger signal more accurately when, returning to Leon's house one morning, she was met by an agitated Fern. "We was broken into," she said at once. "I didn' hear nothin', Miz Garnet. And the baby slept through it all, too. They ransacked your room . . . I don' find nothin' missin'. Reckon that Delphine woman wanted to get hold of some of your hairs, or somethin' to take to a conjure woman."

Garnet's clothes were torn and scattered about the room. Her perfume and rouge pots were emptied and jewelry cases were dumped on the floor. Nothing appeared to be missing until Garnet found her empty writing case. All of her personal papers—marriage certificate, baby's birth certificate—were gone.

"Let's clean up the mess," she told Fern. "And we won't tell Mr. Montbeliard." It had been Delphine, of course. But why had she taken only the documents?

Garnet had her answer a few months later.

Sebastian had sailed away with the fleet, part of the first joint land-sea assault on an enemy stronghold in history. Surfboats had put ashore a force of over eight thousand men at Veracruz without the loss of a single life.

Garnet hoped that Sebastian would return to New Orleans. She was sure he would, if he had the chance. He had given her Ned Hake's address in New York and told her if she was ever in need to get in touch with him. Meantime, he would write to Ned and Deborah, his wife.

"What will you tell them?" Garnet asked. "Ned will remember who and what I am."

"That you are a dear friend. Ah, Garnet . . . what a woman you are. Why, if I weren't married to Emily . . ."

She stopped his words with a kiss.

Leon was still an exciting lover, but Garnet missed Sebastian. Leon's lethargic presence, when he was not using his fine, lean body to make love, was no substitute for the exhilarating company of Sebastian, whose enthusiasm and zest for living infected everyone around him.

The day everything came to an end, Garnet was in bed with Leon. He lay back on the pillow, amber eyes half-closed. *"Chérie . . ."* he murmured. Wake me if I fall asleep. I must leave soon."

"You have to go back to the plantation?"

"I must be on my way before dusk."

"What is your wife like?" she asked suddenly. Odd, she had a feeling that they had run out of time and wanted to clear up all the trailing ends of their relationship.

"Beautiful . . . and cold. Like the wives of all men who are forced to take a mistress," he answered sadly.

"But you love her?"

"More than my life. It is why I come to you . . . why I went before to Delphine, *chérie.* So I do not have to force myself upon my delicate wife."

They heard Fern scream the moment before the footsteps came thundering up the stairs and the door burst open. Erik Gunnar, red eyes glowing like an angry wolf, sprang into the room with a blood-chilling curse on his lips.

Garnet did not see Leon move, yet before Gunnar uttered another word, Leon's arm had snaked out to the

169

nightstand and the pistol was pointed squarely between the hate-filled red eyes.

Gunnar took a step backward. "I'm calling you out, Frenchman," he said thickly. "Dawn, tomorrow. Now, get out of my wife's bed."

"M'sieur, I believe it is you who will leave," Leon said softly, cocking the pistol. "My seconds will make the arrangements with you tomorrow."

Garnet covered herself with the sheet as Erik Gunnar clenched his fist and smashed it into the door, splintering the wood. He gave a last glowering look at the pistol in Leon's hand and left the room.

It took both Cassie and Fern to restrain Garnet from riding out to where the duel would take place beside a misty bayou. She begged Leon not to go. "Please—he isn't a gentleman like you. He won't abide by the rules." She sobbed and pleaded to no avail.

"*Chérie*, we have chosen seconds. They will be there to see the rules are followed. A man cannot ignore a challenge."

Leon kissed her and wiped away her tears. He did not tell her that Gunnar had demanded they fight like common pugilists, with fists only. Leon had exercised his privilege as the party called out to make his own choice of weapons. It was to be pistols at twenty paces.

"Honey, let the men settle it in their own way," Cassie put in, offering Garnet a scent-drenched handkerchief to cry into.

"Erik will kill you, Leon. Please—if you must go, then kill him before he has a chance to kill you."

Leon raised his eyebrows in horror. "*Mon Dieu!* Have you no sense of honor?" he said lightly. "Go and make yourself pretty for me. I shall return in an hour."

But he did not return in an hour. His seconds came riding back to tell her Leon was dead, and with his last words he instructed them to ride and warn her to beware of her husband's wrath.

Garnet buried her face in her hands. When Cassie went to comfort her, she was pushed away. Garnet's eyes glittered as she raised her head, but there were no

170

tears on her cheeks. She went to the nightstand and withdrew the pistol Leon always kept there.

"Take the baby and Fern back to your place," she told Cassie. "I'll face my husband in my own way."

She squeezed the trigger the moment he appeared. There was an ear-splitting explosion and she was thrown backward by the recoil, choking on the smoke. Erik's eyes widened in astonishment and he clutched his shoulder as blood spurted. He staggered forward as she half-lay on the bed, staring in fascinated horror at what she had done.

"Garnet . . ." His eyes glazed and he crashed to the floor, rolled over, and looked up at her with unseeing brown-red eyes. "I loved you . . . I cared for you—"

The blood was soaking into the carpet in an ever-widening pool. Almost without realizing what she was doing, Garnet pulled a pillow from the bed to place under his head. "Lie still," she said. "I'll go and fetch a doctor. I'll take care of you, Erik Gunnar, but after that, we're quits."

Cassie came to visit her in a cloud of eye-watering perfume. She stood tight-lipped in the hall, demanding to know if it was true Garnet was caring for Leon's murderer.

"Didn't you hear?" Cassie cried angrily. "Gunnar turned and fired on the nineteenth step. Leon never had a chance. Honey, what are you thinking of? You shot him and now you're taking care of him when you should be running for your life."

Garnet could not bring herself to tell Cassie that apart from a few pieces of jewelry, she was penniless. Nor could she ask for Cassie's help after depriving her of her closest friend and business partner.

"Cassie . . . I'm sorry—I know how you felt about Leon. I'm sorry I brought tragedy to you and to his family. . . . It was Delphine, you know, who wrote to Erik telling him we were here." Garnet had been up all night and her mind was numb.

Cassie stormed away without another word, tears streaming down her cheeks.

The doctor had removed the bullet and Erik now lay in the bed she had shared with Leon. The red glow in his eyes had dimmed and he watched her warily as she entered the room. He was proud of her, despite his pain. She had nerve; he had to give her that. Someday she'd pay for what she did . . . but not now. "Garnet, baby, thank you for bringing the doctor," he said huskily. "Garnet—let's try again. I swear to you I won't lay a hand on you. And I'll never mention the other men you've had. Garnet—I saw our daughter . . . she's the most beautiful thing I've ever seen. Why didn't you tell me? I can't believe she's mine. She's the first thing in the world that was ever wholly mine. Let me make a home for you both. Listen—I've got money now. . . ."

Never was a man so transformed, Garnet thought in the following days. Erik Gunnar idolized the tiny pink and white bundle that was his daughter. He was gentle and loving with the child, respectful with his wife. As his wounded shoulder began to heal, he made plans. They would return to New York, away from any possible repercussions of the duel. He had no intention of hiding out in the back streets of New Orleans for long. He had changed, Garnet thought. And, after all, he was the father of her child. He agreed to let Fern accompany them.

In New York they moved into their first house, and Erik returned to sea. When he came home after a voyage, he would shower the baby with unsuitable gifts, but he paid scant attention to Garnet and never spoke to her about his ships or voyages. He was a brutal and crude lover, and there were times when Garnet felt he was punishing her with his body, but since he never actually struck her with his fists, she did not complain.

She was, however, troubled by a recurring dream. In the dream she was running down a strange street, blinded by smoke. There was a pounding in her ears. The thunder of hooves. Then all at once a figure materialized in the smoke, beckoning to her.

In the morning she could never recall who the figure

was, but she thought perhaps it was Leon . . . dead because of her.

The war with Mexico was drawing to its inevitable conclusion. Garnet had a home, a husband, and a child, and only occasional thoughts of the elegant Frenchman who had been her friend and lover. She remembered Leon sadly and thought of the contrast between his exquisite lovemaking and the bruising attentions of Erik. But neither of them had ever treated her as a human being in the way Sebastian did. . . Still, life went on and few people ever got everything they wanted out of it.

One morning in the autumn of 1848 her doorbell rang. She was expecting Erik to return from a voyage and he was already overdue. One of the owners of his ship was standing outside.

"I'm sorry, Mrs. Gunnar," the man said. "But your husband has been arrested."

Garnet drew a deep breath. "He killed someone?" she asked.

"He's accused of killing a whole cargo. We'll hire the best lawyers, of course."

"What do you mean—a whole cargo? Animals?"

"Black slaves. It's illegal to import them, and a navy captain has accused our ship of dumping a slave cargo into the sea when the ship was intercepted. All lies, of course. And we might be able to get a lighter sentence, since your husband tells us the navy captain had an old grudge against him. His name is Sebastian Balmain."

Garnet did not attend the trial. She waited at home with the baby for Sebastian to bring the verdict and knew before he spoke that this time Erik would serve his full sentence.

"What can I do?" Sebastian asked.

She looked up at him and a distant flame flickered and died in the depths of her green eyes. "We'll be all right. I can go to work."

"Garnet, ah, Garnet." He slapped his brow with his open palm. "If only I'd known you were married to him." They had been over it all before and both knew it would have changed nothing.

"Why didn't you tell me, in New Orleans?"

"I thought I was free of him then. Besides, I knew you were married, Sebastian, and I didn't think our relationship was such that I should trouble you with my . . . deeper problems."

Sebastian took her hands and drew her close to him, holding her in an embrace that was protective rather than passionate. "You said you want to be far away before he is released from prison. You could go to California—wait for me in San Francisco. Garnet, I'm no longer a poor sailor. Remember the man I told you about—Knute Kolvoord? I worked for him in Liverpool. I just got word that he died and he's left me a tidy sum of money—enough to buy two or three of Donald McKay's clipper ships. Garnet—I'm going to be a shipowner."

Garnet looked up at him and smiled. "I don't know whether to rejoice for you or not, Sebastian. I'm not sure you'll be happy staying ashore and playing the part of a businessman. You're a sailor and you won't feel complete without the wind in your face and a deck under your feet."

His expression was serious as he struggled with his conscience. "Garnet, I've no right to ask you to be with me in California, because I must go to England and fetch my wife. And I have to tell you now that Emily means the world to me. . . . God, I don't know how it is I can love two women, but, Garnet, I do. I want you —I want to take care of you."

She slipped her arms up around his neck and he bent to kiss her. "I'll go with you, Sebastian—to the ends of the earth, if I have to . . . but why San Francisco?"

"I'm taking our first clipper around the Horn myself. I'll stay in San Francisco and Ned will handle things here. We need a man in both places. Someone has to sell the cargoes in California and find cargoes to ship back. The west coast is where fortunes will be made now that gold has been discovered in the Sierras. Everything that floats is racing around the Horn with emigrants and supplies."

Garnet felt his eagerness and enthusiasm and her own response to his nearness. She wanted him and she loved him and wondered how she could have borne Erik's brutal presence. "I want to be legally free of Erik. I believe the fact that he is going to prison is grounds for divorce. I never want him to have the right to come near me or Cerise."

Sebastian was startled by her calm announcement. Most women feared the stigma of divorce more than death itself. As did most men of the time, Sebastian believed marriage was sacred and divorce the ultimate disgrace. Still, he admired Garnet's courage. He thought uneasily that he could never end his own marriage in such a way.

"We'll find a lawyer," he said gravely. "Take care of it before I leave for England." He swung her up in his arms and kissed her thoroughly. She felt the familiar surge of desire and at the same instant the imperious cry of the baby in the next room.

As Garnet disentangled his arms and lips that night in 1848, she knew all at once how she could bind Sebastian to her forever, irrevocably. She would give him what the faraway and shadowy Emily had not given him. A child.

BOOK II

San Francisco—
1853

A hush fell over the assembled guests as the carved mahogany doors opened slowly to the accompaniment of an engagingly amateurish fanfare of trumpets. Two liveried footmen pushed the serving cart slowly, hands preserving the precarious balance of the six-foot model of a ship, the bow of which preceded them majestically into the dining room.

Every eye in the crowded room was fixed, however, not upon the graceful lines of the clipper, but on the tiny swathed bundle lying face down on the teak deck, struggling to raise a head that wobbled alarmingly on a neck and body only six weeks separated from his mother's body.

Almost hidden behind one of the burly footmen, the hand of the anxious nurse strayed toward the baby's back.

"Ladies and gentlemen!" Sebastian roared as the discordant notes of the fanfare faded. "I present my first-born son, Noah, and my new ship . . . soon to be the fastest clipper to race around the Horn. I give you the *Monarch Butterfly*."

The moment the announcement was complete, the nurse picked up the baby, who promptly gave an ear-splitting yell of disapproval, fixing black eyes in his father's direction over the starched white shoulder.

Sebastian laughed. "You see—he liked being on the deck of my ship. I named him well. A toast to my son . . . and to my ship."

The women, in elegant ball gowns of every hue of the rainbow, who were outnumbered by the men in embroidered vests and ruffled shirts, thronged forward to examine the clipper and the child as the tinkle of wine-glasses mingled with the excited murmuring.

Even Sebastian Balmain had outdone himself this time. There had been no hint from behind the garish gingerbread walls of Mariner's Castle, as Sebastian called his remarkable home, that Emily Balmain had even conceived a child. Yet here the infant was presented with Sebastian's third clipper ship at the most dazzling ball the lusty young city of San Francisco had seen.

As the men slapped Sebastian on the back, congratulating him and accepting his cigars, the musicians struck up a lively reel. Footmen passed among the guests with champagne, and the dining hall of the house overlooking the bay hummed and throbbed as men celebrated their own success along with his; for every man present was either making a fortune in the gold fields, or in the supplies that came by way of the tall ships in the harbor. Their houses were the finest, their women the most beautiful, their futures entirely secure.

As Sebastian bellowed to friends and roared with laughter, basking in the fellowship of his peers, no one noticed that his wife, the frail-looking Emily, sat alone and silent, staring down the long banquet table over the ravaged dishes and carelessly discarded napkins abandoned by the guests moments before. She fixed her great dark eyes on the child in the nurse's arms but did not smile, nor did she rise to go to him despite the fact that her arms were unconsciously reaching, her hands outstretched across the damask tablecloth that was stained by a red streak of spilled wine beside her untouched plate of food.

One or two of the women drifted over to her and kissed her pale cheek, but it was clear that Sebastian was being given most credit for the arrival of his son and heir. Emily remained at the table as silent Chinese houseboys began to clear away the dishes and couples drifted through the double doors to the adjacent ball-room to dance.

There was still a score of admirers about Sebastian, his clipper, and his son, when the doors at the opposite side of the dining room burst open. Blinking in the brightness of the chandeliers stood a formidable figure, wearing a foul-smelling fisherman's pullover and salt-stained bell-bottoms. Two servants plucked ineffectually at the giant of a man in an attempt to pull him back into the hall. He raised one brawny arm and sent one servant staggering into the room, sliding over the waxed parquet within inches of the serving cart bearing the model of the clipper.

The moment's silence that followed the arrival of the gate-crasher was more shattering than the fanfare that had filled the room only minutes earlier.

His face was handsome, despite the unkempt beard that was a shade lighter than the tangled brown hair escaping from a filthy watchcap. The attention of everyone in the room was riveted by the wild hatred blazing from eyes that seemed to glow fiery red as they came to rest on Sebastian.

"So, you're out of prison, Erik Gunnar," Sebastian said, raising his glass in a mockery of a toast. "Get my son out of here," he added in a swift aside to the nurse as he stepped between her and the uninvited guest.

"You miserable bastard," Gunnar said in a voice surprisingly soft for his fearsome appearance. "I came to tell you I'll get you for what you did to me. Oh, I'm not going to kill you in front of witnesses and swing from one of your Vigilance Committee ropes. I'm going to ruin you, Balmain. You'll never know which of your ships have men of mine aboard, bent on sabotage."

One of the guests at Sebastian's side slid a small pearl-handled revolver from the inside pocket of his velvet jacket.

"Put that away, Latham," Sebastian said quietly. "There'll be no shooting in front of my wife. If Mr. Gunnar has finished delivering his message, he can either leave of his own free will, or I will personally throw him into the street."

Gunnar's mouth slackened slightly, and a small dribble of saliva escaped into the matted beard. The servant who had been knocked backward into the hall had re-

181

gained his balance and leaped onto the man's back, clutching at his throat in an effort to pull him down.

In the moment before Sebastian barked an order to the servant to back off, Gunnar flung up muscle-knotted arms and seized the servant's neck, sending him flying through the air as though he were a rag doll. The man landed with a splintering crash in the middle of the clipper ship model. He scrambled to his feet, blood on his mouth, as the broken masts fell to the floor with a clatter. The rigging of the model was smashed beyond repair, but the fine polished hull and decks were unmarked by the impact.

Sebastian did not take his eyes from the malevolent red stare of Erik Gunnar, who wiped his fists down his chest in a gesture of disdain, then turned on his heel and strode back to the front door, kicked it open, and disappeared into the thin sea mist creeping silently up the hill.

The frozen figures in the dining hall and clustering at the doors of the adjoining ballroom came slowly back to life. The music, stilled by the outburst, resumed. The two footmen swiftly bore away the broken clipper, and the bloodied servant faded from view. Champagne glasses were refilled, the pearl-handled revolver was pocketed, and its owner moved close to Sebastian's ear and whispered to him.

Sebastian smiled and said, "No! You scoundrel. I'll handle it in my own way and my own time."

At the end of the banquet table, Emily still sat motionless. Stark fear for her husband and son was etched on the lovely heart-shaped face. She twisted a wisp of a lace handkerchief between her fingers and half-rose from her chair.

Sebastian glanced at her, as though only just remembering she was present. He went to her and took her hand to draw her to her feet. "Come, my dear. Our guests are anxious to dance and they're waiting for us to lead them."

She smiled up at him adoringly and tripped along at his side, feet skimming the floor beneath the rose satin flounce of her dress. Every one of the guests watching them sighed with envy. Few husbands and wives treated each other with such devotion and respect.

In the early hours of the morning the remaining guests were too drunk or too sleepy to notice both their host and hostess had quietly withdrawn.

Emily was propped on a mound of pillows in the center of the huge bed Sebastian had had specially made. A slim volume of poetry was cradled in her delicate white fingers and her lips moved soundlessly as she savored the well-known words. There was no need for the book, but it gave her something to hold and prevented her nervous fingers from straying to the long braid of hair that lay heavily over her bosom, now softly rounded from the birth and nursing of her son. Unless her fingers were occupied, Emily found they would tie her hair in knots that had to be cut from the dark silken tresses.

The pillow at her side and carefully ironed white sheets were smooth and untouched. The bed linen was changed daily, including the embroidered case on her husband's pillow that had not been touched by his bristly black hair for several months.

Emily jumped at the discreet knock on her door. There was a pause and then the door opened to admit the nurse, the blanket-wrapped baby in her arms.

"It's two o'clock, mum," the girl said in her lilting Irish voice that always reminded Emily how young the girl was, despite her mothering manner.

"Yes, Maureen, thank you." Emily unfastened the pink ribbons on her bedjacket, her fingers delighting in having a purpose. "You'd better heat some milk. I don't think I'm going to have enough," she added, holding out her arms for her son, who chewed his fist and whimpered hungrily.

"Yes, mum. A real little man, he is, your Noah," Maureen said proudly. "Such a little thing like you to have such a big bouncing boy. I expect it was the party tonight that made you tired. The milk don't come down proper when you're tense, my mam always used to say." She placed the baby at his mother's breast and departed.

Emily bent to place a kiss on the pulsating spot on

183

top of her son's head where the first down of silken hair was darkening the tiny skull. Once, long ago, she had kissed the top of another dark head of hair. That was when her husband slept beside her.

She had always loved the time just before dawn when she would awaken and feel the comfort of his presence in the great bed beside her. In those precious moments while he still slept, she could timidly reach out her restless fingers and touch him, kiss his hair, and creep closer to the enveloping warmth of his nearness. If he began to stir, she would quickly roll back to her own side of the bed, because if she did not, he might awaken and his rough mouth and encroaching beard would raise little red spots on her upper lip and always the lust would come rushing between them, from nowhere it seemed, and he would join their bodies in intimate and painful ways.

Of course, when it was all over, there were the delicious moments when she could relax in his embrace and luxuriate in the affection and pleasure of caresses that were without passion. But those moments were fleeting, and if she tarried too long the whole disgusting ritual would begin all over again.

Emily winced. The baby's sucking became more furious as her milk began to diminish, and carefully she disengaged him to place him at the other breast.

At least she was safe from her husband's assaults on her flesh for a while. If only she did not yearn for his nearness, the touch of his hands tenderly stroking her hair, the wonderful closeness of another creature in the night when old demons came to haunt her dreams. Grandfather's staring eyes as his frantic mind was imprisoned in a helpless body . . . the memory of his groping nocturnal touch when she was a child. The first glimpse of Cyril's mutilated hand . . . their terrible wrenching parting. The nightmare of the voyage to America.

Sebastian and his friend Ned Hake had formed their own shipping line. Then, Sebastian's old employer, Knute Kolvoord, had died the same month the Mexican-American war ended. He had left her husband a substantial bequest, which was quickly invested in one of Donald McKay's clipper ships.

By the time Emily joined Sebastian in America, news of the discovery of gold in the new territory of California was already reverberating along the eastern seaboard. Before Emily had time to catch her breath, she was aboard a clipper with Sebastian, who would allow no one else to skipper his pride and joy in the race around the Horn to bring cargo and passengers to the gold fields.

Her hand drifted from the baby to her husband's pillow and she sighed. She loved Sebastian so much, but she was afraid of him. If only there was a way to have the affection and closeness without the painful lovemaking. She must soon invite him back to her bed and again be at the mercy of his brute strength and voracious sexual appetite. Emily felt she was less than he deserved. Sometimes when he made love to her she thought it was like being caught in a storm at sea. The great tide of his passion was awesome. She longed to be swept away as he was, but she was never able to let go of her tenacious grip on reality.

There were moments when she felt vague longings stir in her senses, but these came when she read a particularly poignant stanza of verse, or heard a hauntingly lovely melody. They rarely coincided with her husband's caresses, and when they did they were so elusive they had disappeared before she could lose herself in them.

The baby was now two months old and it was time for her to ask Sebastian to move back into her bedroom. There was another urgency. It would be easier to tell him what she must soon tell him while they lay together.

She could not keep the news to herself much longer.

Sebastian had glanced at her closed bedroom door before slipping out of the house. Walking through the mist that crept up from the bay, he remembered how lovely Emily had looked and how proud of her he had been. There wasn't a man in San Francisco who did not envy him.

He had never been able to overcome his awe of his wife, nor was he able to understand the hold she had over him. He knew only that he strove mightily to reach impossible goals for her sake. He felt that as long as she was at his side, he was inferior to no man. If, along with the sense of power and achievement, he felt a nagging undercurrent of strain—akin, perhaps, to that of a small boy forced constantly to parade about in his Sunday best—then Sebastian accepted this as a small price to pay for possessing a wife who demanded perfection of herself, also.

Letting himself into the modest house behind its white picket fence at the bottom of the hill, he was not aware that he escaped to Garnet's less exacting presence with the light step of a man relieved of a great burden.

The gaslight from the fog-shrouded street barely illuminated the small vestibule, and Sebastian muttered an oath as his boot connected with the elephant-foot umbrella stand.

"Is that you crashing about down there?" Garnet's voice called as a sliver of candlelight pierced the gloom of the staircase. "Be quiet, for heaven's sake. You'll wake the children." Her voice was low and filled with hidden laughter, despite the reprimand.

Sebastian fumbled with the parlor door. He was lighting a lamp when Garnet joined him, a brilliant red silk kimono pulled hastily over a fragile nightgown.

"You might have left a light burning, in this fog," he growled, dropping into an armchair.

"I didn't expect you tonight. What with the soirée and—" She hesitated, but it had to be said: ". . . and the possibility you'd be paying a visit to the Barbary Coast to settle the unfinished business with the gatecrasher." She perched on the arm of his chair, the red silk slipping from a well-turned thigh, and bent to kiss his mouth.

So she not only knew Erik Gunnar was in town, but also that he had visited Mariner's Castle tonight. "Who brought you that bit of news?" he asked, one black eyebrow arching up.

"I slipped Hwui in among the extra servants you hired for the occasion," she answered frankly. "I knew I wouldn't be able to count on you telling me what the women wore and who got drunk and who got insulted and called out . . . or which women are cuckolding their husbands."

"And the inscrutable Oriental relays all that gossip? Incredible." Sebastian reached up and caressed her cheek with his hand, reassurance as well as fear for her in his touch. "Gunnar didn't come to see you first?"

"No," she said quickly. "Hwui tells me his ship docked only today—yesterday, I guess it is now. What are we going to do about him? I don't want him coming near the children."

"Don't worry about him. I've a feeling he won't be staying long. I'll have Mr. Tang keep an eye on you until Gunnar sails."

He could feel her tension and knew it was more than Gunnar's presence that caused the rigidity of her spine, the fingernails that dug into the chair, and the grimly pursed lips. Garnet did not close herself in against threatened trouble; she met it head-on in the same way Sebastian dealt with danger. Yet he could feel her withdrawing into herself. He rubbed her arm gently. "Don't worry. Everything will be all right."

"I'm not afraid of Erik, or any other man," she snapped.

Sebastian was momentarily startled by her tone. Then he realized that if her Chinese servant had relayed in detail all that had taken place tonight, he would also have told her about Noah. Oh, God . . . Sebastian groaned inwardly, wishing he had not delayed telling her until now.

He pulled her down into his lap and kissed her lightly on the lips, stroking her hair. Not knowing what to say, he tried to convey with his touch that she was still important to him, that nothing had changed. He had never believed that Emily would be safely delivered of a healthy son.

"She's not strong enough," the doctors told him. "One or both of them will die." Sebastian had thought of his mother, dying to bring Mark into the world, and his fear had been so great that he had been unable to speak of it to anyone, least of all to Garnet.

The doctors suggested Emily go to bed for her entire pregnancy, and Sebastian allowed everyone to believe his wife was ill. With a touch of the superstition he had picked up from shipmates, he believed if no one knew she was carrying his child, then perhaps both would survive the ordeal of birth.

Distract her, Sebastian thought, *get Garnet thinking about her own children—not Emily's baby.* He cleared his throat and asked, "How's Missie's cold?"

"Cerise, if you please. She has begun to insist on being called by her real name. No more 'Missie.' She's better. I suspect the sniffles were a direct result of the invitation to attend Larry Winfield's birthday party."

"You shouldn't have insisted that she go. Get your pretty backside into the kitchen and make me some coffee and I'll slip upstairs and look in on Rual."

"You saw him this morning. He's still there." The welcome and laughter in her voice were momentarily subdued and he looked at her sharply. Framed against the background of the lamp, his gaze heavy with fatigue, it seemed she peered at him from a long tunnel enclosing the vague shapes of her past life. The sawdust-floored saloons, the second-rate hotels. The men who had wanted her, possessed her.

"You're angry," he said.

"When have you ever seen me angry?"

"Never. When you're with me you treat everything as a joke. But there's a volcano inside you, Garnet, and no one knows it better than I. Perhaps I should have told you about the baby; is that why you're angry? I was afraid if anyone knew, she'd lose this one, too . . . as she lost my first son."

Garnet rose from the arm of the chair deliberately and moved without haste to the door, glancing at him over her shoulder through the sweep of auburn hair that was burnished by the lamplight. "Your first-born son is asleep upstairs, Sebastian," she said softly before she went swiftly to the kitchen.

He caught up with her as she poked the smoldering embers of the stove back to life. His hands went about her waist and pulled her around to face him. "I'll always see to Rual's welfare, Garnet, and yours. I need you both." His lips were hot and dry, but her mouth welcomed him and her hands fondled him with increasing urgency as she sought to forget the long, lonely evening. His fatigue fled before the passion that rose swiftly, born of memory and touch.

The red kimono and delicate lawn nightgown were a red and white heap on the kitchen floor and he was breathing against her breast, his tongue involuntarily seeking the silk-like areole with its diamond center that grew and hardened instantly.

Her, laugh, low and husky, was muffled in the mane of his hair as she bent to kiss him. "Can you wait until we get upstairs?" she asked, fingers entwined in his hair to pull him up to look at her.

"No," he said and slipped his hand under her knees and shoulders to lift her to the scrubbed wood table, his fingertips moving appreciatively down the length of her body before turning to his own buttons.

She lay on the table, her head cradled under one hand, watching him undress. Her eyes always widened in mock horror when he revealed himself to her, her full lips parting as a pert little tongue expressed its anticipation. It was the gesture of a whore and sometimes he promised himself he would censure her for it, but he never did after that throbbing in his loins had plunged into her soft body and been caressed in the way only she knew how to caress. Her rhythms and tides flowed with his and their lovemaking was so perfectly balanced and in tune that the moment one began to slip over the brink, the other immediately followed in a simultaneous joyous release.

"You've probably broken my back, you great oaf," she said a few minutes later. "Next time you want to make love on the table, you go on the bottom. Get off me and I'll make your coffee."

"Don't want coffee," he mumbled near her ear. "Sleep . . ."

"Not here, you don't." Her elbow was sharp in his side and he rolled quickly away from a probing knee.

Their tension gone, they went naked up the stairs,

teasing each other and chuckling, exchanging stage whispers as they tiptoed past the two closed doors.

Seven-year-old Cerise was sound asleep and did not hear. Even in deep sleep there was a vitality about her pert features, and Sebastian's heart often turned over as he looked at the child, for that was how Garnet must have looked once, before she lost her innocence.

Four-year-old Rual stirred and opened his eyes briefly as the sound of his father's voice intruded upon his favorite dream. His toy sailing boat had miraculously grown to full size and he was standing on deck, commanding his crew to set sail. At the end of their voyage they would find the treasure. Rual smiled happily as he drifted off to sleep again. In repose his chin still jutted stubbornly, and craggy contours lurked beneath baby cheeks. His black hair stood up in defiant peaks against the pillow. If Louisa Balmain had been alive, she would have sworn it was Sebastian, four years old again.

—≼{ CHAPTER 17 }≽—

Erik Gunnar dragged himself to the surface of his drunken stupor as the boot crashed into his ribs. Rolling onto his back, he caught the full force of the fish-reeking water dousing his face. Shaking his head to relocate his eyes in sockets that felt strangely loose, he looked up the length of immaculate fawn-colored breeches, unfashionably tight over muscled thighs. An embroidered blue silk vest and well-tailored broadcloth jacket next met his gaze. The ebony cane with its silver knob that was as much a part of Sebastian's dress as his polished leather boots was being slapped impatiently against a gloved hand.

For all the dandified dress Sebastian had taken to wearing, his large body bulged with muscle, his skin was sun-swarthy, and there was still a rough edge to his voice that hinted of self-made wealth.

On the other side of Erik Gunnar's stained pallet stood the monumentally huge Chinese known as Mr. Tang by everyone, including his employer. Mr. Tang dropped the water bucket to the ground, by Gunnar's head. It made a loud clatter.

"How dare you invade my home, you misbegotten bastard," Sebastian said levelly. The brilliance of his blue eyes was accentuated by the rich blue of his vest as sunlight flooded into the hut through the splintered door. Outside the clear sky was a reflecting canopy over an indigo sea. The blueness of everything assaulted his bleary stare, and caused Erik Gunnar to blink and shake his head again.

"I went to jail twice because of you, you swine," Gunnar muttered into his beard, keeping a wary eye on Mr. Tang.

"You went to jail for murder," Sebastian amended. "Now I'm going to overlook last night's little play on the condition you leave San Francisco today and never come back."

Gunnar struggled into a sitting position, cursing as his head exploded into the target for a hundred pounding hammers. Since neither Sebastian nor the Chinese had touched him, he cursed the bad whiskey, ran his hand through his wet hair, cleared his throat, and spat. "I'm not leaving. And you'll have to answer to the law if you kill an unarmed man."

"I gave my word to Garnet that I wouldn't kill you or have you killed." Sebastian's eyes glittered. "Now get on your feet, damn you."

Gunnar dragged himself to his feet, lurching slightly. He was an inch taller than Sebastian, yet Sebastian seemed to tower over him. It was an illusion created by the proud cast of his head, the arched black brows, the eyes like blue steel.

The ebony cane was tossed to Mr. Tang in the second before Sebastian's gloved fist crashed into Gunnar's whiskey-soaked beard, jerking his head backward but not budging his body. The blow brought Gunnar back to life. He roared as he swung his fist, but Sebastian's head was not where it was supposed to be. There was a whistle of displaced air; then Sebastian's glove caught him on the nose and he felt the warm blood trickle.

"Sebastian!" The woman's voice came unexpectedly, and both men turned to where Garnet stood silhouetted in the doorway.

"How long have you been there?" Sebastian asked, breathing heavily.

"I arrived a moment ago. Hwui came for me. Sebastian, if Cerise finds out about him . . . I'll never forgive you."

There was a moment of silence, broken only by the panting of the two men. Gunnar grinned, showing a chipped front tooth. "Mrs. Gunnar . . ." He tried to bow, but staggered against the Chinese, who remained motionless.

"That's not my name anymore," Garnet snapped.

"No. His lordship, there, paid for you to divorce me, didn't he? Oh, yes, I got the word when I was locked up and couldn't do anything about it. I didn't see why he went to the trouble, though . . . since he didn't want to marry you himself. He just wanted to take you for his whore."

Sebastian's fist shot out again, catching the side of his jaw, but Garnet sprang between them before Gunnar could retaliate. "Sebastian, please. I just want him to stay away from Cerise."

Sebastian's hand ran through his black hair in an angry gesture. "You shouldn't have come here, Garnet. Mr. Tang will take you home."

"Mr. Tang will do nothing of the kind," she responded. "I came to warn Erik that if he comes near Cerise I'll shoot him myself. And this time it won't be in the shoulder. Erik—let Cerise have a life not spoiled by what her parents were."

Gunnar licked the trickle of blood that ran from his gums over the broken tooth. "I made an honest woman of you, Garnet. I didn't deserve to be cast aside like a dead albatross—just because I was locked up."

"It wasn't only because of that," Garnet said quickly. "You forget the times you beat me. I warned you I wouldn't take it from you or any other man."

"And God knows there were plenty of other men."

"Stand aside, Garnet," Sebastian said. "I'm going to thrash him within an inch of his life, and then he's shipping out on the first ship sailing today."

"I'll go," Gunnar said thickly, "because there's things I have to do. But I'll be back for my daughter one day. You can keep your whore; I don't want her. But Cerise belongs to me."

Sebastian was already ushering Garnet through the door, arm about her shoulders. "Come on, I'll take you home. You shouldn't be wandering around Telegraph Hill by yourself. This part of town is crawling with scum."

Outside in the muddy street a surefooted tom cat negotiated the wooden-plank sidewalk around the sprawled body of a sailor, sound asleep and oblivious to the damp chill of the morning air. Garnet paused and extended her hand toward the cat, but it gave her a haughty glance and proceeded on its way.

Sebastian's carriage looked as out of place as a chariot among the ramshackle buildings and tents. Behind it stood the buggy he had given Garnet.

"Mr. Tang will take the buggy. Come on."

"The sun is up, Sebastian. Perhaps I'd better go alone," she mocked him.

"Look, I know you're upset. I didn't know he was out of jail, either, much less that he would show up here."

She allowed him to help her into the carriage and let her shawl slip from her head as she sat down. The auburn hair fell free and unfettered in an unfashionable profusion of soft waves. "How did he get here?"

"On the *Cyrus Lee*. It's a three-hundred-ton whaler some fool filled 'tween decks with emigrants and lost half of them coming around the Horn. It's beached on a mud flat—the crew as well as the passengers are in

193

the gold fields by now. But there's a British whaler sailing for the Sandwich Isles today. Since Gunnar has a taste for whalers, we'll accommodate him. Mr. Tang has orders to see he's on her."

"How did he find us here?" Garnet asked. She resisted as he tried to take her hand into his.

"The whole world is beating a path to California, Garnet. He could have come by chance. But I expect he came after you. I would have, in his place."

Her expression softened and she glanced at him from beneath gold-tipped eyelashes in the age-old manner of the coquette. "Would you, now? Well, it's too early in the morning for your flattery."

He grinned and succeeded in trapping her hand.

When the carriage came to a halt in front of her house and he swung her from her seat over the fence, depositing her on the crazy-paving walk, she asked, "Will you be coming tonight?"

"I'll try." He avoided her eyes.

"Suit yourself. It's immaterial to me," she said quickly and sped up the walk before he could answer.

The broken remains of the replica *Monarch Butterfly* had been taken to the warehouse he used as an office. Sebastian's anger flared again as he looked at the splintered masts and thought of the trouble he had gone to to have that model built to the exact miniature specifications of the ship Ned would soon be sending on her maiden voyage. Sebastian would have liked to be in New York when the full-sized clipper sailed. This time they had to beat the record.

He ran his hand lovingly over the smooth hull of the model. Was there anything more beautiful than that ship? He was still seething at the heresy contained in Ned's last letter. The idea that a filthy steamer could ever replace the clipper was ludicrous. Why, by the time a steamer stowed all the fuel it needed, there was hardly any room left for cargo. And this was apart from the fact that steamers were so much slower. Just another fad, Sebastian told himself, like the trains that

194

young fool was trying to run from Sacramento to Folsom. Steam. What foolishness.

Staring at the tiny clipper, Sebastian fancied he could feel the wind in his face and that peculiar relief of leaving cares on a distant shore. He was no longer worrying about Garnet or Erik Gunnar, who represented situations he could understand and deal with. The malady that plagued him was more complex. Emily and his marriage.

His marriage seemed to have eroded in the way the sea eats at the land. Grain by grain, piece by piece. If there had been storms to weather, Sebastian would have fought the elements and ridden the tidal wave, knowing that even the roughest seas eventually gave way to calm waters.

But there were no storms. His wife was as sweet, lovely, and loyal as ever. They were surrounded by friends, success, and the promise all the good things of life had to offer. They had been blessed with a son.

There was little more to life than any man had a right to expect.

The days of near-starvation in the grim Liverpool boardinghouse, when Sebastian trudged dismal streets in search of work, were but distant memories. Surely few men had achieved as much as he—and no man had a wife with the beauty and grace of Emily.

Why, then, did Sebastian feel their happiness was somehow slipping through his fingers?

The broken model rattled suddenly, as though answering him. A moment later it danced across the table. There was a low rumbling noise, growing louder. Several maps and charts which were hanging on the walls crashed to the floor.

Another tremor. There had been many of them since Sebastian arrived in San Francisco. He put out his hands to steady the model of the ship. They were felt more keenly on the shifting ground near the waterfront. Much of this ground was man-made, filled with sand dredged up from the bottom of the bay.

Mariner's Castle was built on firmer foundations,

high on a hill. Nevertheless, Emily was always nervous when the earth shook. Perhaps he should go to her.

The floor lurched under his feet as he stood up and tried to walk. He was thrown off balance, clutching at the edge of his desk as the plaster of the wall split and cracked. Everything was shaking violently now and he knew that this was not like the other tremors. He was flung about the room, narrowly escaping the heavy furniture that careened about.

Sebastian crawled across the floor while the giant unseen hand shook the building. Clouds of dust and plaster showered from above. In the depths of the earth the fearsome rumbling grew louder. He threw himself into the street as the roof collapsed with a grating roar. He was engulfed in dust and pelted with broken tile. Blinking, he could see that up on the hill several houses had also collapsed, their brick-built chimneys falling as well as the flimsy wood.

Fear clutched his heart. His son, Noah—and Emily, still weak from the birth—were up on that hill. For a few seconds it was like trying to battle a giant wave at sea, fighting to stay upright in a dizzily spinning world.

Then the first tremor gradually subsided. He was racing home, clambering over fallen walls, ignoring cries for help from beneath piles of debris.

At first he thought Mariner's Castle was completely wrecked, but as he drew closer he saw that only one wall had collapsed, exposing rooms of disordered furniture as though a child had smashed a dollhouse. It seemed incredible that one wall could make so much splintered wood.

Maureen was clinging to an upper-story doorjamb, screaming hysterically. Mr. Tang reached the debris before Sebastian and began to fling aside wooden beams and broken furniture.

"Mrs. Balmain and the baby . . ."—Maureen screamed, catching sight of Sebastian—". . . are buried under there. . . !"

A hoarse cry escaped his parched lips as he pulled frantically at the boards. He and Mr. Tang worked silently, side by side, until they came to a tangled mass of dark hair protruding from the rubble.

Emily's body was protectively curved over her son, who lay in her arms. The mattress from the bed had formed a buffer between them and the falling masonry, and it appeared they were unhurt. Sobbing with relief, Sebastian placed his hand on Emily's head, turning her gently to face him.

He was startled to look into her dark eyes and see the anguish written there that was more than physical pain. Her suffering was deep in her soul, the agony of a discovery too terrible to bear.

⊷⊰⊱ CHAPTER 18 ⊰⊱⊷

Cyril and Dai looked with amazement on the bustling port of San Francisco, unable to believe their eyes at the changes that had taken place since California became part of the United States. Remembering the sleepy village of Yerba Buena, it did not seem possible that so much building could have been accomplished in a few short years.

The discovery of gold almost immediately on the heels of the Mexican war was known to them, for hadn't they had trouble finding a ship to get here? Droves of sailors had abandoned their vessels and headed for the Sierra gold fields. But this conglomeration of jerry-built houses, beached hulks of ships, and tents spreading up the hills surrounding the bay clearly indicated that San Francisco was itself a boom town.

"Maybe I'll buy a shovel," Dai said, a dreamy expression settling over his melancholy features, "and see what all the fuss is about."

"Judging by all the construction here, more men

must be getting rich supplying and entertaining the miners than are making fortunes in the Sierras," Cyril said thoughtfully. "The last time we were here, there was but a handful of houses."

"These buildings look so flimsy. Shouldn't wonder if most of them fall down," Dai predicted gloomily.

Beneath Cyril's calm facade, his heart was beating excitedly. He could almost feel Emily's presence, out there somewhere in the crowded town. "Can't imagine why people stay here instead of proceeding to the gold fields. Are you serious about going after gold? You're a bit late, Dai. I should think most of the better claims have been staked by now."

"Oh, I'm sure I'll die poor. But if you're going to hang around here with your sister, then I'll need something to keep me busy." Dai's voice was heavy with self-pity.

"You could go back to sea," Cyril pointed out. "You don't have to make a fool of yourself scratching in the dirt."

"And you could have stayed in London and made something of yourself. You were on the brink, boy *bach*. But, no, you had to throw it all away because your nervous sister calls and you come running. Pining and homesick, wasn't it? And aren't we all?"

"I'm going ashore," Cyril said curtly, turning his back.

"And what about the big bruiser?" Dai persisted, following. "Does he know you're coming?"

"I'm sure Emily told her husband." In their cabin Cyril was unpacking a new white silk scarf he had bought before leaving England, carefully unfolding the protective paper. He draped the scarf about his neck and tossed the tasseled end over his shoulder.

Behind him, Dai watched with acute agony in every line of his face. Unseen by Cyril, Dai stretched out his hand toward his friend, then dropped it to his side, sighing. Dai had once tried to embrace Cyril, and the gesture almost cost him the friendship of the man he loved dearly. Cyril had recoiled from Dai's touch with such horror in his eyes that Dai knew he could never

198

speak of his true feelings. Yet Cyril did not care for women. He should have been a priest, Dai reflected gloomily, as celibacy came so easily to him.

A short time later Dai watched from the rail as Cyril disappeared into the crowds thronging the muddy streets of the blossoming town on the bay.

Cyril had no trouble finding Mariner's Castle. It was as pretentious and ugly as he expected it would be. Built of brick, it was two stories high, of unknown architectural design, and decorated by hideous cupola, gargoyles, and sundry gingerbread trappings. A ship's wheel was mounted on either of the double front doors, and a ship's bell announced the arrival of visitors. Hawsers tied to irregularly cut tree stumps marked the area in front that was evidently to be a courtyard someday.

The front door was opened by a monumentally huge Chinese servant, who seemed as taken aback by Cyril's appearance as Cyril was by his. They stared at each other for a second.

"Mrs. Balmain, please. I'm her brother," Cyril said at last.

The Chinese gestured for him to enter the hall. Cyril waited, hat in hand, while the man moved up the wide staircase.

Looking around at the interior of the house, Cyril saw that if the outside was all Sebastian's, the tastefully furnished interior had to be Emily's doing. Scorning the ugly and cumbersome contemporary furniture that cluttered a room rather than furnishing it, Emily had filled the house with French and English antiques. Thinking of the grim house in Liverpool with its massive Victorian pieces, heavy draperies, and gloomy colors, Cyril reflected that Emily had indeed stepped into a different world here in California.

But despite the graceful furniture and sunlight flooding the hall where he stood, Cyril sensed an oppressiveness about the house. There was sadness here.

Emily's letter had been a plea for help, he knew, despite the careful wording. He had shown the letter to Dai, to explain why he must leave for San Francisco.

Dai's interpretation—that Emily was pining and home-sick—had, for once, not been a melancholy exaggeration.

"If you are ever again in the Pacific . . ." Emily had written, ". . . and, my dear, I do so hope you will be soon—perhaps you could bring me news of all that is happening in England. Sometimes I feel I am on a different planet, so hungry for the sight of an English meadow, or the sound of an English brook, or the scent of violets, I am. Oh, to hear a nightingale again . . . to watch a swan drift majestically upon a sparkling lake. Cyril, if you leave now—this minute—you will be here in time for the birth of my child."

Someone appeared on the landing above, Cyril was disappointed that it was not Emily. A ruddy-cheeked girl wearing a starched apron came hurrying down the stairs. "Mr. La Flair, sir? I'm Maureen, Mrs. Balmain's maid. I'm to take you up . . . but, sir, before you go . . ."

"Something is wrong," Cyril said, feeling a pang of alarm. "What is it? Is Mrs. Balmain ill?"

"A few months ago, sir . . . there was a bad earthquake. Mrs. Balmain and the baby were buried in the rubble. She weren't hurt bad . . . a broken leg . . . and the little fellow wasn't hurt at all."

Cyril's breath was expelled slowly. "Her leg—it still prevents her from walking?"

Maureen looked at her feet. "It won't seem to mend. Mr. La Flair, sir, she might not be quite as you remember her."

"Take me to her, please." Icy fingers were plucking at Cyril's spine. He moved toward the staircase, not waiting for Maureen to lead the way.

"Poor little thing," Maureen whispered as they reached the upper floor. "Having the baby pulled her down—and then the fright of being practically buried alive."

Emily was lying on a mound of pillows in the largest bed Cyril had ever seen. Her dark hair was plaited in two fat braids and her eyes were so large in her shrunken face that he felt he would drown in them. She

200

was laughing and crying at the same time as she held out her arms to him.

Gathering up her wasted body, Cyril felt a great surge of anger. Surely childbirth and a broken leg could not have caused such emaciation. She was little more than a skeleton. Bony fingers stroked his cheeks, ran through his straight black hair. Her breathing was so labored that Cyril felt he must gently disentangle himself from her embrace.

"Now what's all this?" he asked. "You have not been fighting the good fight, Emily." He forced himself to smile at her, although he wanted to weep.

"Cyril, oh, my darling. I shall be strong again now. I felt it the moment you came into the room. I was afraid you would never come to me. . . . It's been so long, my dearest, I was sure you had forgotten your poor sister."

"And I was afraid Sebastian would glower and yawn at the sight of me," Cyril answered with a wry smile.

Emily's eyes darkened until they were almost obsidian orbs. "You may go, Maureen," she said, looking over his shoulder.

"Shall I fetch the baby, mum?" Maureen asked eagerly.

"Later, perhaps," Emily said. "Not now. My brother and I wish to be alone."

As soon as the maid departed, Emily interrupted Cyril's question about her son with a breathless narrative that left Cyril reeling under its impact.

"My husband no longer loves me. I think perhaps he hates me. I didn't know what to do. Oh, Cyril, I've been so afraid—I didn't dare get out of bed for fear he might cast me out of his house."

Cyril decided he had better wait until she was finished before giving her the news about her grandfather. It was clear Emily's recital had been bottled up inside her for some time.

". . . and coming to this wild place. Oh, Cyril, you can't believe what it's like here. There is absolutely no law whatsoever. A Vigilance Committee—that's what they call it. Actually, it is merely a group of ruffians

201

only slightly better than the thugs and murderers they hang so readily. And the politicians are unbelievable. Sebastian says it's the growing pains of a young city." Her expression softened. "He is so honest himself that he sees only the best in others. He worked so hard, racing his clippers around the Horn. And, Cyril, his efforts to improve the lot of sailors—do you know his ships are the only ones coming into port that are not immediately abandoned by their crews? He was instrumental in getting the law passed that prohibits the flogging of sailors." There was both pride and puzzlement in her voice.

"I suppose I just wasn't strong enough to be his wife, Cyril, although I tried so terribly hard. I couldn't understand some of their ways . . . and then I miscarried his first child. He insisted I go to bed for my entire pregnancy with Noah. I did it—to please him. I would have done anything he asked. I would gladly have died for him. You see, I believed all of his spare time was taken up with his fight for sailors' rights. How foolish he must have thought I was."

Cyril picked up her tiny hands and pressed them to his heart. "But why do you believe he hates you?"

"He loves another woman."

"He has taken a mistress?"

Emily nodded. "He has children by her. He boldly keeps them in a house not a stone's throw from Mariner's Castle. I found out about her the day of the earthquake. . . . You see, the previous night this terrible man burst into our home—"

She was panting with exhaustion. Cyril squeezed her fingers to interrupt the distressing story. "Emily, hush, dear. Rest now. There will be plenty of time to tell me the rest later. Our first concern must be to get you back on your feet. In a little while you must tell me what the doctors are doing for your broken limb."

Her great haunted eyes filled slowly with tears. "I was trying to die, Cyril. I prayed I would . . . so he could be free."

Cyril caught his breath. "Please, dearest, don't speak so. How can I bear it?"

Emily's pathetically thin fingers trailed up the length of his white silk scarf and touched his cool cheek. She had bottled up her feelings for so long that she was unsure how to express them. Her love for Sebastian, her joy in giving birth to his son . . . she had been unable to cope with his betrayal.

He had been the great shining knight who rescued her from the tower of the sinister guardian. Strong, invincible, uncorruptible—the force of good over evil. Even though she had never understood her husband and knew that more than their upbringing separated them, she had idolized him. He was her pillar of strength in an uncertain world.

Emily had prayed for death when the floor collapsed beneath her feet and she felt herself plunging to the ground. She had protected the baby with her own body, and her last thought before losing consciousness had been that Sebastian would realize how much she had loved him when she gave her life for his son.

She came to her senses moments later. Even before she was aware of the hands lifting the weight from her back, she had a vision of Sebastian's mistress . . . *who had borne his first son.* All of Emily's suffering during her pregnancy and long delivery, it had all been for nothing. Sebastian already had his first-born.

If she could have spoken her feelings to him . . . if he could have explained to her . . . but they had never communicated. They had been two people moving in separate spheres, together, yet apart. She was so far from home and filled with fear that he would simply ask her to leave. She had written to Cyril and then retired to her bed, hoping that either Cyril would come or she would die before Sebastian came to tell her their marriage was at an end.

"Mistress is downstairs for dinner," Mr. Tang announced to Sebastian when he arrived home that evening.

Sebastian looked at him in amazement. "You're joking . . . no, you never joke. But quite apart from her leg, she's too weak."

"Her brother is here," Maureen said, coming from the kitchen bursting with the news. "Oh, 'tis wondrous to see the change in milady in just a few short hours, sir. Himself carried her down the stairs and she's as lively as she can be."

Handing his hat and cane to Mr. Tang, Sebastian said, "The elegant Cyril, I see." Stormclouds were gathering in the blue depths of his eyes. He did not go to the dining room, but instead ran up the stairs, three at a time.

The earthquake had buckled the floor of their bedroom. Emily had fallen with the debris, the baby clutched to her breast. When the house was rebuilt, Sebastian moved into the room next to hers.

He took off his shirt and tossed it on to the bed, thinking of the past months. Since the day of the earthquake, Emily had eaten no more than what could minimally sustain her, and she had withdrawn into her frail shell of a body, oblivious to everyone around her.

The doctors Sebastian brought in were helpless to treat her withdrawal. They had set her fractures, bound up the torn tendons, and shrugged disbelievingly at the suggestion her mind might be more damaged than her body. A touch of hysteria, they said. One doctor recommended that Sebastian forcibly place her on her feet and demand that she walk. Reluctantly, Sebastian had picked up her wasted body, feeling sweat bead on his own brow at that moment when her eyes expressed an unbearable anguish. He put her on her feet. Her leg buckled, she twisted sideways, and fell heavily. Sebastian dismissed the doctor.

It seemed to Sebastian that she was enclosed in an invisible tower. Yet there were times he felt her great haunted eyes beseeched him to break through to her. Sometimes he was reminded, chillingly, of her grandfather's eyes watching him after the old man's stroke.

Everything was going wrong. Not just Emily's health. There was also the problem of the competition. In the year 1853, now drawing to a close, more than fifty clippers had been launched and it was obvious there were not enough cargoes to fill the holds of the heavily rigged ships. Where rates had been sixty dollars a ton during the early boom of California trading, shippers were now forced to take ten dollars a ton for San Francisco freight.

The *Monarch Butterfly,* Sebastian's pride and joy, had not been able to match the record of the *Flying Cloud*'s stirring voyage around the Horn when she sailed 374 sea miles a day. The *Butterfly* had been severely damaged during a storm due to inept handling, and Sebastian wondered uneasily if Erik Gunnar had paid a crewman to disable her. It was agony for Sebastian to let some other shipmaster take his clipper on her long voyages. If he were only able to sail with her himself . . . why, then she'd show her heels to the *Flying Cloud.*

Repairs to the *Monarch Butterfly* had been completed on the east coast, where Ned frantically searched for a cargo. The Balmain Company would, in fact, have been in serious financial trouble if it had not been for the old McKnight ships which plied the eastern coastal waters, a fact Ned pointed out in every communication.

There was talk of a Panama railroad across the isthmus and steamers from Panama to San Francisco, but Sebastian refused to believe that steamers could ever be a threat to the swift and graceful clippers. He was more concerned with the numbers of clippers being launched and the possibility of sabotage from Gunnar. And Emily.

He sighed, pulling on a clean shirt and peering at his reflection in the dresser mirror. The sun-lines were more deeply etched into his craggy countenance. Smoothing back his hair, which promptly stood on end again, he pondered the dilemma of Cyril La Flair.

Sebastian had always been uneasy about Cyril's relationship with Emily. They had not grown up together, after all. They had met for the first time as adult strangers. That they were related by blood was something about which Sebastian and, he suspected, everyone else had constantly to remind themselves. The bond between the two caused Sebastian even more pangs than the guilt he felt about his own relationship with Garnet.

What a complicated web he had spun for himself, worshipping one woman, lusting after another, and not having the strength to give up either. Instead, he had given up the sea. His head ached with tension whenever that thought crossed his mind. There were days when the sea fever raged in his blood and he would have to lock himself in his office until it passed.

Those were the days he grew impatient with Emily's illness and the sudden quarrels with Garnet flared. He trusted Garnet, but sometimes when he took the more rambunctious of his business acquaintances to her house in order not to disturb Emily, he would find himself quietly seething as the men cast lascivious glances at Garnet. She flirted with them casually and Sebastian was sure it went no further than that . . . but her past was a specter that constantly haunted his peace of mind.

Garnet wore her sexuality like a mantle, flaunting her charms with every movement of her voluptuous body. He resented the fact that she could not, or would not, discard the hip-swinging walk, the lowered eyelids, the provocative thrust of her breasts, when other men were present. He felt these were cultivated gestures, rather than natural ones, and should be for him alone.

Only once had he attempted to subdue Garnet's bright plumage, with unpleasant results. Telling her one evening that he would be bringing several business acquaintances, he had asked that she try to find a more sedate dress to wear. Perhaps, too, she could quietly withdraw after dinner, rather than joining the men in conversation.

Her eyes flashed opal fire. "Oh, no, you don't, Sebastian. I'm not a little gray dove in a gilded cage like your Emily up on the hill. I'll dress as I damned well please. And if I can't talk to you and your friends, who can I talk to? The only social life I have is here. We can't go out anywhere for fear someone will see us and tell your wife. I've never put restrictions on you, so don't try to put any on me. I am what I am, and if you don't like it, I suggest you stay home with that little mouse in her subdued clothes and oh-so-proper ladylike manners. God damn you, Sebastian . . . how dare you—"

He caught her to him, afraid of where the outburst was leading. "Garnet, I'm sorry. I didn't mean to criticize you. You're right; you are a bird of gaudy plumage, and that's the way I want you to be." He kissed her, knowing that his touch was the only way he could really express what she meant to him; knowing, too, that she would respond. This time she did not. She stiffened in his arms, clamping her lips tightly to keep him at bay.

Sebastian groaned inwardly. "I didn't mean 'gaudy' . . . you're beautiful and exciting and . . . Garnet, honey, I guess I didn't want you to hear me explaining to some gentlemen why they'll have to wait a while longer for the money I owe them. There was no market for the last cargo Ned sent, and our business still has not recouped."

She relaxed immediately. "Why didn't you say so, you big ox? Haven't you learned yet that it's easier to solve a problem with someone else's ideas as well as your own? If there's no market for a cargo, we should think of a way to create one."

So the conversation had been effectively steered away from her flaunted sexuality and from Emily. Sebastian tried to avoid discussing Emily with Garnet, whose eyes filled with venom at the mere mention of his wife's name. Later he would wrestle with a guilty conscience and tell himself that it was a form of betrayal not to defend Emily against unwarranted attacks—even from Garnet.

What a complicated business life was. And now there was yet another complication to face. Cyril La Flair. Downstairs with Emily, who had left her bed for her brother after refusing to do so for her husband.

He had delayed going downstairs to face Emily and Cyril, almost afraid of seeing them together, and not knowing why. Putting his anxieties into the back of his mind, he went down to the living room.

Emily was sitting in a chair near the fire, her leg supported by a hassock. Her hair shone above the lace collar of a high-necked gown of deep burgundy. Except for the sunken cheeks and bird-claw hands, her emaciation was hidden under the voluminous tucks, pleats, and folds of her rich-colored gown. In spite of everything, she was heartbreakingly lovely.

Cyril sat upon another hassock at her feet. Leaning forward, arms on bony knees, his waxen features and piercing dark eyes were illuminated by the flickering firelight. Their hands were clasped together, Emily oblivious to the three stumps where fingers should have been.

Sebastian stepped into the room, feeling a sick thrill of horror at the sight of them so close together.

Cyril rose immediately at Sebastian's approach, his dark eyes blazing with dislike, and his lip curling slightly. His greeting, however, was polite. "Sebastian . . . how are you?"

"Well enough," Sebastian muttered, looking past Cyril to Emily, who gave him a tremulous smile and a silent message of apology that angered him. Without ever accusing him, she made him feel guilty.

Sebastian glanced back at Cyril. "You docked today? How long will your ship be in San Francisco?" The question inferred that Cyril would depart with his ship.

"I came as a passenger, not a sailor," Cyril replied.

"I see. I take it your fortunes have changed since we last met?"

"My compositions were enjoying some small success in London."

"Yet you left it all behind to come here. I suppose my wife asked you to come, although she apparently forgot to mention it to me." Sebastian's eyes met Emily's for a second.

Emily bit her lip. "I was going to tell you, Sebastian. But you've been so busy . . . and I didn't know if Cyril would be able to come—"

Cyril smiled at her and, watching, Sebastian felt as though an invisible shield had dropped between him and the two of them.

"I'm afraid, dearest sister," Cyril said, "I would have come without an invitation, the moment I learned you had a son. I adore children. I suppose not having any

208

of my own, I look upon other people's children as mine, too. They are all so filled with promise and the glorious, soaring belief that anything is possible in the future. I feel that each child comes into the world capable of being another Michelangelo . . . or Brahms . . . or Beethoven—perhaps a new Shakespeare is being born at this moment."

Sebastian was not listening. *Her* son, he was thinking. To Cyril, Noah is Emily's son—not mine. Something stirred again in the back of Sebastian's mind, a vague warning buried in the far caverns of his hidden thoughts. *Send him away . . . before it's too late.*

"I have not yet offered my congratulations on the birth of Noah," Cyril was saying. "Your son is beautiful. Eyes like Emily's . . . and have you noticed his fingers? Extraordinarily long. A pianist, I'm sure."

Sebastian almost laughed aloud. Noah came from a long line of seafarers. How they would all laugh to hear Noah described as "beautiful"! A word for an effeminate type like Cyril. Still, perhaps that was the warning he should heed. He must get Noah to sea at an early age, away from the influence of Emily and Cyril. Make a man out of the boy, before they turned him into a sissy.

Mr. Tang appeared in the doorway and bowed. "Dinner is served," he announced.

There was an awkward pause as Sebastian and Cyril looked at Emily. Then Cyril lifted her into his arms. She wrapped her arm about his neck.

Sebastian turned and strode toward the dining room, anger written in every step. A slow flush was spreading upward over his face as he took his place at the head of the table. He immediately reached for the decanter of wine, filling his glass until it spilled over the rim, then draining it with a single gulp.

Assisted by Mr. Tang, Cyril placed Emily at the other end of the table, her leg supported by a hassock. Then he took a chair beside her.

"Sebastian, I brought sad news, I'm afraid," Cyril said as Mr. Tang began to serve the soup. "It's Emily's

209

grandfather—Job McKnight died just before I sailed from Liverpool."

Feeling two pairs of dark eyes scrutinizing him, Sebastian murmured what he hoped was an appropriate comment, "A merciful release, Emily."

"Yes," Cyril agreed quickly. "I saw to it that a wreath was sent in your name, although I did not attend the funeral. I went to the house later. I spent some time with your half-brother, Sebastian. Young Mark is a very . . . interesting boy."

Sebastian's attention was caught. "He's about fourteen or fifteen now, isn't he?"

"Yes. But he seems much older. A remarkable intellect. Tall for his age. Bright blue eyes, like yours. He is keenly interested in the shipping company. Mollie Flanagan was boasting to me—privately, of course—that Mark is such a genius that a professor friend is having him admitted to the university next year, despite his tender years."

"He'll own all of the McKnight ships now that the old man's dead," Sebastian said thoughtfully. *Including the ones the Balmain Line is using for coastal trade,* he thought. The clippers were losing money . . . and without the McKnight schooners . . . "England seems a very long way from this coast," he said aloud. "If it weren't for the distance, I'd like to meet young Mark."

Emily was silently remembering Mollie reading the tea leaves. What had she predicted for her charge? A remarkable life—great peril? And something so awful in Emily's own future that Mollie had not been able to bring herself to speak of it. Well, perhaps it had already happened. She wondered if Sebastian would be relieved when Cyril told him he was taking her away. She smiled sadly at her husband. How strong and handsome he looked.

Mr. Tang appeared with the entrée and the meal proceeded as though the past months had never happened, despite the undercurrent of anger between the two men.

Sebastian was both angry and hurt that Cyril had been able to do what he had not—bring Emily from

210

that remote place her mind had taken her since the earthquake. Cyril decided when she should return to her bed, and Sebastian bit back an angry remark as his wife disappeared up the stairs in the arms of her brother.

Sebastian took his glass of brandy to the fireside and stood staring at the chair where Emily had been sitting, conjuring up in his mind the vision of the two dark heads close together, the intertwined hands. His attention was caught by a sheet of paper that had slipped between the seat and the arm of the chair. He picked it up and read it slowly, twice:

> *"Oh, lift me from the grass,*
> *I die, I faint, I fail!*
> *Let thy love in kisses rain*
> *On my lips and eyelids pale.*
> *My cheek is cold and white, alas!*
> *My heart beats loud and fast;*
> *Oh, press it to thine own again*
> *Where it will break at last."*

A pounding hammer struck the anvil of his anger with each word he read. Sebastian did not know the poem was the work of the English poet Shelley, nor would it have made any difference to his state of mind if he had. He sensed the undercurrent of eroticism in the lyrics, and in his mind there was only one reason a man presented such words to a woman. That Cyril had given the poem to Emily, rather than the other way around, Sebastian did not doubt.

Cyril came downstairs to find Sebastian contemplating a piece of parchment that curled and then sizzled in the flames of the fire, a glass of brandy in his hand and a cigar clamped between his teeth.

Cyril strode purposefully toward him and, facing him, squared his shoulders. Cyril was almost as thin as Emily, his skin drawn tightly over sculptured bones. The black coat and trousers, relieved only by the white silk scarf he was still wearing, incongruously, since he was indoors, made him look smaller and more ghostly than ever. Sebastian looked down at his wife's brother through a red haze of brandy, firelight, and anger.

Before Sebastian could gather his wits about him, Cyril plunged to the attack. "I find my sister's health a matter of extreme concern. I am appalled that she has been neglected to the brink of death, it appears. I shudder to imagine what might have happened had I not arrived in time."

"Would you have me force-feed her?" Sebastian growled. "She refused to eat—or speak—until you turned up. She showed no interest in anything, not even her child."

"She is desperately unhappy. Did you make no attempt to learn why? Could you not guess?" Cyril demanded. "You must allow me to take her home, as soon as she's strong enough to travel."

Sebastian looked down at Cyril in shocked amazement. "Are you mad? This is her home. And I, my friend, am her husband. Much as you wish you were."

Cyril's dark eyes flickered with a cold flame. Slowly he pulled the white gloves from his pocket and, with a deliberately contemptuous gesture, slapped Sebastian's cheek. Sebastian's mouth opened in surprise as his hand went to his face, touching the imaginary imprint of the glove in disbelief.

"I'm calling you out, sir," Cyril said, the timbre of his voice filling the room with his challenge. "Your insult is intolerable. You may have your choice of weapons. My seconds will be here first thing in the morning."

Sebastian was still staring, his hand on his cheek, when the front door closed quietly and firmly.

CHAPTER 19

Sebastian patiently untangled the rigging of Rual's toy clipper, while Garnet brushed her daughter's red-gold hair. From time to time Garnet glanced in Sebastian's direction, sensing that he was deeply troubled, but knowing that as always he would wait until the children were in bed to tell her his problem.

This time, Garnet was sure, it was more than the frail Emily's health or the problems of too many fast clippers competing for too little cargo now that the first flush of gold fever was abating.

"Ouch!" Cerise cried, as Garnet came to a sticky knot in the bright and unruly curls. "Mama . . . you're hurting me. I do think I'm old enough to brush my own hair," Cerise added impatiently, squirming away from the punishing hairbrush. Honey-gold eyes looked up at her mother. "You're thinking about something else," she accused.

Garnet laughed. "Now what could be more interesting than a mop of curls? You'll dazzle all the young guests tomorrow, my sweet, if you'll just remember not to scowl and stamp your feet."

"I don't want to go," Cerise said fretfully.

Sebastian looked up. "Not another birthday party?"

"No, not a birthday party. So I shouldn't have to go, should I, Papa?" Cerise had always called him that, and neither Garnet nor Sebastian had ever corrected her. "It's that awful Larry Winfield. His cousin came from . . . where did he come from, Mama?"

"South Carolina," Garnet said. Her eyes met Sebastian's defensively. "By the time Cerise is grown up,

213

this wild town will have been tamed, Sebastian. And I mean to see that my baby knows the right people."

"The richest people, you mean," Sebastian said, but he grinned so the remark was without malice.

Garnet's eyes flashed with the fire of opals, despite her level reply. "This is a brawling infant of a city, Sebastian. Today's opportunists will be tomorrow's finest families."

"What's an oppor . . . opport . . ." Cerise wrestled with the word while wriggling out of range of the hairbrush.

"That's what you're going to be, my pet," Garnet laughed. "And tomorrow afternoon you are going to the Winfields' party to meet the young gentleman from South Carolina—what's his name? Austin Gentry."

"I knew Latham Winfield was from the South," Sebastian said. "I didn't realize he left a family there. Funny how San Franciscans all seem to arrive in the world fully formed and without a past."

"Like us," Garnet observed. She pulled her feet up under her on the chair in her favorite and most unladylike pose. "Winfield's sister apparently married into the Gentry family. Like the Winfields, the Gentrys are shipowners, but they also own a large plantation, apparently, and God knows how many slaves."

"He's coming on a ship," Rual said, his blue eyes gleaming brightly. "Wish I could sail on a ship."

Sebastian picked up the boy and swung him onto his shoulders. "All in good time. Now I'm going to take you up to bed and tell you a story."

" 'Round the Horn," Rual squeaked excitedly. "Tell me 'bout coming 'round the Horn."

As their voices faded, Garnet gave her daughter a playful slap on the rump. "It's time for you to go to bed, too, young lady. I want you clear-eyed and wide awake for the party tomorrow. And you will be polite to Larry Winfield and his cousin, or I won't write to England for that book you want so much."

"You just want to be alone with Papa," Cerise said sagely. "Can I read in bed?"

"No! You'll ruin your eyes," Garnet said. Her full

lips twisted into a wry grimace. Cerise's passion for the written word was exceeded only by Rual's passion for ships. Funny, neither Garnet nor Erik Gunnar had much love for books. Cerise must have been a throwback to her schoolteacher grandfather, Garnet reflected. She would have made a perfect daughter for the bookish Emily. Garnet began to straighten up the living room after her daughter departed. She wondered if Sebastian's apparent gloom was because of Emily, after all. No one else could plunge him into despair in quite the same way.

Garnet battled both jealously and despair. She knew from Sebastian and from the gossip about town that Emily had gone into a decline. At first Garnet had secretly rejoiced that Sebastian's wife, who had so dazzled San Francisco society when she first arrived, was no longer the most gracious hostess in town. She had been jealous of Emily in those early days and could not help flirting with Sebastian's business friends in an attempt to prove a one-man-one-woman affair was an impossible trap.

Garnet heard that an evening at Mariner's Castle was a magical event. Emily, they said, was not only beautiful and utterly charming, but was also an accomplished pianist, and often entertained her guests. In a raw, new society, Emily had brought Old World courtesy and concern for everyone's comfort that was in sharp contrast to the boisterous social life the young city usually offered. Emily, they said, made everyone feel like a king or queen. Since she had such great expectations of people, they felt compelled to live up to her image of them.

Hardest for Garnet to bear, however, was the knowledge that Emily idolized Sebastian. This information was given by Latham Winfield, who made it clear on several occasions he would happily replace Sebastian as Garnet's protector. "Emily worships the ground he walks on," he told her. "I doubt he'd have come this far without her at his side. She looks up at him with those big trusting eyes, expecting him to move mountains . . . so he does. We do what's expected of us, don't you think, Garnet?" His glance had been shrewd. "If someone important to us believes we're invincible—we are. Or if they believe we're no good . . ."

Garnet had tried to put his words out of her mind. Latham Winfield was attracted to her and no doubt wanted to fan the flame of her jealousy of Emily.

Then, all at once, Emily had gone into seclusion. They said her health had failed. Sebastian avoided Garnet's eyes and mumbled, "Oh, she's all right—she's getting better," when Garnet asked. He had never said she was pregnant.

Garnet heard Sebastian's booming laugh upstairs. He was telling Rual a bedtime story. A cold knot formed in her breast again. Sebastian had been so happy when he returned from a trip to the east coast to find she had given birth to his son . . . but the arrival of his legitimate son, born in wedlock and announced to the world with more pomp than the birth of a crown prince . . . that had filled him with more pride than he had ever shown before. Sebastian was so damned transparent, Garnet thought. He had been happy, but guilty, when Rual was born.

She could hear his footsteps on the landing as he called "Good night" to the children. She composed herself, green eyes inscrutable and opaque. Sebastian would never know the true depth of her feelings for him. She would never let him know she suffered the torment of the damned when he left her to go to Emily. Knowing Sebastian, he would pity her, and Garnet would rather die than inspire pity in any man. Especially a man she loved.

Perhaps he would tell her why, after Emily's broken leg had mended, his wife had not resumed her position as San Francisco's leading hostess. Garnet wondered if perhaps Emily had so enjoyed spending the months of her pregnancy in bed that she had been glad of an excuse to do so again. Garnet shivered suddenly as she remembered the day of the earthquake. *Someone walking on my grave,* she told herself.

Sebastian came clumping down the narrow staircase. He stood behind her, lifting her hair from the nape of her neck to plant his warm kiss. She felt her spine tingle all the way to her toes. She turned to face him, reaching up to pull his mouth down to hers.

They stood close together, alternately kissing and nibbling for a long minute. Then Sebastian went to the door and closed and locked it while Garnet closed the draperies against the prying eyes of the night. "I gave Fern the night off," she said over her shoulder.

Silently they dealt with buttons and hooks and laces, leaving their clothes in a heap on the floor. Garnet lay down on the fireside rug, pulling a pillow from the couch for her head and another for her hips. When Sebastian kneeled between her legs, she was ready for him, guiding him with a tender touch. He moved inside her, grew, surged, and exploded. Afterward, she lay in his arms, waiting for him to tell her what it was that cast its shadow over him.

"Emily's half-brother arrived from England," Sebastian said at length. "Emily got up . . . dressed . . . came down to dinner—for the first time since the accident." He always referred to it as "the accident" and never mentioned the earthquake.

"Well, that's good, then, isn't it?" Garnet asked softly. "Perhaps now she'll start to get well again."

Sebastian sat up, reached over her for his coat, and pulled a cigar from the pocket. Garnet took one of the tapers from the brass canister on the hearth, lit it from the blazing log, and held it for him.

"He called me out. The little runt challenged me to a duel." Sebastian choked on his cigar smoke. Garnet stood up and poured him a glass of brandy. "You'd better tell me the whole thing, from the beginning. Then we'll decide what's to be done," she said quietly.

Emily gripped the edge of the chair until her knuckles were translucently white. Maureen watched apprehensively as her mistress pushed the chair forward, then swung her leg stiffly to try to follow. Maureen caught Emily as she winced with pain and toppled slowly to the bed.

"You're just too weak, mum."

217

"Maureen, I *must* walk. I must go to him."

"Then let Mr. Tang carry you," Maureen begged.

Emily pulled herself upright and again reached for the chair. "Mr. Tang has refused to take me. I regret to say that you are the only friend and ally I have in this house. I must persist. If I am unable to walk today, then I shall keep on trying until I can. Meantime, Maureen, you will be my emissary."

"How's that, mum?"

"You will take messages to my brother and bring me word of him. And no one else in the house is to know."

"Oh, mum, I'm afraid to go roaming around the streets by meself. Them Sydney Ducks and Hounds is all over the place."

"Nonsense. I heard Mr. Balmain say that the Vigilance Committee has cleared all of the lawless element out of town." An abandoned ship had been converted to San Francisco's first jail, and there had been an abundance of hangings, but in her isolation at Mariner's Castle, Emily could not know that the problem of lawlessness in the young city was far from solved. Seeing the girl's frightened eyes, however, Emily added gently, "Besides, I wouldn't dream of asking you to go out at night alone. You shall go in broad daylight on the pretense of making some purchases for me."

Maureen let out her breath with a visible sigh of relief.

"I think I hear the baby stirring, mum. Shall I fetch him?"

"Yes. Bring Noah to me. He will think it is great fun to watch his mama fall down as she tries to walk. . . . No, don't scold me! I must try again. And I want Noah to be with me all the time. He is beginning to take notice of what's happening around him, and we must exert the right influence on his life."

Maureen started for the door, then stopped. "You won't try to walk again until I get back?" she asked anxiously.

"I'll wait," Emily promised, "as long as you assure me again that Mr. Balmain refused to face Cyril in a duel."

"I swear to God," Maureen said, crossing herself. "A very sad-looking fellow came first thing this mornin' and said he was Mr. Dai Williams. *Die* Williams—that's what he said his name was. And as lively as a corpse, he was, too. 'I'm after being Mr. La Flair's second,' he says. And Mr. Balmain says, 'Tell the little fool that dueling is against the law and he'd better forget the whole thing, as I have.' And the melancholy looking gent says, 'Yes, that's good.' And Mr. Balmain says, 'And tell him, too, that if he comes near my house or my wife again, I'll tear him limb from limb with me own two hands.'"

Emily closed her eyes and swallowed hard. "Very good, Maureen. You may go," she said faintly.

They had quickly found places for themselves in a town swarming with rich, lonely, and homesick men. Cyril and Dai were hired to entertain in a saloon on the Barbary Coast. Cyril played the piano and Dai sang in his deep, true baritone. The fact that Cyril's piano arrangements had to make allowance for three missing fingers, and the unbearable heartbreak in Dai's voice, actually worked for, instead of against, them. Every man in their audience was newly arrived from some other part of the world, and most of them had left families and sweethearts behind to come and seek gold. While they enjoyed the boisterous and bawdy entertainment supplied by buxom, hard-shelled ladies, when they listened to Cyril's haunting music and Dai's sweetly melancholy ballads, they could brush away a tear in the smoky darkness and know they were not alone in longing for loved ones far away.

At the end of an evening, there was always a collection of coins and even a little gold dust atop Cyril's piano, since neither he nor Dai would accept the drinks offered.

Dai had seen the ruddy-cheeked Irish girl, Maureen, slip into the saloon just before opening time and converse in whispers with Cyril. Tightly folded notes sealed with sealing wax would surreptitiously change hands, but Cyril never confided in Dai the contents of any of the messages he exchanged with Emily.

Persuading Cyril not to storm Mariner's Castle had been a major task that had left Dai exhausted. "He won't fight you, *bach*," Dai told Cyril. "He refuses. He says dueling is against the law. But if you go to his house, then will he tear you limb from limb with the full approval of the law, look you. So there now, calm down, and accept your fate. A long time dead we'll all be, nevertheless."

Cyril had paced angrily, black coat flapping about his lean frame, his dark eyes living coals in the shadowed sockets. "I must get Emily away from him. I must go up there and take her away. Oh, Dai, I'm deathly afraid for her . . . she's so frail."

Fortunately, the Irish maid had arrived with the first of Emily's messages before Cyril could leave on his fool's errand. After reading the note a smile of grim satisfaction hovered for a moment on his marble lips. But then just as suddenly it faded, as Cyril muttered something about there not being money enough.

The money they were paid by the owner of the saloon and the generous tips they received were scrupulously divided, but Cyril's share always dwindled despite the fact that he spent very little on himself. When Dai censured him for his personal asceticism, Cyril's dark gaze grew remote. He needed, he said, a great deal of money for a particular cause, and must of necessity hoard his earnings.

They were planning something, Dai knew for a certainty. But what? Something that needed a great deal of money. With his customary penchant for looking for the darkest motives, Dai wondered, in terror, if they were planning to pay someone to do away with Sebastian. Life was cheap in this fledgling city. There were unsolved murders every day.

Many ex-convicts from the Australian penal colony had found their way to San Francisco and quickly formed gangs—the "Sydney Ducks" and "Hounds" being the most notorious. For the right price there was little that could not be bought from those thugs.

Yet Cyril and Emily were gentle souls, Dai reasoned. But, then, again, gentler souls than theirs had been moved to dark deeds by forbidden passions. At last, unable to bear the suspense, Dai ransacked Cyril's belongings one day when he was at the piano. He found the bundle of letters from Emily and began to read:

I can bear all the loneliness, knowing it will one day end. Of course I understand, my dear, that we must deal with the mundane matter of money. How I wish you were not so proud! Grandfather assured me there would be an annuity for me and I would not hesitate to ask Sebastian for it, if you would only give your approval. Sebastian has always handled all of the money, so I'm not sure exactly how much is involved . . . but surely enough for our simple needs?

I asked him again—via Maureen—if you might be allowed to visit me. The message came back that our "relationship" was an "unhealthy" one! Isn't that incredible? I believe it is more unhealthy that Sebastian has not seen his own half-brother for years. Perhaps if they were to meet, he would be able to understand the bonds that tie us that can never be broken.

I will not speak to him again—not until he allows you to come to me. My own punishment is actually greater than his, for I do love him, Cyril. But, dearest brother, I love you, too.

Keats' immortal lines hang heavily on my mind today. . . .

*But to that second circle of sad hell
Where 'mid the gust, the whirlwind, and the flaw
Of rain and hailstones, lovers need not tell
Their sorrows. Pale were the sweet lips I saw,
Pale were the lips I kissed, and fair the form
I floated with, about that melancholy storm.*

Dai's brow knitted into a perplexed frown. He was right that the lack of money was all that was keeping them from . . . doing what? Cyril had once confided that he considered money to be merely a necessary evil, and it's source was of little consequence to him. With one important exception. He would die before touching a penny of old McKnight's money.

Breathing a sigh of relief that Cyril would not let Emily ask for her inheritance money, Dai's gaze again drifted over Keats' poem. He was not sure what Emily had in mind in quoting it, but it seemed to him that the bonds that bound Emily and Cyril were much deeper and more mysterious than either of them realized.

One evening when Cyril and Dai took their places at the piano, their attention was caught by a handsome woman with a mass of auburn hair that fell almost to her waist. She was dressed in a well-cut velvet gown of deep jade-green, and except for the unfettered hair and lack of an escort, she might have been one of the prettier matrons from Nob Hill.

After the shouts of approval and table-thumping appreciation of their ballad had died away, the woman came to them. She moved with a provocative hip-swinging walk and returned the comments of the watching men in the same vein. At the piano she leaned on one elbow and fixed emerald-green eyes on Cyril.

"What are you up to, Mr. La Flair?" she asked in a husky, slightly teasing voice. She glanced only briefly at his mutilated right hand resting on the keys.

"I hope I'm entertaining the guests, madame," Cyril said. He knew the identity of the woman instantly. Balmain's mistress.

"You play better with seven fingers than most pianists in this town with ten," she said. "Your music . . . I've never heard anything like it. I'm no expert, but I should think if you wrote it, you're wasting your time here. You'd do better in the east . . . or in Europe. I'd say, in fact, that a man who plays for tips is here for another reason altogether."

"I have no idea of what you speak. If you'll excuse me, I must resume playing."

She was placing a slip of paper beside his hand on the keyboard. "My address. Come to my house at midnight or later. I'll be waiting for you. This may surprise you, but you and I want the same thing, and I believe we can do each other some good."

When Cyril went to the rear of the saloon and reached for his hat and coat, Dai quickly followed. "Don't go, *bach,* maybe it's a trap."

"Mind your own business, Dai," Cyril said shortly.

"You think that woman will help you get your Emily away from him, but—"

Cyril had disappeared into the foggy night before Dai could finish.

The house was an inconspicuous white-frame structure behind a picket fence, as unlike the garishly splendid Mariner's Castle as the darkly beautiful Emily was from the gaudily pretty Garnet. An oil lamp burned in the window to guide him up the mist-shrouded walk.

She was still wearing the green velvet dress when she opened the door and led him to a simply furnished sitting room. "Thank you for coming," she said after the door to the room was firmly shut.

He had been surprised by her speech. He had expected the rather disjointed and vague speech of the actresses and singers who flocked to the gold coast in a day when few "nice" women traveled alone unless they were being met by a husband.

"You know who I am?" she asked, gesturing for him to be seated.

He stood by the fire, warming his hands. "Yes."

"I know you haven't seen Emily lately. But that maid of hers carries you messages. If you are hoping to take Emily back to England . . . perhaps I can help you."

"So that you can take her place in that monstrosity of a house up on the hill?" Cyril asked coldly.

The green eyes flashed defiantly. "Yes. She hates him and she's making him miserable. I love him and I want respectability for my children."

"And what about Emily's child?"

"I believe," she said, smiling softly, "that a child belongs with his mother. Will you sit down and let me tell you my plan?"

Cyril regarded her silently for a long moment, his

dark eyes boring into hers with such intensity she felt he must surely be probing the depths of her soul. Then he slipped his overcoat from his shoulders and sat down. "I would form an alliance with the devil himself to rescue Emily from her present fate. I shall, therefore, be happy to do business with . . . the Scylla."

He was considerably taken aback when Garnet tossed her hair back over her shoulder and said, "So that's what you call me. Scylla . . . a sea monster who snatches sailors from their ships and devours them. Woman above the waist, and a pack of ravenous hounds below." Her voice crackled like crumbling autumn leaves, deep in her throat.

"I'm sorry. I didn't mean to hurt you. But you have caused considerable pain to someone who is very dear to me."

"How could you know I would know what a Scylla was?" she asked lightly, pulling her feet under her on the chair.

--·⊰ CHAPTER 20 ⊱·--

Garnet scanned the faces of the disembarking passengers, peering from beneath the veiled black bonnet that concealed her bright auburn hair. As usual, the ship had brought a variety of gold-seekers, speculators, merchants, gamblers, and prostitutes.

She smiled beneath the disguising veil as one ship's officer, undoubtedly new to boomtown on the bay, tossed a fifty-cent piece in the direction of a skinny youth. "Carry my valise to the nearest hotel, boy," the officer commanded.

The boy let the coin drop into the mud, then casually pulled two coins from his pocket and threw them at the officer. "Carry it yourself, my man," he drawled.

San Francisco was being built, burned or torn down, and rebuilt on a foundation of gold. Fortunes were made and lost, and a new society, devoid of old values, social or occupational, was coming into being. Some successful miners were convinced it was unlucky to return to the gold fields after a visit to San Francisco unless they had spent every ounce of gold they brought with them.

Garnet saw the gaudily dressed woman start down the gangplank and she smiled and waved, then realized Cassie would not recognize her under the black veil and shawl.

A moment later they were in each other's arms and Garnet's eyes were watering from the assault of the pungent perfume as much as from emotion. She quickly drew Cassie out of the path of the rushing passengers.

"Garnet, honey, why the widow's weeds?" Cassie asked. "I hardly recognized you." She herself was an impressive figure in a bright red dress with matching coat, bonnet, and gloves. Her shoes had also been dyed to match her outfit, but were already splashed with mud.

"I wanted to be sure I wasn't seen. I'll explain later. Come on. I've a buggy waiting."

"I've a trunk in the hold."

Garnet glanced about anxiously. "I'll wait for you in the buggy."

By the time her trunk was loaded into the buggy, Cassie was bursting with curiosity. "Now, what's all the mystery?" she demanded as Garnet urged the horse forward.

"I don't want Sebastian to know about our business. To be honest, Cassie, I don't want anyone here to know about our association."

Cassie sniffed into a lavender-scented handkerchief. "You've gone respectable," she said accusingly. "I don't know if I'd have come all this way if I'd known you weren't going to be my partner. But then, I was never happy in New Orleans after Leon died. And your letters were full of all those wild stories."

"I didn't exaggerate. I promise, we'll make more money in a week here than a year in New Orleans. And I *am* going to be your partner—behind the scenes. I hope you won't mind, but I'm taking you directly to a hotel."

"I'm not to see your children?" Cassie's face fell. "I was so looking forward to seeing Cerise. Is she still as pretty as when she was a baby?"

"More so. Cassie, I'm sorry—but I did tell you it was a business arrangement I was offering you. I want Cerise and Rual to have a different kind of life than I had. Here's the hotel. Wait until someone lifts you over the mud."

Cassie tried to keep the hurt from showing. "And I thought the streets here with paved were gold. Why, they aren't paved at all."

Within the privacy of Cassie's room, Garnet tossed the black shawl and bonnet to the bed, with a shiver. She had worn black only once before—for Tom—and that had been years ago. "I am wearing widow's garb to disguise myself. Most of Sebastian's friends know me," she said by way of explanation.

"And I thought he was wealthy," Cassie said, pulling a three-inch hat pin from her red bonnet and removing the frothy concoction of feathers and tulle. She adjusted her golden wig and sat down.

"He made a fortune on the first clipper cargoes. But he squandered so much building Mariner's Castle and furnishing it in the manner he felt the aristocratic Emily deserved . . . and he is generous with me, Cassie—though I itch to manage his money and business sometimes and show him how wasteful he is. But all that is neither here nor there. I need money for a plan of my own that I can't ask his help for."

Cassie looked at her shrewdly. "I don't understand you, Garnet. You're living in a town where the men outnumber the women maybe fifty to one. Why haven't you married a rich miner? You told me you were divorced from Gunnar—why do you want to get back into the saloon and gambling business when you don't have to? If I had your looks—"

226

Garnet's green eyes took on a feline inscrutability. "I haven't time to answer a lot of fool questions just now, Cassie. I have to get home before Sebastian comes for dinner, so could we please discuss business? I've got a place all picked out. I want it to be really high class. What about the girls—did you find any?"

Cassie kicked off her mud-splattered shoes. "A couple will follow as soon as we send them the money. I spent our whole stake on the fancy furniture you wanted. It will be unloaded from the ship tomorrow." She sighed and flexed silk-clad feet. "You think we really need to get into the bawdy-house business? Wouldn't liquor and gambling be enough?"

"The men in this town will pay almost any price to sleep with a woman. We can retire in a year if we do it my way."

"You must have a mighty good reason for wanting to get rich fast. I'd feel better knowing what it was."

"All right, Cassie. I want to be Mrs. Sebastian Balmain. Emily's brother is here, playing piano in a saloon and saving pennies in the hope he can get Emily back to England. Only he's never going to make it on that pittance."

They were interrupted by a knock on the door; two bellboys struggled with Cassie's heavy trunk. It would have been tempting to go through the dresses Cassie brought, but Garnet wanted to be at home before Sebastian arrived.

She was still breathing heavily from having bathed, changed clothes, and checked with Fern to see that dinner was ready, when Sebastian arrived. He ate dinner with her and the children at least once a week and, Garnet suspected, later went home and had a second repast.

After giving him a quick kiss, Garnet bent over the table, straightening silverware and catching her breath, as Sebastian hugged the children and listened to their excited babble.

". . . and that awful carrot-haired Austin Gentry pulled my hair and pinched me on the bottom," Cerise

227

told him indignantly. "So I punched him in the nose and made it bleed."

"Good for you, honey. But what did Mrs. Latham say when the fur and feathers started to fly?" Sebastian asked, grinning.

"Oh, Austin Gentry told her he had walked into a door," Cerise said coolly.

"I see. A real Southern gentleman."

"No! He's a nasty boy with carroty hair and I hate him."

Sebastian smoothed back Cerise's own red-gold curls and pondered on the clashing of two redheads with like temperaments. He frowned suddenly, thinking of two other like temperaments. Emily and Cyril. Their spirits seemed to be two halves of the same whole, sharing the same dreams, joys, and despair. It was as if Emily's soul had taken a second body—and that body was Cyril.

"Did you bring my boat?" Rual asked, sapphire-bright eyes gleaming with anticipation. Sebastian's hand was behind his back and his smile widened as he brought forth a rakishly rigged clipper.

Rual's mouth opened and he reached out his hands in silent awe. As small fingers closed reverently around the smooth hull of the ship, Garnet went to kiss Sebastian's cheek. "Sailors!" she sighed. "How is everything?" Emily's name was never mentioned in front of the children, but Sebastian knew what Garnet was really asking.

"Still not speaking to me. But she's making a determined effort to get back on her feet. Mr. Tang tells me she is taking a few steps each day. She's eating again, too."

Later, when the children were in bed and they lay in each other's arms and were satiated with their love-making, Garnet's fingers idly traced the stubborn contours of Sebastian's face and she whispered, "Why don't you let her go to him? She's getting well again for his sake."

Sebastian's large frame stiffened in every muscle and he sat up abruptly. "What are you saying, Garnet?" he demanded. "Do you know what you're saying? He is her brother. *They are blood-related.*"

"There are unions of the mind, you know . . . as well as of the body."

"Not between men and women, there aren't. Besides, she's my wife."

A furrow appeared in Sebastian's brow. There had been many nights after he left Garnet's arms that he had gone home to pace the silent hall of Mariner's Castle, in turmoil as he strove to cope with his feelings for the two women in his life. He worshipped Emily as a goddess, placing her on a pedestal above all other women, so in awe of her beauty and purity that he had never been able to find the words to tell her of his feelings. Emily was goodness and fidelity, and even the punishing silence she had maintained since Cyril arrived had not killed Sebastian's love for her.

She had quietly pleaded with him to allow Cyril to visit her, and when he had refused, she had again withdrawn into her shell.

Garnet's hands were moving over his body, expertly finding the response she sought. How many men had taught her those caresses? Unwillingly, Sebastian thought of Emily, who had never known any man's body but her husband's. "Garnet, there's nothing between Emily and her half-brother . . . nothing sexual. But their attachment is still unhealthy. Better I keep them apart. It's him I'm worried about—not Emily. I know her; she is too pure of mind and spirit to ever sleep with a man not her husband."

Garnet closed his mouth with her kisses before he could twist the knife any deeper in her heart.

The Red Garter, usually known simply as "Cassie's Place," was the talk of the Barbary Coast. The gambling rooms were honestly run, the liquor served was the finest, and the surroundings were tastefully elegant. A restaurant was added for the convenience of the patrons, and it was soon evident two upstairs rooms were insufficient.

An exotically lovely Mexican girl named Consuela was proving to be a major attraction, although most of the "hostesses" worked only until they landed a rich husband.

Within a month of opening, Cassie considered insisting on a members-only rule, since their space could not accommodate the numbers of would-be patrons. As it was, clients were not admitted unless they had bathed and were elegantly dressed, and Cassie kept raising prices to keep the lower elements out. Nevertheless, one afternoon when Garnet called, Cassie told her flatly they would have to look for a larger place, or institute the members-only rule.

Garnet had no intention of turning the Red Garter into a private club. The growth of their business had exceeded her wildest expectations, but more than that, the challenge of scaling even greater heights in a man's world appealed to her.

Garnet removed her widow's veil and closed the window curtains of Cassie's private room. "I know. I've been thinking about it and I believe the only way to get what we really want is to build. That way we won't have to pay exorbitant rent to a landlord and we can have the location we want."

Cassie poured two glasses of blackberry wine and they sat on the satin-upholstered couch. Cassie slid a heavy account book on to the coffee table in front of her and flipped through the pages, while Garnet made notes and drew plans for their new establishment. Their conversation was brisk and the expression of their ideas concise.

Later that day Garnet stopped briefly at the saloon where Cyril worked. "We'll have to wait a little longer," she told him as soon as Dai had discreetly withdrawn. Cyril was at his piano, as usual, going over some arrangements. "I'm going to have to build a bigger place, and all of our capital will be tied up for a while."

Cyril sighed. "I'd hoped to have enough money of my own . . . but alas, something always seems to come up."

"How would you like to work for Cassie in the new place? We might as well pool our resources. Perhaps instead of paying you, we could put your money in the bank. We'll double what they're paying you here."

"Dai Williams?"

"Him, too."

Cyril's dark gaze was momentarily a study in ironic satisfaction, but Garnet could not know he was contemplating the poetic justice of the situation. "Very well," he said. He turned to cough into his handkerchief. Since coming to the damp mists of San Francisco, his old trouble with quinsies had come back and he was experiencing that difficulty in swallowing that heralded another attack. He would have to conceal it from Dai, or his friend would promptly make one of his scalding poultices.

It took nearly a year for Cassie's new and much larger establishment to be finished and opened. In addition to Cyril and Dai, there was a troupe of comely veterans of the English music halls whose dances were somewhat risqué and who performed comic skits. The hostesses, who had grown in number to ten, mingled with the patrons in the gambling rooms and saloon bar, and discreetly disappeared upstairs from time to time.

Within six months of the opening, Cyril unobtrusively slipped up to the private rooms and waited for Cassie's silent partner in her disguising widow's weeds to arrive.

There was no need for him to tell Garnet why he wanted to see her. "You're ready?" she asked.

"Yes."

"Good. Let's make plans."

Two weeks later, Sebastian came crashing into the white frame house behind the picket fence. Thunderclouds raced across the blue eyes and his roar of pain and rage stopped Garnet's breath in her throat.

"What is it?" she asked, her hands gripping the folds of her skirts tightly.

"Emily . . . she's gone," he said hoarsely. "And La

231

Flair, too. Vanished into thin air, both of them. Oh, God, what shall I do?"

"Sit down. I'll get you some brandy." Garnet's voice was shaking.

"Someone in this town helped them. By God, when I find out who . . . the Welshman won't talk, but I'll find out . . . Garnet, oh, Lord, I'm so afraid they're on a ship. I've searched everywhere. They must have slipped aboard last night while I was here with you."

Garnet handed him the glass of brandy, not daring to look into his eyes.

Sebastian drained the glass. "They took my son with them. Noah is gone, too," he said in a strangled voice. Then, without warning, he covered his face with his hands and his muscular frame shook with silent sobs.

--◄{ **CHAPTER 21** }►--

Sebastian spent months combing San Francisco and the nearby gold towns, searching for Emily and his son. Obsessed with finding them, he neglected his business and his second family. He would stop to see Garnet, stare unseeingly at the puzzled children, and start to speak only to forget what he had meant to say. He was drinking heavily.

Garnet slept poorly, and when she did fall into an exhausted slumber, her old dream came back. She wondered if it was Sebastian hidden in the black smoke, and if the thundering hooves represented his flight away from her.

One evening, beside herself with worry for his sanity and her own, Garnet clutched at him when, moments after arriving, he stood up to leave. "Sebastian, for God's sake, stay with me a while," she begged. She had never pleaded before, believing a clinging woman would drive a man away faster than the plague, but she was desperate. "It's Rual . . . he doesn't understand why you don't play with him anymore. You hardly speak to him . . . and you and I . . . we haven't made love since . . . since—"

Sebastian's eyes were streaked with red as he looked down at her. For a moment she was reminded, horrifyingly, of Erik Gunnar. Sebastian shook his black mane of hair as though trying to clear his head. His breath reeked of whiskey. "Since Emily took my son away," he finished for her.

"Rual is your son, too, God damn you!" Garnet shouted. Her hand flew to her mouth. *Oh, God,* she thought, *I'm a screaming shrew. I'm losing him!*

Sebastian's eyes were unfocused and he was not listening. "I've questioned every ship's master. I can't believe they sailed from this port. But they must have. . . ." He looked at Garnet, seeing her wild-eyed stare for the first time. She was angry with him. Of course. How arrogant he had been to expect two women would share his life. His present pain was well-deserved. Was Garnet about to leave him, too?

In his pride he had never wanted to acknowledge that Garnet regarded him as a dispensable part of her life. But the fact was there, no matter how far back in his mind he pushed the thought. He had always known she would one day move on to another man, another life, without a backward glance. As she had in the past. Perhaps that time would come when Rual was grown and she no longer needed him. Sebastian watched his son's growth with a mixture of pride and apprehension. But Emily . . . sweet, faithful, loyal Emily . . . his wife. That she should desert him—that was the blow he had least expected.

"Garnet, I came to tell you—" His voice trailed off again.

"What, Sebastian, what did you come to tell me?"

"I'm going to England. They must have gone to England. I should have seen it before. He didn't come

233

to visit her; he came to take her home. I'm going after them, to bring them back."

"No!" Garnet's face was ashen. "Please, Sebastian, let her go. Don't you see? She doesn't want to live with you anymore. She hates you, she'll never forgive you—"

He had started for the door but paused and turned slowly. "She doesn't hate me. It was the accident. She and the baby were buried alive. It did something to her mind. In time . . ."

"No!" Garnet screamed. "Not in time. Never. It wasn't the accident. You big fool, don't you know— didn't you guess? She found out about me and Rual— that day of the earthquake."

Realization flooded into his eyes, and with it a hideous possibility. "That was the day after Gunnar crashed the party—good God! Was it he who told her? No one else would have . . . but how could he have got past Mr. Tang? Impossible. If she found out that day, it must have been when Mr. Tang and I went looking for Erik Gunnar. . . ." Sebastian paused, remembering bits and pieces, fragments of gossip that had reached his ears. His friends hinting that the woman didn't live who would willingly share her man with another. Not without a fight . . . and women didn't always fight fairly.

A cold chill moved slowly down his spine. He stared at Garnet, studying her expression, the fear in her eyes. Her face was naked with emotion: defiance, horror, guilt.

"You . . ." he said slowly. "You told her."

"No! No . . . I didn't." Desperation was in her voice and her touch as she ran to fling herself into his arms.

His hands closed around her shoulders and he pushed her away, his mouth twisting into a grim accusing crescent. "Then how do you know it was the day of the earthquake that she began to hate me?" He shook her roughly, so that her hair whipped her face. "Tell me how you knew if it wasn't you who told her! Damn you, Garnet—"

Garnet felt his hands on her throat, saw the terrible rage blazing in red-rimmed eyes, and everything was spinning into a misty haze when the tiny whirlwind of fists and feet fell upon Sebastian.

Rual was sobbing and punching his father's legs, kicking at his ankles. "You let my mother go! You're hurting her! Stop it, stop it!" the child cried.

Garnet struggled to remain conscious, her hands plucking at Sebastian's tightening fingers.

A moment later the air was rent with piercing screams and there was a great crash of breaking china. The pressure on Garnet's throat stopped abruptly and she reeled backward, collapsing into the nearest chair.

Sebastian was staggering and shaking his head and all about him were the broken remains of the vase Cerise had flung at him. Her scream faded as she ran to her mother's side, burying her face in the soft mass of Garnet's hair. They were both trembling violently.

Rual was making a valiant effort to control his frightened tears. He placed himself between his mother and father and, chin jutting, blue eyes blazing, glared at Sebastian. "We want you to go away. We don't like you anymore."

Sebastian brushed his hair back from his brow, smearing blood across his hairline. He blinked, as though awakening from a nightmare only to find a reality more terrible. His expression hardened as he looked at Garnet, and he strode to the door without another word.

The next morning Garnet was awakened early by Fern. "Miz Garnet, you got a visitor. It's that big Chinaman who works for Mr. Balmain, and he won't go away."

Garnet struggled to sit up. Her neck was stiff and her mouth dry. Her voice was a hoarse croak as she asked Fern to hand her a robe.

Mr. Tang was waiting in the hall. He handed her a bulky envelope, bowed, and departed.

"Make me some coffee, Fern. Don't wake the children yet." Garnet went into the parlor to open the letter. A thick wad of money fell to her lap and she picked up the brief note that accompanied it.

Sebastian wrote:

Garnet,

*I have instructed my bankers to make a similar
sum available to you each month. If it's not
enough for your needs, please see Mr. Moffatt.
I'm sailing for England today. Forgive me for man-
handling you. I'd been drinking. The guilt is more
mine than yours.*

Garnet gathered up the money and pushed it back
into the envelope. When Fern brought her coffee,
Garnet took a sip and said, "I want you to take that to
the bank. See the manager and tell him it's to be deposited in Sebastian Balmain's account. Get a receipt."

"Yes'm." Fern's eyes were fixed on the bruise on
Garnet's neck. "You all right, Miz Garnet?" Fern had
not been home during the altercation with Sebastian,
but she had guessed what happened.

"I'll be fine. When you get back I'll get dressed and
go see Cassie."

Cassie noted that Garnet was very pale and that she
wore a high-necked gown with a froth of lace at the
throat that looked as if it had been hastily tucked in
place.

"You look like a woman who got the worst of an
argument," Cassie observed. "You might as well tell
me what happened. I'll find out, anyway."

Garnet drank several glasses of wine, despite the
early hour, and told Cassie everything.

"Well, then . . ." Cassie said when she had finished.
"Maybe it's time my silent partner came out from behind the widow's weeds and took an active part in the
business. Why not, Garnet? Dress up and circulate.
You'd enjoy it; you know you would. I never could
understand how you spent all your time in that little
house waiting for that big ox. He never takes you anywhere. You only entertain his business friends—never
their wives. What do you get from it all?"

Garnet tossed back her hair and examined her reflection in the gilt-framed mirror above Cassie's cluttered
dressing table. "I love him," she said. "It was enough."

"And now? He'll be gone for months, maybe years. What will you do now? Come on, honey, you might as well go to work. Try to forget him."

"No. I can't, Cassie. There are the children to consider. They were accepted into all the best houses in town so long as I didn't flaunt my relationship with Sebastian. I must go on as before. When Rual and Cerise are grown up and on their own, I shall live as I damn please. But not now. Cerise is going to marry the richest and most powerful man in this town; I swear it."

The sea was a bright blue-green and the warm breeze carried the scent of fragrant blossoms. A white beach shimmered in the sun, crowded with beckoning coconut palms, their graceful trunks bowing before the tradewinds. The lush green foliage beyond the beach gradually gave way to mist-shrouded hills.

Already the lagoon was filled with glistening brown bodies, swimming across the coral reef toward the ship. Garlands of flowers trailed in the clear, warm water as the islanders brought the traditional Sandwich Isles greeting to the newly arrived *malihinis*.

Emily clasped her hands in delight. "The air . . . it's so heady, I feel I shall swoon from it." Her thin arms went across her breast as she hugged herself for sheer joy. "Oh, Cyril, dearest heart, look at the flowers they are bringing. Look at those beautiful people. . . . Oh, to move through the water as gracefully as tropical fish, as they do."

Cyril smiled, turning to lean against the rail and watch Emily's reaction as the islanders swarmed aboard the ship. Dripping garlands of flowers were heaped about the necks of passengers and crew. Emily was soon bedecked with half a dozen *leis,* and her pointed little face almost disappeared behind orchids, hibiscus, and ginger blossom. His own white silk scarf was discarded as a lovely young girl placed a string of seashells abbout his neck and then a flowered *lei*. "*Aloha,*" she said, her smile revealing perfect white teeth.

"*Aloha kakahiaka,*" Cyril responded.

237

Emily clapped her hands. "Bravo! Oh, how clever of you to speak their tongue."

He moved to her side and placed his arm about her shoulder to ward off further eager bearers of *leis*. "Come, let us go below and see if Noah has awakened. We must prepare to go ashore."

"And how shall that be accomplished?" Emily asked as they made their way through the chattering and giggling reception committee.

"They'll take us in a boat—skimming over the coral teeth that would tear the hull of the ship if we anchored any closer to shore."

"Honolulu . . ." Emily said softly, her voice caressing each syllable. "It has such a romantic sound." She felt as though she had just awakened from a nightmare to find spring sunlight flooding her bed.

"We may not stay on this island, Emily. There are other islands, and I would like to avoid the main harbors where the ships drop anchor . . . here, or the whaling port of Lahaina, for example. But we shall explore all of the islands in time." Cyril left unsaid the thought that her husband might sail one of his clippers into those busy ports. The burden Cyril would have to bear was the knowledge that although Emily believed herself to be a discarded wife, whose disappearance would be a relief to her husband, that in actual fact Sebastian did not want to lose her and might very well come after them.

Cyril would have told her anything and convinced his own conscience of the justification of the means he was using so that they could be together. He no longer tried to analyze his feelings for Emily, nor the fact that he could forget his strong code of honor and resort to devious methods because of his love for her and need to care for her.

Emily breathed deeply of the scent of the blossoms encircling her slender throat, running her fingertips lightly over interwoven petals. She walked with a slight limp, but Cyril kept his arm about her, rendering support. She turned and looked into his dark eyes, glowing with happiness. "We have died and gone to heaven," she announced passionately. And Cyril laughed and bent to brush her cheek with his cool lips.

They went below to her cabin and swept a sleepy and bewildered Noah into their arms so he could have his first glimpse of their island paradise.

No one saw Emily blink away a tear as they left the ship. It symbolized her wrenching parting from Sebastian. Not even the memory of his faithlessness could dim the bright image of her lost husband in her mind. Emily knew beyond a shadow of a doubt that the fault was hers, although she was not sure exactly why.

Only days away from the Sandwich Isles, a different drama was at that moment beginning.

The black hump of the big bull whale broke the surface a split-second after the cry rang out from the masthead.

"Blows! Flukes! Ah, blo-o-o-ws!"

The watch below was hailed on deck as the excitement of the hunt pulsed through the ship. The first mate, Mr. Gunnar, was already in the boat on the starboard quarter. "Lower away!" he shouted the instant the last of his six man crew scrambled aboard.

Deep indigo seas swept up to meet the small boat and the oarsmen began to pull as soon as they touched the surface, clearing the ship with a few strokes.

The whale blew just as two cows, one trailing a calf, breached to the leeward. A fair breeze had sprung up and Gunnar quickly ordered the sail hoist. Three boats from the bark-rigged *Gray Treasure* set their course toward the distant gam of whales.

From the masthead a code of signals with colored waifs guided the small boats as they strove to be the first to beach their craft on the black bulk of the whale.

The sperm whale blew, dead ahead, its vaporous breath roaring from the spiracle. They could see wrinkled rubber-like skin as the hump burst above the water. Gunnar quickly turned over the helm to a crewman so that he might change ends of the boat and prepare to heave the lance as soon as "Wood to blackkin" was called.

239

Sail and oars closed the distance rapidly. Gunnar stood at the ready, lance in hand, as the boat was beached on the broad back of the whale. He swung, the lance buried itself five feet into the whale, and the men were rocked violently in the flurry, doused with seawater and blood.

A second later they were clear, the boat tossing in the churning white water as they played out the line and fought to stay afloat. Now came the crucial minutes, waiting to see if the carcass could be taken in tow or would sink. Every man tensed, knowing full well that of ten whales killed, they would be lucky to get one back to the ship.

"Mr. Gunnar, sir—there!"

The dead sperm whale was tossed up on a swell. They had killed the large bull.

With their ship downwind from the kill, the men began the hard pull back, inching the great carcass through the water with back-breaking toil, their hands already bloodied from hauling whaleline. As long as they kept the boat slowly moving forward, the whale's great body would follow.

At last they were alongside their ship, and the operation of sweeping and fluking, making the whale fast alongside, was begun. A chain went around the tail end, just in front of the flukes, and was hauled taut through a hawspipe.

The hunt over, the hard labor was about to begin. Cutting tackle and cutting stage were rigged and lowered. Sailors with long-handled spades flensed the whale and the tackle began to rip away the blubber along the line hacked by the twenty-foot-long spades.

As they worked on their precariously swaying platform, blue sharks moved in, attracted by the spreading red tide of blood. One thrashed in a frenzy on the surface, its jaws fastened into the whale meat. Slashing at the sharks with spades was little deterrent. Soon the water was sliced by fins as the sharks moved in from every direction. The men worked faster now, the whale's body rotating in the water as it was peeled of its blubber.

Erik Gunnar paused for a second in his labor to wipe the sweat from his brow. His brown-red eyes reflected the bloody sea and he silently calculated his share of the twenty-three whales the *Gray Treasure* had taken.

The skipper had promised them a few days in the Sandwich Isles, and while it was not San Francisco, Lahaina would be a welcome break for the men, who had not seen a mainland port for nearly three years. Perhaps, Gunnar reflected, as he caught a shark with his spade, driving the metal into the creature's wicked teeth, he would send a small present to San Francisco for Cerise. He had been working on a piece of scrimshaw, painstakingly carving the likeness of his ship into a bit of polished whale bone.

He thought of his daughter often, her mother rarely.

<h2 style="text-align:center">⊱⊰ CHAPTER 22 ⊱⊰</h2>

The River Mersey was slate-gray beneath a light drizzle and overcast skies. From the deck of the ship, Liverpool's streets appeared as narrow and architecturally unappealing as Sebastian remembered, although within days he would be aware of the great building boom that was just beginning. St. George's Hall had been opened the previous year, a Corinthian-style building designed by Harvey Lonsdale-Elmes, to the city's great pride.

Sebastian changed into a suit before going ashore. The months at sea had eased his pain and he felt strangely at peace. He had worked his passage as an ordinary seaman, slipping back into the role as easily as if he had never left it. Stopping off in New York to see Ned and his wife, Sebastian had been unable to explain why he had decided to sail on a ship other than his own.

"Why didn't you wait for the *Monarch Butterfly* to arrive in San Francisco and sail on her? God knows I have a hard enough time finding capable skippers and crews, Sebastian. What were you thinking of?" Ned demanded. He had felt for some time that he carried the company, which did not even bear his name. Sebastian had made him a partner, but refused to change the company name.

Ned's wife, Deborah, was wearing the same faintly disapproving look.

"I had to get out of San Francisco. I was at the end of my rope," Sebastian answered. "I just signed on the first ship. And I want to be on a packet for Liverpool as soon as I can, so let's get down to business."

He only half-listened to Ned's complaints that the clippers were losing money. Everyone was talking about steam.

"Steam! I'll never trade my beautiful ladies for smelly steamboats," Sebastian said. "Steamers are slow and half their cargo space is taken up with fuel. You think you have trouble getting sailors for the clippers . . . wait till you hear how hard it is to get stokers for steamboats."

"Then while you're in England you'd better have a word with your half-brother," Ned said, his expression bleak.

"About what?"

"About the McKnight schooners. He sent me a letter asking me to return them. If we have to send them back, we're in deep financial trouble."

"Where are they now?"

"Two are down in the Gulf and the third is here."

"Why do you suppose he wants them back in Liverpool?"

"Because he's converting the McKnight Line to steam. There's talk he's fitting out what they call "luxury" liners—fancy furniture and accommodations to transport the rich back and forth across the Atlantic.

242

I expect he's selling all the old McKnight ships to raise capital."

Remembering the conversation, Sebastian paused for a moment when the cabbie deposited him in front of the gaunt brick house in Princes Park. The years had not mellowed the austerity of the architecture. Above him was the window overlooking the park where Emily had whiled away the lonely days of her imprisonment. For a moment the sun broke through the clouds and gilded the dark glass, and Sebastian fancied he could see a ghostly face watching him. He hesitated, afraid to approach the door and be told she was not here.

The front door opened before he could knock. A tall young man with straight dark hair, a light complexion, and bright blue eyes stepped out. His forehead was unusually high but was balanced by a square jaw. Although he was lean for his height, he carried himself with almost military precision. His eyes were alive and intelligent and took Sebastian in with a single sweeping glance. He held out his hand.

"Brother Sebastian, I take it? I am Mark McKnight."

Sebastian accepted the handshake, which was firm but aloofly businesslike.

"I was just leaving for the office, but business can wait. Let's go inside."

Sebastian followed through the vestibule, along the hall, and into the damp parlor. The rosewood piano, covered with gray bloom, still stood against the wall. The wallpaper bulged damply behind the monstrously huge aspidistra plant. Sebastian shivered and assured himself he would not be intimidated by an eighteen-year-old boy.

"Is Emily . . . my wife . . . has she come to see you?"

Mark did not answer for a second or two, and Sebastian had the uneasy feeling that the boy's mind was working like some giant machine, sifting and sorting information and impressions. "So that's why you came at last," Mark said. "I'm sorry, if your wife is in England I was unaware of the fact. She hasn't been in touch. May I offer you a drink?"

"Whiskey, if you have it." There was no reason for Emily to return here, Sebastian was thinking.

"We should have some Scotch. Mollie likes a wee drop to help her sleep."

"Mollie Flanagan is still with you?"

"Of course. Did you imagine I would turn her out to pasture because I am no longer a helpless babe? She's the only real family I've ever known."

Sebastian caught the note of disapproval. "I did write and tell you that if you ever needed anything . . . or if you wanted to come home—"

"Home?" Mark raised a perfectly formed eyebrow. "Your mother was American."

"But I was born here, old chap . . . of an English— or, rather, a Scottish—father. That's all right; I didn't mean to infer that you've neglected me. Mollie tipples a little these days, and I was merely letting you know I'll tolerate no criticism of her while you're here."

"You wrote Ned that you want the schooners back. May I ask why?"

The blue eyes snapped to attention. "I'm pooling all of my assets for our conversion to steam. You don't need them, surely? I understand you own several clipper ships . . . beautiful vessels, a tribute to Yankee design. Pity they came on the scene too late."

"Too late for what?"

"Why, to be a commercial proposition, of course."

"That's the opinion of a steamboater," Sebastian said stiffly. "Aren't you a mite young to be making such decisions about your father's ships?"

"Not at all. My father very astutely made me his sole heir. I can be advised, but not overruled. And no age minimum for my running the business was set. He had, of course, hoped to live long enough to hand me the reins himself." He paused, then added "The whole company has drifted into stagnation while I was away at university, but I'll soon have things moving again."

There wouldn't be a McKnight Line if I hadn't stepped in and put it back on course after your father's stroke, Sebastian thought. But aloud he said, "Your schooners will be returned with all speed."

244

Sebastian sipped his drink and contemplated his half-brother, the thought flickering on the edge of his mind that Mark had been blessed, or cursed, with the combination of his father's canny intelligence, Louisa's tight control on emotion, and the polish of good schools. Since this was wrapped in well-bred handsomeness and the boy exuded a restless vitality, it seemed that Mark McKnight at eighteen was already a dangerous force.

"I'll instruct the servants to prepare a room for you," Mark said.

"No, thank you. I plan to leave right away for London." Sebastian had already decided Cyril must have taken Emily there. It was logical, for Cyril had lived there once.

"Perhaps you'd like to see one of our new liners while you're here. I have a steamer we expect will make thirteen knots on her maiden voyage. And I believe you'll be surprised at the passenger accommodations. We're a long way from your packet days when passengers were jammed 'tween decks like so much ballast."

"No. I believe I'll take a train to London today."

Mark gave a slightly condescending smile. "I see your aversion to steam doesn't extend to the locomotive engine. You'll admit a train is preferable to spending days in a horse-drawn carriage?"

Sebastian merely glowered and stood up to leave.

"I'll take you to the railway station," Mark offered, "if you'll wait a moment while I have the carriage brought around."

He opened the door too quickly for Mollie Flanagan to step out of sight. She tottered slightly, her florid face flushed, and a strong smell of wintergreen preceded her into the room.

"Come in, dear," Mark said. "We have a visitor you will no doubt remember better than I."

Sebastian caught the smell of whiskey the wintergreen had not quite masked when Mollie spoke. "So ye've come back, Mr. Balmain, now that himself is gone. Well, Mark can manage quite nicely, thank you, without you nor nobody else."

"Now, Mollie," Mark said, but he smiled affectionately. "Sebastian is in England looking for his wife. He has not come to interfere in our business."

"So Emily left you, did she?" Mollie's eyes glinted. "I'm not surprised. Never saw a more mismatched couple than you two. And as for Mr. Balmain interfering . . . well, he can't do that, because your father made sure everything went to you. And quite right, too. The way them two—"

"I was just going for the carriage," Mark said, deftly steering Mollie to a chair as she swayed slightly on her feet. "I shan't be long, Mollie." He kissed her cheek affectionately.

The carriage took them on a roundabout route so that they could pass the McKnight Line office. Mark apologized and said he had to make a stop to instruct his clerks. Sebastian refused the invitation to go inside and waited in the carriage, studying the sign fastened to the door:

McKNIGHT LINE
STEAM TO NEW YORK
THE FULL-POWERED SCREW STEAMER
PANDORA
TO SAIL
19th MAY
SIX GUINEAS
FULL DIETARY
APPLY WITHIN, OR TO
JAMES BAINES & CO. TOWER BUILDINGS,
WATER STREET

When Mark reappeared he remarked casually, "We shall have four identical ships and a weekly service to New York. I could use a good man on the other side of the Atlantic, if you're interested."

Sebastian grimaced. "You'll not get me aboard a steam kettle. Hellish creations of Lucifer. I remember when they tried to steam across the Atlantic on the *Savannah* and she used her sail for twenty days of the crossing and her steam engines for three and a half.

And a semaphore station that saw her coming in belching smoke thought she was afire and sent a cutter out to the rescue."

Mark laughed. He was a striking-looking young man with his face set in the slightly bored expression he wore, but when he laughed the resulting animation was magnetic. "Nevertheless, my dear brother, the first real challenge to your clippers has been declared for May 19."

Sebastian turned to look out of the window. Office boys were scurrying across the street with their rolled bills of lading. Frock-coated men in tall hats stopped to converse about the movement of ships and cargoes. Occasionally a brawny sailor with faded eyes and weatherbeaten skin came strolling up from the docks.

Images flickered in Sebastian's mind. Knute Kolvoord and Job McKnight. Years of toil and banishment from the sea to make a home for Emily. Emily . . . brown velvet eyes, shining dark hair framing alabaster features. The perfectly modulated and thrillingly vibrant voice that had the power to make tiny nerves tingle with a force both sensual and spiritual.

He thought of the miracle of the birth of Noah, his son. Emily had suffered so terribly giving birth to the child, yet had never uttered a word of complaint. She had labored for two days and the midwife fled in panic, saying Emily would surely die. Holding her hand, watching her frail body contorted with fearful contractions, he had been astounded at her courage. She did not cry out, although every one of her fingernails cracked from being dug into the bedposts in her agony. When it was all over and his son was squalling beside her, Emily opened her eyes and Sebastian saw the shadow of pain lingering in their depths, but it was eclipsed by the love shining there. "Have I given you a healthy son?" she whispered weakly.

Sebastian nodded, his throat constricted with emotion, and squeezed limp fingers.

"My dear . . . it's all right. I would gladly have died to give you your son," she said. Sebastian had gathered

247

her into his arms and known there was not another woman like her in the universe.

It never occurred to him that Garnet might have suffered as much bringing his other son into the world, for Sebastian had been at sea, bringing a clipper around the Horn, when Rual was born.

Oh, God, Sebastian thought. Where are you, Emily? Where have you taken my son?

Sebastian's lips came together in pain as he choked on the bitten-back exclamation of her name. He was no longer listening to the polished and slightly amused drawl of his half-brother.

In London Sebastian learned the name Cyril La Flair was well known in musical circles. A promising composer. His music was at once a celebration of life and an acknowledgment of the tragedy lurking beneath the surface of even the most mundane of existences. His own tragedy, of course, was the loss of his fingers, which ended a career in the concert halls. He had left London abruptly and not returned. He has a half-sister, you know, to whom he is devoted. And you, sir, you're an American? Did you know Cyril's half-sister, Emily? She lived in a small seaport called San Francisco.

"No," Sebastian said. "I am merely looking for Cyril La Flair."

The letter from Ned reached him after he had spent several futile months in London.

Ned wrote:

The McKnight schooners were returned. The *Monarch Butterfly* sailed for California with more ballast than cargo. The California trade is dead; there is simply too much competition. It's as difficult to get crews as cargo. We are facing bankruptcy. If you don't plan to return, will you please give me the authority to run the company?

Every man-jack in our employ knows you've lost interest. I'm including part of an entry from the *Butterfly*'s last log, to illustrate the problems I'm facing:

July 23—let men out of irons because needed

their service. Cape Horn north five miles, coast-line covered in snow. At six squally, in lower and topgallant studding sail. High seas running, ship very wet fore and aft. Suspended first officer from duty because of continued neglect of duty. Discovered mainmast had sprung.

Sebastian, there is much more. What am I to do?

Sebastian signed a power of attorney and sent Ned a note to the effect that he could do what the hell he pleased. Then Sebastian wandered down to the river.

The salt tang of the sea crept up the Thames, borne on a fresh breeze and lurking in the rigging of the homeward-bounders. Incoming sailors were stowing sail or standing ready at the lines. Some were hanging over the rail. Voices drifted over the water, raised in song—a chantey, sung by the crew of a British clipper as she neared the end of her long voyage from Australia.

A lump formed in Sebastian's throat as their voices rose in chorus: *"Oh, whiskey is the life of man . . . whis-key, Johnny . . ."*

Sebastian closed his eyes. He was lying out along a yard, reefing sail, while Irish O'Toole sang in his clear, true voice. Sebastian blinked. Emily was not in London. He would never find her. He had tried so hard, for her sake. Tailor-made clothes and careful with the table manners. Books. Worked hard to become rich and successful so she would be proud of him.

"Oh, I'll drink whiskey, while I can . . . whis-key . . . Johnny—"

The house—Mariner's Castle, built with loving care, filled with the finest furniture from England and France, carried around the Horn in his clippers. He had cultivated friends, entertained lavishly . . . and thrown it all away because he had not been strong enough to resist Garnet's earthy lure.

"Damn," Sebastian said aloud. He felt toward Garnet something of the love a parent feels for a wayward child. While he loved the woman, he hated her morals.

249

Women who sold their favors were no good. It was as clearcut as that.

The fact that he was only truly happy when he was with Garnet and had never really been at ease with Emily was something he did not consider. In order to love a woman completely, he thought, it was necessary to have no doubts about her faithfulness.

Two boardinghouse runners were dragging a drunken sailor toward the gangplank of a waiting ship. Sebastian watched them maneuver the man aboard the ship. "Damn," he said again. "I'm not a lubber."

He followed the runners up the gangplank, knowing neither where the ship was bound, nor caring. After a voyage or two he would return to San Francisco and Garnet. Emily was lost to him. Someday Noah would come looking for him. Blood was, after all, thicker than water.

--✠{ CHAPTER 23 }✠--

Garnet was in the private room of the Red Garter. Her foot tapped and her fingers strummed in tune with the music drifting upstairs.

A door at the rear of the room led to a stairway that went down to the kitchen so that she could enter and leave without being seen. The door leading to the landing was kept locked and only Cassie had a key. Since the other rooms on that floor were used by the girls and were also always locked when in use, no one suspected that behind that particular door all of the business of the Red Garter was conducted.

The walls had been soundproofed as much as possible, and the music helped drown out the sounds of the most profitable entertainment provided by the Red

Garter, but Garnet could hear soft cries of delight from the next room.

She got up from her desk and went to the window, lifting the heavy satin draperies to look at the flickering lights below. It was a moon-drenched night and the sky hung like a velvet canopy over the silver surface of the sea.

A night meant for love, not loneliness. The thought kept hovering on the edge of her mind, and her body was warm beneath the silk gown. She had not lain with another man since coming to San Francisco with Sebastian. Months had elapsed since he left to bring Emily and his son home, and still Garnet waited, tortured by sensual longings and surrounded by women whose business was the gratification of the senses.

She went back to the ledgers on the desk. Laughter on the other side of the wall. A man's laugh, then the giggling of a girl. Garnet fancied she could hear the creaking of the springs of their bed. She moved away from the wall, concentrating on the music. Since the departure of Cyril and Dai, the music was neither as beautiful nor as sad. Garnet moved in time with fiddle and piano, her lips forming the words soundlessly, body swaying rhythmically.

The door opened suddenly and Cassie came into the room in a cloud of jasmine. She stopped, her eyes taking in Garnet's pose. "You poor little thing," she said softly. "You're so lonely you could die from it, aren't you?"

Garnet said shortly, "I've been waiting for ages. I got tired of going over the books. Lord, we made a profit this month. You think we should lower our prices?"

"If we do, the customers will think we're cutting back on quality. Why don't you find yourself a new man? Even if *he* comes back, you think it will be the same? Honey, you know it can't be."

Garnet sighed. Cassie knew all there was to know about her, and there was no use hiding her feelings. "I guess I keep hoping, even though I know you're right."

"He'll bring his wife back and they'll forgive each

other and be cozy—and you, my friend, will be out in the cold. Lord, I've seen it enough times in the past. Men want their wives to be pure, even if they go to a hot-blooded whore on the side. When it comes down to it, it's the whore they'll give up first, because they can always find another."

"But you, Cassie . . . you left your husband because he brought home a mistress. So has Emily. You didn't go back—maybe she won't, either."

"Baby, even if she doesn't come back, it won't be the same for you and Sebastian. You've wrecked his marriage, and he won't be able to forgive you for that. Either way, you're the loser. You should make a new life for yourself while you're still young enough."

Garnet glanced down at the burgundy silk dress she had worn under the enveloping black shawl. Had she, she wondered, deliberately worn it tonight? "Perhaps," she said, "I'll go downstairs for a while, just to listen to the music and be with people. But I don't want to be recognized. Will you lend me one of your wigs, and maybe an ostrich plume, and I'll bend it over my eyes?"

"How about that little sequined veil on my red hat? You know, sometimes some of the Nob Hill matrons come in wearing hats and veils. They're all so curious about what goes on. I swear we could make a fortune if we put peepholes in the girls' rooms." Cassie laughed and pulled open the door. "I'll run up to my room and get what we need to disguise you . . . back in a minute." She disappeared into the hall and Garnet smiled and lifted her auburn curls up on top of her head experimentally. She wondered how she would look in a blonde wig.

"Very becoming," a voice said from the doorway.

Garnet whirled around. Latham Winfield stood on the threshold. *Damn, Cassie didn't lock the door.*

"This room is private, Latham," she said, letting her hair fall.

He stepped into the room and closed the door. He was good looking in a somewhat shrewd and cynical way. "I was waiting for Consuela to be free." His speech was slightly slurred and his red-rimmed eyes were roving speculatively over her body. "But I'll pay five hundred dollars for your favors."

"Get out, Latham. You're drunk."

"A thousand dollars," he said.

"Sebastian will kill you."

"Sebastian isn't coming back to you, Garnet. He told me before he left if Emily would take him back he would swear on his mother's grave never to see you again." He advanced toward her.

Garnet tried to dart past him, but he caught her. He laughed softly as his arms went around her and his hands found her breasts.

She struggled and her dress tore. She broke free and sprang backward, her eyes searching the room for a weapon. *Cassie, for God's sake, come back!* Garnet picked up the paperweight on the desk and hurled it at him, but he ducked and it crashed harmlessly against the wall.

No use screaming—between the soundproofed walls, the music, and the carnal sounds from the other rooms, no one would notice. Garnet picked up a vase and flung it as he came toward her again. The vase broke over his upraised arm and the sharp pain made him curse. He slapped her and her face jerked backward under the impact. She pounded at his chest with her fists. They both crashed to the floor, panting.

His face was just above hers, eyes hooded, and his erect masculinity strained against her thigh. Slowly his mouth came down on hers and his hand closed over her breast. She lifted her hands to push him away, but it was too late. Her own treacherous body was responding to him, seeking release from the tension and loneliness of the long, deprived months.

When he began to slide her dress down, she raised up her hips to help him. By the time he had removed her pantalettes and was beginning to undress himself, they were both staring worldlessly at each other. Neither noticed as the door opened soundlessly and Cassie looked in briefly before withdrawing.

Garnet looked at his naked body, the hard chest, well-muscled thighs, and erect manhood. She did not

253

see his face, only his body. Her own need was a tightly coiled spring in her pelvis and throbbing nipples. Her hand reached up to touch his organ, to bring it to her lips.

He pulled away after a moment, bent to kiss her breasts, to move to her inner thighs, to send his tongue seeking her sweet, musky warmth. Then his hands were under her and he was lifting her to meet his thrusts as he entered her and drove deeply, twisting and turning. She was moaning, writhing, arching her back to seek even deeper sensations.

The moment her climax shuddered away from her, she felt shame, excruciatingly, humiliatingly. Latham Winfield meant nothing to her; he represented only a body to serve a passing need, an appetite to be appeased. He was no more important than the meat she had eaten for dinner. She turned her face away and did not look at him as he got up stiffly, muttering something about next time they should have a bed.

"Just go," Garnet said, her voice muffled in her tangled hair. She lay where she was, naked and shivering, until she heard the door close. She was pulling on her torn dress when Cassie returned.

"Don't say anything," Garnet said sharply.

"I brought the wig and veil. You still want to go downstairs?" Cassie asked gently.

"No. I'm going home." Garnet snatched up her black shawl and fled through the rear door.

Cassie stood watching the closed door for a moment and a tear slid down her rouged cheek. A generous number of twenty-dollar bills were stacked neatly on the table near the door.

Out in the street Garnet ran blindly, ignoring the men who called after her. At the corner she paused to catch her breath as a group of sailors made their way up the hill from the wharf. She did not look at them as a drunken voice hailed her from the direction of the Red Garter. "Wait! What you running from Cassie's place for? Come on back, honey, I'll take care of you."

A miner, staggering and leering, caught up with her. His arm went about her waist.

All of her shame and anger—at herself, at the world —were in the blow she gave him. He reeled into the street with a howl of pain.

The next moment Garnet was surrounded by a laughing crowd of sailors. "A hundred dollars on the redhead!" one shouted. "She'll lick him easy! Go on, girlie, hit him again!"

The miner said hastily, "I don't want trouble with you men. She just came a-running out of the Red Garter. I was looking for some fun, that's all." He backed away nervously.

"Garnet—" a voice said behind her.

She turned and met the wolf-red stare of Erik Gunnar. "The Red Garter . . . I've heard of it. That where you sell it now?" he asked.

Huddled beneath her black shawl in a dimly lit waterfront tavern, Garnet said again, "Please, Erik, don't ask this of me."

"She's my daughter, too," he said. "Just let me meet her. I swear I won't tell her who I am." He drained his glass. "Though why the hell she should be more ashamed of having me for a father than you for a mother is beyond me. I may be an ex-convict and a lowdown sailorman, but her mother's a whore at the Red Garter."

"She doesn't know that . . . I mean, I'm not a whore there—I own half-interest in the place. But I've kept in the background. No one knows. Cerise goes to a private school—she's invited to all the best homes in the city. Erik, you want her to be a lady, don't you? She's so pretty and bright, she can be anything she wants to be. Please don't spoil it all for her."

"I just want to see her." He caught her wrist across the table, holding it in his knotted fingers. "You can tell her I'm an old friend. Bring her to one of the restaurants tomorrow." His fingers moved over her slender wrist. "You haven't lost your looks, Garnet. What happened to Balmain—he walk out on you?"

"No," she said quickly. "He's away on a voyage."

He laughed softly. "He walked out on you. That's why you're a silent partner at the Red Garter. Besides, that clipper of his was beating down the coast about the same time my whaler reached the bay."

"The *Monarch Butterfly?*" Garnet asked, her heart leaping.

"The very same. If he's aboard her, he's home by now. We docked this afternoon."

Garnet was on her feet, jerking her hand free of his grasp.

"You bring my daughter to the Blue Dolphin Café tomorrow at noon—you hear?" he called after her.

Sebastian was not at her house. Garnet awakened Fern and then shook the sleeping Cerise. He must have gone directly to Mariner's Castle, she thought. Was Emily with him?

"Wake up, baby," she said to her daughter. "Come on, you're going to spend a couple of days in Monterey."

Fern came into the room, carrying a valise. "You want me to pack for all of us, Miz Garnet?" she asked sleepily.

"No. Just the children and yourself. I want you to take them down to Monterey on the first stage heading south. It's almost dawn, and I think there's one at seven. Remember Consuela—the Mexican girl who worked for us when we first opened? She married a man from Monterey. Tell her I want you and the children out of the way for a few days; there may be trouble here."

Fern's eyes widened in alarm. "Then I'll deliver the chillun and come back."

Garnet smiled tiredly and patted Fern's arm. "No, you stay with the children. I can take care of myself."

She watched the stagecoach leave, waving good-bye until it was out of sight, then walked slowly in the direction of the waterfront.

The *Monarch Butterfly* stood out among the other ships at anchor like a swan among the ducks. She was a beautiful vessel, with her graceful lines, masts, and spars etched against a silver daybreak. The delicate prow thrust forward as though impatient to conquer new oceans. For a moment Garnet wished she could reverse roles with Sebastian. She would sweep him aboard the clipper and sail away with him, never to return.

The first officer was coming down the gangplank when Garnet called to him. "Is your captain aboard?" The man turned to look at her. "Cap'n Styles? No, ma'am. He went ashore."

"Styles? Oh . . . Mr. Balmain didn't sail with you, then?"

The first officer shook his head. "No, ma'am. Mr. Balmain is the owner—he has never sailed with us. I did hear he brought the first of his clippers around the Horn himself—but he's never sailed on the *Butterfly*."

Garnet's shoulders slumped and she sighed a despairing sigh as she retraced her footsteps. Before she crawled wearily into her bed, she spoke to Hwui, the Chinese handyman who came in to help Fern. "I want you to watch a man for me. His name is Erik Gunnar. I don't know where he's staying, but you can find him. He came in on a whaler. He's big and bearded and has strange red-brown eyes. Give him this." She handed him a note stating briefly that she and Cerise were leaving San Francisco. "I want to know the minute he leaves town."

The days passed nervously. Garnet did not dare leave the house for fear of running into Gunnar. At length Cassie sent her a message asking why she had not been to the Red Garter. Garnet waited for Hwui to make his daily visit and report on the whereabouts of Gunnar, and when the man told her in his halting English Gunnar had been staying aboard his ship making ready to sail, she decided to visit Cassie.

She did not notice the dark figure detach himself from the shadowed vantage point across the street as she alighted from her buggy at the kitchen entrance to the Red Garter. The man disappeared quickly in the direction of the waterfront.

Garnet waited in the private room while one of the kitchen helpers went to announce her arrival to Cassie. A few minutes later Cassie burst into the room. "My God, Garnet—why did you come here now?" she demanded breathlessly.

"What kind of greeting is that? You sent me a message—"

"But *he's* downstairs!"

"Erik?"

Cassie looked blank. "No, not Erik. *Sebastian!*"

Garnet collapsed weakly into the nearest chair. "But —I went to the *Monarch Butterfly* and they said he wasn't on it."

"He wasn't. He came in on a brig as a crewman."

"Did he ask for me, Cassie? You didn't tell him I come here—I own the place?"

"Relax, honey. He just came in as a customer. He ate in the restaurant and now he's in the bar, drinking and watching the show."

"He's alone?"

"Yes."

"He didn't come to my house," Garnet said heavily. "He came here. . . ." An unsettling thought crossed her mind. "Emily . . . ?"

"She couldn't have come back with him," Cassie said, "or else he would be at Mariner's Castle—not here."

"I mustn't let him see me here—I'll go home, wait for him there."

Cassie caught her arm. "Garnet, he isn't coming back to you. Accept it. Go away somewhere—do anything, but don't go and sit waiting for him when he won't come."

There was an urgent tapping at the door and the two women exchanged startled glances. The staff of the Red Garter had strict instructions never to interrupt Cassie when she disappeared into this room.

Cassie opened the door a crack and looked into the

frightened eyes of one of the girls. "There's trouble downstairs. I thought you should know."

"Let the bouncers handle it."

"I don't think they can . . . it's that big sailor . . . Latham Winfield pulled a gun on him."

Cassie felt the door wrenched from her hand as Garnet sprang forward with a cry of dismay on her lips. "What happened?"

The girl looked from Cassie to Garnet. "Winfield is drunk . . . he said something—very loudly—about spending the night with the choicest piece of . . . you know . . . we had. Next minute the big sailor laid him flat on his back and Winfield pulled a gun. The big sailor knocked out the two bouncers and everyone is yelling and screaming and trying to hide. . . ."

"Stay here, Garnet. I'll handle it," Cassie said.

But Garnet was already pushing past them and hurrying down the wide staircase to the scene of confusion below.

Most of the patrons and girls had cleared a wide area for the two men. Sebastian stood amid splintered tables, glaring down at Latham Winfield, who still lay on the floor, his pearl-handled revolver pointed at Sebastian's chest. Draped over the bar were the two bouncers.

"You drunken, lying bastard . . . put the gun down and get up. I'm going to teach you . . ." Sebastian shouted.

"I'll put the gun down, Sebastian—when you calm down. How the hell did I know you were here when I asked for Garnet?" Winfield made no move to rise. "I tell you she's one of the whores here!" He looked up and saw Garnet coming down the staircase. In the sudden hush that fell, Sebastian turned and saw her, too.

Garnet's hand gripped the banister as Sebastian's stricken eyes met hers. His mouth opened slightly and his fists clenched and unclenched at his sides. He stared at her, disbelievingly, blinking as though to make her image fade from view.

She found her voice at last. "Sebastian . . . it isn't what you think . . ."

His eyes were torn from her in a slow and painful gesture. His massive shoulders rose and fell in resignation as he turned to offer his hand to Latham Winfield. Pulling him to his feet, Sebastian said, "I'm sorry, Latham. I shouldn't hit a man for telling the truth." He turned and strode from the room, crashing through the doors into the street.

Garnet hesitated only a split-second, then hurried after him. She caught up with him just beyond the canopied entrance.

"Sebastian—wait. Aren't you even going to let me say a word in my own defense?" She was breathing rapidly.

He turned and looked at her with dull eyes. "You don't have to defend yourself to me, Garnet. I'm a sinner myself."

She searched his face for a moment, seeking something there she could not find. Then her eyelids fluttered once and her own eyes were opaque. *Save your pride. It will be worse if you beg and plead . . . don't grovel. Don't let him know you won't be able to live without him . . . he'll feel pity and guilt but it won't change anything. At least keep your pride intact.*

"Is it all over between us, Sebastian?" she asked quietly.

"I don't know, Garnet. I need to be at sea for a while. Get things squared away in my own mind. I'll be taking the *Monarch Butterfly* out, soon as I find a cargo or some passengers."

"You didn't find Emily, or your son?"

"No. But it's not them I'm sailing in search of. Reckon I'm looking for myself."

She drew a deep breath and her chin went up. "Good luck, then. Stop by and see me if you ever come back this way." She turned and walked back into the Red Garter with a slow, hip-swinging walk.

Sebastian watched her go, grinning faintly and shaking his head. *What a woman!* She didn't give a damn about him or any other man. Sebastian envied her cool acceptance of the fleeting nature of human attachments. He would miss her desperately, long for her caress as much as he longed for Emily's serene and graceful presence in his life. Garnet, Garnet . . . if it had been just one man, he thought; but a whorehouse. . . . Ah, well, the gods knew how to punish a man for his misdeeds.

In the shadows, the red stare of Erik Gunnar was fixed on Sebastian's back. Gunnar motioned for the sailor at his side to keep silent.

Gunnar had been summoned when the man he had sent to watch the Red Garter had come to report that Garnet was there. Gunnar had not expected the scene that followed. He had been at the door when he heard Sebastian bellow like a wounded moose.

Gunnar smiled grimly. Garnet and his daughter would keep. This was too good an opportunity to miss. Balmain alone on a misty street. No powerful Chinese servant or friends nearby. He nodded to the man at his side and they moved forward on silent feet.

Sebastian did not feel the blow to his skull that felled him. Lights exploded in his head and then he was in a black void.

---- ·◄{ **CHAPTER 24** }►·-

The hard-eyed skipper looked at Sebastian slyly and gestured toward the papers in front of him. "Your mark's on there. You were drunk when you signed on; that's why you don't remember. Might as well make the best of it."

"If I walk the same deck as Gunnar, one of us will be a dead man before the voyage is over," Sebastian said.

"What if I make you second mate? Seems a pity to waste all your experience. Food will be beter than in the fo'c'sle, and Mr. Gunnar will have to work with you. Look, Balmain, this is a whaler, and you won't see a mainland port again for a couple of years. Might as well be one of my mates and get a bigger share of the profits."

Sebastian stared out of the porthole at the blue-green swells of the Pacific. "The thought of killing those gentle beasts turns my stomach."

The skipper shrugged indifferently. "You'll get used to it."

In front of skipper and crew, Gunnar and Balmain maintained a curt and uneasy truce. In private, their enmity was fed by their inability to give rein to their lust for blood. Sebastian made his position clear during the first meal they shared in the officers' saloon. "There'll be no beating or flogging the men."

Gunnar's crafty red stare went over Sebastian carefully. "You're too soft, Balmain. Been ashore too long. Women will do that to a man, 'specially a whore. Wears a man out."

Sebastian's hand tightened around the tin mug of coffee he was holding and the metal bent in his grasp. He ignored the hot liquid that ran over his fingers. "I was at the Red Garter myself—the night before you. The stowaway is as hot-blooded as ever."

"Shut your filthy mouth, or, by God, I'll shut it for you."

"Why don't you try?" Gunnar invited softly. "And see how fast Mr. Second Mate Balmain is put back where he belongs—in the fo'c'sle. You're not on your navy ship now with your officer's braid, Balmain. Remember that. And before we're done, you're going to have a taste of what I went through. You got any idea what it's like to spend years of your life locked up? Bad enough for a lubber—but for a sailor it's a living death. Gives a man time to think what he'd do to the one who put him away." Gunnar laughed aloud. "You think I brought you aboard just for the pleasure of setting about you with a rope or my fists? Hell, no, Balmain. That isn't the plan at all."

Sebastian ignored him. He bit into a dry biscuit and chewed savagely.

Nothing had changed, he thought despairingly as the days passed. Crewmen were still at the mercy of brutal officers, and the few half-hearted laws that had been passed ashore for the protection of sailors were largely ignored at sea. As the small vessel sailed southward in search of whales, Gunnar's orders were increasingly punctuated by blows. Before long he was carrying a knotted rope at all times.

Skipper and crew were on edge as the ship failed to find any prey. The captain considered putting back into the Sandwich Isles for fresh water when they were caught in a storm. Giant swells tossed the small whaler about helplessly for nearly a week as the men, drenched and battered from flailing canvas and splintered yards, fought to keep her afloat. By the time the violence of the elements abated, the ship was hopelessly off course.

Cursing and pounding his fists, Gunnar strode about the deck, driving the exhausted men to make the necessary repairs and replace tattered canvas. Coming up on deck one morning, Sebastian found Gunnar had brought out a cat-o'-nine-tails and was flogging the youngest crewman.

Seizing the cat from Gunnar, Sebastian flung it overboard, then turned to face the angry red stare. "This time there'll be no mates to help you, Gunnar. You men over there—get to the skipper's cabin and lock him in. Keep him there," he ordered. "Nor a skipper with a pistol at my head," he added as Gunnar sprang at him.

They were both older, slower, but the fight was as vicious as any they had had in the past. After a time Sebastian was no longer aware of the pain when Gunnar hit him, or of his own satisfaction as his fist connected with flesh and bone. They were both bleeding and panting.

Swinging, grappling, charging one another, grunting with pain and gasping with fury, neither knew how much time passed. Then all at once Sebastian realized that Gunnar was down on the deck and he was sitting on his chest, hands on his throat. He saw the bulging red eyes as the crewmen yelled, "Kill the bastard, Balmain . . . go on, kill him!"

Almost at the same instant, the shout came from the masthead, "Land, ho!"

Sebastian hesitated, then released his grip and Gunnar's head rolled limply. "You had enough?" Sebastian asked, panting.

Gunnar nodded, his eyes glazed.

"No more floggings or beatings?"

Gunnar shook his head weakly.

Sebastian got up slowly and went to the rail. On the horizon was a small deserted atoll. There were many such islands in the Pacific. Most were far from shipping lanes, and vessels would come upon them only when blown off course, as they had been. Sebastian walked, in an elated daze of victory, toward the skipper's cabin. He could taste blood in his mouth, but Gunnar had been beaten and humbled.

The captain regarded him coldly when the cabin door was unlocked. "You realize what you've done? You've ruined the discipline of the ship. I should have left you in the fo'c'sle. This is the thanks I get. You've destroyed my first mate."

"Then make me first mate," Sebastian said.

The captain's eyes flickered over him. "I'll think about it. Meantime, put a boat over the side and go and see if there's water on that island."

At high tide the atoll was barely a mile across. A barren volcanic island devoid of life, despite the freshwater spring in the small central valley. The men who dragged the boat up on the black cinder beach and filled water barrels were glad to return to the ship.

From the captain's cabin, Gunnar watched the men rowing back toward the ship. One eye was closed and he held a blood-soaked rag to his nose. "That's your answer, then," he said to the skipper. "You either string him up or we maroon him on that island." Funny how things worked out, he thought. It had always been his plan to give Balmain a taste of imprisonment.

Shanghaiing him aboard the whaler had merely been the means to transport him to South America, where it was easy to get a man thrown in jail.

"He could be picked up—eventually," the skipper said. "God, what isolation . . . there isn't even a tree on that bit of land."

"Probably don't get a chance to grow, with the winds here. Still, there's fresh water, and he can fish in the sea. And you know as well as I do that it isn't likely another ship will find that small bit of land."

"What about the crew? They like him."

"Break out the pistols. They'll soon change their minds about whose side they're on."

The skipper looked again at the bleak atoll. "He'll probably go mad, after a time."

Sebastian did not go mad. He survived. But the year he spent on the small island, alone, filled him with a need for revenge that blotted out all other thoughts from his mind.

When at last a ship was blown off course and he was picked up, he could think of nothing but finding Erik Gunnar. Emily, Garnet, and his sons by them were pushed into the back of his mind by the all-consuming hatred of the man who had condemned him to a living death.

The ship that picked him up was bound for Valparaiso, and from there he took another ship to New York. Ned greeted him as though he had been resurrected from the dead, but he had gloomy news. The Balmain Shipping Company was bankrupt.

"There was nothing else for it. I couldn't get cargoes and I couldn't get crews. The creditors moved in and sold all our ships—everything. All except the *Monarch Butterfly*—she came in from her last voyage so badly damaged she was declared unseaworthy. She's in a yard in Boston. They'll decide whether to have her broken up for salvage or try to repair her—then the creditors get her, too."

"No, they don't," Sebastian said quietly. "I do."

"You can't—even if we repair her and you get her

out to sea, you'd be seized the minute you entered any American port."

"Then I'll steer clear of American ports until I've raised enough money to buy her back legally . . . aye, and maybe pay off the rest of our debts. Now I want you to find out where a certain whaler is. . . ."

Ned waited until the repairs to the *Monarch Butterfly* were complete before he took news of the whaler and Gunnar to Sebastian.

"She was lost with all hands," he said. "But Gunnar wasn't aboard. Last anyone heard of him, he was in the China seas."

Ned did not meet Sebastian's eye. It was only a small lie, after all. Gunnar was on another whaler, in the Pacific. But Sebastian was less likely to lose the *Monarch Butterfly* if he sailed the China seas . . . and while he had the clipper, there was always the chance the Balmain Shipping Company would regain its former glory. Ned intensely disliked his reduced status in the world.

--✠{ CHAPTER 25 }✠--

"They are magnificent," Emily breathed. She leaned forward, her dark eyes glowing with admiration as the shining bodies of the dancers leaped and twirled, fiery torches brushing perilously close to bare bronze flesh.

The setting sun blazed gold and red and the silhouetted coconut palms were graceful ballerinas against an aquamarine sky and darker sea.

Behind the men, the grass-skirted *wahines,* naked above the waist, swayed sensuously. Flower garlands swung seductively, revealing firm young breasts, while bare feet, ankles encircled by flowers, moved soundlessly on the black sand of the volcanic beach. Their hands told the story of the dance, while their hips told a story as old as humanity.

"Civilized savages," Cyril whispered. "Compassionate barbarians. They are a social contradiction. Intelligent, yet illiterate. Fierce warriors who deck themselves with flowers."

"Emelē," the small boy at her side said, pronouncing her name *eh-me-LEH*. "See, Emelē." He pointed as the leader of the troupe of dancers sprang into the center of the group brandishing an enormous curved sword. She jumped, pretending to be startled by the flashing blade of the great knife, and the boy laughed and clapped his hands in glee.

His name was Kekoa, and he had moved into their grass shack along with his older sister, Luana. Cyril had tried to buy, or at least rent, the shack from its owners, the parents of Kekoa and Luana and several other children. They had all been puzzled by his offer of money, shrugged, and grinned broadly, then dissolved into giggles as they set about building another shack for themselves so the *haoles* might have somewhere to live.

When two of the children moved in with Emily and Cyril and the baby, everyone seemed to accept the arrangement. Emily had Luana to help care for Noah, and Kekoa became Cyril's devoted shadow. On Sundays he would accompany them across the island to the missionary's chapel, where Cyril would play the piano for the congregation.

Honolulu was growing into an attractive town, but Cyril and Emily rarely left the pleasant beach where, like the islanders, they lived on the bounty provided by the sea and the verdant land.

At dusk on many evenings, the blowing of the conch shell and lighting of the torches signaled that the feasting was about to begin, and Emily and Cyril were always invited. After two years on the island of Oahu, Emily still gazed with awe at those splendid bodies and repeated, "They are magnificent!"

Noah ran as wild and free as the island children, unfettered by clothing or shoes in the gentle climate. His small body was tanned and his hair was black as night. With his dark eyes, he was almost indistinguishable from the other children until one noticed the more delicate contours of the face and the retroussé nose.

Noah could already swim and ride the great breakers beyond the coral reef with practiced ease, thanks to Kekoa, but it was clear he had inherited from his mother her love of music. For all his tender years, he would sit enraptured when Cyril played the piano, and nothing could keep the child from the throbbing drums and rhythmic dancing of the *luaus*. Music was the first passion of his life.

Cyril was having a piano sent from the mainland, but it seemed it would never arrive, so long was it taking. Meantime, they lingered in the chapel after services and Cyril taught Noah simple scales and sonatinas. Cyril had devised a way of using his right palm and the edge of his hand to strike notes in place of his missing fingers.

There was a chorus of sighs from the waiting diners at the present *luau* as the underground oven was opened. The pig that had been slowly roasting since dawn was carefully lifted out by a team of cooks. The *ti* leaves were unwrapped and the aroma of the meat brought an appreciative murmur from the hungry dancers and spectators. Lava rocks had been placed in the cavity of the pig and the meat was so tender it fell into pieces as the *ti* leaves were peeled away.

Along with the roast pork was a great variety of fish, shellfish, fruit, vegetables, and the native dish called *poi*, which Emily found a little bland. She and Cyril had enjoyed almost perfect health since their arrival, and it seemed there had never been a time of winter chills and bronchial coughs for either of them.

Days drifted away languorously. The soothing breath of the tradewinds whispered scented melodies. The sea was always warm. Long hours to remember half-forgotten poems and lovely music were theirs. The idyll was perfect in every detail.

"If you eat too much, you'll get as fat as the royal

women and I shall lose you to a great big Kanaka war-rior," Cyril teased as Emily fell ravenously upon the food. The mature island women were of statuesque proportions and were much in demand as wives to the even larger men. Many of the men were close to seven feet tall, and their wives only slightly shorter.

Emily smiled and looked around for Noah. He was squatting in front of a great pile of food and happily pushing it into his mouth with his fingers.

"Are we going to leave with Reverend Hawkins in the morning?" Emily asked.

They had been planning to explore the other islands for some time. Now one of the missionaries was to be taken by outrigger canoe to Maui, and they seized upon this opportunity to join him.

"Yes, so please don't overtire yourself tonight," Cyril said. "Kekoa is going with us, by the way."

"Do you suppose that is news to me?" Emily laughed. "I don't believe I've seen you without Kekoa in tow since we landed on your island paradise."

Kekoa grinned. He was nearly as tall as Cyril, despite his tender years, which he estimated as ten or so. The islanders were vague about their age. Cyril fondly ruffled the boy's curly dark hair.

Cyril loved the boy as a son, Emily knew, lavishing as much affection and attention upon him as on Noah.

There had been a time, shortly after Kekoa and Luana moved in with them, that Emily had watched the lovely island girl with some dismay. Luana fluttered her lustrous lashes at Cyril and the invitation in her eyes was unmistakable.

The islanders wore clothing more as a form of adornment than for either protection or modesty, and Luana's golden breasts were frequently glimpsed behind the flower *lei*. Her hair hung like a sleek black waterfall to her waist and she always wore a blossom near her right ear, which Emily learned meant that she was un-attached and looking for a man.

In the settlements now sternly under the influence of missionaries, the women were beginning to wear voluminous dresses to cover their bodies, and their casual enjoyment of sex was discouraged; but the missionaries could not be everywhere at all times. On this side of the island, the young missionary Josiah Hawkins had fought a losing battle with the comfort of near-naked bodies and the playful pleasures of the flesh.

Because of Josiah's failure to convince his flock of the folly of their ways, he was now to be sent to the island of Maui, and a more experienced minister was to take his place.

Josiah's young wife had died on the long voyage to the islands, and Emily felt that perhaps his grief had caused him to neglect his duties. She had hoped when he arrived that he would persuade the women—especially Luana—to wear clothes. The girl would lean seductively over Cyril when she served his food and had more than once removed all of her scant clothing in his presence to stroll down to the beach for her daily swim.

At last Emily could not bear the tension any longer. She had taken Cyril's hand and led him to a secluded grove where a waterfall cascaded diamond-bright over dark lava rocks, falling into a clear lagoon. All around them the lush growth of trees, plants, and vines whispered the siren song of the island paradise. The air was fragrant with the perfume of hibiscus, orchids, and plumerias.

"What is it, dearest one?" Cyril asked, sensing her agitation. "Aren't you happy here?"

Emily's eyes did not meet his as she absently plucked a plumeria blossom, then dropped it as though it were a hot coal when she remembered the islanders used plumerias only for burials.

"It's all like a beautiful dream," she whispered, "that is so perfect I am afraid it cannot last. I shall awaken and it will have dissolved with the dawn."

Cyril picked up her hand, pressed it to his lips, and held it imprisoned against his heart. "What is troubling you, dear heart? It is more than the fear that happiness cannot last."

Emily could feel her color rising, but she knew she must not lose this opportunity. "Cyril . . . the girl, Luana—she's beautiful, isn't she?"

"Yes," Cyril agreed, puzzled. "And so is her brother, Kekoa. Are you still worried that we are somehow exploiting them? They are free to leave, you know . . . but I do believe they enjoy being with us—learning from us, as we learn from them."

"Luana . . . looks at you with more than friendship in her eyes." Emily's blush now stained her cheeks. "Cyril, my dearest, I could not bear to share your mind with another woman. But I was married, and I know that men need physical release . . . oh, dear. I am trying to tell you that it's all right . . . if you and Luana—"

His fingers went under her chin, lifting her face so that their eyes met. "I do not lust after Luana's body— or that of any other woman, Emily," he said quietly. A small muscle twitched in his cheek and his eyes seemed to have collapsed into their shadowed sockets. Emily saw for one frightening second an unbearable longing in the depths of his gaze that tugged at some answering chord deep in her own consciousness.

He let out his breath slowly, his fingers tracing the line of her cheek, following the marble whiteness of her throat. "When we first came here, there were nights when I walked the beach while you slept, Emily, tortured by longings I knew could never be fulfilled. When Josiah arrived, I even talked with him about overcoming temptation. Having lost his wife, he, too, was troubled by the sensual quality of the very air here. But we both agreed that just as Roman Catholic priests take a vow of chastity and manage to live their lives removed from the pleasures of the flesh, so, too, could we. I told him that we were blood-related and could hope for no more than a union of mind and spirit and soul."

Emily was crying, silent sobs shaking her narrow shoulders, tears scalding her eyes that were only a misting of dew compared to the terrible weeping of her heart.

They never spoke of the incident again, but as Luana's grasp of English improved, the girl was frankly curious about the "marriage" of two people who did not share a bed. Luana assumed, as did everyone else, that

271

Cyril and Emily were man and wife and Noah was their son.

"Eh-me-LEH . . . you get the insides sick when you birth the child?" Luana asked one day when Cyril had gone down to the beach to watch the island men ride the big winter surf on their boards. *"Maopopo ia 'oe?"* she added, frowning. "Why don't you sleep with your man?"

Emily blushed. "Luana . . . he is not my man in the sense you mean," she said slowly and carefully. "We are half-brother and half-sister. We had the same father."

Luana still gazed blankly. "You don't love him?"

"I love him with all of my heart," Emily declared.

"Then why don't you sleep with him?"

"I told you . . . we are half-brother and half-sister."

"I do not understand," Luana said, shaking her head. "The royal kings and queens of our islands always marry with brothers and sisters to keep the line pure."

Emily's fingers flew to her hair and she began to tie tight little knots. "It is forbidden to us, Luana. What you call a *kapu*. It is a *haole kapu*."

"Haoles are strange people," Luana said, genuine puzzlement in her dusky eyes. She unwrapped the short-skirted *pau* she wore and added, "I'll go and watch the surfboards now." She grinned impishly. "Maybe some fine fellow will give me a ride."

Emily watched the girl's naked body disappear down the palm-lined pathway to the beach. No doubt some fine fellow would be very happy to share his board with Luana. The boards were large and tremendously heavy, and only the biggest and burliest men were able to carry them to the beach and paddle out to catch the waves.

That evening the Reverend Josiah Hawkins had come to the *luau* and announced he was to be sent to the island of Maui.

"My bishop believes an older and more experienced man is needed here," Josiah told them. He was blond, with pink cheeks that had repeatedly blistered in the tropical sun, despite the wide-brimmed hat he always wore. "But I suspect that I offended some of our people in Honolulu and my banishment is more the result of that."

"Oh? What did you do?" Cyril asked, taking a bite of the *mahi mahi* fish and smiling rapturously at its delicate flavor. "Did you suggest your God-fearing friends stop meddling in island affairs? Point out the ridiculous costumes they insist be worn are ugly and cumbersome and totally unnecessary in this climate?"

"Or, perhaps," Emily put in, leaning forward, "you told them that the sailors who come thronging ashore from the whalers should not behave in such a reprehensible fashion?"

Josiah sighed. "What the white man hath wrought here does seem to be an offense to both God and the native. But no . . . actually, I protested the fact that the Christian Chinese are not allowed to attend services."

"Are they not?" Cyril asked in surprise. The Chinese had been imported to work on the sugar plantations, Cyril knew, and were on the islands on a five-year contract.

"It isn't the fact they are Chinese," Josiah said, "but that there is sickness among them. The sick were turned away from the chapel for fear of their infecting others in the congregation."

"Frankly, I can understand that concern," Cyril said. "Both the Caucasians and the Orientals have brought so much sickness to these islands, and the natives have no immunity."

"I heard there had been rampant sickness among the Chinese," Emily said. "Is it smallpox again?"

"The islanders call it *mai pake*—the Chinese disease," Josiah replied, lowering his voice. "But the missionaries fear it is a disease well known in biblical times."

"Good God," Cyril said.

"I don't understand, which of the ancient diseases do you mean?" Emily asked, glancing from one grave face to the other.

273

Josiah hesitated a second and looked over his shoulder cautiously before answering. "Leprosy."

Everyone was up early preparing to sail to Maui. All of Kekoa and Luana's relatives gathered on the beach for *alohas*. Flower *leis* were exchanged and the gods were called upon to watch over the travelers. Even the *haole* god was urged to bring their loved ones safely home again.

The outrigger canoe had been at sea for only a few hours when a sudden squall darkened the skies and warm tropical rain began to fall. The rugged islanders kept the outrigger moving over the increasingly surging swells for a time, but then a strong gust of wind caught them and they were hurtled across the foaming surface of the ocean, propelled by unseen currents.

Cyril gathered Emily and Noah into his arms, draping his coat around them. The islanders, who were constantly in and out of the water, ignored the rain.

"We will be blown off course," Cyril told Josiah. "They will not fight the surge of wind and current now, but as soon as the squall passes, they will again head for Maui."

Josiah nodded, but his face was pale green and his lips moved in silent prayer.

As capriciously as the wind had risen, it dashed across the surface of the sea and disappeared. Gradually the swells diminished and the rain abated to a light drizzle. An island loomed ahead.

A bleak peninsula, backed by forbidding mountains, appeared through the misty rain. Silence fell upon everyone in the outrigger, even the children.

Emily's arms tightened about Noah. She stared at the gloomy land mass, reluctantly mesmerized. "What a dreadfully lonely place," she whispered, as though afraid the sound of her voice would disturb the deserted shore. "So . . . desperately sad. Which island is that?"

Cyril shivered visibly and drew her closer, sharing her sense of foreboding. "Molokai." His voice cracked on the word, and he said again, "Molokai . . . we shan't be stopping here. As you can see, it is difficult to land on the peninsula because of the rough surf."

They could see that the peninsula jutting into the ocean was battered on three sides by stormy surf, while the south side of the island was walled off by towering mountains that were too sheer to climb. It was a place of total isolation.

"*Pōloli au,*" Noah said, breaking the spell.

"In English, please, dear," Emily insisted.

Cyril laughed and ruffled Noah's black hair. "He says he is hungry. Kekoa, what did you bring to eat?"

Kekoa fumbled in his pack. He held up a ripe yellow mango and sliced it neatly in two, despite the violently rocking canoe. He and Noah devoured the fruit, juices running down their chins. The Reverend Josiah Hawkins rolled his eyes toward the heavens and clung to the side of the outrigger.

If Molokai had appeared forbidding, the island of Maui was even more abundantly fertile than their own island of Oahu.

Divided in two parts by an isthmus, Maui was a study in contrasts of climate and vegetation. It was said to be the home of Pele, the fire goddess, who had, according to island myth, fought a losing battle with the goddess of the sea. The giant crater Haleakala was a desolate, burned-out reminder of that clashing of all-powerful gods. The ancient lava flows to the sea were now covered with trees and flowers. Sugarcane and pineapples had been planted. It was difficult to behold the green profusion of vegetation and remember that Maui had boiled up from beneath the sea, starting life as a barren cinder, black and bare.

Reverend Hawkins was bound for the whaling port of Lahaina, on the leeward side of the island. Emily and Cyril had already decided to stay for a time with the young missionary before sailing on to the big island of Hawaii.

They looked with some trepidation at the bustling town of Lahaina, which was crowded with sailors. Cyril estimated that at least five hundred whaling vessels lay at anchor. Although it was early in the day when they arrived, the streets were filled with drunken and roistering sailors.

"We had better go directly to the mission house," Josiah said, glancing about nervously.

The door of what was apparently a hotel, being built of wood, burst open in front of them. Several sailors reeled into the street. Emily stopped dead in her tracks, her eyes widening with fear as she gazed on a white man with a bushy beard and wild eyes. He was as tall and burly as many of the islanders, and for a moment Cyril thought she was frightened because the whaler was built somewhat like Sebastian, her deserted husband.

"Cyril . . . that man." Emily clutched at his arm to try to get him to detour around the group, who were watching Emily's approach with interest. "It is the same man who broke into our home in San Francisco . . . the one who swore vengeance on Sebastian."

Josiah cleared his throat and adjusted his clerical collar. "If you will allow us to pass," he said to the nearest sailor.

They fell back for the minister, their eyes fixed on the beautiful white woman. Especially the red-hazed eyes of Erik Gunnar, who strove to clear his fogged senses and remember where he had seen that lovely face before.

--*{ **CHAPTER 26** }*--

Rual Wade came storming into the house, blue eyes flashing icy sparks, black mane of hair rearing in every direction.

Garnet looked up from the hem she was pinning on Cerise's new dress and her heart turned over as her son stood with the light behind him in the doorway. He was a young Sebastian in every bulging muscle and craggy plane of his tanned face. He grew more like his father every day.

"He wouldn't let me get my kite," Rual announced angrily. "It was caught in that Monterey pine in front of the house."

"He's been up to Mariner's Castle again, Mother," Cerise said, golden eyes looking disdainfully at her brother's unkempt appearance. "You look as though that big Chinaman dragged *you* through the pine tree."

Garnet straightened up, removing the pin from between her teeth. "I asked you to stay away from that house, Rual."

Rual shrugged, moving his wide shoulders in a gesture so typical of his father that Garnet felt an old pain tug at her heartstrings.

"I can't help it if the wind carries my kite up the hill," Rual said. "I don't understand what right that Chinaman has to keep me away from my father's house."

"It does seem odd that Mr. Tang guards the house, after all this time. Surely Sebastian will never come back," Cerise said. She had stopped calling him "Papa" on the day she broke the china vase over his head. Later Garnet had explained to the two children that Sebastian was Rual's father only.

"Rual, for the last time, stay away from Mariner's Castle," Garnet said.

Cerise said, "I don't see why you're so fascinated with that place, anyway. It's a joke to most people in town. It looks like a sailor's drunken dream of a house."

"It does not!" Rual shouted indignantly. "Anyway, I like it because it's the closest thing to a landlocked ship. If Mother would let me go to sea . . ."

"We'll have no more of that," Garnet said sharply. "You're too young."

"My father was at sea at my age. And I'd think you'd want a sailor in the family, after all the time and money you put into your Ladies' Seamen's Friend Society. If you won't let me go to sea, who in our family will go into your Sailors' Home?" Rual inquired darkly.

Garnet laughed. Three years earlier, in 1857, they had leased the old Mercantile Hotel on Front Street and renamed the building the Mariners' Home, at Garnet's suggestion. The other ladies of the society had at first agreed, since Garnet was their most generous contributor. Later they had tactfully suggested it be renamed the Sailors' Home, to avoid any possible confusion with that strange house . . . Mariner's Castle.

During the empty years following Sebastian's departure, Garnet had worked hard, behind the scenes, to make the Red Garter successful, but it had not been enough to fill the lonely hours. She joined some of the other matrons in forming the Ladies' Aid and Protection Society for the Benefit of Seamen. Since this was immediately confused with the Ladies' Aid, they changed the name to the Ladies' Seamen's Friend Society.

"Is Larry Winfield coming over today?" Garnet asked Cerise.

Cerise frowned. "I hope not. Austin Gentry is coming to take me for a ride."

"They had a fight over her last Saturday," Rual said. "Austin gave Larry a bloody nose."

"They were not fighting over me!" Cerise exclaimed, picking up a cushion to toss at Rual, who dodged it and renewed the attack.

"Yes, they were so—you flirt with both of them. Everyone says you're the worst flirt in town and you'll come to a bad end . . ."

"That's enough," Garnet said, but a smile plucked at the corners of her mouth. "I'm sure they were not fighting over Cerise. Perhaps it was another argument about states' rights. Aren't the Winfields Abolitionists? And don't the Gentrys own slaves back in South Carolina?"

Cerise's honey-colored eyes were carefully disinterested.

Garnet was instantly alert, studying her daughter with a knowing eye. "Cerise, baby, I don't think you should

278

play off one against the other. Larry Winfield is a much better prospect for you. His father is the richest man in town, and Larry's such a sweet boy . . . while that Austin Gentry—I believe the Gentrys only send him to visit the San Francisco branch of the family when he gets into some kind of scrape at home. Honey, he's a wild one—and he's a Southerner and a slave-owner, and there could be a war between the Southern states and the North." There was real fear in Garnet's eyes now.

Rual leaned back in his chair, satisfied that he had diverted his mother's attention from his excursion to Mariner's Castle. He had always been fascinated by the great monstrosity of a house his father had built for the beautiful and mysterious Emily. There were many legends about both the house and Sebastian. He was, some said, searching the world for his lost Emily, doomed like the Flying Dutchman to sail the seas endlessly. But Rual knew his father was at sea simply because that was where he wanted to be.

For Rual's part, he knew he was, as Garnet liked to put it, his father's love-child. She would hear no word of criticism about Sebastian and once had slapped Cerise for making a derogatory remark about sailors in general, and Sebastian in particular.

Rual remembered a black-haired giant who made boats and played with him and taught him to tie knots and the name of each sail aboard every kind of ship. He remembered a deep, rumbling laugh and huge hands with black hairs growing on the backs of them. Hands that were strong, yet soothing. Patient, loving hands, that only once had been used in anger. . . . Rual sometimes had nightmares about the day he had come upon his father choking his mother, because he loved his father, and even that memory could not taint the love and longing for his return.

He had been too young then to understand, but later Cerise told him that Sebastian blamed Garnet for Emily's disappearance.

There had been times . . . not many . . . when, in the heat of a youthful argument, one of their friends had called them ugly names. No one ever repeated this folly.

Rual had learned early in life that his strength exceeded that of all his contemporaries. After a boy had been thrown to the ground and sat upon by Rual, he was not likely to arouse Rual's wrath again.

Cerise was as quick to take offense as her brother, and she could reduce another girl to tears with her barbed tongue. Nor was she above slapping or kicking a boy. Since boys were raised to believe girls were frail and delicate creatures, in constant need of protection, and since it was quite unthinkable to strike one, Cerise usually had the upper hand. Besides, she was the prettiest girl in town, and the most popular . . . and girls who were pretty and popular were allowed an occasional tantrum.

Rual asked Garnet many times what had become of his father. Usually, Garnet's eyes would take on that familiar feline opacity and she would change the subject. Once, however, she said, "Rual . . . you are so like him it frightens me. No, I don't know where he is, and I've never heard from him. I did write to Ned in New York, a year or so after Sebastian sailed away."

She was standing at the window, watching the pale mist creep up the street from the bay.

"Yes, yes," Rual said eagerly. "Did he reply?"

"He said the Balmain Shipping Company was bankrupt. The clippers were sold to pay their creditors . . . all except the *Monarch Butterfly*—because your father arrived in time to slip her out of the harbor before anyone realized what he was going to do. He just disappeared with her."

Rual's blue eyes brightened. "The *Monarch Butterfly* was the most beautiful clipper of all. I remember her —I still dream about her sometimes."

"They believe he took her to the China seas. She couldn't come back to America or she'd be seized to pay debts." *If it weren't for that, he would have come back, at least to see you, my son.*

"Do you think my father ever found them . . . Emily and Noah?" Rual knew he had gone too far. The veil descended over his mother's eyes. "Where is Cerise?"

280

she asked abruptly. "Run and ask Fern if she's in her room."

Garnet lived in daily fear of her daughter's awakening sexuality, recognizing in Cerise her own sensual nature. Garnet worried that Cerise would succumb to temptation before she was safely married. Cerise should have been a boy, Garnet thought, with her quick mind and hot temper and the hidden fires of her sexuality. They were traits that could see a young lady undone.

Cerise was sitting in the fog-shrouded carriage only a short distance from her home, with Austin Gentry's arm about her, her hair in disarray and the buttons on her basque unfastened.

Austin's carrot-colored hair hung thickly about his velvet collar, and his red moustache tickled her nose as he sought to plant a kiss on her elusive lips. He was highly aroused and becoming impatient with her.

"Come on, Cerise, honey, just one little old kiss. Then I'll take you on home." His slow drawl was husky with passion, and his hazel eyes were melting with desire for her.

Cerise had not resisted when he unbuttoned her basque, but she would not allow him to put his hand inside her bodice. She had permitted him to brush her lips lightly with his, but drew back when he tried to press his advantage. "You will take me home this minute, Austin Gentry, or I shall never go riding with you again," she declared. Despite her reprimanding tone, her golden eyes glinted invitingly.

"Honey, baby, sweet thing . . . you know I have to leave San Francisco soon. How can you let me go without one little old kiss? Ah, Cerise, why won't you elope with me? Marry me, darlin' . . . before I die from lovin' you."

Cerise smoothed her unruly red-gold curls and buttoned her basque. She lowered her eyelashes and glanced at him from beneath their gold-tipped fringe. "Perhaps next time you come to San Francisco."

"Hell's bells, Cerise," Austin said in exasperation. "Don't you understand, darlin' . . . there ain't going to be no next time. There's going to be a war, sweet thing, and I'll probably get killed and I'll never know what it's like to love you."

"I thought you loved me now," Cerise teased.

He put his hand on her breast. "You know what I mean, honey."

Cerise moved his hand, but not too quickly.

"Reckon you never did appreciate how hard it was for me to get my family to let me come here. They never did stop regretting that first time they sent me to Uncle Latham when my baby sister was born . . . 'cause after that, all I ever wanted to do was sail on any Winfield or Gentry ship headed this way. Cerise, honey child, you know I've loved you since you were a little girl in a frilly dress, giving me a bloody nose at Larry's party."

Cerise pouted slightly. "But I'm not ready to get married yet. I haven't had any fun."

His eyes lit up mischievously. "Cerise, darlin', you won't know what fun is until you get in bed with me . . . and you can do that legally if you marry me."

"Mother would never allow it," Cerise said lamely. Austin Gentry was the most exciting boy she knew. The combination of long, hard thighs, a rogue's grin, and the flamboyant red hair were irresistible. Then, too, his soft Carolina drawl and impeccable Southern manners charmed every female he met. There were the added allures of vast family wealth, a slightly tarnished reputation with women, and the glamour of being "from out of town."

"I've a mind to kidnap you," he threatened darkly. "Sweep you up on my horse and ride off with you."

Cerise laughed. "All the way to South Carolina?"

"You're a witch, and I declare you'll be the death of me," he said gloomily. "Come on, I'd best take you home before your mother sets about me with a switch. Reckon you'll be sorry you turned me down again, after I'm gone and the war starts and . . ."

"If I hear another word about war, I shall get out of this carriage and walk home," Cerise said. "I never want to hear anyone say 'Abolitionist' or 'states' rights' again as long as I live. What has any of it to do with us here in San Francisco? It's all so far away."

"I'm sorry, darlin'," Austin said quickly, pressing her fingers to his lips.

Inwardly, Cerise groaned. She would have liked nothing better than a swift exchange of ideas on the prospect of war and what could be done to prevent it, but she knew only too well what was expected of her in the way of conversation. She had been well tutored in the art of flirting with young gentlemen.

Austin held her fingers to his lips, thinking that perhaps he was so bewitched by her he could forgo for a little while the pleasure of thrashing Yankee hides in the war that was inevitable.

The men who were captivated by Cerise seldom stopped to consider there were women more beautiful, mor graceful, and infinitely more accommodating than she. Men looked into those wicked honey-colored eyes, sparkling and tempting and promising untold delights with a flutter of incredibly thick and curly eyelashes, and did not see that the nose was a trifle short for beauty, the mouth too wide for modesty, and the chin definitely too stubborn for compliance. When she smiled her teeth were small and white, and enchanting dimples appeared in her cheeks and chin.

As a small child, that smile had saved her from her mother's wrath and caused Sebastian to sigh and say she was making a rod for her own back raising a girl whose willfulness and high spirits would be her downfall.

Garnet privately encouraged her daughter. Cerise would never have to depend on employment or charity for her daily bread if Garnet had anything to say in the matter. From the time Cerise was twelve years old, Garnet began to train her daughter in the delicate art of captivating men. The girl's red-gold hair was treated with coconut oil and brushed to make it shine luxuriously. She was discouraged from eating rich foods which would cause her tiny waist to spread or her delicate complexion to blemish.

When the time came, Cerise would marry the most powerful man in town. She would marry into a family so aristocratic that she would be forever protected from scandal and hardship. She would never have to live as Garnet had lived.

"It's just as easy to love a rich man as a poor man," Garnet told her daughter. Over and over again. But Garnet really meant a powerful man, for Garnet herself was as rich as any man in town.

Cerise enjoyed the company of men, was impatient with the idle gossip of the girls and women she knew, but Garnet warned her repeatedly that men did not like women who were more clever than they. Cerise soon realized that while men did indeed like flighty young girls to speak of nothing but the next party and who was whose sweetheart, married women could and did express their opinions on a variety of subjects.

This was one reason Cerise was seriously considering Austin Gentry's proposal. When she told him she had not yet "had her fun," it was merely the type of remark young men expected from empty-headed misses who didn't know what they really wanted until a man told them. Austin would be an exciting lover, she was sure, but more than that, he would indulge her every whim. However, the overriding reason she wanted to marry Austin was that she felt it imperative to put a great deal of distance between herself and San Francisco.

Cerise had never told her mother of that shocking afternoon she decided she must leave. Cerise had been making an afternoon visit to one of her friends when the man materialized as she was about to get into her buggy.

He was a giant of a man with bushy hair and strangely glowing red-brown eyes, dressed in seamen's clothes and very much under the influence of drink. His hand went to her horse's reins before she could utter a sound. "Cerise . . . Cerise Gunnar? Please—don't be afraid. I'm your father."

She had learned a great deal that afternoon that she

284

wished she could have remained ignorant about. Cerise had always felt slightly superior to Rual, since Garnet had at least been married to *her* father. Garnet always hinted that her father was dead—but there he was, in all his uncouth glory. A whaler in rough clothes who reeked of fish and rum and blood.

Cerise quickly invited him to ride in her buggy before the prying eyes of any of her friends saw her in the company of a staggering, drunken sailor. She listened impatiently when he told of sending her numerous letters and presents over the years. They had undoubtedly been intercepted by her mother.

But the worst revelation was about her mother. Cerise listened with growing horror as her father told her explicitly what kind of woman her mother was.

She protested, "But that was long ago . . . my mother is respectable now. Why, she works hard for the Ladies' Seamen's Friend Society and other charities."

Erik Gunnar laughed coarsely. "I bet she does. It's only fair, right? Give back a bit of the money sailors spend in her whorehouse."

The Red Garter . . . that place whispered about as being the most luxurious den of iniquity in a city of infamous sporting houses. Erik Gunnar swore that Garnet was co-owner of the Red Garter. It was a fact known to every tar who sailed the Pacific. And if the Nob Hill matrons suspected Garnet's connection with the Red Garter, evidently her charitable works and impeccable personal life-style caused them to close their eyes to the source of her considerable wealth.

Cerise had looked into the peculiar red-brown eyes of her father and known he was telling the truth.

"Don't worry," he said, a maudlin tear slipping down his cheek and disappearing into his rum-soaked beard. "I haven't come to make trouble for your mother. I just want you, daughter. I want you to come with me—I've a little house in Lahaina, in the Sandwich Isles. You can live respectably with me, away from your mother's sin . . . maybe even marry one of the missionaries there. But if Garnet tries to stop us . . . well, I'll drag her into the Red Garter and show this town who really runs the place."

Cerise decided at that moment she must marry Austin Gentry and move to the Carolinas with him . . . if not for her own sake, then for the protection of her mother.

⊰ CHAPTER 27 ⊱

The terse announcement that Cerise Gunnar was going to marry Austin Gentry took San Francisco by surprise. Surprise was quickly replaced by glee. That incorrigible flirt was getting her just desserts. The trail of broken hearts she had left in her wake could take satisfaction from the knowledge she was marrying a man as much a philanderer as she was a coquette.

Then, too, the wedding being arranged so quickly—supposedly because Austin Gentry had to return home on account of the political situation in South Carolina —caused some raised eyebrows and speculation. Did she *have* to get married? they wondered.

The latest escapades of that notorious miss were conveyed about town from highest society to the waterfront dregs by the young men who felt ill used by Cerise. Nob Hill matrons heard their sons swear off women for life because of her heartlessness. The ladies of easy virtue on the Barbary Coast often found themselves acting as surrogates for the tantalizing Cerise.

That her career as heart-breaker had been ended by that red-haired rake from South Carolina was indeed good news. It left Larry Winfield and a dozen other eligible young men who had been mooning over her available to the rest of the debutantes.

Garnet had at first refused to give her permission.

286

Cerise looked her mother levelly in the eye and said quietly, "We could have eloped . . . but I know you always wanted to see me married in a church. I've made up my mind, Mother." She paused. "My father came to see me . . . a few weeks ago."

All the breath left Garnet's body and she slumped down in a chair, her green eyes wary as Cerise continued: "He told me all about the Red Garter. It's true, isn't it? You're that awful Madigan woman's partner."

"There's nothing awful about Cassie."

"Oh, Mother! She's the laughingstock of the town. Those gaudy clothes all the same color from bonnet to shoes, and the ridiculous wig and all that face paint and perfume. Even the other madams laugh at her."

"What do you know about madams?" Garnet asked faintly.

"That's what my father said Cassie Madigan is. I suppose you must be, too, if you're her partner." Cerise sat down on the arm of her mother's chair and bent to kiss her mother's pale cheek. "Mother, I don't care. If I'd used my head, I would have realized that all the money you spent to be sure Rual and I grew up among the idle rich . . . and all you've donated to your seamen's charities . . . had to come from somewhere. Personally, I think it's very clever of you to have made so much money from a sporting house." Cerise bit her lip, then began to giggle helplessly.

"It's really funny . . . I suppose that pompous old Judge Winfield and Banker Moffatt and all those pink-cheeked old gentlemen . . . all the time they were probably clients . . ."

"Cerise, stop it," Garnet said, but her own dimples were showing.

"I c-c-can't help it. . . ." Cerise went into gales of laughter.

"You'd better tell me more about your father's visit. Did he make any threats? Did Rual see him?"

Cerise told her mother briefly what had happened, leaving out her father's threat to expose Garnet as co-owner of the Red Garter if Cerise did not go to live with him. "Apparently he's part-owner of a whaler in the Sandwich Isles. Oh, Mother, he was so uncouth . . . how could you have married him? Can you believe it—he wanted me to go and live in Lahaina with him?"

"What did you tell him?"

"That I'd be in school another year and would think about it. Mother, you must come with me to South Carolina when I marry Austin. Rual will surely run away to sea one of these days."

"No!" Garnet said quickly. "I won't leave San Francisco. If you've set your heart on marrying Austin, I won't stop you. But I won't go with you."

Cerise looked at her mother pityingly. "You still think Sebastian will come back, don't you? After all these years, you're still waiting for him to come sailing back to you." Cerise shuddered. "I hope I never fall prey to that kind of obsession. My life is going to be lived by a logical progression of events over which I shall have complete control."

Garnet felt a chill whip icily through her veins as she looked at her daughter. *Surely,* she thought, *I can't have created such a cold and calculating woman. I only meant for her not to be a slave to her emotions, as I've been. . . .*

Cerise was a breathtaking bride. Her oyster lace gown was supported by hoops, and the sixteen-yard skirt was a masterpiece of tiered ruffles, inset with matching satin ribbons to which tiny seed pearls had been attached. The tight-fitting bodice was gossamer-fine lace over satin, delicately embroidered, and long sleeves ballooned out above tight wrists to reveal insets matching those of the skirt. Her sheer veil fell from a headdress of fresh flowers.

Hardly anyone noticed the dozen bridesmaids in their pastel gowns, as all eyes were fixed on the bride, but the men present occasionally stole a glance at the bride's mother. Garnet was lovely, if a trifle pale, in a muted shade of blue that shimmered with green lights when she moved.

Austin Gentry was an exuberant bridegroom who kissed his bride with far too much enthusiasm, considering the packed church and round-eyed minister. As one wag put it later, everyone was afraid for a moment that Austin thought he was supposed to consummate the union on the spot.

Outside the church only Garnet noticed the carriage with the discreetly closed curtains. Garnet felt a pang of guilt, knowing Cassie was behind those curtains, but Cassie had not expected to be invited to the wedding. Later, when the reception was over, Garnet would take her a piece of wedding cake and tell her all the details.

Garnet watched the flaming hair of her son-in-law disappear into the decorated carriage that trailed old shoes. She said a silent prayer for the couple's happiness, but she could not quell the premonition that the first of her daughter's "orderly progression of events" was a mistake for all concerned.

Cerise had to restrain Austin from leaving the reception the moment the cake was cut. As it was, they departed for their hotel suite with unmannerly haste, according to Cerise.

"Sweet thing," Austin said, nibbling her ear, "we surely have better things to do. Sweetheart, baby . . ."

"Open the champagne," Cerise instructed, pushing him away. "I didn't have nearly enough at the reception, and I want to be thoroughly relaxed before we go to bed."

Austin looked at his bride with some dismay. This was hardly the blushing, terrified, about-to-be-deflowered little virgin he expected. She was composed and businesslike to the point of being brisk. A nagging doubt clawed at the back of his mind.

Cerise calmly unpacked her overnight bag as Austin struggled to pop the cork from the champagne. When he approached her with two glasses, sparkling and fizzing in the candlelight, she casually gestured toward the dressing table. "Put mine over there."

Placing both glasses down, he moved closer to lift her hair and kiss the nape of her neck. Slowly the golden eyes turned to meet his, reflecting the same wicked promise as the champagne. "You can help me with my hooks. Then I'm going behind that screen to finish undressing. I can't imagine anything uglier than a hooped petticoat, and I've no intention of diminishing your ardor."

She reappeared wearing a voluminous ruffled nightgown, her hair loose about her shoulders, and quickly drained both her glass of champagne and his. "Better pour some more," she advised.

Austin did so, then began to undress in front of her. She was so damned desirable . . . even all that white lace could not conceal the swelling breasts and tiny waist above exquisitely rounded hips. But she had not begged him to extinguish the candles, and she kept her eyes fixed on him as he tossed his shirt to the chair and began to unbutton his trousers. He was suddenly very anxious to find out if he had foolishly married someone else's leavings.

He sprang to the bed, catching her by surprise. His lips were hot on hers and his hands tore away the nightgown. She parted her lips and accepted his tongue, watching him with a businesslike glance the champagne had failed to soften. "I'm not exactly sure what I'm supposed to do," she said. "But I know you've had plenty of experience . . . so just tell me."

Austin groaned, then covered her breasts with kisses, stroking the taut skin above the soft golden pubic hair, lightly touching her inner thighs, which relaxed expectantly. He rose to his knees, wrapping her legs about him. "Brace yourself, darlin' . . . I'm a-comin' in," he whispered and hoped with all his might there would be some resistance, somewhere. . . .

There was. She stiffened as his organ tried to gain entry and met the tough membrane of her maidenhead. He withdrew and then thrust again, harder. She gasped and closed her eyes and he hesitated for a moment, then began to work his way deeper into the silken cocoon that gradually accommodated him.

After a moment she opened her eyes and looked up at him, smiling. Her hips began to make small circles, and when he bent to kiss her breasts, her nipples were hard little points. He plunged and soared and thrust and could not stop the climax he felt coming. "I'm sorry, darlin' . . . I was too quick for you, but in a few minutes I'll be ready again," he whispered, his hazel eyes glazed.

"Good. I think I'm getting the idea," she said and rose gracefully from the bed to go to the washstand behind the screen. He could hear the splash of water as he searched the sheet and found the streaks of blood. She had been a virgin for sure. He chuckled. "Son of a gun," he said to himself softly.

He was already erect again when she stepped, naked, from behind the screen. She came to the bed and gazed wonderingly at his manhood, then tentatively put out her hand to touch him.

"You can squeeze a little harder, darlin', it won't break off," he said and, laughing, reached up to pull her down beside him.

For Garnet, events crowded so rapidly one upon the other that she attributed her continual tiredness to the whirl and worry of crisis after crisis . . . and to the fact that her sleep was again disturbed by her old recurring dream. The street in her dream was now vaguely familiar, but the thunder of hooves came before she quite recognized it or the mysterious figure in the smoke, whose face she could not see.

The newlyweds had barely sailed for Panama on the first leg of their journey to the Southeastern coast when the news reached San Francisco that Fort Sumter had been fired upon and the country was plunged into civil war.

A few days later a sea captain knocked at Garnet's door. He held a squirming and furious Rual by the scruff of his neck. "Mornin', Miss Garnet. Caught me a stowaway just as we were about to slip our lines. Thought I'd better deliver him in person."

The world spun dizzily for a moment and Garnet only vaguely heard herself thank the captain.

"I'm going to join the navy," Rual said. "I'm nearly thirteen and they're taking powder monkeys twelve years old. He can tell you." He glared accusingly at his captor.

"Well, reckon that's true enough," the captain said, "But they get their father's permission first."

"If my father were here, he'd give it to me," Rual muttered. "He'd understand. It's my mother who is ruining my life."

They spent the day arguing. Garnet had not felt well for several weeks but kept going because of the wedding preparations. She had been looking forward to a rest. "All right, Rual," she said at last. "Let's compromise."

"What do you mean?" He ran his hand through his hair and succeeded in making the bristling mane more tousled than before. Another of his father's gestures, thought Garnet. She blinked away a tear. Sebastian had been only a small part of Rual's life, yet he was more his father's son than he was hers.

"I know you hate school, and love the sea. Supposing I write to Ned Hake in New York? I could send you to him to learn about running a shipping line. You can learn navigation, too. Then in a couple of years you can go to sea—not as a powder monkey, but as a midshipman."

Bright blue eyes regarded her suspiciously. "I thought Ned sold all of my father's clippers except the *Monarch Butterfly*. That's what you told me."

Garnet's lips curved slightly and her eyes were a luminous green. A look of such feline satisfaction spread across her features that Rual had the uneasy expectation she might at any moment begin to purr.

Instead, she said, "That's true. I gather the bankruptcy hit Ned hard. I'm sure he would be more than happy to teach you all he knows if I were to supply the capital he needs to get the Balmain Shipping Company going again."

"You would do that? You have enough money?"

"More than enough. But I wish the country weren't at war. Rual, you must give me your word you won't go to sea for at least two years. By then it should be all over—at least that's what the men here say."

"Don't worry, all the fighting will be in the South. I'll be as safe in New York as here."

"I'll go and see Banker Moffatt today," Garnet promised.

Garnet stopped in to see Cassie after leaving the bank and Cassie convinced her that she must see a doctor. "You're as white as a ghost. And you're still having those dizzy spells, aren't you?"

Garnet nodded. "I'll go, as soon as I've taken care of things. Cassie, I want to sell my share of the Red Garter. Will you buy me out?"

"Of course. I wouldn't want to run this place with anyone else, if you're bent on leaving." A worried furrow appeared between her brows and she mopped her throat with a perfumed handkerchief. "But why do you want to sell?"

Garnet explained about Rual's proposed apprenticeship to Ned and the Balmain Shipping Company. "With Cerise married and Rual in New York . . . I thought I'd just take things easy, perhaps spend a little time with the Seamen's Society."

"What about Mariner's Castle? You going to sell it, too?"

Garnet blinked in surprise. "I don't own Mariner's Castle."

"You've been paying the taxes on that white elephant ever since Sebastian left . . . and seeing to the upkeep and paying the big Chinaman. Oh, I never said anything because it was none of my business."

Garnet sighed deeply. "I'll go on taking care of it. I suppose I could let it go and then step in and buy it for back taxes, but I always hoped that one day . . ." She stared into space and Cassie spoke to her several times without receiving an answer.

"Garnet?" Cassie touched Garnet's hand in alarm. "You all right, honey?"

The doctor diagnosed "female problems" and gave her a tonic. It only made the dizzy spells worse, and soon Garnet stopped taking it. Her brief hours of sleep were filled with disturbing dreams—the old nightmare was back regularly, but now there were others, too. Sometimes she dreamed Sebastian had returned; then, suddenly, he would change into Tom—dear, lost Tom from so long ago. She would awaken, shedding tears of joy, to find her bed empty, her arms stretched out to welcome a loved one who wasn't there.

She worried about Cerise and the days would not pass quickly enough until her daughter reached her destination and sent word back of her safe arrival. There was much to be done in transferring the Red Garter to Cassie, and in the matter of the arrangements to be made with Ned in New York.

Eventually, it all became a tumbling mass of detail in Garnet's mind. Once she found herself walking up the hill to Mariner's Castle. She stood at the front door, with its weathered ship's wheel and tarnished brass bell, and did not know why she was there.

She had financed the house for years, yet had never set foot inside it. It should have been her house. Hers and Sebastian's. They had been so right together. They would have been happy. If only he had not met Emily and fallen under her spell.

Garnet pushed the door and found it was unlocked. There was no sign of Mr. Tang, the only caretaker of the house. Inside the furniture was covered with white shrouds, and a cobweb trailed icily across her brow. Utter silence closed in on her when the door swung shut, for after the earthquake, Sebastian had seen to it that the walls were stoutly rebuilt.

Somewhere off in the distance, Garnet fancied she could hear the echoes of voices from long ago—her own voice and Emily's, in their only confrontation.

Garnet had been angry and afraid that morning. News of the lavish party, culminating in the announcement of the birth of Noah Balmain, had hit her like a thunderbolt. Sebastian had never even hinted Emily was with child. Garnet had been stunned, sickened, and terrified. What about Rual? What about herself? In the few minutes she had slept that night, her old nightmare had returned: the dash down the smoke-filled street, the thunder of hooves, the shadowy figure that beckoned so insistently, luring her toward some unknown and terrible fate.

To add fuel to the fire, Erik Gunnar had found them in San Francisco. The minute Sebastian left her after dealing with Erik, Garnet had walked up the hill to Mariner's Castle. If Sebastian could dispose of Erik, then Garnet could dispose of Emily Balmain. It was time to sort out who belonged to whom.

At first the Irish maid Maureen would not allow her into the house. The perky girl bristled indignantly when she opened the door, and it was clear she knew who Garnet was. When Garnet refused to budge from the doorstep until she had spoken with Mrs. Balmain, the girl at last told her grudgingly that Mrs. Balmain was taking the air in the rear garden.

Garnet opened the gate and found a pleasant garden with trimmed hedges and a profusion of flowers spilling over brick walks. Emily was sitting beneath a rustling elm tree, a book in her hands. She looked up as Garnet approached, the sunlight dappling her creamy skin and burnishing her dark hair with dancing lights.

The blending of dark and light, sunlight and shade, fair skin against a dark dress, shadowed foliage and bright blossoms, created a living oil painting. Garnet saw Emily through Sebastian's eyes for one heart-stopping second. Sebastian's wife was more beautiful than the deep red roses and saffron daisies lying in the basket at her feet. Her exquisite features were lit by a mysterious inner radiance, and her large expressive eyes were as vulnerable as a fawn's.

Emily smiled shyly and rose to her feet. "Good morning. Were you looking for me? I am Emily Balmain." Her voice was perfectly modulated, giving her words lyrical resonance.

Garnet stared, tongue-tied. Nothing she had heard had prepared her for the reality of such a fairy princess, one whose aura seemed to eclipse all of nature's other creations. Garnet faltered for a moment, then stepped forward. "I am Garnet . . . Wade."

Emily was politely attentive but gave no hint the name meant anything to her.

She looks too tiny to have given birth to a child . . . there is something about her that is strangely inviolate . . . it's no wonder Sebastian worships her . . . worships her *and uses* me *. . . she is the madonna, and I'm the whore.*

Garnet's chin went up. "I thought we should meet now that you have a son, also . . . to be sure we understand who Sebastian's first-born son is."

The velvet eyes were still wide and trusting, the delicate heart-shaped face was inclined slightly to the side, and a strand of hair like a satin ribbon fluttered away from a tiny ear as exquisitely formed as a shell. In the instant before she spoke again, Garnet had a sudden vision of a fragile china statuette shattering under the impact of a mailed fist.

"I bore Sebastian a son, also. I've been his mistress longer than you've been his wife."

The words came ringing down the years as Garnet stood in the deserted hall at Mariner's Castle. At the time she had admired Emily's composure. Sebastian's wife had turned pale as death, but she had not raised her voice. She listened quietly and attentively as Garnet ripped the fabric of her marriage to shreds. Then she begged to be excused, as she was feeling faint.

Garnet had been prepared for almost anything but that terrifying politeness. She had stumbled out of the peaceful garden feeling like some evil priestess who had just committed the ultimate sacrifice. She paused for a moment on the street in front of the house, wondering if there was some way she could return and undo what had been done. But Emily had disappeared into the house.

I did it for Rual, Garnet kept telling herself. She was holding on to that thought when she reached her own house and watched, disbelievingly, as the picket fence suddenly rippled, snake-like, and the gate jumped in her hand.

She could hear the low, rumbling roar of the earth tremor and lurched toward the house, forgetting everything but the urgent need to reach her children. It was the following day before she heard that part of Mariner's Castle had collapsed and Emily and her baby had been buried in the rubble.

"Who is there?" a voice called from across the shadowed hall. Garnet remembered where she was and turned and stepped through the front door before Mr. Tang emerged from the kitchen.

She managed to hide her illness from Rual and kept going on taut nerves and surreptitious gulps of brandy until the day he sailed, as a passenger, on his voyage to New York.

A letter arrived from Cerise, describing a plantation that was incredibly huge—a veritable municipality, run by hundreds of slaves. A world so different from the rough-and-tumble, brawling young city of San Francisco that Cerise would need time to decide what her feelings were about the wealth and indolence of the Gentry family. She wrote:

> *I had thought that we lived a life of ease and plenty . . . but here, one even has a small black girl to wave one's fan! I really see why Mr. Lincoln wants to abolish slavery, Mother . . . but it is a sinfully marvelous way of life for a select few!*
>
> *Austin has positively heaped me with jewels and baubles and clothes, and I have only to express the slightest wish and it is fulfilled so extravagantly that I hardly dare open my mouth.*

Garnet gave a sigh of relief. Cerise would be secure with a wealthy and adoring husband. She would never have to work in a saloon, or care for other people's children as Garnet had.

A month later a more ominous letter arrived. Austin Gentry had enlisted in the army. He had kept it from Cerise at first, pretending he was merely training for the militia. But now he had been sent north and there was heavy fighting in Virginia. His father and most of the men in the family had also enlisted. His mother, a

297

permanent invalid, had moved in with relatives in the country for fear Charleston would be shelled by Yankee gunboats.

Garnet had been feeling dizzy and faint all day and she read the letter with mounting apprehension. She had not looked beyond her daughter's marriage to a wealthy man. What if her husband were killed? What if the South lost the war? What would become of Cerise?

All of Garnet's money was now tied up in the Balmain Shipping Company, to ensure Rual's future, except for what she kept to live on and maintain Mariner's Castle. She must make sure that Cerise would have financial security, if necessary. . . . Her lawyer and banker would know how to handle it.

"You're not going out, Miz Garnet?" Fern said, her face knitted with concern as she came upon Garnet tying her bonnet strings. "You've been rushing about all day long. You should be resting," she protested.

"Just one more errand, Fern. Then I'll lie down and rest." Garnet put out her hand to steady herself as the familiar vise-like darkness squeezed the light from her eyes for a second. Her heart was pounding uncomfortably and her limbs were numb. The fresh air would probably be good for her.

Since Cerise and Rual left, she dreamed often of Tom. Her first love . . . big, friendly, Teddy-bear Tom, who leaped over walls and dashed across streets to express his sheer joy with life. The two of them would be laughing and running through the park, along the riverbank, hand in hand. What if he hadn't been killed? she would think upon awakening. She would have married him, and lived happily ever after. . . .

Sebastian—whom she had loved not wisely, but too well—had been something like Tom. Even Erik, whom she married in a fit of pique merely to hurt Sebastian, resembled Tom physically. Had she, she wondered lethargically, been trying to replace Tom in marrying both of them?

She had had her old nightmare the night before, and for the first time she recognized both the street and the beckoning figure. The street was in San Francisco, but the dark figure had never walked these streets. It was Tom, her first love, her first lost love.

Garnet was thinking about her dream, trying to make some sense of it, as, spurning her buggy for the short walk downtown, she strolled toward the bank.

Feeling a wave of dizziness, she paused before crossing the street. Blinking in the sunlight, she saw the silhouetted figure on the other side of the muddy street. A big, broad-shouldered man. A giant of a man. All the passersby moved aside to let him pass. Sebastian! His name sprang to her lips and her heart fluttered alarmingly.

She was running across the street, feet sliding in the mud, when she realized it was not Sebastian she saw, but Tom. Tom . . . smiling and tossing his hat in the air . . . beckoning to her to come to him . . . hurry, hurry, he beckoned.

Garnet did not hear the shouted warning, nor did she see the men who tried to reach her in time. The stagecoach came clattering up the street and there was a blurred thrashing of hooves, skidding of wheels, and a limp green velvet bundle lying forlornly in the mud when the coach and horses came grinding to a halt.

The first man who reached her brushed the auburn curls from her face and was surprised to see she was smiling. "Tom . . ." she said, then slipped away.

BOOK III

1861

──⊰{ **CHAPTER 28** }⊱──

Ned Hake's wife, Deborah, did not approve of Sebastian's bastard coming to live in her house. Ned responded that he would give lodging to the devil himself in order to be his own man again. The Balmain Shipping Company was reborn. Did Deborah realize that Ned would have a free hand until Rual's eighteenth birthday?

"And what about his father?" Deborah demanded.

"Sebastian isn't likely to come back. He knows he'll lose the *Monarch Butterfly* if he does."

"But Mark McKnight will tell Sebastian the boy is here—that the company is solvent again." Mark occasionally made an Atlantic crossing on one of his steamers and brought news of Sebastian from time to time.

"Mark will tell Sebastian you're buying ships. He'll wonder where the money came from. And if Sebastian comes back, he'll fritter all the money away again. You know how he is—he's a sailor, not a businessman." She spoke in short, indignant bursts, keeping her voice low so Rual would not hear.

"Mark probably won't make any unexpected visits now that we're at war with the South," Ned said. "And I still have Sebastian's power of attorney."

"I don't see why you couldn't just start a new company for yourself and the boy."

"Because, my dear, Rual's mother was adamant that we retain the Balmain name. It is her money that's bailing us out, after all. Besides, Sebastian's name will carry more weight than mine with prospective shippers. He still has many friends. They blamed me for the bankruptcy, not him. They don't even condemn him

303

for running off with the *Monarch Butterfly,* because every one of our creditors receives payments on account, from all over the world."

Ned had not been in touch with Sebastian since he spirited the clipper away and had not pressed Mark McKnight for details when he mentioned that from time to time Sebastian went to England.

"You know, there's also Rual's sister, or half-sister, I suppose she is," Ned said thoughtfully. "The Wade woman's other child, Cerise. She apparently married into the Gentry family, who are Southern shipowners as well as plantation owners. Once the war is over, Rual could have some interesting connections there."

"I wonder where Emily and her brother took Sebastian's legitimate son," Deborah mused. "Do you think they are still in California?"

"Hush. Don't let Rual hear you. He idolizes his father, and I gather the existence of the legitimate son is a constant agony to him."

Mark McKnight was watching the hostilities in America with keen interest. A blockade of the Southern ports had been ordered by President Lincoln, and the Confederate States had responded by getting several cruisers to sea and sinking an impressive amount of Northern tonnage.

Maritime insurance rates soared. The Atlantic was a dangerous cauldron and there were fears that neutral ships would get caught in the American conflict. There had been outrage in England when the Federals stopped a British ship, the *Trent,* boarded her, and seized two Confederate commissioners bound for England and France. For a time the country hovered on the brink of war, and many upper-class Englishmen were openly in favor of an alliance with Jefferson Davis' new nation.

The death of Queen Victoria's consort, Prince Albert, sobered the white heat of outrage. In the ensuing period of mourning, the Federals quickly apologized to England for the incident, released the Confederate commissioners, and smoothed out diplomatic relations.

A government proclamation forbidding British subjects to carry contraband or participate in the American conflict had little effect. English ships were running the blockade into Southern ports and English sailors made haste to volunteer for service aboard Southern blockade runners to reap the enormous profits to be made carrying war supplies to a nation of planters and farmers, and transporting Southern cotton back to Lancashire.

The McKnight steamers carried fewer passengers on the Liverpool-to-New York crossing now, and Mark began to consider diverting some of his ships to Bermuda or the Bahamas, which were transshipment ports for Southern goods.

"Pack me a bag, Mollie," he said one day late in 1861. "I'm going to America."

"Don't go, lovey," Mollie begged. "Not while there's a war there. Your mother was American, Mark. Maybe they'll conscript you into the army," she added tearfully.

Mark smiled and patted her hand. "Don't worry. My half-brother is serving in their navy, and they're only taking one member of each family." It had always been easier to make up a story for Mollie than to argue with her.

Mollie looked doubtful. "Sebastian? When did you see him?"

"He was in London the last time I was there. Hanging around the concert halls looking for Cyril. Poor old Sebastian is going to turn into a music lover in spite of himself. Anyway, he told me it would be his last visit for a time, as he was going home to enlist in the navy. He served in their navy during the Mexican war, you know."

"Which side is he on?" Mollie asked. She was not sure what the American war was all about.

Mark laughed. "The North, of course." *Which is why I shall perhaps help the South,* he thought with amusement. His keenly competitive nature had always been frustrated by a lack of competitors. Sebastian was the only man Mark had ever met who did not stand in awe

305

of his wealth, intelligence, and power. Few young men had risen so swiftly to the top, with or without inherited wealth. The price Mark had paid was the lack of challenge and direction left to him. His life was a constant battle against tedium.

Sebastian was the last of a vanishing breed, Mark thought. His half-brother treated him like a troublesome younger brother dogging the footsteps of the older boys. And his archaic views on the superiority of sailing ships over steamers had, on the few occasions they had argued the point, ended with Sebastian obstinately unconvinced.

The Atlantic crossing was uneventful, and New York seemed little changed by the war raging to the south. At the home of Ned Hake, however, there was a definite change.

Mark found himself face to face with a strapping youth who was Sebastian with the years of toil and worry lifted from his features. For once, Mark's *sangfroid* faltered as he stared at the bulging muscles, and the craggy features exuding energy and power.

Ned introduced the boy as Rual Wade and was quickly corrected. "I am Rual *Balmain*," Rual amended.

Deborah rose immediately, her face flushed, and said, "I must see to dinner."

The moment she departed, Ned said, "You can't call yourself that, Rual." To Mark he added, "This is Sebastian's boy, but not his legitimate son."

Rual looked at Ned with ill-concealed dislike. "My name is Balmain, like my father's."

Ned frowned, but did not issue a reprimand. Mark's quick mind digested the fact that any obligation appeared to be on Ned's side.

Rual added, "I dislike being rude, but part of your agreement with my mother is that I adopt the name."

Ned looked as though he wished they would both disappear as he turned to Mark and said, "I hope you won't mind sharing a room with Rual. We've only one guest room."

"As long as Rual doesn't object. I shall be leaving

for Bermuda tomorrow." He could have gone to a hotel, but he was curious about Sebastian's son.

What a complicated morass of bloodlines his mother had created when she married Job McKnight, Mark reflected as he followed Rual up the stairs to the guest room. And Sebastian added to the family jigsaw of half-brothers by siring sons to two different mothers. And a daughter . . ,

Upon entering the room, Mark's attention was immediately caught by the silver-framed photographs standing on Rual's dresser. He stared at the girl with the bold, challenging eyes and luxurious hair spilling about her shoulders. Despite the grainy quality of the picture, those eyes bored into his with the impact of a pair of dueling pistols. Mark stood transfixed, unable to tear his gaze away. The girl wore a low-cut gown and displayed a slender throat and rounded shoulders. Her chin was slightly tilted, adding to the challenge of her eyes. *To hell with you,* she seemed to be saying.

"My sister—Cerise," Rual said. "She's married."

"She lives in San Francisco?"

"No. She married a Southerner. I haven't heard from her since the fighting started."

"I may be visiting the South," Mark said, and it seemed his voice was coming from far away. Reluctantly, he tore his eyes from the photograph to study the twin frame next to it. An older woman. She, too, had an arresting face. Pert, vivacious, with an impish smile hovering about sensually full lips that both mocked and invited. Like the girl, she had a wild mass of wavy hair.

Mark's mind raced, sorting impressions and questions. He had never been so moved by a mere picture. Was it, he wondered, the temptation of forbidden fruit? That curse of their star-crossed family? Cyril and Emily —living in some remote place, in the worst kind of sin. But Mark was not Cyril. The woman hadn't been born who could bewitch a McKnight, certainly not one who was not only married, but also was his half-brother's daughter. *Forbidden love,* a small voice repeated.

"Perhaps," Mark said, "I can call on her and see that she's all right. You must give me her address."

"Yes, I wish you would. You see, I'm not sure if she received word about Mother . . ." His voice broke and he turned away quickly.

Mark offered the appropriate condolences when he learned the boy's mother had been killed in a street accident. Then he looked back at the two photographs and thought privately that Garnet would never be dead while Cerise was alive.

For the first hectic weeks of her marriage, Cerise had found herself whisked about to a bewildering array of Austin's relatives. The Gentry clan were shipowners in Charleston and Wilmington, planters in both North and South Carolina, and politically active everywhere.

According to the rules of Southern hospitality, the newlyweds were expected to visit as many relatives as possible, staying as long as they wished, before settling into their own home. Had it not been for the secession of the Southern states and resulting war to force them back into the Union, Cerise and Austin would have spent a full year honeymooning and visiting.

Austin's father owned a fleet of ships that carried Southern cotton all over the world. He maintained a house in Charleston, and in addition owned a plantation on the Ashley River which was run by a steward. Austin's mother had been an invalid since the birth of his younger sister, Dahlia, and Austin spent much of his childhood with relatives. Austin's mother was now ensconced in the home of his Uncle Will and Aunt Rose Gentry. Their gracious manor house stood on a vast plantation near Columbia, the state capital of South Carolina. It was here that Austin left Cerise, for several weeks, telling her he was off to look in on a family business, while actually he went to Charleston to enlist in the Confederate army.

Cerise was furious when she learned he had deceived her. "Why did you lie to me?" she demanded on the day he confessed, in answer to her surprised queries about the crisp gray uniform whose jacket he was in the process of buttoning. The were in their bedroom preparing for the farewell party for several young and not so young Gentrys who were departing for Virginia. All of the neighboring planters and, it seemed, half the population of Columbia had been invited.

Austin grinned engagingly and ran his hands over her shoulders and breasts. "I didn't want you worrying, sweet baby. I wanted us to enjoy our honeymoon until the very last minute. Come on, now, don't be mad at me, honey."

She twisted out of his embrace. "Austin, for heaven's sake, will you stop treating me as though I'll have the vapors if I'm faced with anything more formidable than chosing what to wear!"

A perplexed frown replaced his grin. "But, sweetheart, I knew you were dead set against me joining the army." He was becoming more and more puzzled by the abrupt change in his bride. It was as though a changeling had been slipped between his sheets. Without warning she had dropped the sweet and rather vacant coquetry that had so captivated him. He saw that indeed the little girl who had stamped her foot and boxed his ears had not, as he had once fondly imagined, grown into an elegant and fragile gentlewoman, in need of his protection.

Cerise stormed back and forth in the room. "Of course I'm against such foolishness. What sense does it make to try to settle political differences by blowing off the heads of strangers? But that doesn't mean you should go through an elaborate charade because you disagree with me . . . treating me like a stupid child."

"Now, sugar plum, we'll whip the Yankees and I'll be home before you know it. Don't fret your pretty little head."

She watched his reflection in the mirror as she savagely thrust a hairbrush through her hair. He was devastatingly handsome in the gray and gold uniform, with his flaming red hair and teasing eyes. She wanted to tear off her ball gown and spend the evening making love, rather than face the legions of guests gathering downstairs, especially as he was to leave the following morning. But she was too angry to express the wish. Besides, she had discovered that although he was always as ready to make love as she, perhaps more so, he did not particularly care for her to initiate the proceedings.

"I don't know why you didn't just leave me in San Francisco. Here I don't know a soul, and you are rushing off to war." She smoothed the skirt of her dress and the gold satin shimmered.

Austin relaxed. This was easier to deal with than a wife who expressed strong—and opposing—views on masculine matters. "Why, you won't be lonely, honey. You can stay here with Aunt Rose and Dahlia and you can visit . . ."

They were interrupted by a timid knock on their door and Dahlia's hesitant and breathless summons: "Austin, Cerise . . . Mother wants you to stand in the receiving line."

Dahlia was a shy fifteen-year-old, very much in awe of her older brother and his self-assured wife. Her hair was golden, barely touched by the flamboyant red of her brother's, and lacking the fire of Cerise's red-gold locks. When she walked down the stairs on Austin's arm, with Cerise at his other side, Dahlia looked like a pale copy of the striking couple she accompanied.

"You must go and see Mother," she whispered, "before she falls asleep. She'll want to see Cerise's dress."

Cerise tended to forget the presence of the frail woman with wisps of white hair who never left her room and received guests only for measured minutes.

The plantation house was being invaded by gray and gold uniforms and a dazzling array of ball gowns. Cerise felt uncomfortable standing between Aunt Rose and Uncle Will, a softly spoken gray-haired man who treated every woman as though she were a fragile jewel. The family were receiving their guests with the charm that seemed to come naturally to all of them, and conversation flowed over and around Cerise's head. They inquired of friends and relatives and new babies and rheumatic elders. They spoke of crops and cotton prices and overseers. While the women were present, none of the men mentioned the war, despite the fact that the majority of them were already in uniform.

Cerise wanted to stamp her foot and scream at them that they were all fools hell-bent on destroying themselves in the madness of war. Instead, she bit her lip and smiled until her face ached. She studied the faces of the other women and saw reflected there such pride in their men and blind faith that their way of life would prevail that she felt a sudden twinge of pity for them. Surely they could not know how deadly the peril they faced really was.

More than once she wondered if she would have married Austin had she known the hotheaded Southerners would really start a war. She liked Austin, enjoyed his lovemaking, and was proud of his good looks. But she did not feel overwhelming love for him and did not expect to.

"You must come and visit us," one of the matrons was saying, and Cerise searched her mind in vain for the name of this particular aunt. She murmured politely.

The musicians began to play, a trio of black slaves dressed very differently from the field hands she had seen wending their way back to the quarters at dusk. These three grinned broadly and plucked fiddle strings and strummed banjos with lighthearted joy. How can you smile, when you are slaves? Cerise wanted to ask. Austin took her hand to lead her out for a reel.

During the empty months that followed, she remembered that evening many times. The music, the dancing, the blithe disregard of danger. Most of all, she remembered the too-short hours in their room when the party ended, when they made love with new poignancy, unable to sleep for the need of each other, clinging like drowning people to the only solid reality in a sea of uncertainty. In their kisses and caresses and breathless joining of their bodies, they sought to drive away the demons of war and separation.

Then Austin was gone, and so were most of the men. Women with brave but tearful smiles and an army of black slaves were left behind. All of them seemed to know what was expected of them, and to be content to wait for their returning warriors. Except Cerise, who had expected marriage to give her a purpose in life, and was disappointed that it had not.

It did seem, that autumn, that the arrival of Mark McKnight was ordained by mischievous fates.

--❧ **CHAPTER 29** ❧--

Cerise was writing a letter to Austin, telling him of the death of her mother, when Dahlia knocked on her door.

"There's a gentleman to see you, dear," Dahlia said breathlessly. "An Englishman. I explained that you are in mourning, but he said he had come a great distance and would like to pay his respects personally. He said he came from your brother in the North, and I know you've been worried about him. . . ."

Cerise was red-eyed from crying. She had been crying steadily for three days and there seemed no end to her tears. Too late, she realized how much she had loved her mother. She had never understood her, but Garnet had been the one person Cerise loved better than herself. Now she was gone, forever.

As Cerise rose, absently smoothing her wrinkled black gown, Dahlia started to suggest perhaps the visitor could wait while she changed clothes, but the soft suggestion fell on deaf ears as Cerise murmured, "Rual . . . I wonder if he knows about Mother."

She paused, halfway down the curved staircase, when she realized Mark McKnight was standing in the hall watching her descent.

Tall and lean, black-haired, keen blue eyes, and a slightly quizzical expression. Even while standing still, there was a restless energy and impatience about him.

What a relief, Cerise thought, to see a young man in impeccably tailored clothes that were not a uniform.

"Mr. McKnight? I am Cerise Gentry."

He was bowing over her outstretched hand when he looked up at her suddenly, his startlingly blue eyes penetrating the mist of grief that blurred her vision, and she saw that he was handsome. Probably arrogant, too, Cerise thought, from his bearing and bold glance. Caught in that glance, she barely heard his words of commiseration.

"You were in New York? You saw Rual? Oh, forgive me—we can go into the drawing room and I'll send for refreshments. You must have had a trying journey." She gestured toward the Gentrys' black butler who hovered in the background, and he moved forward to take Mark's coat and hat.

Seated opposite him in the drawing room, Cerise compared Mark to Rual and saw subtle similarities. Where Rual's eyes were blue and rebellious, Mark's were blue and searching. Rual's black hair was a bristling mane, while Mark's was smooth upon a classically well-shaped head.

As though aware that she was silently appraising him, Mark said, "Rual had a photograph of you. What a pity it is not possible to take pictures in color. Forgive me if I appear to stare. Your hair and eyes are so gloriously different in color from Rual's, it's hard to believe you are brother and sister."

"We had different fathers," Cerise answered, hardly aware of what she was saying. In the long silence that followed her statement, she had the uneasy feeling he was pouncing on this piece of information like a tiger upon unwary prey.

That first time, Mark McKnight stayed exactly long enough to be polite without being forward.

Mark's cool self-assurance and faintly bored air were the external defenses he had cultivated over the years to hide a sensitive soul that had been badly bruised in childhood. He had spent a lonely boyhood, constantly out of step with his peers because of his advanced intelligence. His first week at school, his teacher had discovered he could already read. He went rapidly through standards one, two, and three before astonished teachers found the class level to which he could best relate.

Surrounded by boys three years his senior, he had been resented and bullied unmercifully. Smaller stature did not stop him from fighting back. Finding he was no match for his classmates physically, he resorted to verbal defense, which enraged them further.

To make matters worse, after his father died, Mollie Flanagan became more open in her enjoyment of the bottle. On several occasions she passed out cold in the street and Mark had to pay a hansom driver to pick her up and carry her home. While he found he could put up with his classmates' abuse of his own person, he could not bear to hear ill spoken of his beloved Mollie. When anyone called Mollie names, Mark flew into the fray with little thought for his own skin.

Had he been a more self-effacing child, in time the other boys would have tired of their sport, but despite his tender years and smaller stature, Mark had a valiant nature that refused to concede to superior size. It seemed to him later that there was never a time in his childhood that he was not recovering from a bruised jaw or blackened eye. Despite this, he was so handsome that people turned to stare at him on the street.

He never told anyone that one beating he had endured had resulted in permanently impaired hearing in one ear. Since this sometimes resulted in his ignoring a remark addressed to him, he was thought snobbish and cold. He compensated for what he believed to be his own body's weakness by fine-tuning all of his other senses and by excelling in everything he attempted.

In his early teens he grew rapidly, and with his newly acquired height there was less of a gap between himself and his university peers. But he never forgot those early years and offered his friendship guardedly. No one ever really got to know him, despite the wide circle of acquaintances who were only too happy to call the handsome and intelligent young man their friend.

314

Women flocked about him and he enjoyed their company. He moved with an older, faster crowd and imitated their world-weary sophistication. After all, it was a defense against revealing to anyone that the specter of his lonely childhood, and lack of a real family, still haunted him.

Not even to himself did he admit that deep down he was afraid that since he had caused the death of his mother by his own birth, someday he would be destroyed by a woman. It was an irritational fear that his cool logic would not have been able to accept. Even he did not know why he approached women in the same way he took on any new project . . . define the problem, plan the strategy, move inexorably to victory. He began to wonder, after a time, why the conquest of women brought less satisfaction as he got older.

Several months after Mark's first visit to Cerise, a United States official in Bermuda suspected that the McKnight steamer *Belle* was bound not for Nassau, as her supercargo claimed, but for the beleaguered Confederacy. Mark encountered obstacles in the way of obtaining coal and supplies, as well as attempts to get the crew to desert.

A day after leaving Bermuda, the *Belle*'s bow was clearly pointed in the direction of the American coast. Several other significant changes were being made. Two four-and-a-half-inch rifled guns were mounted in the forward ports and two boatguns on the quarterdeck. The "ladies' saloon" was converted into an armory, shell room, and magazine. Every man aboard was armed with a British Enfield rifle.

Finally, a bill of sale changed hands.

"I'm curious," the captain said to Mark as he signed the bill of sale. "Why did you stay aboard? It's almost certain we will encounter Federal blockaders."

The young Englishman's expression was inscrutable, and when he spoke there was a faint note of boredom in his voice. "A new experience for me, nothing more."

"I'm glad so many of your countrymen are on our side."

315

"The upper classes are, of course," Mark replied. "We have many blood ties to your Southern states, as well as a tendency to side with the underdog in any conflict. But I'm afraid many people in England still see the issue as slavery. We ourselves abolished slavery thirty years ago and find its practice today abhorrent."

"But you personally don't see the issue as slavery?"

"Lincoln has said that he wants only to maintain the Union, while Jefferson Davis is equally determined to form a new nation. Excuse me, Captain. I'd like to go on deck and get some air."

Staring out across the dark water, Mark thought about Cerise. He had to see her again. He told himself his goal was merely seduction. She was, after all, married. Even in her mourning clothes, red-eyed from weeping, she had been more exciting that any woman he had ever known. There had been plenty of women, all discarded with cool efficiency after their surrender. The chase was what made them interesting. For Mark the challenge of acquiring something had always been better than actually achieving his goal.

He was bored with his ships, bored with life as one of the most eligible bachelors in England. In a way, he envied his half-brother, Sebastian. Old Sebastian had a singlemindedness of purpose and clearly defined aim that made his life simple. Mark smiled as he thought of their last meeting.

The big sailor with his bulging muscles had been incongruously out of place beneath the crystal chandeliers of the foyer of the concert hall. He had shifted his feet uncomfortably when Mark and several of his friends approached.

"I was going to stop in and see you in Liverpool," Sebastian said, after introductions had been made.

Mark was amused. Sebastian's demeanor was that of a boy caught in the schoolroom on a Saturday. "Let's have supper after the performance," Mark suggested. "How did you like the first part of the rendition of Cyril La Flair's music? Was it not interpreted with rare dual perspective? I felt the orchestra was perhaps a bit heroic in scope for the soloist's lyrical appproach."

Sebastian's somewhat faded blue eyes glazed, and one of Mark's friends murmured in his ear, "Cut it out, Mark."

Later they went to a small café in Soho and Mark kept Sebastian's glass brimming with ale. He was careful not to mention Cyril again, and after a while Sebastian relaxed and brought up the subject himself. "On the program," he said, slurring his words slightly, "they said Cyril La Flair had been lost at sea. Where did that story come from?"

"A romantic sponsor of concerts who wanted to hang a tragic label on Cyril—to make his music more appealing to impressionable young girls and weepy old matrons. Posthumous fame is always easier for an artist to acquire."

"He probably wrote that music for Emily," Sebastian said, gulping down another glass of ale. "I went to the London police, you know. But they couldn't help me. I'm going home. Time to get back into the navy. They'll need men . . . always hard to get enough men for the navy."

"You'll take the *Monarch Butterfly* back to America?"

Sebastian smiled. "She's far away, in safe waters. Someday she's for my son, Noah. By the time he's a man, I'll have paid off all the debts and she'll be free and clear."

"Would you like passage on a McKnight steamer from Liverpool?"

Sebastian slurped the head off another glass of ale. "Might as well get used to steamers, I reckon. More than likely they'll put me on one when I enlist . . . especially when I ask for sail."

"Most of your navy ships use both steam and sail," Mark pointed out. "So you'll be able to wrestle with your flapping canvas."

Sebastian leaned forward, confidentially. "Should have done what my father did—taken my wife to sea with me. Been master of my own ship, instead of a lubber ashore." He blinked. "How happy we'd have been, Emily and me . . . and *he* wouldn't have come between us."

The ale, rather than Sebastian's true feelings, was responsible for casting the impression that the search for Emily was still his life's major quest—that and the fact that seeing Mark again had reminded him of her.

Actually, Sebastian had found himself in London quite by chance, after taking his clipper to Kolvoord's yard in Moulmein. He had been asked to captain a ship to England and had reasoned that after he had delivered the cargo there it would be easy to cross the Atlantic to enlist in the U.S. Navy. Seeing Cyril's name advertised on a poster, he decided to attend the concert.

Sebastian had survived on the small and lonely island because he had been too angry to die. Anger, and the burning thought of punishing Gunnar for marooning him, had kept him going. When he thought of Gunnar, his blood raced and his senses quickened. Conversely, thoughts of the women in his life served only to depress him, and he tried desperately to prevent them from arising at all.

As time went by, his search for Gunnar became less intense, but whenever he found himself in a strange port or wherever sailors gathered, it would be about Erik Gunnar that he asked first.

There had been times he thought of returning to Garnet, but San Francisco was on the far side of the earth, and he could not take the *Monarch Butterfly* to an American port. Besides, it was possible that after all this time Garnet had forgotten him. He wondered with a stab of old pain if she were still selling her favors at the Red Garter. No, better not to go back.

Emily and Garnet . . . in the neat compartments of his mind were his beliefs that he had loved Emily and desired Garnet and that the two emotions were totally different and separable.

He had never really understood women. He knew only that they aroused different feelings in a man. Some made him more gentle, more protective; others brought out baser instincts. Then there was the rare woman who

318

inspired a man to be more than he thought himself to be. Emily, his sweet lost wife, had been such a woman.

Looking back, Sebastian realized he would have spent his life in the forecastle if it had not been for Emily. Yet with Garnet he had been more comfortable. With Garnet he never had to worry about saying the wrong thing, using the wrong fork . . . or shocking her. He could tell Garnet his most private thoughts, relate the most ribald of jokes, enjoy her body and revel in the knowledge that she enjoyed his.

At sea, during peaceful night watches, Sebastian sometimes thought of the two women. When he arrived in port and caught sight of a big bearded sailor, his rage smoldered as he remembered Erik Gunnar and the long lonely year on the barren atoll. But thoughts of finding Emily, or returning to Garnet, or revenge on Gunnar all began eventually to fade. Sebastian thought instead of his son, Noah.

"Must be getting old," he muttered, as his thoughts drifted again to the longing he felt to see his son. "When a man thinks of his link to the future—his immortality —I reckon he must be getting old."

"I beg your pardon?" Mark asked.

"It's all I have to leave him, you see," Sebastian said earnestly. "The clipper . . . and my love for the sea."

"Ah," Mark said, nodding. "I see. It's a painful subject, Sebastian, but would it help to remember what kind of a man Cyril La Flair is? My own boyhood would have been bleak, indeed, if Cyril had not been a part of it. I missed him terribly after you returned and took Emily back to America with you. Cyril left for London, as you know, and I saw him infrequently after that. I realized later that Cyril rarely had any money and probably could not afford to make the journey to Liverpool." Mark paused, noting the hardening of Sebastian's jaw, and realized what he hoped were words of comfort were having the opposite effect on Sebastian. "I'm just trying to say . . ."—he finished lamely— ". . . that Cyril loves children and has great patience with them."

"Blood will tell, in the end," Sebastian growled. "My son will be a sailor, like me. I named him for the greatest sailor of them all, didn't I? His inheritance from me will be my love of the sea . . . and the *Monarch Butterfly*."

Mark almost envied a man whose wants were so simple: a tall ship, fair winds, and a son to carry his name forward. He remembered the conversation now as he stood on the shadowy deck of the *Belle* and watched the crew throwing tarpaulins over the engine room hatch to hide the lights that might give away their presence to Yankee gunboats.

They would creep down the shore at night, close enough to risk running aground, and hope to remain out of sight of the blockading squadron patrolling about a thousand yards offshore.

Mark was at the captain's side when the first ominous shadow appeared on their port bow, moving slowly toward them. They held their breath, hoping that the *Belle*'s slim silhouette would not be observed against the dark shoreline.

Seconds later, a second Federal ship appeared.

Gliding by, they had almost passed the two ships when the hoarse shout rang out across the water. "Heave to! Stop that ship, or I'll sink you!"

Without waiting for the captain's reaction, Mark grabbed the speaking tube to the engine room and yelled, "Pile on the coal and give her every ounce of steam!"

A calcium rocket exploded into white light over their heads, and a second later the cruiser's guns put a shot across their bow. They were drenched with water as the *Belle* shot ahead. The second Federal vessel was rapidly closing and the two ships steamed bow to stern, perilously close to the rim of white surf.

"Damn it, we may run aground," the captain said, "but I'll not give them the ship."

Another shell screamed overhead. The black ribbon of water between the two ships was now so narrow they could hear the boatswain's shrill pipe and barked

320

orders. Shouts and curses were hurled from one ship to the other.

Suddenly a shell found its mark, and the foremast shattered into a cascade of splinters, falling to port. The captain quickly ordered the ship's carpenter to cut away the spar. Seconds later another shell ripped into the bunkers.

The needle on the steam gauge crept to full pressure and then beyond. The *Belle* was pulling away from her pursuers. Now deadly grape and canister spewed across the *Belle*'s decks as the Federal made a desperate last attempt to stop the blockade runner.

Looking shoreward, Mark saw the white surf closer than before. Over the roar of exploding shells and the mournful howling of the wind, he heard the thunder of waves breaking on the dark shore. Racing aft, he found the helmsman draped limply over the wheel, surrounded by a spreading pool of blood.

Pulling the helmsman free, Mark swung the wheel hard over, and the ship's headlong dash into the destructive surf was stopped with only seconds to spare.

As the *Belle* steamed into the safety of the river, there was a warning roar from the Confederate shore batteries and an answering chorus of cheers and Rebel yells from the crew. The captain and Mark went below for a glass of rum.

"The cargo is intact and we can repair the ship," the captain said, raising his glass. "And you, my friend, can run the blockade with me anytime you wish. You didn't tell me you knew practical seamanship. I thought you were just a businessman."

Mark's normally sleek hair was windblown and his clothes were salt-caked and disheveled. His eyes glowed with a blue flame. "I begin to see," he said slowly, "why Sebastian made haste to rush home."

Mark arrived at the Gentry plantation near Columbia to find a festive war benefit in progress. Guests, primarily female, were donating items of gold and silver and pewter to the cause. Rose Gentry received him

321

graciously and was properly grateful when he quickly donated a handsome gold watch and chain. Glancing about the crowded room, he could not see Cerise. "I don't see your daughter-in-law. I hope she is not indisposed."

"My son's wife is still in mourning, Mr. McKnight. Perhaps you had forgotten it's been less than a year since she lost her mother." Rose Gentry's charming Southern accent expressed no hint of censure, but Mark noted her choice of words—"my son's wife"—and interpreted the subtle warning accurately.

He smiled disarmingly. "Of course. Perhaps I could visit with her privately—to be sure the rules of social conduct are maintained."

Rose hesitated, then led the way to a drawing room away from the main hall of the sprawling plantation house. "I'll send Tannie with refreshments. Do please be seated, Mr. McKnight."

A slim black girl brought a decanter of wine and a platter of assorted cheeses. She remained in the room when Cerise appeared a few minutes later, and it was clear she had been ordered to chaperone the visit.

Cerise wore a high-necked black dress and her hair was piled in a knot of curls on top of her head. As she came through the doorway, the sound of a fiddle, the tinkle of glasses, and a burst of laughter from the main hall accompanied her. Mark recognized immediately the look in her tawny eyes. It was an expression he had seen in the mirror occasionally when he examined his own reflection.

"I'm surprised to see you back here, Mr. McKnight. How nice to see you again . . . on the eve of my departure."

"You're leaving?"

"I've imposed long enough on Aunt Rose's hospitality. I intend to travel to Virginia to be nearer my husband."

To be nearer your husband, Mark wondered silently, or to be away from the restraint of relatives who would strangle you with their social taboos? He could see her fingers tapping lightly on the arm of her chair in time with the muted music drifting through the closed doors.

"I understand there was heavy fighting—Manassas, wasn't it? And Port Royal has been captured by the Federals. Are you sure your husband will welcome your arrival in Virginia? From what I've seen of your Southern gentlemen, they fear the prospect of putting their ladies in danger far more than they fear the mighty dragon to the north."

"Mr. McKnight—"

"Mark—please call me by my first name. I hope we shall be friends."

Her golden eyes met his and he felt his pulse quicken. "There is something you can do for me," she said, "since you are a neutral and can come and go as you please."

"Anything. Anything at all."

"A cryptic note arrived from Rual. Apparently he has run off and joined the navy. He felt since Mother died he was no longer bound by the promise he made to her not to enlist. Could you possibly find out which ship he is on? At least if I knew which ship, I could stop imagining the worst every time I hear of another sinking."

"I'll do my best. Of course, I shall need to know where you will be so that I can let you know."

"If Austin won't let me stay near his regiment, I shall probably go to Charleston and reopen his parents' house there. His mother has been fretting about leaving it un-attended. Tell me, are they as fiercely patriotic up north and as cocksure as they are down here?" She leaned forward, her eyes lighting up with eagerness. It must have been some time, Mark thought, since anyone had spoken to her of anything but the perpetuation of her grief.

"I'm not sure New York is a typical Northern city," he replied. "Last year at the onset of hostilities, their mayor suggested the city be declared an open port and be allowed to trade freely with both sides."

Cerise dimpled and her lips curved into a smile. "How gloriously venal of him!"

Mark grinned. "Isn't that a strange attitude for a lady whose husband is fighting for his nation's honor?"

"I don't approve of war."

Mark's eyes flickered in the direction of the black servant, Tannie, who stood dispiritedly waving a palmetto fan, her eyes heavy with fatigue. She was little more than a child. Despite his careful air of neutrality, the American war between the states occupied most of his thoughts nowadays. Mark found himself torn between admiring the courage and gallantry of the Southerners, and deploring the existence of slavery.

"I find myself both fascinated and repelled by war," he said. "I was a schoolboy during the Crimean War, but I remember my blood racing with pride when our headmaster called an assembly to tell us of our various victories. Then when the fever of pride subsided, I would wonder about some of the actions of the military leaders—and the cost of the victories in human suffering and loss of life. The famous charge of the Light Brigade is a classic example. Cerise, I'm afraid your Confederacy may be yet another Light Brigade, charging bravely but foolishly against the big guns of the North."

Cerise sighed. "Maybe you should try telling them that. I've tried. They listen politely, but you know they're thinking: Why, we must humor Austin's strange wife, who has never been told that ladies don't join in the men's conversations. Actually, my mother spent years telling me ladies didn't argue, or express divergent views in front of gentlemen, but, Lord, listening to men's foolishness and biting one's tongue does get so tedious."

Mark laughed, enjoying her frankness. Her outspoken and lively conversation was a breath of fresh air in a world of stale coquetry. He felt he wanted to talk to her without stopping for weeks. He was captivated by her intelligence and wit no less than by her beauty.

Further conversation was forestalled by the appearance of Aunt Rose Gentry, who had privately decided her daughter-in-law should return to the grief-stricken solitude of her room.

A week later Mark was in New York, where he visited Ned and learned Rual was indeed serving as a powder monkey aboard a navy ship.

"I couldn't stop him," Ned said.

And probably didn't try very hard, Mark thought. "Perhaps we could try and arrange for him to be transferred to the same ship as Sebastian," he suggested. "It would mean a lot to both of them, I'm sure." *Odd,* he thought, *that I should be the reuniting element in this strange family.*

As though reading his thoughts, Ned asked, "I take it you've stayed in this country because of family matters? I don't want to be inhospitable, Mark, but we're at war with the South. I'm a bit uneasy about your traveling back and forth. There are rumors that some Englishmen are spying for the Confederacy. Not that I'm accusing you—"

"I can assure you I am not a spy. In any event, my only real interest is my family ties. Sebastian is my half-brother, and while we hardly know one another, I do feel concern for him and his family . . . Rual and Cerise."

"Cerise is not Sebastian's daughter," Ned said, his expression carefully bland. "I've never met her, but from her picture she seems a beauty. Pity she has a husband. I expect otherwise she would find a handsome young English blockade-runner irresistible."

"So you know," Mark said. "Why didn't you say so instead of babbling about me being a spy?"

"Well . . . I was wondering. How about taking some goods through the blockade for me? I understand the profits can be enormous."

Mark looked at him levelly, trying to keep the contempt from his voice as he answered, "Not even carrion feed on their own dead. I'm sorry, I can't help you. I take only food and other civilian items through the blockade, and those I only sell at cost."

Ned flushed and turned away, thinking that Sebastian and his half-brother were more alike than they knew.

--◄{ CHAPTER 30 }►--

Sandwich Isles—1862

Luana came forlornly into the shack. She wore a drooping and faded flower on the back of her head, and Emily knew this indicated her current love affair was over.

"Luana, we are going to make another voyage to Maui to visit the Reverend Josiah Hawkins. Would you like to come with us?" Emily asked.

Luana brightened. "I can come? And Kekoa, too?"

Emily smiled her assent.

Cyril looked up from his music, his eyes lingering on Emily's face. As always when she smiled, he wanted to hold his breath as though it would prolong the magic of the joyous singing of his own heart. Listening to Emily speak softly to Luana, telling her of their planned visit to Lahaina, on Maui, her hauntingly melodious voice was a symphony to his mind's ear, and the love he felt for her was poured into the notes he wrote rapidly onto the staff drawn on the paper in front of him.

The piano he ordered had never arrived and was presumably lost at sea. He still traveled to the missionary's chapel in order to play his compositions, and it was his mounting rage at the puritanical restrictions imposed upon the islanders that prompted his suggestion they sail to Maui to visit Josiah.

Cyril knew nothing of the hierarchy of the Church, but he believed there had to be some higher power to curb the present missionary's zeal. Josiah had agreed that the Church's teachings should be adapted to the nature of the islanders and their surroundings and culture. Josiah would know which bishop could persuade him to temper evangelism with understanding.

"Look, I've finished my dress," Emily said, holding up the brightly printed cotton material. She had fashioned it in the free-flowing and voluminous style of the muumuus the missionaries insisted the women wear. Secretly, Emily hoped Luana would follow her example and cover those golden breasts.

Emily disappeared behind the coconut-frond screen Kekoa had made for her and reappeared wearing her bright dress, her hair loose about her shoulders. When she raised her hands to pull her hair back into the bun she usually wore, Cyril said, "Don't . . . leave it loose. If you must wear that foolish dress, soften the effect with your hair."

"The dress is much cooler than the gowns I brought from San Francisco," Emily said, blushing.

"And modest." Cyril smiled. "Whatever you wear, dearest, you are the fairest flower of all."

Behind them, Luana knitted her brow, perplexed as always. Strange *haoles*. Every time they looked at one another, their longing was like the burning lava that flowed from the fire goddess on the big island. Yet, still, after all these years, they fought it.

On the island of Maui there was a plant that grew only on the mountaintops which took from seven to forty years to mature. Luana thought that the love of these two *haoles* was something like the silver sword plant. It would surely take as long to blossom.

They were about to capsize; Erik Gunnar knew they could not prevent it. Damn, he shouldn't have disregarded all the warning signs: the black cat, the albatross.

The whale, in its death throes, thrashed in the bloody water.

The men felt the boat rise on the rushing wake, tilting and splintering as the huge tail slammed into the wood.

The six men were plunged into the sea, battered by loose planks and the writhing whale. Their own blood mingled with that of the great mammal in the warm green water.

Erik went down, kicking away from the body of the whale before attempting to surface. He could not see clearly because of the spreading cloud of blood and swam blindly in a direction he hoped was the opposite to that which the whale, still trailing his lance, was taking.

At last, lungs bursting, he shot to the surface and gulped the life-giving air. Treading water, he saw the scattered debris from their boat. Two men were swimming toward the other boat rowing to their assistance. There was no sign of the whale on the churning surface of the sea, or of the other men. It was possible they had become entangled with the lines and were being dragged under fathoms of water by the diving whale.

He was farthest from the approaching boat and, after resting a moment, began to swim toward it, his eyes searching the blood-streaked water for signs the wounded whale was about to breach again.

Too old for this game, he thought, kicking with legs that felt like lead. Should have given it up . . . don't need to do it anymore. He had waited in vain to hear from his daughter. He had sent her several letters and then returned to San Francisco. Now, swimming slowly to safety, Erik Gunnar thought of that visit.

Garnet was dead. Even now it was difficult to think of her in the grave because she had always seemed so vital and indestructible. *Must be mellowing in my old age,* he thought. But that was before he learned Cerise had married and left San Francisco.

He had been hurt. She should have told him. He

had a brief vision of walking up the aisle, his daughter on his arm, to give her away at her wedding. He felt cheated.

The boy Rual was gone, too. Balmain's bastard. And San Francisco, city of a thousand strange stories, still speculated on what had become of Balmain's wife and legitimate son. There was even a story circulating that Balmain sailed the seas endlessly, searching for them. Gunnar thought of the barren atoll in the South Pacific and the lone figure on the beach, and he smiled to himself.

Right from the beginning, Erik thought, Garnet had been the main cause of their enmity. After all, he had been no worse an officer than many others. He had never felt guilty for disciplining sailors to make sure the owners' cargoes arrived on time. It had been unjust of Balmain to accuse him of tossing a slave cargo into the sea. Not that he hadn't been running slaves illegally . . . but they had been flung overboard on the skipper's orders, not his. Unfortunately, the old man had been killed when the navy ship intercepted them and the crew gleefully testified that the first mate was responsible.

His arms ached as he neared the boat. His thoughts were interrupted by the shouted warning of the oarsmen. He blinked and looked around. A gray fin was slicing swiftly through the water, aimed directly toward him.

Sucking in a breath, Erik put his head down and hurtled through the waves, arms crashing through the rolling swells, every nerve straining to close the distance between himself and the boat.

He was alongside, reaching up to the outstretched hands, not seeing the horrified eyes of the men fixed on the water behind him, when he felt the slight bump against his leg.

They had his hands, hauling him up, when the agonizing pain registered in his brain. Looking down, he saw the shark's jaws fastened around his thigh. The fish jerked its head, trying to bite through his flesh, and

329

Gunnar saw his blood running in small rivulets between the pointed teeth.

He pulled one hand free of his clutching rescuers, balled it into a fist, and smashed it into the shark's rheumy eye, while his yell of pain and fear reverberated across the bloody sea.

A moment later he was over the side of the boat, lying on his back staring at the cloudless sky as someone tied a tourniquet around his thigh.

Returning from a shopping expedition along the narrow streets of Lahaina, Emily almost collided with the Reverend Hawkins as he came dashing out of the mission house.

"Why, Josiah! Why such haste?" Emily asked. "Have you heard from your bishop at last in response to all of Cyril's complaints?"

"Emily . . . they sent for me. I must go to the harbor. A whaler came in with an injured man who is not expected to live. They want me to comfort him in his last moments."

"I'll go with you," Emily said at once. "Where are Cyril and Kekoa?" She fell into step beside him, taking two quick little steps to each of his strides.

"They went fishing. Emily, I'm not sure you should come. Apparently the injured whaler was attacked by a shark."

"Oh, the poor man," Emily said, turning pale. "But of course I must come."

"His captain had to amputate his leg, and you know they use the crudest methods at sea. I'm not sure you'll be able to stand the sight."

They dashed past the whalers' marketplace, and the strolling crowds made way for the minister and the madonna-like woman dressed in native garb. "Don't worry, Josiah," Emily said breathlessly, "I shan't faint, I promise."

"I understand they took him into the Pioneer Inn. . . ."

He was conscious, but his eyes were wildly red and he raved incoherently. Emily bit her lip and bent to wipe the sweating brow of Erik Gunnar, knowing who he was, but feeling only compassion for him.

No one expected him to live. There was nothing to be done except attend him until he died from infection, loss of blood, or shock. Learning that he had a house in Lahaina, Emily had him taken there. She and Luana moved in to care for him, despite Cyril's protests.

By the time his fever abated, Emily knew most of Erik's story from his delirious ramblings. When at last the doctor proclaimed him to be out of danger, Erik realized where he had seen the angel of his fevered dreams before. His mind went back to the night he first arrived in San Francisco and heard that Sebastian was throwing a lavish party. The woman with the angelic face had been seated at the head of the table, alone. Surely . . . it couldn't be . . .

Returning to the mission house visibly upset after calling on Erik, Emily went immediately into Cyril's comforting embrace.

"My dearest, what is it? Has he had a relapse? Come, let me get you some juice to drink." He led her to a chair and gently untangled her clutching hands.

"He is much improved. But Cyril . . . he knows who I am! He told me the woman—Garnet—was killed in a street accident." Emily gulped some of the passion-fruit juice Cyril placed in her trembling fingers. "And Sebastian . . ."

Cyril stiffened, feeling a cold chill in the pit of his stomach as she said the name that had been between them like a hovering tornado every second of every day.

". . . they say he is sailing around the world, searching for his son." Her voice was a frightened whisper. "He wants Noah back. Oh, Cyril, what will we do if he finds us? I couldn't bear it if he took my son from me."

Cyril took a deep breath. "Emily, there is a war between the American states. I'm sure your husband is back in the navy. But wherever he is, there is little chance he will find us here. I was too careful. No, dearest, Sebastian won't find us here."

"Of course, you're right," Emily said, but she was still trembling. "You know . . . the woman, Garnet, had a daughter. I thought she was also Sebastian's child, but Erik told me she was *his* daughter. The poor man, all he can think of is seeing his child again. Oh, Cyril, it never occurred to me that Sebastian would be longing for his son, just as Erik longs for his daughter. I always felt I was relieving Sebastian of an unwanted burden, allowing him the freedom to be with his other family. Oh, Cyril, I never dreamed how I might be hurting him. I didn't want to hurt him—I wanted him to be free of the burden of living with me when he loved her. I just wanted to be with you, Cyril . . . somewhere peaceful and quiet . . . and I've always thought of Noah as being—" She stopped herself in time. She had been about to say that she thought of Noah as being Cyril's son, but she was afraid to put the thought into words for fear it would give away that shameful secret longing that was always with her.

Cyril stroked her hair. "Someday we will tell Noah about his father. We'll send him to visit Sebastian—but not while there is a war. You know, Emily, we must see that Noah has musical training—beyond what I can give him in this primitive place. I've been thinking about it, and I've wondered if perhaps when the Americans end their war, we could send him to visit Sebastian—then on to London or Paris."

Emily gazed at him fondly, her tapered fingers reaching out to touch his gaunt cheeks. "Yes, of course, Cyril, dearest, you are always so right about everything. Oh, my dear, do you truly know how happy you've made me. How can I express what you mean to me?"

Cyril looked into her eyes and heard his own voice, as though from far away, and he was not sure if he were speaking aloud or if Keats' poetry were calling to him from some distant shore:

The shut rose shall dream of our loves, and awake
Full blown, and such warmth for the morning's take,
The stock-dove shall hatch her soft brace and
*   shall coo*
While I kiss to the melody, aching all through!

No, he had not spoken the words, for Emily was saying to him, "How grateful I am that you have been more than a father to Noah. He is a . . . very competent pianist, isn't he?" she asked with modest maternal pride.

Cyril hugged her, placing a kiss on top of her head, and she did not see the tear that slipped down his hollowed cheeks and came to rest on her silken hair like a drop of dew upon dark grasses. "Noah is a genius. You haven't heard his latest composition. He has so magically captured the sound of the tradewinds lightly drifting over murmuring seas . . . whispering through rain-washed trees. . . . There is even a passage where I am sure I can hear the sound of a flowered *lei* trailing across the lagoon . . . yet there *is* no such sound! Such is your son's genius."

Emily nestled closer to him, smiling happily, her fears forgotten and her heart so full of love it must surely burst through her ribs. There was never a moment that she did not rejoice in their shared happiness. To have a son whose music would live on long after all of them were gone was beyond her wildest dreams for her time on earth.

Her fingers traced the beloved contours of Cyril's face and she said softly, "Perhaps it's the magic of these islands, Cyril. You know, Erik was telling me that he has done some dreadful things in his past, and yes, he did hate Sebastian. But since he lost his leg and really settled here, he, too, has fallen under the spell of these gentle people and this lovely land. He no longer has hatred in his heart, and he does not even care terribly about his leg. He says he will have someone make him a wooden stump one of these days . . . that perhaps he owed the sea his leg, he'd taken so much from it. The islanders still believe the shark is a god, he tells me—despite all of the missionaries' teachings."

"Emily, dear, having you for a nurse would reform the worst of sinners, I'm sure."

"Poor Erik, he worries so about his daughter. He learned she is in the Deep South somewhere. He met her only briefly as a young lady. Isn't it sad? He spent most of her childhood in prison."

Cyril was silent, pushing into the back of his mind the thought that everyone was in a prison, of one kind or another. He was holding heaven in his arms, yet the bars of a taboo that could never be broken chained his love for her to the prison of his mind.

──⊰{ CHAPTER 31 }⊱──

"You sent for me, sir?" Sebastian saluted.

"There's someone to see you," the skipper replied. "I sent him to your cabin. One of the new powder monkeys. Claims to be a relative of yours. Apparently someone pulled some strings to get him assigned to us."

Sebastian's heart leaped until he did some mental arithmetic and realized it could not possibly be Noah; he was still a child. He went quickly to the cabin he shared with the second officer and pushed open the door.

The boy was examining the charts on the desk and turned as he heard the door open. Unruly black mane of hair, vivid blue eyes making the blue drill shirt and bell-bottoms look faded by comparison. Sebastian stopped abruptly, staring at the image of himself as a boy. "Rual. . . ?"

"Don't worry, I didn't tell anyone I was your son," Rual spoke defensively, watching Sebastian warily.

Sebastian sat down on his bunk. "How is your mother?"

"Mother died—was killed, in a street accident just after the war started. I would have let you know, but I didn't know where you were."

Sebastian stared at him blankly, slowly reassembling

pieces of his life in his mind. Garnet . . . pretty, lively Garnet, with her flaming hair and cat's eyes and the un-ashamed joy she took in her body. She had been his joy, and his downfall. He had intended to go back and see her and the boy . . . someday. Somehow the years had slipped away. He had once searched the China seas fruitlessly for Erik Gunnar, but eventually the goal of paying off his debts and being free to take the *Monarch Butterfly* back to America replaced his need for re-venge. Someday, he had promised himself, he would find his son, Noah. And if he didn't live that long, then at least the *Butterfly* would be an inheritance.

Standing in the cramped cabin with Rual, Sebastian fought for composure as his numbed mind tried to ac-cept the fact that it was too late to go back to Garnet. He barely realized what the boy was telling him.

"She kept up your house—Mariner's Castle. And she got the Balmain Shipping Company going again. You haven't been to see Ned, or I expect he would have told you."

"Garnet . . . your mother had enough money to do that? Mariner's Castle—I haven't thought about that place for years."

"Perhaps when the war is over you could go and see it." Rual suggested awkwardly. He longed to embrace his father, but the cabin space between them seemed endless.

"You say the company is solvent? There are ships?"

"A small fleet of schooners—thanks to Mother." *He could shake my hand . . . touch me.* "She worked hard for seamen's rights, too— founded a sailors' home in San Francisco and a Seamen's Friends Society. You wasted your life searching for a will-o'-the-wisp and ignored the real woman in your life."

A slow flush spread over Sebastian's face and he said angrily, "Mind your tongue, boy. I'll not be lectured to by a lad still wet behind the ears." He was not sure what the boy meant by chasing a will-o'-the-wisp.

"I'll get back to the fo'c'sle," Rual said, his glance sweeping over Sebastian's uniform and saying more plainly than words that he was holding his tongue because a powder monkey did not speak his mind to the ship's first officer.

Sebastian did not try to stop him. He was thinking of a small boy with flailing fists who defended his mother against a threatening giant who must have terrified the child. *Garnet, ah, Garnet . . . if only you could have been as pure as Emily*. He was so numb with pain that he did not notice Garnet's son had watched him intently throughout the brief interview with a tiny flame of hope burning and then dying in his vivid eyes.

Staring at the empty cabin, Sebastian wondered if Noah looked like Rual. He hoped he did.

Rual stumbled up on deck, furiously blinking away the tears that would not stop. He would die of shame if any of the men saw him crying like a baby.

His heart had surged with pride when he saw his father. He made an impressive figure in his officer's uniform, dwarfing every other man aboard. Except for the touches of gray in the black hair and the deep sun lines around the vivid blue eyes, Sebastian was exactly as Rual remembered him.

Clutching the ship's rail, staring at their wake, Rual thought of the years he had waited for this moment, imagining in detail what their reunion would be like. The slow realization dawning in his father's eyes, the rush of joy at seeing him again, the words, "Rual—my son—thank God we've found one another at last!"

Rual had disregarded Ned Hake's warnings that a man usually did not want the world to know he had sired a bastard. It would be different with his father and himself. He had kept his father's memory alive in his mind, never loving him less for going away. Rual knew that his father belonged at sea. Yet in the instant Rual stood in the cabin with his father, all of Ned's warnings came to mind and Rual spoke defensively, not revealing his real feelings.

Would it have been any different had he flung himself at his father, embracing him? In his heart Rual sadly acknowledged that it probably would not have been different. It was true what Ned said. Sebastian

336

loved only the lost Emily and her son, the legitimate son, Noah.

Rual wept into the lonely wind and when he at last raised his head it was as though a veil had been lowered over his face. No one aboard this ship would know that Sebastian was his father. And no one would ever learn that the only thing Rual wanted out of life was to regain his father's love. Least of all, Sebastian.

Cerise's journey to Virginia had been a disastrous confusion of crowded trains, detours to avoid the fighting, and then a dismal hotel where, at last, she waited for Austin. She saw him for only a few minutes before his regiment was due to move northward. He was not pleased to see her. He was afraid for her safety. Firmly, but lovingly, she was told she must return to South Carolina immediately.

"Please—let me stay here. Perhaps you can come and see me sometimes? Austin, I'm not afraid of the war. I'm more afraid of what will happen to our marriage if we're separated."

"Sweet thing, honey, baby," he said, his tired eyes crinkling longingly as he looked at her, "all I want in the world is to be with you. But I've got to make a secure place for you and for all of us. We've got to win this war, darlin'. . . . Listen, don't get mad, honey. We're going to whip 'em. Pretty soon we'll be marching north, and ain't nothing going to stop us."

There had been time for no more than a lingering kiss.

Charleston, Cerise thought, as she entered the crowded rail station, bracing herself for the long trip back to South Carolina. *The Gentry townhouse in Charleston—I'll go there. Surely it won't be as isolated as the plantation. I'll head back to Columbia and see Aunt Rose and Dahlia, then go on to Charleston.*

"How did you know where to find me?" Cerise asked when Mark was shown into the drawing room of Austin's parents' house in Charleston. She dismissed the

337

gray-haired butler, Moses, but did not invite Mark to be seated.

"Tracked you down from the Gentry plantation near Columbia. You came to Charleston with two Negro servants—Moses and Tannie. Your aunt and mother-in-law believed you would stay only a few days and supervise the packing of some of the valuables; they are concerned that you plan to stay indefinitely."

She watched him defiantly and was about to retort when he hurried on. "I brought you news of Rual. He's serving on the same ship as his father. No need to express your gratitude. Do me the honor of coming to dinner and the theater with me and we'll call the matter settled." He smiled, sure of himself, and Cerise felt another prick of anger.

"Mr. McKnight, I am a married woman. What you suggest is preposterous. The idea of you visiting me is preposterous. I believe this whole situation is . . ."

"Preposterous?" he suggested. His eyes never left her face, yet her body felt naked. There was a peculiar tingling in her fingertips and toes and she was afraid he would know the effect he was having on her. How she would have loved to dress up for him . . . go out and be a part of the wildly gay social whirl that only wartime and peril and imminent parting could produce. She was lonely and he was so handsome in that cool aristocratic way that just begged to be taken down a peg or two.

"You are alone here except for the servants. You surely must be going out of your mind with boredom. So why do you resist your natural impulse to accept?"

"It isn't proper—"

"Nonsense! You don't give a damn about what's proper any more than I do. You have the restless eyes of the rogue female, so don't play the part of the sheltered belle when you don't mean a word of it."

"You are insufferable. Please leave immediately."

Mark sighed regretfully. "Allow me to tell you what I've learned about people in general, and our respective families in particular." He tossed his hat to the nearest chair and sat down on the sofa, patting the seat beside him for her to join him.

338

Cerise remained standing, but she made no move to ring for the butler.

"You see, I had a nurse . . . good old Mollie Flanagain brought me up after my mother died and her views of life were somewhat distorted by her belief in vengeful saints and colorful Irish curses. However, she knew a great deal about what went on in our family and we often discussed our various destinies. My memories of Sebastian's wife, Emily, are blurred with the years, but I remember a storybook princess with a voice that caressed the senses like a magical musical chord. Her half-brother, Cyril La Flair, was a strangely brooding, rather frightening figure to look at, but he was transformed into a dashingly romantic prince whenever he was near Emily. They were both almost luminously intense in looks and demeanor. Together they gave the impression of being mythical beings inadvertently glimpsed by mortal eyes."

Cerise raised her eyebrows quizzically and Mark continued, almost apologetically: "Emily always appeared to be enclosed by an invisible wall—yet sometimes her eyes seemed to beseech for someone to break through and touch her."

"And you think Cyril was the one who broke through?"

"I'm sure of it. And she did the same for him. Watching him when he was near her was like looking at an El Greco painting that magically came to life. You know El Greco? The Greek renaissance painter who painted those mysterious, elongated portraits—spiritually compelling, but vaguely inhuman. . . . I was only a small boy when Sebastian and Emily sailed away and Cyril left for London . . . but I never forgot how they were when they were together—Emily and Cyril. They seemed to shine upon each other, somehow."

"You were probably too young to realize that their love was a sin. That aura you thought you saw about them was the temptation of forbidden love!"

"No!" Mark said sharply. "There was nothing evil about them. I don't believe they had sexual feelings for one another. They simply needed to be together."

"You don't really believe a man and woman can live together and never be tempted sexually?" Her tawny eyes mocked him.

A querying glint rose in Mark's eyes. "We're drifting from the point I was trying to make," he said finally. "When you and I discuss sex, I would prefer it to be on a personal basis. The present subject is my half-brother, Sebastian, and the two women in his life—and Cyril La Flair. I'm not sure how you feel about all of them, but let me tell you how I do. I knew and loved Emily and Cyril. Cyril was a slightly built man, but he was filled with courage of a special sort. I'm not sure how I knew this, because he rarely spoke of himself. He used to tell me stories—Roman and Greek myths . . . fairy stories—but somehow I always associated the fearless heroes with Cyril. If there was a prince in the story, it would be Cyril. And Emily was always his princess."

"But why are you telling me all this?" Cerise interrupted.

"Because it was right for Cyril and Emily to run away together. It was only with one another that they were truly happy. That is the only conclusion I can come to after much thought on the subject and many discussions with Mollie. And Sebastian . . . well, he is a different kind of man entirely. His kind of courage and honor is perhaps easier to understand. I like him tremendously, although I'll be frank and tell you my feelings for him are tinged by rivalry—he is my older brother and I feel the need to compete with him. I never knew your mother, Cerise, but I have a feeling she and Sebastian were right for each other, too."

Cerise bit her lip and looked away. "My mother died a very lonely woman, waiting for Sebastian to return to her."

"I'm sorry, Cerise. But do you understand what I'm saying? Sebastian and Emily were opposites—and as we all know, opposites do attract. But they are rarely happy together. Emily and Cyril were kindred spirits—and I think perhaps Sebastian and your mother were, too, if only all of them could have realized it."

340

"Isn't this all beside the point, since Mother is dead?"

Mark leaned forward, his eyes fixed on her face. "I'm suggesting that perhaps we can learn from it. Cerise, you're a very perceptive and intelligent woman. you know as well as I that history repeats itself endlessly because humanity is too stupid to learn from past mistakes. It's the same way with personal relationships." He paused, blue eyes watching her intently, their challenge not concealed. "I believe you and I are very much alike and could bring a great deal of happiness into each other's lives."

"You continue to ignore the fact that I'm married," she pointed out incredulously. Unconsciously, she had taken a step backward, away from him.

"I haven't met your husband, but I've traveled in your country, and I know your Southern aristocrats. With your own words, you have also given me clues as to the kind of marriage you have. You don't belong with a man who will pamper you and shield you from life. You need someone to allow you loose reins, to develop your own . . ."

Cerise picked up the bell and rang it furiously, interrupting Mark in mid-sentence. When the butler appeared, his eyes wide with alarm, she snapped, "Mr. McKnight is leaving. Show him out."

Mark had the last word, however. After he had departed, Cerise found a carriage-load of those household items that were in short supply due to the Yankee blockade. Accompanying them was a scribbled note:

I'm not sure I should do this—blockade-run supplies will prolong the killing, which I believe should be stopped as soon as possible, so that we can attend to the business of living.

Sometimes Cerise found she had trouble remembering what Austin looked like. Except for their brief meeting in Virginia, he had been home on leave only once, during the first year of the war. And they had been strangers then, except when they were in bed.

His letters were short, poorly spelled, and mostly passionate avowals of his love for her. She thought perhaps she would conceive a child during his leave and that would relieve the stupefying monotony of her existence, but she did not.

Like the other ladies of her class, she volunteered her services at the military hospital, where she rolled bandages and wrote letters for wounded soldiers; then she went home to her lonely room wishing that she could go out dancing with the unmarried girls. She missed her mother, and Rual, and her San Francisco friends. She longed to talk with someone whose topic of conversation was not the Glorious Cause.

When Federal ships crossed the bar and fired on Fort Sumter, she listened to the roar of cannon and hoped it signaled the end of the war. She did not particularly care which side won, as long as it ended. But the Federal ships were driven off and she hoped that Rual had not been aboard one of them, and, if he was, that he was not hurt in the engagement. The hospital was full of mangled boys not much older than he.

From time to time various Gentry relatives visited her and begged her to return to their plantations, pointing out delicately that it was not proper for her to live alone.

"I like it here," she responded. "Frankly, plantation life makes me uneasy. I can't help but feel that the blacks will rise up against their owners soon, knowing help is on its way from the North."

Her relatives paled at this heresy and departed hastily, puzzled by a woman who, while not exactly a Yankee, certainly did not fit their expectations as a proper wife for Austin Gentry.

She did not admit even to herself that she lingered in Charleston because of her freedom there to receive Mark on his frequent visits. Although those visits usually ended with an indignant dismissal on her part, she was always glad to see him and engage in lively conversation made the more stimulating by the undercurrent of flirtation. Recklessly, she disregarded convention in allowing him to visit her at all, although

he came discreetly after dark and she consistently refused to accompany him to restaurants or the theater.
She refused to consider what would happen if any
gossip about her were to reach the ears of the Gentry
family in the country.

She thought of Mark often and realized guiltily that
he occupied her thoughts more than did her departed
husband.

One evening one of the other young matrons who
worked at the hospital with her begged Cerise to help
with a ball she was organizing.

"It's for the Cause, honey. All I want you to do is
help collect the donations. You don't have to dance or
anything . . . but you could stay for the refreshments,
such as they are, what with all the shortages. Anyway,
you spend so much time alone—"

She had worn Cerise down eventually.

At first she busied herself with the collection of
jewelry and small valuables being donated. She watched
the men in uniform and girls in two-year-old ball gowns
fill the dance floor.

Then a deep blue enchanted twilight fell.

*I'm here without my husband . . . I'm still in mourn-
ing for my mother,* she told herself as she turned her
back on the gaiety.

Cerise felt his presence behind her and her heart
slowed to a painful, powerful throb as she heard his
voice. "May I have the honor of dancing with the most
beautiful woman present tonight?"

Mark led her out into the center of the floor and the
violins sighed the opening strains of a waltz. There was
the warmth of his hand on her waist and the first
swaying, tentative steps; then the tempo of the music
quickened. Spinning, reversing, the lights and other
dancers dissolved into a blurred mass of movement.

When the music stopped they were near the doors
and Cerise broke away and went swiftly outside. Mark
followed, pausing as he came upon her leaning against
the veranda rail.

Her face was lifted to the sky and the starlight
touched her profile as though in homage. Their aware-

ness of each other was as tangible as the faint fragrance of mimosa hanging in the warm air.

"Why do you run from me?" he asked. "Our mutual attraction can have only one conclusion."

"My life was to be planned and orderly," she replied, not turning her head. "Why did you have to disrupt it?"

"I also had a well-ordered existence. I realize now that's all it was—an existence—until I met you." His hand found hers. She withdrew it.

"You're beautiful."

"I'm married."

"We are two among millions. What draws us together if not some mystical design in the cosmos?"

"We must go back inside."

"I thought women followed their hearts, not their heads. Alas, for my illusions."

"Men are the romantics. Women can't afford to be. We must conform to the rules and standards you make for us. In biblical times the adulteress was stoned to death. Society still condemns the harlot. She is pilloried on public scorn . . . a disgrace to her community, her family, herself—"

He moved closer. "It's possible to break the marriage ties legally."

"But not morally." Her eyes, large and moist in the deepening dusk, held his for a tormented second before she ran back to the house, leaving only the lingering fragrance of mimosa.

One afternoon as she was leaving the hospital, she found him waiting for her in a hired carriage.

"Why, Mrs. Gentry," he said, springing down beside her and bowing deeply, "imagine meeting you here! What a surprise!"

Cerise forced a smile for the benefit of the other young matrons with her. She made the proper introductions, and the stir the handsome young Englishman was making among them was not lost upon her. There was nothing for it but to accept his offer of a ride home, before he said something outrageous that would be pounced on by the watchful women.

The carriage bore them along streets lined with steep-roofed houses, beneath rustling palmettos, and the sunshine was mellow.

"I would have thought you'd have left Charleston by now," he said as soon as they were alone. "You must realize that although the city has no real strategic value to either side, it will be both viciously attacked and hotly defended for its symbolic importance."

"Because it was here the first shots of the war were fired?"

"Exactly. In fact, I have grave doubts as to the fate of the entire state of South Carolina when the Federals succeed in crushing the rebellion."

Cerise regarded him from beneath curling gold-tipped eyelashes. Although the glance was flirtatious, her mind was recording every word he uttered, every fleeting expression of the chiseled features, and each gesture of his hands.

You are too perfect, Mark McKnight, she thought. *No one man has the right to be as devastatingly good looking, rich, successful, and intelligent and analytical as you are. The flaw has to be that you lack compassion. You have studied the war and reached certain conclusions, but are unmoved.* Aloud, she said, "The South is far from beaten. It's presumptuous of you—a foreigner—to pick a winner as cold-bloodedly as you might wager on the outcome of a big fighting match."

Mark's eyes flashed in eager anticipation of a verbal battle. Part of her fascination lay in her readiness to disagree with him. He thought again that in an age of simpering coquettes she was like a breath of fresh air in a musty room. It was, he decided, partly because she was secure in the knowledge of her beauty and allure. To attract a man she had neither to agree with his views, nor grant him any favor, mental or physical. The excitement of the pursuit of such a woman intensified his desire for her.

"Simple logic," Mark said, "decrees that the side

with the greater resources, in men and material, must prevail. That side is the North."

"Then it will be a long war," Cerise snapped, tossing her hair back over her shoulder in the challenging way she had. "Because to win they'll have to kill every last Southerner. You don't really know our men, Mark McKnight. They are not cold Englishmen. They are hot-blooded rebels who will never surrender."

Mark leaned forward, one black eyebrow raised. "Even when they run out of ammunition? When there is no food for either the army or the civilian population?"

"The blockade-runners will keep us supplied," Cerise said confidently.

"Ah, yes," Mark said softly as their carriage came to a halt in front of the Gentry townhouse. "Some of whom are cold Englishmen. You have fallen prey to a common misconception, by the way. Those who are capable of great depth of feeling must of necessity keep their emotions hidden behind an impassive exterior. Otherwise, you see, the impact on those volatile types with all of their fire on the surface would be shattering."

He swung his long legs down to the pavement below and turned to help her down, his eyes mocking. Cerise wondered why he was reacting so strenuously to her teasing barb about English coldness.

In the instant his hands went around her waist and she was suspended between carriage and ground, his face just below hers, he said, "If we could be alone for a while, I would be happy to demonstrate the hidden fire beneath my cold exterior."

"You disappoint me," she said, trying to hide the sudden tension that gripped her at his nearness. "You're just like other men, after all. Sooner or later you must reduce every thing to a . . . personal level."

He put her gently down on her feet. "I've never tried to disguise my 'personal' interest in you, Mrs. Gentry." *Why else do I neglect my business, my comfortable and familiar life and everything that was important to me before you came along?*

She struggled free of his helping hands and moved quickly toward the house. She walked gracefully, the billowing skirts supported by wooden hoops swaying beneath a tiny hand-span waist. There was a flash of lace-edged pantalettes as she climbed the steps to the house.

Mark watched her, a smile of admiration and pleasure lighting up his face. He was careful to bestow such glances only on her back, afraid if she were to see him looking at her in that way she would be aware of the intensity of his feelings for her. He was unsure how Cerise would use such knowledge.

Realizing she was about to disappear into the house, he quickly went after her, taking the steps three at a time. "Please think about what I said," he said as he reached her side, "about moving somewhere safe. Don't stay in South Carolina until the war comes to you."

She had not invited him in, but he lingered hopefully as the black butler opened the door in response to her impatient knocking. Moses was properly impassive when he saw Cerise was accompanied by a guest, but he was quick to announce, "Mist' Austin is in de parlor, Miz Cerise. He was just fixin' to go to de hospital lookin' for you."

"Austin! He's here?" Cerise was running across the hall as the parlor door burst open at the sound of her voice. The next moment she was swept into the arms of a red-haired Confederate officer, resplendent in gray and gold, despite the holes in the soles of his boots.

Mark watched the passionate reunion with eyes icily blue and a hardening of the jaw that was in contrast with his normally aloof expression. His hands were clenched into fists in the pockets of his coat and he did not notice the butler waiting to receive his hat.

At last Cerise broke free of the long kiss and turned to introduce him. Mark noted, with some satisfaction, her defiant glance. She had been well aware of the effect the embrace was having on him.

"Austin, this is Mark McKnight," she was saying. "And I think we should go into the parlor while I explain who he is."

Austin exhibited the customary courtesy of his countrymen, but there was no doubt he could hardly wait for an explanation as to why his wife was coming home, alone, with a handsome stranger who was not wearing a uniform in this, the third year of the war.

"Mr. McKnight is related to Rual," Cerise said as soon as the door closed between them and Moses, "although I'm not sure exactly what the relationship is." She dimpled suddenly and her eyes lit up like golden lamps in the darkening room.

She has, Mark thought, watching her, *the wickedest eyes I've ever seen. Surely in those amber depths there is the will to defy convention.*

"I am Sebastian Balmain's half-brother," he said to Austin. "Since I am a British subject and free to come and go as I please, I've been keeping your wife informed as to the whereabouts and welfare of her brother, Rual."

"I see," Austin said. He unbuttoned his jacket and sat down, long legs stretched in front of him. "You must know, then, that a Federal fleet of ironclads is at this moment steaming toward our harbor."

"I landed in North Carolina. It's no longer possible to get through the blockade to Charleston. Do you believe the Federals will invade the city?"

"Our intelligence believes they plan a siege and bombardment. They're hauling a long-range gun to Morris Island. My wife will have to leave immediately." Austin turned to Cerise, who had pulled her chair as close to his as she could get it. "Honey, you must go and stay with Aunt Rose. I've only three days' leave, so we must put Moses and Tannie to work packing at once."

Cerise's face fell. "But why can't I stay here? At least I can make myself useful at the hospital. At the plantation there is absolutely nothing for me to do. I shall go out of my mind."

Austin glanced in the direction of their guest in a way that plainly said he would prefer their conversation to be private, but Mark did not take the hint.

"No, honey, you can't stay here. Besides, if it's

just work in the hospital you'll miss, you can go into Columbia. Cousin Billy and Beulah have a house there, and the university has been converted into a military hospital—you could stay with them and volunteer there."

Moses knocked on the door to announce dinner and Austin said, "You'll join us, sir?"

"Delighted," Mark murmured.

"Bring a smoking jacket for Mr. Austin," Cerise said to Moses. "He'll be more comfortable, and Tannie can mend that tear in his uniform jacket."

"No—don't bother, Moses," Austin said quickly, buttoning up his coat.

He was surprised at the food waiting on the sideboard, knowing how desperate the situation was for both soldiers and civilians because of the tightening Yankee blockade. There was fresh meat, gumbo, and even a bottle of wine.

"Why, honey, where did you get all this?"

"Since it wasn't here this morning, I assume Mr. McKnight brought it."

"I'd heard that many of your countrymen were running the blockade," Austin said stiffly. "From the continued rise in food prices, the profits must be enormous."

"Utterly fantastic," Mark agreed. "There surely would be no other reason for a man to risk getting blown to bits by Federal gunboats." His eyes were fixed on Cerise.

"The Confederacy could use ammunition rather than wine, but I reckon there's more profit on wine?" Austin asked sarcastically.

"Exactly. Besides, if I brought in bullets, I should have all the men they killed and maimed on my conscience. I am not a war-lover."

"Merely a war profiteer?" Austin suggested, shaking his head as Moses approached with the opened bottle of wine.

"Austin"—Cerise broke in hurriedly—"this isn't like you. You're forgetting that not only is Mr. McKnight our guest, but he's also a neutral."

There was an awkward silence as the two men re-garded each other and their unspoken thoughts hung in the air. Sitting between them, Cerise felt like a bone lying between two dogs. She was angry with both of them, and more than a little envious. They were free to do as they pleased. Come or go, fight or withdraw. Even declare their rivalry over her, if they chose. And she? She would be sent to Columbia for safe keeping.

Later, when they were alone in their bedroom and Mark had departed—not having been invited to spend the night—Cerise looked across the room at the stranger who was her husband. She sat at her dressing table, brushing her hair as he lounged on the bed with the glass of wine he would not accept at dinner cradled in his hand.

On his last leave they had slipped away to their room at every possible opportunity and made love so many times Cerise was almost embarrassed to face the family at mealtimes. Tonight she felt no desire and was both puzzled and apprehensive. She kept thinking about Mark, no matter how she tried to put him out of her mind. It occurred to her with a shock that she actually knew and understood him better than her husband.

Mark had undoubtedly been running the blockade, not for profit alone, but because he was attracted to her . . . and, she suspected, for the sheer thrill of danger. These were motives she could understand—Austin and the rest of the Southerners who were ready to give up everything, including their lives, for a cause that was lost from the start, one that seemed gallant, but was foolish. She could not feign the patriotism that made no sacri-fice too great, no hardship too severe, and, feeling out of place among people who put their Cause above their own comfort and safety, she was drawn to a man who pursued his own aims as ruthlessly as she wished she were able to pursue hers.

Fighting a sense of panic whenever she thought of Mark, she went to Austin and took the glass from his hand, then flung herself into his arms. He winced as her hands went under his jacket and she drew back, startled. "What is it?"

"I'm sorry, honey . . . here, help me off with the coat. I've got a minor flesh wound. That's how come they gave me a furlough."

His shoulder and ribs were bandaged. Cerise bit her lip, feeling more guilty than ever. "Why didn't you say something downstairs? The way I clung to you in the hall, I must have hurt you."

His face crinkled into a smile, despite the pain in his eyes. "Help me out of my clothes, sweet thing, and we'll figure out what to do next."

Cerise tried to put everything out of her mind but the memory of the pleasures they had once shared. She caressed him gently, kissed his lips and his eyes, pressed her mouth to his chest, ran her fingers over his thighs until he was fully erect. He was lying on his back and she moved to take the dominant position, but his hands closed about her waist and he said, "Now, honey, I told you it was just a flesh wound. Heroes only get shoulder wounds, right? I can still take my proper place on top."

She lay back and parted her thighs and tried to hide her dismay when, as he fumbled, she imagined a dark stain seeping through the bandage. Her own flesh felt cold and dry and she did not want him. She told herself it was because of his wound, that she was afraid he would tear it open, but the image of Mark's face kept superimposing itself over her husband's worried expression. He pushed his organ inside her and she cringed because the entry was dry and painful. After moving slowly for a moment, he began to perspire and, giving up, rolled over on to his back. "Give me a minute, sweet thing . . ." His breathing was labored.

"If you would just let me . . . be the . . . the active one," she said in a small, tight voice. *Perhaps then I could summon my own desire* . . . but she knew, with a feeling of dread, that it was neither his weakness from the wound, nor his insistence of male dominance that had driven desire from her mind. It was a much more deadly malady.

Austin did not mention Mark until the following morning. "You will not receive McKnight in the future," he said abruptly.

"Oh, and why not?"

"Don't argue with me, honey. You know it isn't proper for him to be visiting you. Don't force me to call him out."

Cerise bit back her angry retort. She lay stiffly beside her husband in bed, wishing he had not come home to her.

"Now everything's going to be all right, honey—soon as we win the war. Don't fret your pretty little head. Why, one Johnny Reb can lick a dozen Yankees any day of the week." He boasted and teased and made little exploratory journeys with fingers and lips as, in the bright new morning, he felt renewed strength and vigor and the surging of desire that had not been appeased the previous night. But she could neither submit nor cooperate. She wriggled away from him, angry that it was his right to order her to the plantation, forbid her to see a man who was more a companion to her than her husband had ever been.

She made the excuse that she must go to the hospital to explain that she would be leaving almost immediately. On the way she reflected that it had always been that way between them. Austin never talked to her about anything but the most superficial of his feelings and the most banal trivialities. She had no idea of his deepest feelings, nor he of hers. He humored her as an affectionate father humors a precocious daughter despite the fact that she still regarded him as a swaggering little boy.

Out on the street, she realized she had forgotten the rolls of bandages she had taken home for Tannie to launder. She let herself into the house through the piazza, which was hidden from the street by high walls. She went quickly in the direction of the servants' wing, now occupied only by Tannie and Moses.

At the end of the hall she paused as she saw someone else was knocking at Tannie's door and, with a familiarity bred of long practice, pushed open the door and entered the room.

Cerise reeled back into the shadows, a sick feeling of both horror and guilt enveloping her. Austin had just entered the maid's room and closed the door. That it was not the first time and that a wife who refused to accommodate a husband had to share the blame were two thoughts that raced through her mind and kept her riveted to the spot. Then she heard a giggle, followed by Austin's voice, murmuring lazily. The words were a shock, for although Cerise had never heard them before, their Anglo-Saxon descriptive bluntness conveyed better than any picture what was going on behind those closed doors.

CHAPTER 32

On the Gentry plantation near Columbia, the women rejoiced at the news that Lee was in Pennsylvania and the Yankees were rushing to the defense of Gettysburg.

Draft riots had erupted in New York following the signing of Lincoln's Draft Bill, and rumor had it that there had been a thousand Yankee casualties from the riots alone.

Cerise remembered her mother's stories of the famous Five Points riot, when she had first met a man named Tom, her first love. The Irish, whose National Guard unit had caused the Five Points riot, were now rioting at the prospect of being drafted and the fear that freed Negroes would take their jobs. Disturbingly, Cerise thought about Mark and his oft-repeated refrain that history repeats itself and continues to do so unless people learn a lesson from it.

With the Southern victories, the hope was born again that England would ally herself with the Confederacy. This latter fact tempered Aunt Rose's indignation at the reappearance of the young Englishman, Mark McKnight, after Austin had assured her there would be no more cause for alarm in respect to his wife's association with the man.

"What can I do?" Aunt Rose inquired of Dahlia, after ordering the butler to set another place at dinner. "If we are going to be allied with England? And he did bring such a handsome contribution to our larder. Why, I don't remember when we had so much food. And I did so need the thimbles and needles and thread. . . . Honey, we mustn't let your mother know he's here."

Torn between wanting to keep all of McKnight's gifts and the feeling she was betraying her nephew's trust in regard to his wife, Aunt Rose wrestled with her conscience and sought her niece's approval.

Dahlia, who was secretly in love with a boy serving with Lee and who could think of nothing but his safe return, made noncommittal sounds.

Cerise and Mark, meanwhile, were walking and talking together. Cerise had made no pretense of annoyance at Mark's arrival, being only too glad to see him again and not caring who knew it. With Mark she felt alive, vitally concerned with everything happening in the world, eager to share her thoughts and ideas. Even when they quarreled, which was often, she was more stimulated by him than any man she had ever known. Telling herself she regarded him only as a friend and would not allow their relationship to drift from a platonic state did not blind her to the dangerous ground they were treading. But when faced with the choice of a temptation-free existence and never seeing Mark again, her heart rebelled. She could and would keep a tight control over herself—and him—and nothing improper would occur.

They strolled together in silence for a little while, savoring each other's presence without the need for words. Then Cerise asked, "Is there any hope for an alliance with England? "How did you perceive the sentiments in Parliament when you were there?"

"I don't think there'll be an alliance. Of course, if Lee gets a foothold in Pennsylvania, I believe England will at least recognize the Confederacy as a nation . . . perhaps be more open with the aid they are already giving. There is concern about England's seagoing commerce, because of the blockade. It's odd, but the same conditions that brought about the war of 1812 between England and America are again ripe—in reverse. English ships are in jeopardy and Englishmen are still outraged that the Federals actually boarded an English ship and seized two Confederate commissioners. So sympathy is with the South."

"If England did come into the war on our side," Cerise said slowly, "there's no doubt the Confederacy would win."

Mark glanced at her sharply, aware of her personal association with the South. Before she had referred impartially to North and South without placing herself on either side, her anger directed only at the bloodshed and privation war brought.

"England could never ally herself with a government that endorses slavery," Mark said.

"But the South will free the slaves themselves, in time. You know as well as I that the issue isn't really slavery—"

She's beginning to sound like them, Mark thought with a cold feeling of dread. He was silent, collecting his thoughts.

"Austin is with Lee in Pennsylvania," Cerise said. "He's serving under Brigadier General Lewis Armistead, but that's all I really know."

"Why did you marry him?" Mark asked abruptly. They were walking along the road bordering the cotton fields where the slaves worked in the hot afternoon sun. Cerise's parasol shadowed her face, and before she could answer, he went on: "Don't lie and and tell me you loved him, because I know you didn't—and don't."

The parasol dipped, covering her eyes. "I saw my

mother destroyed by love," Cerise said shortly. "And I vowed I'd never be a slave to it. I wanted to be free—I thought of marriage as an escape from all the restrictions of being a single girl. It was the rite that magically conferred womanhood. Austin adored me; he was handsome and full of fun and very rich. It seemed a perfect match."

"Thank you for being honest," Mark said quietly. "You know that I love you, of course."

He spoke the words for the first time in his life. He felt his heart expand at the wonder and revelation of the purity and selflessness of his love. She was more important to him than his life. He knew that he would never love another woman as hopelessly as he loved Cerise. Yet despair was there, too, written in the suddenly drooping shoulders and long sigh that shuddered from her.

She looked straight ahead, did not slow her pace.

"Please—say something," Mark begged, "before I make a complete fool of myself in front of all of these black workers. I've always thought of myself as being a reasonably honorable man, Cerise. I know it wasn't honorable to pursue a married woman—although there have been others in my life. I suppose there will always be those couples who seek a diversion from the bonds of matrimony. But I knew you were not one of those women. Cerise, I'm trying to say that I believe I've known from the moment I first saw you that if I couldn't have you, I would want no other woman."

The parasol was between them again and her voice seemed muffled by the lace and ribbons. "Oh, Mark . . . perhaps if we had met sooner—before I was married. Who knows? But it's too late."

He caught her wrist, pushing the parasol out of the way, and jerked her around to face blazing blue eyes that were filled with longing and a desperation she had not seen there before. "Our lives are only an instant in the eternity of time. It doesn't make any sense to forfeit happiness because of traditions we don't believe in."

"I do believe in marriage! And Austin loves me—"

"He can't love you as I love you because he doesn't know you as I know you. I watched you together; he sees only a woman whose body he craves and whose beauty is a credit to him. He has no concept of what goes on in your mind and doesn't care to know. Oh, Lord, Cerise—can't you learn from what went before? Your mother and Sebastian—Cyril and Emily. Our own respective fathers—you and I, we were both children of *mésalliances*. But it doesn't have to be that way for us now."

"Let go of me, please. The field hands are watching us and Aunt Rose will come running from the house any moment and swoon at our impropriety." She could not meet his tortured gaze.

"Tell me you love me," he demanded.

Her eyes were suddenly bright with unshed tears, glistening like golden dewdrops. "Austin was wounded. That's why you thought—he was different—because..." She fumbled for words.

"He was different because he's been fighting for two years," Mark said. "A soldier—in being prepared to kill—must also be prepared to die. If you didn't know and understand him before, it will be even harder when he comes home bitter and disillusioned because it was all for nothing."

"The South is going to lose," she said. It was more a statement than a question.

"Yes," he answered quietly. "The blockade is strangling you. Soldiers can't fight without guns and ammunition, food, medical supplies. You simply don't have the capability of producing all you need. Your men are fighting with unbelievable courage and daring, but eventually your lack of manufacturing facilities will defeat them, not the enemy. What is particularly sad is that in fighting so fiercely, they will prolong the war... perhaps for years. Casualties on both sides are already appalling."

"I'm glad you're not a part of it," Cerise said vehemently.

He stared at her for a moment, a strange raw pain flaring in his eyes.

357

"Oh, I know you've been bringing supplies through the blockade," she said quickly. "But that was just an excuse, wasn't it? To come and see me—and vicariously enjoy the thrill of danger without having any real stake in the outcome."

A pulse showed itself briefly in his temple. "Do I appear so shallow to you?"

"Not shallow. Practical. You take risks for yourself, not for a political cause. And you know even if you are caught, you're a foreigner—a neutral—so probably nothing will happen to you."

He frowned. "To the brave go the fair . . ."

"What?"

"Nothing. I was thinking aloud. Perhaps I'm not quite so unmoved by the war as you believe. I've always felt that war is the ugliest of human pastimes. I swore I would never be a part of one. But you're right about my blockade-running. I do feel guilty about perpetuating the conflict by bringing supplies through the blockade. And while I admire the courage of the South, I can't endorse a system that depends on enslavement to survive."

"Slavery *is* wrong . . ." Cerise began, trying to suppress a sudden image of Tannie in her husband's arms.

Mark was not listening. His eyes seemed to be focused on some distant horizon. "The war has to be ended. How can we find our own peace while your husband is at war? How can I fight for you against a man who is fighting for his country? Oh, God, Cerise—I've been so besotted by you I didn't see what I was becoming."

She looked at him as his eyes slowly met hers again, seeing the love that mirrored her own feelings so perfectly it was as if their very souls had touched.

"I never expected to love a man," Cerise said heavily. "What a cruel joke." She jerked her hand free of his grasp and raced back to the sanctity of the house.

CHAPTER 33

A boiling cloud of smoke and dust engulfed Cemetery Hill. Muskets, knapsacks, and bloody fragments of human flesh were tossed into the swirling mass.

There were no cheers, but a mournful roar like a single gasp of agony from hundreds of parched throats rose from the entire field.

On the hill were wrecked caissons, dead horses, and men sprawled in the grim stillness of death.

The living defenders and the men who charged up the hill fought in the blinding, impenetrable fog of powder smoke . . . smoke from cannons and rifles that was stabbed by red flashes of fire illuminating the waving flags and silhouetted men.

General Armistead, slouch hat poised atop his sword, was leading the Confederate contingent that broke the Federal line. Still waving his sword, the black felt hat now slipped down to the hilt, he grasped one of the dead Cushing's guns. He yelled for his men to charge, then fell, mortally wounded.

Behind him, Austin Gentry felt the explosion of pain rip through his body and he went down, choking, all the fires of hell searing his brain as his body sent back quivering messages of pain. It was as though a dozen red-hot nails had been driven into his legs and lower abdomen.

The sounds of battle around him faded, returned briefly, then faded again. He did not know that the climax of the battle had just passed, that he had been a part of the Confederate wave that had almost turned the tide, but that tide was now ebbing. The broken charge was drifting back down the dark slope, stumbling over human debris.

Military formations had been broken, but the men retreated defiantly, ready to turn and fight if the Federals attempted pursuit. They made no attempt, having exhausted themselves repulsing the supreme effort Lee made; they were content to let the enemy go.

Virtually all of the men who had followed Armistead, however, were either dead or had been taken prisoner. Austin Gentry was not among the thousands of wounded being taken back by wagon train to Virginia.

News of Lee's retreat from Gettysburg plunged the Gentry plantation into deep gloom. Besides Austin and Dahlia's beau, half a dozen Gentry men were serving under Lee. There were no able-bodied men, other than black slaves, left on the plantation. Even Uncle Will, a man well past his prime, had volunteered. He had departed wearing the uniform he had worn in the Mexican-American war.

The field hands labored under the direction of a black foreman. Aunt Rose ran the house and supervised the slave quarters with the unflagging energy and iron will of the head of a large corporation, which indeed the plantation was. Everything of value that could be donated to the Cause had been donated. The women's clothes were as worn and patched as those of the slaves. But at least the plantation residents were not starving, like the city-dwellers. Their gardens produced vegetables, and there was pork for the household and chitlings for the slave quarters.

Cerise and Dahlia stayed in the Columbia townhouse of some Gentry cousins, Billy and Beulah. Cousin Billy proved to actually be Dr. Gentry, now serving the wounded on the former university campus. Cerise and Dahlia worked long hours at the newly converted hospital, and visited the plantation only when Aunt Rose sent an urgent summons for their presence. Moses would drive the carriage into town and, if they were at the hospital, would patiently sit outside until they emerged from performing their duties. Then his cap would leap into his hand and he would say gently, "Miz Rose requests the pleasure of the young misses' company."

It occurred to Cerise that Aunt Rose sent for them from time to time to be sure the frail Dahlia was not overtaxing her strength. She had become even more quiet and withdrawn after the Gettysburg casualty lists were released.

Austin's name was listed, and beside it was written "missing in action." The Gentry family had lost two other members in that fateful battle. They all rallied around Cerise, assuring her that Austin was a prisoner; she must never think of him as being dead.

Just before the summer drew to a close, the carriage arrived at the hospital, and although Moses remained seated in it, Mark McKnight alighted and went inside. He found Cerise sitting beside the bed of an incoherent youth with a powder-blackened face. She was dispiritedly waving away the flies that descended in black clouds whenever her exhausted arm slowed the waving of the palmetto fan. Her golden eyes were dull and her hair straggled limply down her back, tied back with a rag. There were bloodstains on the white apron she wore and her dress clung to her back.

Mark wore a tailored suit, a spotless shirt, and polished boots. He was sleekly well fed and immaculate. Looking up to see him wending his way through the rows of broken bodies, Cerise felt a stab of resentment. It wasn't fair that there were men who were well fed and well dressed while others died miserably or survived the battle only to perish of wounds and exposure and sickness.

"Miss Nightingale, I presume?" he said, his face lighting up as he saw her.

"What are you doing here? I hope you brought quinine and not wine on this trip," she said, batting viciously at a buzzing bluebottle fly.

"Put that down and come outside with me for a moment. You look absolutely exhausted," he said. "And if you'll look closely, you'll see that your patient no

361

longer cares whether the flies land on his face or not."
He bent to pull the sheet over the boy's staring eyes.

Her fingers were trembling with fatigue and waves
of hopelessness and despair mingled with nausea at the
stench of blood and death all around her. She stood up
stiffly and he took her arm to lead her outside into the
sunshine.

"I suppose you went to the plantation," she said,
"and got Aunt Rose into a state again."

"Not so much of a state that she refused the new
dress I brought for her," he answered with a wry smile.
"I brought one for you, too. It's in a box in the carriage."

"I hope it's black," she muttered. "No doubt I shall
hear any day that I must go into mourning for my
husband."

"He's a prisoner," Mark said. His voice was expres-
sionless, and his eyes studied the cart that had just
come to a halt at the hospital doors. It was jammed
with wounded men, their arms and legs forming a
bloodstained tangle.

Cerise drew in her breath and closed her eyes for a
second. "You're sure?"

"It took a great deal of detective work and much
wining and dining of Federal officials, but I found him.
He was badly wounded in the charge up Cemetery Hill.
He's in a prison hospital, I assure you."

Stretcher bearers were untangling the wounded men,
carrying them into the hospital, where surgeons sharp-
ened knives and saws in readiness for the hacking off
of shattered limbs.

"Come on. The carriage is over there. You're going
home for a bath and a rest. Then you're going to put
on the new dress I brought and I'm taking you to my
hotel, where the chef is preparing the food I brought.
No—no arguments, or I'll have to use force. I'm sure
you'd never be able to explain to your fellow nurses
why that foreign fellow picked you up in his arms and
made off with you."

She climbed into the open carriage with him and
Moses urged the horses forward. Mark told him, "Drop

us off at the house. Then you can go on back to the plantation. Be sure to thank your mistress again, on my behalf, for allowing you to bring me into town."

"My reputation will be ruined here, too," Cerise said gloomily. "Thanks to you, I'm a scarlet woman all across the state."

Mark merely smiled and leaned back in the seat so he could watch her.

"I wish you wouldn't stare at me so," she whispered fiercely, with a glance at the impassive back of Moses. "People will notice."

"But you just said your reputation is already ruined," he pointed out. *Even in a threadbare dress, her hair tied back with a strip of bandage, and her face glowing with perspiration, she is more vitally beautiful than any woman I know,* Mark thought.

How many times he had returned to England and flung himself into a romantic liaison with some lovely young woman, trying to forget the only woman in the world he really wanted. Cerise, with the wicked golden eyes and blazing red-gold hair, the glory of which paled beside her inner fires. He had never waited so long, nor endured so much to possess a woman. Yet it was not merely her body he wanted. He wanted to surrender himself to love. To love and care for this woman. Who belonged to a man lying in a prison hospital who would never walk again. Questions clicked into place, re-shuffled in his mind, and offered the same hopeless answers.

Cerise was surreptitiously lifting the tissue paper from the dress box on the seat beside her. A glorious jade-green taffeta shimmered into view. She caught her breath.

Mark pretended not to see her fingers lightly touching the green dress. "Rual was home on leave. I didn't see him, but Ned said he'd grown and looked well, though I gather putting him on the same ship as Sebastian may have been a mistake. They don't get along too well. Pity, they are the spirit and image of one another. Well, here we are. I'll wait in the parlor while you bathe and rest and change into your new dress."

"I'm not going with you," Cerise said, but there was doubt in her voice and she picked up the dress box reverently and handed it to him before he helped her out of the carriage.

She lingered in front of the mirror, hardly recognizing the reflection that smiled back at her with dimpled delight. Under the lamplight, mysterious golden glints appeared in the taffeta, setting off her eyes, while the predominant jade-green contrasted with her red-gold hair, now burnished from being washed in the scented soap—yet another gift from Mark—and rubbed vigorously dry by Tannie.

Cerise had not been able to look into Tannie's dusky gaze for some time after Austin's leave ended, knowing that the girl had lain with her husband, and resenting her for being able to bring him pleasure when she, his wife, had not. Eventually, reason had prevailed. Cerise knew that any blame in the matter lay squarely with Austin and herself, and not with Tannie. Tannie was a slave who had no choice in the matter.

Surprisingly, Dahlia had urged Cerise to go out to dinner with Mark. She had gratefully accepted the black silk mourning dress with jet beads decorating the bodice that he had brought for her. "How did you know . . . that I lost someone dear to me at Gettysburg?" she whispered, her eyes filling with tears.

"You were to have been married on his next leave, weren't you? You should bring your grief out into the open, let others comfort you. It will help," Mark said gently .

Listening to the compassion in his voice, Cerise thought again that every time she saw him he revealed another facet to his personality that endeared him to her. How she wished he would show some despicable trait—or even return to being the aloof and selfish young man she had first met—so she could quell her growing love for him.

"Go with him," Dahlia urged. "He has been so kind to us. What harm will it do? It surely isn't helping Austin for you to stay home worrying about him . . . and with Mark's connections in the North, perhaps he can get Austin exchanged later on."

Dahlia refused Mark's invitation to dine with them, and when they left, she was proudly wearing her new mourning dress. A small framed photograph of her lost love had appeared on the piano.

They dined in the candlelit hotel restaurant and Cerise drank champagne and felt light-hearted and young for the first time in months. Then, without realizing she had agreed to go, she found herself in Mark's room. He was handing her another glass of champagne and watching her over the rim of the glass, silently adoring her with his eyes.

"One glass. Then you must take me home," she said, feeling her heart begin to pound in slow distinct cadence with his.

"Stay with me. Let us have just one night together. You see, I'm going away . . . I won't be back for some time."

"No. I can't. You don't understand. It would be the first step down the road my mother traveled. Oh, she tried to live respectably for my sake and Rual's—but the other children would whisper sometimes, things they heard from their parents. Once a woman loses her reputation, she can never regain it. I don't want my children haunted by the specter of my past."

His arm went around her waist and he led her to the couch. She was conscious of the warmth of his fingers through the jade taffeta and the electricity that flowed through her body at his nearness.

"It isn't your reputation you're worried about, or you wouldn't be here with me. You're afraid if we make love you'll never be able to live with your husband again."

"All right," she flared back, "I am attracted to you. I admire your mind, enjoy your companionship, worry about what you're doing when you are not with me. I do want you. There, I've said it all. . . . Are you satisfied?"

He took the glass from her shaking fingers and placed it on the table, then reached out and began to unbutton her basque, slowly and deliberately. "I love you," he said. "At first I was attracted to a pair of challenging eyes in a photograph. When I met you, I found to my surprise and delight that apart from your lovely body— the mere sight of which fills me with desire—even our minds were perfectly in tune."

"Because we are both despicably selfish characters, perhaps?" she suggested, her breathing growing uneven as he laid bare her breasts and caressed them. "Yes," she went on, recklessly allowing him to fondle her, although his touch was sending molten sparks coursing from her inner thighs and contracting secret muscles in a tight pain of need. "That must be it—we are both ruthless. I work at the hospital merely to fill my empty hours so I shan't die of boredom, knowing I believe the war is foolish and wrong. And you—you bring wine and taffeta through the blockade . . . move about freely in the North and South as an observer to all of this carnage . . . for the same reason! Just to escape boredom. Oh, we are both doomed to hellfire. . . ."

He pressed her back against the couch and covered her mouth with his, parting her lips gently but insistently, slipping his tongue between her teeth. She closed her eyes and lost herself in the kiss.

His fingers were tantalizingly slow and gentle as he slipped her dress down the length of her body, kissing her lingeringly as each inch of her flesh was bared. When his lips and tongue reached her inner thighs, she cried out softly, seizing his head and pulling him back to kiss her lips. She felt she was drowning in his kiss and could not bear it when he pulled away from her to remove his own clothes.

His body was lean, with a well-developed chest shadowed by dark hair, and broad shoulders. She watched the candlelight flickering over the contours of his body, naked and beautiful, and she was overwhelmed by the intensity of her feelings. His eyes were peacock-blue and filled with the promise of wild delights as he lay down beside her.

There was no time or space or dimension, only the searching awareness of smooth, warm skin transmitting sensory messages of love. When at last he entered her, they were both lost in joyous abandon and were whole at last.

The clock on the mantle began to chime midnight. She stirred beside him, struggling to escape his encircling arms. "I must go."

"You can't. You're mine and you know it. Come away with me—back to England. There's still time. I'll do anything you want me to do." He sat up, his black hair falling over his brow, the lamplight shadowing his shoulders and bare chest so that he looked like a Grecian statue coming suddenly to life. "The war of attrition will begin now. Gettysburg was just the beginning. Each side will suffer heavier and heavier casualties in order to inflict them upon the enemy. You can't stay here; you must come away with me."

She slipped from his grasp and out of bed and his words died in his throat as he looked at her: her long, creamy limbs, the full breasts that emphasized the narrow waist and flat stomach, her hair falling about rounded shoulders. Her skin was flawless and seemed to glow in the lamplight.

"If I go now, perhaps I can still look Dahlia and her cousins and the servants in the eye tomorrow. It's just midnight. I can never see you again, Mark. Please don't ever come back, because I am powerless to resist you, and if you love me you must help me be strong. When the war is over I am going to try to be a good wife to Austin. I *will* make my marriage work—I will!"

She raised her tear-stained cheeks and he saw the resolve in her eyes and recognized it only too well. He had seen the same determination reflected in his own mirror many times. She was the other half of his own spirit and soul and would destroy herself before she would deviate from the path she had set.

CHAPTER 34

"We've been ordered to make a strong demonstration before Charleston," the skipper told Sebastian, "in order to draw the Confederates' attention away from General Sherman's march from Georgia."

"We'll need to mark the obstructions in the channel before we can do much good in that respect," Sebastian answered.

"Begin to locate the obstructions and mark them immediately, then."

"Aye, sir."

"The boy . . . Rual Balmain, who came aboard with you. He's your nephew, is he? There's a remarkable family likeness. I thought at first he was your son, but he said he was not."

Sebastian muttered something unintelligible and made his escape from the captain's cabin. So Rual denied being his son. Well, he couldn't blame him for that. They'd been at loggerheads since they met aboard that first ship . . . too stubborn and bull-headed for his own good, that boy, Sebastian reflected, oblivious to those traits in himself. There was a lot of Garnet in Rual, he thought, the craggy planes of his face relaxing in sweet remembrance of her for a moment.

She would have been proud of the boy. He had become a midshipman through his own efforts; Sebastian had no part in it. And he'd served honorably in a dozen engagements. Damn it, Sebastian was proud of him, too. If only there was not that freezing silence between them. If only he could bring himself to tell the boy that he had loved Garnet, in his way.

He no longer believed he would find Emily. He still dreamed of her sometimes, though in his waking hours her face was becoming harder to recall. But Noah . . . his son . . . Sebastian was convinced that one day Noah would come looking for him. As soon as he was old enough. Noah would bind up the wounds. Sebastian had done his penance for his sins, and his reward would be the reunion with his son. Noah, his true son, his legitimate heir. What plans he had made.

When the war ended Sebastian would build up his fleet of ships. By the time Noah was a man, the Balmain clippers would be sailing every sea lane. The *Monarch Butterfly* was safely hidden in Burma. *I kept her for you, Noah. I presented you to the world from the deck of her model, and, by God, when you're a man you'll sail her with me.*

In the middle of January, 1865, their ship was engaged in locating channel obstacles when Sebastian came upon Rual unexpectedly below decks.

Rual had grown even taller, and he bulged with muscle. Sebastian felt he was looking into a ghostly mirror whenever he saw the boy. "Everything shipshape, midshipman?" He never knew what to say to the boy. How did a man look at a sixteen-year-old and say, "Look—I slept with your mother and brought you into the world . . . but I can't accept you into my life until I've made my peace with my son born of marriage and commitment."?

"Aye, sir," Rual answered, standing aside to allow the first officer to pass. His bright blue eyes flickered with an emotion Sebastian did not recognize. Was it hatred? Did the boy hate him for walking out on his mother?

There was a sudden grating crash and they were flung to the deck. Water rushed immediately through a hole in the bulkhead. Everything slanted dizzily and they were plunged into darkness. Seawater swirled around them as Rual struggled to pull himself free of the splintered bulkhead.

"We're going down fast," Sebastian gasped. "Must have been hit by a torpedo."

Rual was on his feet, knee-deep in water. "Can you get up? We've got to get out of here."

"No. Something's trapping my legs. Go on. You get out of here. I'll work myself free." Sebastian pulled himself up, straining to push the wreckage that held fast his legs.

Rual turned to grasp the imprisoning planks and his hands closed over metal. Shells . . . they had burst through the bulkhead and jammed in deadly profusion over his father's legs. Each second the water rose with terrifying swiftness. Rual hurled the first shell over his shoulder, then the second, working feverishly as Sebastian fought to keep his head above water.

In the instant before Sebastian's head disappeared under the murky water, he shouted, "Rual, for God's sake, save yourself so I can face your mother when I meet her. . . !"

"Take a breath and hold it!" Rual yelled back. "Damn you, don't you die on me! I love you, Father!"

He didn't know if Sebastian heard the last words, which had been wrenched from deep inside him and which echoed as unexpectedly in his own mind as they must have in his father's.

Picking up shells and heaving them away, he lost track of time. How long could a man live underwater? Why the hell had they wasted so much time before acknowledging one another?

Then all at once the water was working with him, floating the shells free. His hands closed around his father's shoulders and dragged him, choking and coughing, to the surface.

"Hold onto me, while I find a way topside," Rual gasped, putting Sebastian's arms over his shoulders and reaching upward to find a way through the imprisoning deck. There was now only a foot of airspace left.

Groping along in the darkness, Sebastian clinging to him and trailing his injured legs in the water, Rual reached upward and at last felt only air. The next moment the ship groaned in her final agony and slipped over to her starboard beam and they were both swimming, feeling the pull of the sinking ship trying to take them with her.

They were separated in the churning, flotsam-filled

370

maelstrom. Rual thrashed his arms about wildly, seeking his father, but his hands connected only with debris. He was not sure how badly injured Sebastian's legs were, or how long he would be able to swim.

In his anguish, Rual shouted aloud, "Where are you, you old bastard?"

A head popped out of the water in front of him, bristling black hair standing in defiant spikes. Sebastian grinned and winced at the same time as he fought to stay afloat.

"You've got it all wrong," he said between gasping breaths. "It's you who is the bastard."

The men who had been on deck and who were now being pulled into waiting Confederate boats were astonished to see the two men who lay on their backs, floating and shouting with laughter as they waited to be picked up. When they reached for the younger of the two, he said, "No—take my father first. His legs are hurt."

A minute later, lying in the boat while someone felt for broken bones, Sebastian looked up at Rual and his eyes filled with tears.

Hours passed before the harried Confederate surgeon was able to examine Sebastian's injured legs. Rual crouched beside his father in the crowded prison, keeping silent vigil when the faded blue eyes closed in exhaustion, listening when Sebastian talked.

Learning about Erik Gunnar's treachery and hearing the horror in Sebastian's voice when he spoke of the long, lonely year on the deserted atoll, Rual felt his own blood chill. He understood now why his father had disappeared so abruptly, but not why he had never returned to them when he was rescued.

After a time, Sebastian moaned in pain and began to speak deliriously of a bawdy house. Rual turned away, not wanting to hear. Then Sebastian said, distinctly, "The Red Garter." Rual felt a jolt of recognition.

He thought of the Red Garter's madam, the flamboyant Cassie Madigan, with her gaudy clothes and eye-watering perfume. There had been a time when Rual

371

and the other boys would follow her down the street, cat-calling and whistling, until someone chased them away.

Once Larry Winfield had dared Rual to slip inside the Red Garter and see what went on there. Austin Gentry, who was older than all of them, had casually offered to go with him. Before Rual realized what was happening, the dare had been backed by a collection of everyone's allowances.

Getting inside the Red Garter had not proved difficult. There was a rear door leading to the kitchens and they slipped inside when the Chinese chefs were busy with dinner. The boys hid behind the bakers' racks and peered through a hatchway to the dining room.

The ground floor was disappointingly more like a grand restaurant and fancy saloon than the bawdy house they expected. Crystal chandeliers glinted above spotless white tablecloths, and rich brocade covered the walls. Elegantly dressed patrons were dining or drinking at the adjacent bar. A group of musicians played upon a central dais.

Then Austin noticed that occasionally one of the hostesses would saunter up a wide staircase in the company of a man. Huddled in their cramped position, the two boys tried to see what was at the top of the stairs, but could not.

"That must be where they do it," Austin whispered. "There's a fire escape outside. Maybe we could get into one of the rooms."

Rual had seen enough, but Austin was not to be deprived. Half an hour later they were clinging to the cold iron fire escape and Austin was working on the window frame with his penknife. The room beyond the window was dark and deserted. Rual felt some of his bravado fading. At length Austin grunted in satisfaction and the window slid up.

Cautiously they crept across the room, bumping into a large empty bed. Austin was easing the door open when he stepped backward so abruptly he collided with Rual, who jumped in panic.

"Someone coming this way," Austin whispered

hoarsely, shoving Rual back. They dived under the massive bed as a woman came into the room. She went to the nightstand and turned up the lamp, then called out, "Come on in, honey. Don't be shy."

Lying on the polished wood floor on their stomachs, the two boys saw a pair of high-heeled silver slippers topped by trim ankles. A moment later a pair of mud-spattered boots stood beside them.

There was a moment's silence, during which a slim foot slipped out of one of the silver slippers and the other foot went up on its toes. The boots were planted firmly astride and did not move. There was a long sigh. Then the boots turned and the crash of bedsprings announced that the man was seated on the bed.

First one and then the other silver slipper was kicked aside. A shimmering mass of red satin enveloped the feet, then was picked up. White petticoats and pantalettes were next. The boots, meanwhile, were eased from the man's feet.

The two boys looked up in dismay as the bedsprings creaked again and bulged alarmingly close to their heads.

"Oh, honey, that's a beauty," the woman gushed.

Austin shoved his fist into his mouth to keep from laughing aloud, while Rual buried his face in his coat sleeve and shook with silent chuckles.

From somewhere above, muffled by the mattress, came the man's voice. "No . . . turn over, honey . . ." This was followed by creakings of the springs and unintelligible grunts of pleasure.

The sounds became more frenzied and the woman was crying out, little gurgles of joy and admiration. The bedsprings jumped and bounced. Austin was now lying on his back, looking upward as the springs jiggled perilously close to his face. His eyes were wide with mock alarm and he was gasping with the effort to keep quiet.

At length the bouncing of the bed reached a crescendo and they heard a great sigh of relief come bursting from the man. Gradually, the movement above ceased.

"Come on, now, darlin', don't fall asleep." The woman's voice was tentative. "Go on—out you go."

The man's bare feet hit the floor with a slap, followed by the woman's. Several minutes elapsed before she was able to persuade him to dress and leave. There was a brief argument when the man said there were other things he would like to do, but this ended when the woman pointed out sweetly that he'd have to take care of the financial arrangements downstairs first.

Both boys relaxed when they heard the door open and the man depart, still protesting he was not yet finished. A moment later the silver slippers were beside the bed and the woman snapped, "All right—get out from under the bed and show yourself."

Too surprised to do anything else, they crawled out. They were confronted by a hard-eyed young woman wearing only her high-heeled silver slippers. The two boys stared in fascination at her pubic hair.

"Did you enjoy yourselves?" she asked sarcastically, placing her hands on her hips. "I hope so, because that's going to cost you. You think anything is free at the Red Garter?"

"How did you know we were there?" Rual asked, his eyes wide. Her breasts glistened slightly in the lamplight.

"I heard you. You're lucky he didn't. Guess he was busy with other things. But me—well, I can tell you how many flies there are on the ceiling. Empty your pockets, both of you. Let's see how much money you've got before I scream for the bouncers."

Her eyes glittered greedily as she saw that Austin had a great deal of money in his wallet. She was reaching for it when his hand closed over her wrist. "Bet I could make you forget there's flies on the ceiling," he said slyly.

She laughed. "You're just a kid."

"Try me."

Her head jerked in Rual's direction. "He's even younger than you are. You ought to be ashamed, bringing a little kid like him into a place like this."

"You can have all the money in my wallet—if you let me do it to you," Austin said. At his side, Rual gasped at his audacity.

She grinned. "All right. Get the kid out of here the same way you got him in."

"He stays," Austin said.

"What?"

"So he can tell my friends I did it."

She hesitated, her lips parted, considering.

"All right," she said at length. She kicked off the slippers and lay down on the devastated bed. Rual's eyes bulged as she parted her thighs and raised her knees slightly. He felt a stirring in his own groin as Austin pulled off his trousers with such haste he fell to the polished floor with a crash.

Unabashed, Austin picked himself up and got on the bed. He waved his organ wildly in the general direction of the parted thighs.

"You know what to do with it, sonny?" the woman asked in a bored tone. "Or do you want me to help you?" Expertly, her hand went out and caressed him. She continued rubbing him for a few seconds as Austin groaned and tried to push past her hand into the dark furry nest awaiting him. The next moment it was too late. The woman smirked with satisfaction as Austin cursed in boyish fury.

On their way home through the dark streets, Austin said to Rual, "If you tell anyone that I came before I got it in, I'll cut yours off."

"Yeah—" Rual said, laughing. "And who'll hold me down for you?"

But he had dutifully backed up Austin's claim of extraordinary prowess. By the time the story had circulated among all of their friends, the woman in the Red Garter had begged Austin to stay with her forever; she couldn't live without him.

While he watched over his father in the Confederate prison, Rual remembered the incident. Had his father been enamored of one of these whores there? Rual wondered sadly.

-ᵈ{ CHAPTER 35 }ᵇ-

Sherman is coming! The distant rumble of cannon
pounded on the nerves like a nightmare pulsebeat.

Neither rain, mud, nor cold could slow the relentless
blue tide sweeping toward Columbia. Word of the forty-
mile-wide swath of devastation left in the wake of the
advancing Yankees was spreading panic through the
state's capital city. Confederate forces, severely de-
pleted and desperately short of equipment after four
bloody years, offered only rear-guard resistance.

State officials, Confederate troops, and private citizens prepared to evacuate the city as the Union forces
reached the west bank of the Congaree.

All day the trains ran, whistles blowing, while wag-
ons rattled through the streets carrying people and
goods fleeing to the uncertain safety of the country.
They passed wagon loads of wounded men, bouncing
over the muddy streets, dazed faces and broken bodies
soaked by the drizzling rain as dark clouds blanketed
the city, adding to the gloom.

Cerise and Dahlia watched the confusion and turmoil from their window. The thronging crowds carried
squalling children, bundles of clothing, family heir-
looms. They seemed to move in all directions at once.

"Moses will never be able to get through the crowds
with the carriage," Dahlia said.

Tannie immediately began to whimper.

"Stop that!" Cerise said sharply. "And hurry with
that pocket." The black girl's fingers were trembling as
she picked up her needle again to sew the pocket into
the hoop skirt lying on the table in front of her. It had

been Cerise's idea to conceal their few valuables beneath their skirts.

"We should have gone with Cousin Beulah last week," Dahlia said, her eyes clouded with fear. "I'm sorry I persuaded you to stay." Dr. Billy had finally collapsed of exhaustion and Beulah had taken him to friends in the country to rest.

"You were right—we were needed at the hospital," Cerise said, giving her sister-in-law a smile of encouragement that was not a true reflection of her own feelings. She was wondering tiredly what would happen to the wounded and sick troops if the Yankees decided to shell the town. In spite of herself, Cerise felt a mounting rage toward the enemy Yankees. Her anger was more difficult to bear because of her love for her brother, presently serving in the Yankee navy. *But at least Rual is not one of the murdering, burning hooligans with Sherman, thank God.*

The war years had taught Cerise to respect and admire the quiet courage and dignity of Southerners. Above all, she admired their code of honor. Perversely, now that the defeat of the Confederacy was a certainty, Cerise wished passionately that she were a man so that she might take rifle in hand and ride out to meet the invaders.

She turned away from the window. There was no way they could get through those jammed streets to the hospital. Dahlia was convinced that Moses would appear with the carriage to transport them to the safety of the Gentry plantation when the first distant sounds of cannon announced the closing enemy. Cerise wondered privately if every black slave had not already deserted the plantation.

Trunks and valises stood around the room in various stages of packing, but there seemed little point in continuing to stuff them with household items.

"Did you pack the silverware?" Dahlia asked Tannie for the third time. The girl nodded dumbly, eyes wide with fear, as Dahlia repeated, "We must be ready when Moses comes for us."

There had been no mail for days. Cerise continued

to hope she would hear from Mark, although there had been no word from him since their one evening of love. Official word had reached her that Austin was a prisoner of war, presently in a hospital being treated for severe leg and abdominal wounds. A short note, written for Austin by a Yankee nurse, arrived soon after the official announcement. He was fine, and would be coming home to her. And he loved her. Cerise thought of all the similar notes she had written for wounded Yankees. At least Austin would have food and medicine. There was little of either for the wounded men in Southern hospitals, and even less for the civilian population. Yet Southerners bore their deprivations with quiet dignity. Cerise wanted to weep with both compassion and fury. She prayed for some miracle to turn back that terrible blue tide from the North.

The end was near and there was an awful, mind-destroying inevitability about it. And when it was over, what then? She would care for her husband, try to nurse him back to health along with the devastated fortunes of the Gentry family. *Oh, my God, Mark ... how I love you! How I want to be with you! Where are you? Why haven't you at least written to me?*

The alarm bell rang shrilly, spreading further panic in the street. Tannie screamed and Dahlia clutched at Cerise, who shook her impatiently. "It's probably a fire. Some drunken fool no doubt tossed a cigar butt into a pile of cotton. There were two cotton fires yesterday."

In the vacant fields and lots, all of the town's cotton lay in piles, ready for burning, but it was feared a wind might spring up and blow the sparks into town. General Beauregard felt that as the railroad had not been destroyed, there was no need to burn the cotton. The previous day's fires had been accidental.

"Oh, look," Dahlia said, tears streaming down her face, "I can't bear it . . ."

Following her gaze, Cerise saw a dispirited group of Confederate cavalry riding by, slumped wearily on their horses, their once proud uniforms tattered and mud-stained. Abject misery and defeat were written on each exhausted face.

378

"They're leaving us!" Dahlia cried. "The Yankees are coming!"

Cerise said quickly, "They won't kill women when they get here."

Dahlia turned wide and frightened eyes toward her. "But what if they . . ." She glanced over her shoulder again at the whimpering Tannie and added in a low voice, ". . . *you know what*—"

"I haven't heard of one single case of women being raped," Cerise said, disregarding Dahlia's blush at the mention of the word. "They say Sherman is burning everything behind him and plundering the plantations . . . but I haven't heard of a single—"

"Tannie—go to the kitchen and see if there's any coffee left," Dahlia ordered quickly.

When the girl departed, Dahlia looked at Cerise reproachfully. "You know you shouldn't say things like that in front of the Negroes. They are so easily frightened."

Cerise threw up her hands in exasperation. "I swear if I live here a hundred years, I'll never understand Southerners. Dahlia Gentry, you stand there worrying about frightening a black slave when they are the reason your people went to war—"

"Now, Cerise, you know that was just one of the issues," Dahlia chided. "And anyway, it is certainly no reason to let poor Tannie know that Sherman's men are rampaging across the state."

Tannie came back from the kitchen bearing a pot of the bitter brew made from parched rye and sweet potatoes that served as a substitute for coffee. There was also a thin hominy gruel.

"Come and have breakfast," Cerise said. "Staring out the window won't bring Moses to our rescue."

"There is a column of smoke. . . . Look, Cerise, over there. Oh, my goodness. Is it the Yankees so soon?"

"A cotton fire, probably. The reason for the alarm bell. Tannie, you'd better lock all of the doors."

"Yes'm." Tannie rolled her eyes in silent terror as she bolted the front door.

The three women ate their meager breakfast. There

379

was nothing to do but await the arrival of the carriage to take them to the Gentry plantation.

Dahlia clasped the photograph of her dead lover in her hands and Cerise thought of Mark. It helped quell the fear and hatred she felt toward the approaching Yankees. Mark had never returned to her after that one night they lay in each other's arms. But then, she had begged him never to return.

I should have gone away with him, she thought. *What purpose have I served. . . ? What will become of us all?*

They jumped, startled, as someone pounded on the front door. Opening it just a crack, Cerise saw their neighbor outside. "The government stores have been thrown open to the people!" she cried. "Send your Negroes down there quickly."

Tannie was cowering back against the table when Cerise turned after closing the door. "Ah's afraid! Ah don' want to go out there."

Cerise hesitated, looking from Dahlia's reproachful eyes to Tannie's wide and terrified ones. The cannonade seemed closer, each successive rumble of the guns thundering with greater and more terrifying clarity. She snatched up her shawl. "I'll go myself. We need food, the larder is empty, and we've no idea when Moses will get here."

She had barely opened the front door again when the first shell whistled overhead, exploding on the next street. The house shook and plaster fell from the ceiling. Cerise clutched the doorjamb for support as the floor leaped beneath her feet. She watched, fascinated, as a crack crawled slowly up the window glass.

Dahlia was pale with fright. "Oh, please, Cerise— you can't leave us now. What if Moses comes for us while you're gone? He *will* come for us—he must."

"You two go down to the basement," Cerise said. "I'll stay here and watch for him." There seemed no point in adding to their terror by pointing out that the street in front of the house was now totally impassable.

The day dragged by interminably, punctuated by the nerve-wracking explosions as shells fell, some near, some at a greater distance. By nightfall the street was lined with soldiers, drawn up and ready to march. The air was stifling with gunpowder smoke.

They slept fitfully and were awakened by an ear-shattering explosion. The last of the glass fell from the windows.

"Light a candle, Tannie," Cerise said. She could hear the muffled sobs in the darkness. The three women had wearily crawled into the same bed.

"What is it?" Dahlia asked through chattering teeth.

"I'll go outside and see what I can find out. Stay here." Cerise ignored pleas and clutching hands.

The day was breaking on smoke-filled streets. Cerise choked as she breathed the heavy air. Their neighbor's black butler, Henry, was scurrying up the street, carrying firewood. She called to him, asking what had caused the gigantic explosion.

"Our soldiers done blowed up de stores," Henry called back. "Dey is all gone and de Yankees is comin'. De streets is full of corn an' flour . . . all over de ground."

They drank the last of their coffee and Dahlia and Tannie clung to each other as the cannonade opened up again. Just before one o'clock they heard shouting outside. Flinging open the door, Cerise looked into the stricken eyes of their neighbor.

"They've come! They are marching down Main Street and there's a crowd of women and children flying in front of them." She turned and fled back to her own house.

Cerise sped up the stairs with Dahlia and Tannie hard on her heels, to look out of the bedroom window. They were just in time to see the Stars and Stripes run up over the State House.

"Oh, what degradation . . . what a horrid sight," Dahlia whispered, her voice filled with loathing.

The night brought a southern horizon lit by camp-fires and a sky illuminated by the burning of General Hampton's residencce a few miles beyond the town. Sumter Street was lit by burning houses, and in the red glare, drunken bluecoats, shouting and cheering, staggered back and forth between camp and town. A gale-force wind sprang up, wafting the flames from house to house.

"We shall have to try to get out on foot," Cerise said, feeling the heat of the fires through the broken windows. "We can't stay and risk the fires spreading this way."

The jingling of their doorbell did not at first register on their dulled senses. Then Tannie peered through the shattered window and said, "It's Mist' McKnight! Glory be, It's Mist' McKnight!"

Cerise believed for a moment she was dreaming. She was not. He was on the doorstep, swathed in a sturdy tweed overcoat, unperturbed, smiling. "Are you ready to leave?"

She fell into his arms, laughing and crying with relief. He held her closely for a moment, pressing his lips to her forehead.

"A carriage—do you have a carriage?" Dahlia asked eagerly, while Tannie jumped from one foot to the other in her impatience to be gone.

"Well . . . if you can call it that." Mark nodded apologetically to a decrepit cart, to which, incongruously, was harnessed a sleek cavalry horse, prancing and magnificent.

"You stole a Yankee horse!" Cerise gasped. "How marvelous!"

Mark opened his mouth as though to speak, then paused, his expression inscrutable. He bent to pick up the nearest piece of luggage. "I went to the Gentry plantation. They told me their carriage and all of their horses had been commandeered to evacuate wounded soldiers—the army even took old Moses. All of their other slaves have run off. Gather up whatever you absolutely must have and leave the rest. I'll wait for you outside. I'm afraid if I take my eyes off that horse for a second, we'll lose him."

Tannie snatched up two valises. "We is ready now!" she cried.

"Oh, Mark," Dahlia said, a worried frown knitting

her brow, "if they catch you, they'll shoot you for stealing a horse."

"Don't worry, I didn't steal him. He's mine. I just borrowed the cart."

"Oh," Cerise said, disappointment in her tone. "He looks like a cavalry horse—but too well fed to be one of ours."

Mark grinned. "If I'd known of your secret admiration for horse-thieves, I would gladly have stolen one. Come on, I want you all out of town quickly. And if it will help me gain favor in your lovely eyes, I *did* steal some clothing."

Cerise glanced at the too-large tweed overcoat, but did not have time to question him further as he bundled them outside.

Helping them into the cart, Mark said to Dahlia and Tannie, "Cover yourselves with the blankets and don't come out for anything, do you understand? Oh, yes, Cerise—I stole the blankets, too. No—not you, my sweet," he said quickly as Cerise prepared to climb into the back of the cart after Tannie. "I need you up front with me. You are going to have to drive after I leave you."

"What do you mean—leave us?" Cerise asked. She felt something cold and heavy pressed into her hand. Looking down, she saw she was suddenly holding a pistol.

"Do you know how to use it?" Mark asked. "It's for your protection after I leave you on the edge of town."

"I'd like to shoot murdering Yankees with it," Cerise said savagely. "But don't you dare leave us. And where have you been all this time? You never even wrote to me."

He turned, grinning. The fiery glow of the burning city lit up the handsome profile she had missed so desperately all those long months. "But you sent me away forever—don't you remember? You said our love could never be. I was never to darken your doorstep again."

Mark was pulling off the tweed overcoat. Cerise saw to her astonishment that under the overcoat he was wearing the hated blue uniform of the Yankees. She felt a stab of both fear and admiration for him. So that was what he meant about stealing clothes! The cart lurched off down the street.

"What will they do to you if they catch you wearing the Yankee uniform?"

"Don't worry about it. Most of the soldiers in town are too drunk to see past my captain's insignia. Just pray we don't run into someone of higher rank."

"Perhaps you should have stolen a major's uniform?" Cerise suggested, dimpling with amusement, despite the peril that surrounded them.

On either side the devouring fires crackled. Falling timbers crashed. The library was ablaze, the State House already consumed. Thunderous roars signaled the collapse of building after building.

Mark drove the horse with his whip as the heat seared their flesh and the smoke scorched their lungs. From time to time, blue-clad soldiers stumbled into their path, waving bottles and singing ribald songs, but they quickly veered off when they caught sight of the captain's bars on Mark's uniform. Cerise silently thanked God that Mark had had the foresight to purloin the uniform. They never would have got through the Yankee soldiers without it.

Cerise felt a sob rise in her throat as she saw the college buildings had caught fire. All the doctors were on the roof battling the flames, while the wounded who were able crawled outside. Yellow hospital flags lay forlornly on the cold ground.

The common opposite the gate was crowded with homeless women and children, clinging to each other and shivering in the night air.

A harsh Yankee voice yelled, "See what you've brought on yourselves? This is what you get for setting yourselves up as better than other folks."

Cerise felt a tear scald her cheek. She brushed it away angrily. "God damn them!" Her fingers tightened around the gun on her lap.

"Isn't it a bit late to feel the stirring of patriotism . . . or whatever it is you're feeling?" Mark asked dryly.

"After all, this is the end we both predicted. We were above such stupidity, weren't we?"

"The war was wrong and evil . . . but this . . . this is monstrously inhuman. What will become of all those women and children? What about the wounded back there in the hospital who can't crawl outside? They'll roast to death. Oh, God—take me back. Mark, I said stop this cart and take me back. I must go and help them—" She had risen out of the seat, clutching at the reins.

His arm went about her waist, forcing her to sit down. He kept her imprisoned with one arm while handling the reins with the other hand. "Cerise—darling, please don't! I know how you feel, but there isn't anything you can do—"

She struggled silently for a moment. Then as his grip tightened, she screamed at him, "You don't know how I feel! Damn you, with your imperturbable English calm! How can you know how I feel when you have ice water in your veins? Besides, this isn't your war. These are not your people who are suffering so. Oh, I'm going to shoot the next Yankee I see carrying a flaming brand."

"Cerise—" Mark's voice had an edge of authority. "Be still until we reach the outskirts of town. As soon as Dahlia and Tannie are out of danger, we can decide what to do about your sudden urge to kill Yankees. I told you before—I can only stay with you for a little while."

She had forgotten the presence of the other two women, cowering beneath the blankets. "Don't make fun of me, Mark," she warned, "not while I'm holding a pistol. Very well, you can take us to the edge of town. If you have some pressing business to attend to, we shan't detain you further. No doubt there is some high-profit cargo you need to sell. Not too many ships get through the blockade anymore, but I should have known yours would."

Mark ignored the sarcasm as he concentrated on driving the lathered horse.

They were passing through a sea of smoke, filled with

dizzy images. She had not eaten all day and the faintness of hunger added to the nausea caused by breathing the charred air.

Mark made many detours as he found streets blocked with burning debris. Once he had to put his boot into the chest of a corporal who decided he would like a ride back to camp, but after what seemed an eternity, they reached the edge of town unmolested.

The soot-streaked faces of Dahlia and Tannie peered cautiously over their blanket. Cerise turned to look back at the city. Rolling columns of black smoke passed across the copper-colored sky, glittering with sparks and bursting embers.

They could still hear the terrible roar of the conflagration, and within it, the muted cries of those trying to escape. The terrified lowing of cattle added to the pathos. Hundreds of pigeons whirred over their heads in frenzied flight.

Mark had stopped the cart. "Cerise, you can handle the horse from here. You must go on to the Gentry plantation and I must go back. If you'll go on to the plantation, I promise I'll do all I can to help back there."

The blaze was reflected in Cerise's honey-colored eyes, and for a second her gaze was strangely like that of a red-eyed wolf. Mark had no doubt that the woman who sat beside him in disheveled, smoke-darkened clothing, her hair a tumbled mass about her shoulders and her shoulders squared defiantly, would not hesitate to use the pistol she held in her hands.

"Cerise—there are no men on the plantation. You and that pistol are all that stand between the women and Sherman's troops. You must go on to the plantation. You're needed more there than in that doomed town."

Both Dahlia and Tannie burst into tears at these words.

"And you," Cerise said coldly, "you can't come and protect us, of course. Your precious blockade-run cargo is too important."

"I'll come to you as soon as I can." Mark grinned

suddenly and, before she was aware of his intention, leaned forward and kissed her mouth. She stared in astonishment when he released her lips and said, "Besides, you're more than a match for any Yankees you may run into. My money would be on you. Now I'm going to turn the cart onto the road to the plantation and give you the reins. So close your mouth, my love; you're gaping at me. Then tell me you love me."

They had barely started to move, nor had Cerise time to answer before suddenly their path was blocked by a dozen men in gray. It all happened so quickly that she was only aware of the grasping hands pulling Mark down from the cart, disarming him, and the sickening thud of fists connecting with flesh.

She was screaming and fumbling with the pistol as Mark crashed to the ground, vainly trying to defend himself against the five men attacking him.

One of the Confederates leaped up onto the cart beside her and snatched the pistol from her hand. "We're saving you from that damned Yankee."

Cerise grabbed at the man's hands, trying to regain the pistol. "Leave him alone—stop it, you're hurting him!" she shouted. Behind her Dahlia and Tannie sobbed hysterically.

"They is killin' him!" Tannie shrieked.

"Ma'am—please," the Confederate said, ducking Cerise's flailing fists. "Don't you recognize us? We're your own men. Miss Cerise—look at me. You treated my brother in the hospital."

Struggling free of the man's clutching hands, she jumped down and tried to pull the others from Mark. "No! Let him go! He isn't a Yankee!" She was beating on their backs futilely.

They dragged Mark to his feet, savagely twisting his hands behind his back to tie them. His face was bruised and blood ran from his mouth.

"We've got to get out of here before any more of them come this way," one of the Confederates said. "We're not far from the Gentry plantation—they'll shelter us for the night. Finish him and let's be on our way."

387

Cerise flung herself at Mark, wrapping her arms about him protectively. "Are you mad? He's an Englishman—not a Yankee. Mark—tell them. . . . Oh, please, believe me, he was helping us, not kidnapping us."

The man who had taken the pistol from her looked at her doubtfully, then grasped Mark's hair and jerked up his head. "If you're English, why are you wearing that uniform?"

The blue eyes were dazed from the beating, but his voice was firm and distinct. "Because I am a captain in the U.S. Cavalry. I am your prisoner, sir."

Cerise reeled backward, staring at him in disbelief. "No! It isn't true. It can't be. You . . . you can't be one of those monsters with Sherman."

Some of his former nonchalance crept into his voice as he answered, "I thought perhaps my small effort might hasten the end of the war . . . and my return to you. Cerise, don't blame all of Sherman's men for what is happening to Columbia. The fires were started by a few drunks—"

A rifle shot rang out and all was confusion. The man who snatched the pistol from Cerise crumpled and fell, blood gushing from his chest.

"Cerise! Get down!" Mark yelled.

The Confederate stragglers dived for cover as shots whistled about them. In the back of the cart, Dahlia and Tannie cowered in terror as the horse pranced expectantly at the familiar sounds.

Cerise was down on the ground, not sure if she had flung herself there or been knocked down. She had hurt her side in the fall. Mark was beside her, trying to shield her with his body. The dead Confederate was inches away, the pistol he had confiscated lying beside him. She picked it up and placed it in her lap. She was untying Mark's hands when she looked up to see one of the Confederates point his rifle directly at Mark's chest.

The pistol was in her hand and she had squeezed the trigger before she was conscious of moving. The recoil sent an arrow of pain slashing through her side. A moment later they were surrounded by blue-clad troops and were being helped to their feet. Cerise stared, wid-eyed, at the man she had killed.

"Dear God in heaven! I killed one of our own men. For you . . . a murdering Yankee!" She was beating on Mark's chest, pain stabbing her side, sobbing hysterically. Someone pulled her gently away.

"You saved a good officer, ma'am," a voice said.

Mark's voice reached her, from far away. "Cerise, I am going to detail two men to escort you to the plantation. I have to hurry back into town and do what I can to stop that holocaust."

She blinked, his face coming into focus. That face she had so longed to see again. "I hate you. I never want to see you again. You've turned me into a traitor. You let me think you had stolen that uniform."

"I borrowed the overcoat. I didn't know if you would open your door to a bluecoat—" Mark began.

"I killed a good man. I should have let him kill you."

Mark's arms went about her, holding her close. "I'll come for you tomorrow. Cerise, there's something I have to tell you. Your husband is dead. He died of his wounds in the prison hospital."

Cerise's eyes rolled upward and she slumped in his arms. It was only then that Mark realized his left hand was pressed into warm stickiness on her side.

He laid her down gently and turned over his hand, staring at her blood dripping from his fingers.

In the back of the cart, Dahlia called out in a tiny, terrified voice, "If someone will please help me down, I will go to her—"

Several soldiers leaped to help Dahlia and Tannie down. Mark stared at Cerise's limp form, his face ashen. In the moment's confusion no one noticed the wounded Confederate inch his way across the ground toward the fallen gun. He raised the rifle and fired a split-second after Mark gathered Cerise into his arms, holding her close to his chest. Mark felt the bullet slam into her body. All the other sounds and sights of the night were rushing away from him, borne on a wave of agony that he prayed heralded his own death. He did not want to live without her.

But his own flesh was not penetrated by lead. Dahlia was beside him, trying to pry his arms free of Cerise's still and bloody form.

Tannie began to wail, a high-pitched kneening sound. "She's dead. They done kilt Miz Cerise."

--◈{ CHAPTER 36 }◈--

Mark believed the desolation left after the burning of Columbia was a scene as close to hell as anything he would ever encounter, but Charleston was not much better. It had been spared the soldiers' torches because, it was rumored, Sherman had a mistress in the city; but the long siege and bombardment had taken their toll.

There was no shipping in the harbor except for a few quartermasters' vessels and a couple of small steamers. The warehouses were deserted, the wharves rotting. No wall or roof seemed to have escaped the siege guns.

Perched on the crests of dilapidated roofs were rows of turkey buzzards, and from time to time they lazily flapped their wings and stretched their hideous necks.

Mark walked along streets ankle-deep in sand, past charred chimneys, weed-wild gardens, and walls overgrown with moss. There did not seem to be a house that had not been hit. A shell had smashed into the steeple of St. Michael's Church and another had demolished the altar. It was difficult to remember coming to this charming city the first time, early in the war, to visit Cerise. This was where it all started, he thought, where the first shots were fired.

He hated the madness of war. Its futility. The misery left in the aftermath. Above all, the toll in human life. Lives that meant more to loved ones than any political insult or national boundary. Yet he had become a soldier with the same enthusiasm and dedication he approached any other challenge. He would be the best.

The military discipline he had forced upon himself came to his aid after the fateful night he delivered Cerise from the fires of Columbia unto the troopers' bullets. He was an officer and there were men to lead. Try to maintain outward calm. Be alert to looters and deserters running wild. Keep a tight rein on both one's own emotions and the victorious advancing army.

Outwardly he was coldly efficient, maintaining a distant but watchful eye on the men under his command. In the privacy of his thoughts, he relived every moment he had spent with Cerise.

Unbidden, all of the demons of his childhood came back to haunt him. His mother giving her life to bring him into the world. *Cerise cradled in his arms, taking the bullet meant for him.* Mollie huddled over her inevitable tea cup, squinting at the tea leaves. "Danger lurking for you over water, Mark. Promise me you'll stay here. Don't go traveling, lovey. Stay off your Dad's ships. Let the sailors run them. My Mark is too clever to waste himself, isn't he? There's a woman in your cup, Mark. She's trouble. Stay away from her. She'll bring you only grief."

His own voice, high-pitched in a squeak of defiance at the older boys. "Don't you go near her! Leave her alone. She isn't very well, that's all. Oh, Mollie, Mollie, please get up. Please wake up, Mollie. Your dress is getting dirty." Unconsciously, his head jerked in memory of the cuff on the ear.

Their whole family was cursed. Had there ever been a happy love affair for any of them? He wondered.

Miraculously, Cerise clung to life while they carried her to the Gentry plantation. Her blood left a trail across the ravaged earth. The doctor Mark sent for arrived only an hour after they had placed her inert body on a bed. Everyone was sure she was dead, including Austin's mother, who staggered from her own bed to try to help her daughter-in-law, despite her own weakness. Mark insisted there was a faint pulse and worked feverishly to try to stem the flow of her blood.

The doctor and an orderly sent everyone from the room. Mark paced the hall, cursing his own carelessness in allowing the tragedy to happen. When the doctor emerged from the room sometime later, he shook his head sadly.

All the breath left Mark's body. He stood erect, frozen with horror and grief.

"The first bullet merely grazed her side," the doctor was saying. "The second wound is more serious—and I'm afraid it will be fatal. The bullet apparently passed under her shoulder blade—at an upward angle—going right through her body. It's incredible it missed you, as I understand you were holding her at the time. Had she been given immediate medical attention . . . I don't know, she might have had a better chance for survival. As it is, she's lost too much blood. These women are weakened by poor diet—I'm truly sorry, Mark. I understand you know her personally. I've done what I can, but I doubt she'll last the night."

He sat beside her bed for a while, listening to the pathetically shallow breathing. Someone tapped him on the shoulder. "Sir . . . you were to rendezvous with Wood's brigade."

"Yes. Yes, of course. I shall leave at once. Get me a fresh horse, Corporal. We have to try to stop that holocaust in Columbia. Tell the other women I shall return as soon as I can."

Mark doubled back to the Gentry plantation as many times as he dared during Sherman's advance to the sea. He was always refused admittance by a stone-faced Rose Gentry. On his last visit a home-made wreath was tacked to the front door and beside it a black-edged card, stating: IN MOURNING. PLEASE DO NOT DISTURB.

His grief and despair were taken out on his own men. No one dared enter a Southern home on a foraging expedition while Mark McKnight was present. His men were forced to eat jerky when there were hogs and chickens in plain sight on enemy farms. By the time they reached the coast there were men who hinted darkly that the limey captain, good soldier though he had been, yes and a fair officer, too had better beware of his own men. They were tired of his attitude that a defeated enemy had to be treated with such undue respect. Leave them their dignity, indeed. Who started this whole thing, anyway? Officers had caught a stray bullet in the back for less.

"Sir . . ." a voice said at his side. "The prisoners you were looking for—we've found them. Balmain—"

Mark blinked, barely understanding what the sergeant was saying. "What? Oh—yes. Sebastian and Rual Balmain. Take me to them." Neither of them had been prisoners long enough to have reached the state of emaciation achieved by some of the poor devils they had found in Confederate prisons. But then, the Southern troops and civilians weren't much better off. They were all starving to death. "Are they all right?" he asked, falling into step beside the sergeant.

"A little weak, sir, that's all. The older man had leg injuries, but they seem to have healed all right."

Sebastian and Rual sat side by side in the house being used as army headquarters. Both were noticeably thinner and their uniforms in shreds. Two pairs of identical blue eyes regarded Mark cheerfully as he entered the room.

Mark felt like Judas when Sebastian leaped up and began to pump his hand, while Rual slapped his back affectionately.

Sebastian was chuckling. "I didn't believe it when they told me . . . Captain McKnight." The calloused hand squeezed his approvingly. "My little limey half-brother, a captain in the Union Army."

"Reckon between us we did the family's share of bringing this sorry business to an end." Rual said. "Have you been to see Cerise? How is she?"

"Please—sit down. I've sent for some food and fresh uniforms," Mark said.

"The last I heard, she was at her plantation near Columbia," Rual said. "I've been worried sick ever since I heard Sherman's men burned the city to the ground. Is the plantation all right? How soon can we go there? Are there any trains running?"

Sebastian was watching Mark's expression. The anguish in his eyes sent a cold shiver down Sebastian's back. "Rual," he said quietly. "Better sit down. I think maybe Mark has something to tell you."

Sebastian was shocked by the devastation left in Sherman's wake. Silently he reflected that the war at sea had been cleaner. At least the navy had never been responsible for such civilian misery. Rual had remained tight-lipped and silent since leaving Charleston, and, knowing how much he had loved his sister, Sebastian left him alone.

Mark's leanly handsome features revealed no hint of what he might be feeling. He stared expressionlessly at the ashes of a ruined city. Sebastian thought that just as he had in civilian life, Mark still presented a remarkable immaculate and unruffled appearance. Yet there had been that one look of stark pain in his eyes in the moment before he told Rual that Cerise was dead, killed, ironically, by a Confederate bullet.

But the slightly bored, superior facade had again descended. Whatever pain he was suffering, Mark would bear it with British stoicism. He seemed oblivious to the pathetic ruins they passed along the road.

"Was there any need for this?" Sebastian asked, appalled.

"Three generals and God knows how many other officers and men toiled all night trying to put out the fires started by a few drunken troopers," Mark said. "Sherman himself ordered Stone's troops out of the city and replaced them with Wood's brigade. Three hundred and seventy men were arrested. Two killed and thirty wounded. But by then the fires were out of control. Only a shift of the wind saved Columbia from total annihilation." His voice was chillingly objective. There was no way for him to know that he was already in the early stages of the metamorphosis his father had undergone when his beloved first wife died. And if he had known, he would have coldly agreed that history did indeed repeat itself. Wasn't that the whole trouble with mankind?

"If you don't call this total annihilation . . ." Sebastian said, shaking his head as they passed the pathetic bones of a once proud and beautiful town.

The Gentry plantation house appeared to be untouched, although the fields were blackened and deserted. When they went up the veranda steps and into the house, however, they saw that marauding troops had been here, too. Every remaining item of furniture was smashed. Curtains and draperies had been torn from windows. There was a blackened area in the middle of the dining room floor where something had been burned.

An eerie stillness hung over the house. Out of the corner of his eye Mark could see the remnants of the black-edged mourning card. It had been ripped from the door and tossed carelessly into the dust. He moved toward it unobtrusively as Sebastian called out, "Is anyone here? Is there anyone at home?"

A moment later a figure came hesitantly out of a door and moved along the landing above their heads. Dahlia leaned over the banister, her lips moving in a silent prayer of thanks as she recognized Mark. "I'm sorry . . . we were afraid the Yankees—I mean—the soldiers— were coming back. Auntie and two of the slaves are hiding in the pantry—and I ran up to the sick room." She came slowly down the staircase, her eyes lowered. At the foot of the stairs she looked up at Mark and said, "We didn't recognize you. We just saw the uniforms. We've been visited so many times by Yankee marauders. One group of Negroes without an officer took the last of our food yesterday. This morning a group of whites smashed the last of our household goods and took the last of our livestock. There is nothing left and we were afraid . . ." Her voice trailed off and she blushed as she became aware of Rual, who was staring at her in a thunderstruck way.

Mark quickly made the introductions. "Forgive the intrusion, but Rual wanted to come." *To see his sister's grave.* The words refused to come from his lips.

"Are you alone? Where are your men?" Rual asked.

"Austin and Uncle Will are both dead. The others . . . we don't know."

"Don't worry," Rual said. "We'll take care of you."

Dahlia cast a worried glance in the direction of the closed kitchen door. "I'm afraid Aunt Rose is not herself. Her mind wanders . . . it's because of the strain she's been under. I'm afraid if she sees your uniforms it might set her off again."

There was a clatter of broken crockery. The next moment the kitchen door opened and Aunt Rose, followed by two black servants, appeared. Aunt Rose wielded a broom, sweeping broken dishes before her. She herded the pieces of china into a neat pile before looking up at the visitors. She froze when she saw Mark and said sharply to the two servants, "Go and watch the grits. Keep stirring and mind they don't burn, hear?"

"Yes'm," one girl said dutifully and gave the other girl a jab in the ribs when she began, "There ain't no grits—"

Mark pondered the freeing of the slaves for only a second or two, as Rose Gentry had fixed him with a frosty stare. "Mr. McKnight," she said distinctly, "you really must cease and desist from calling on Austin's wife. It is most outrageously improper." She shook her finger at him.

The three men looked at the floor in embarrassment. Mark said stiffly, "Mrs. Gentry, this is Rual Balmain—Cerise's brother—and his father, Sebastian Balmain. We deeply regret intruding at this sad time, but if you would allow us to see . . . to see—"

Dahlia moved to her aunt's side. "Auntie, dear, try to remember. Austin was killed. He won't be coming home again."

Rose Gentry's eyes narrowed. "Nevertheless, it is quite improper for a widow to receive gentlemen callers so soon. Cerise's brother may go upstairs. The other gentlemen may wait in the drawing room."

Oh, God, Mark was groaning inwardly, *she doesn't know who is dead and who is alive, poor demented*

soul. . . . This is what we have done to these women;
God forgive us all.

Dahlia looked at them apologetically. "It was such a shock to Aunt Rose, you see—first having Cerise brought home with bullet wounds, then losing Austin and Uncle Will—not knowing where the others were. And when Mother died, it was just too much for her to bear. . . . Mother had been an invalid for so long, but it was still a terrible blow to lose her so suddenly."

Mark's head jerked upward, his glance sweeping the staircase. "Your *mother?*" he repeated, stunned. "It was your *mother* you were in mourning for?" The next moment he was racing up the stairs, heedless of Rose Gentry's protest.

Rual and Sebastian exchanged startled glances. "Cerise! She's alive!" Rual yelled, and followed Mark up the stairs. Sebastian gestured helplessly to the women, smiled broadly, and went after them.

By the time Sebastian reached the sickroom, the three of them were all talking at once. Cerise was lying on a chaise at the window, a basket of tattered clothes beside her and a needle and thread in her hand. The sun blazed on her hair and although she was pale as a nun, her eyes were bright and clear. She was not able to move her right arm and shoulder, and the mending was going slowly with only one hand. Glimpses of makeshift bandage appeared as she turned her head first to Mark and then to Rual.

Sebastian was not aware of what was being said. He stood in the doorway, staring, his breath caught in his throat. Except for the eyes, which were golden instead of green, the grown-up Cerise was so like Garnet that it took his breath away. The same pert features and wild mop of curls. Even hardship and illness had not taken away the curves of her body. She tilted her chin in that proud and defiant way Garnet used to, daring the world to try to master her. *What a fool I was to leave her,* Sebastian thought. *Ah, Garnet . . .*

Cerise's voice registered on his numbed brain. She

had already expressed her astonishment at seeing him. "Is it all over?" she was asking now.

"Yes," Mark said. "Lee surrendered to Grant at Appomattox."

"And you—will you return to England?" Her voice was cool.

There was a long pause as her eyes met Mark's intense blue stare. Sebastian felt the electricity pass between them. They're in love, he thought. God help them. Do they know where it will lead them?

"That depends—on whether I can persuade a certain lady to accompany me. First I must await my discharge from the military. There will be much to do for a time."

Rual was oblivious to the undercurrents of their conversation. He interrupted to ask Cerise about her wounds.

She smiled at him fondly. "The doctor says I shall be able to get up soon. Aunt Rose sent for Dr. Billy and he's been coming in regularly. We'd have starved without him, because Aunt Rose wouldn't accept any of the supplies you sent, Mark. She also sent your doctor packthe very next day. I'm afraid the war won't be over for Aunt Rose for some time."

"Rual, let's go and unload the supplies we brought," Sebastian said. "We mustn't tire you, Cerise." When Rual hesitated, he said, "Come on, I need some help. And we'll get the roses back in her cheeks faster if we get some food into her."

When the door closed behind them, the mask of politeness faded from Cerise's expression. Mark regarded her warily. He took a tentative step toward her but she stopped him with an upraised hand. "That's close enough, Mark. Since it is probably not in your nature to gloat as victor over vanquished, I assume you've come to distribute your largess out of pity. I believe I speak for the rest of the Gentry family when I tell you we need neither your pity nor your charity."

The hurt showed in Mark's eyes for only a split-second. "I came because I love you. Everything else is incidental to that. Cerise, try to understand why I enlisted on the side of the North."

"What you did—or do—is immaterial to me."

"When your grief for your husband subsides—"

"And what about my grief for what the Yankees are doing to the South? That will never subside."

"But you were against the war from the beginning."

"Damn you, don't cloud the issue with your cool logic. I look around and see blackened fields, burned houses, starving widows and orphans—chaos! And all I see when I look at you is a blue uniform . . . the cause of all of our misery. Why couldn't you have stayed neutral? It's none of your affair—you're an Englishman."

"Half-American," he corrected with a sad smile. "But even if I'd been a Samoan hermit, it would have been impossible to remain neutral. I spent too much time here. I wanted the war to end. I felt compelled to do my small part to help it end."

"And you volunteered for the Union because they were the *right* side," she finished for him, sacastically. "Or was it because Austin was a Southerner and that was the real conflict—the only challenge you were really interested in?"

Anger flared in Mark's eyes. "And you—you feel you must do penance because your dead husband's side lost the war? Or perhaps because you feel guilty about our love—"

"No! Don't call it that—call it what it really was . . . an affair—a tawdry affair. Get out, Mark. Go away and leave me alone. Yes, I feel guilt . . . guilt for Austin, guilt for what is happening to this gracious state. I can still smell Columbia burning, see the hospital flags lying on the ground while the wounded burned to death . . ." She turned from him, her shoulders shaking with silent sobs.

Mark watched her for a moment, tight-lipped. "I love you, Cerise. I'll always love you. Don't make a mockery of what we had by calling it tawdry . . . it was never that."

Her voice was a strangled sob. *"Get out of my life."*

He fought the impulse to go to her, take her in his

arms. It wasn't the right time. Besides, he reflected bitterly, perhaps she was right. Had he endowed himself with noble motives in volunteering for the Union Army when in reality he had been engaging in a private war with Austin?

Downstairs, Sebastian and Rual had brought the supplies into the house. Rose Gentry had locked herself in her room and refused to come out until the Yankees left. Dahlia had found some unbroken glasses and poured everyone a glass of water. Rual stared at the soft-eyed Southern girl and twice stumbled over his feet as he looked at her instead of where he was going.

"We'd better leave," Mark said shortly. "If you'd like to go up and see your sister again, Rual . . ."

Sebastian studied Mark's expression and quietly agreed. Somehow the joyous discovery that Cerise had not been killed, after all, and the resulting reunion had suddenly turned to ashes. The war and divided loyalties were not so easily forgotten.

--⌐{ **CHAPTER 37** }⌐--

Oahu, Sandwich Isles—1866

Cyril had returned from a shopping expedition in Honolulu and Emily searched among the purchased treasures for a newspaper. Their few books were becoming threadbare, and new reading material was always eagerly awaited.

Disappointed, Emily looked up from the spools of thread, needles, tea, and various staples. "You didn't bring the Honolulu paper," she said. "Did you forget?"

Cyril paused a moment longer than necessary before

shaking his head and Emily pounced on his hesitation. "Some bad news? Oh, Cyril, my dearest one, you don't have to shield me from bad news. I am so happy, nothing could ever depress me. Has it to do with the war in America?"

Cyril smiled, in spite of his secret fears. "Had you forgotten, dear heart? The American War between the States ended last year. The slaves you worried so much about are free, although the Confederate raider *Shenandoah* is still keeping the whalers away from our waters."

Emily slipped her arm through his and rested her head upon his shoulder. "It all seems so remote," she confessed. "The rest of the world can never touch us here. But why are you keeping the newspaper from me? Oh . . . Cyril, it isn't . . . ?"

"No," Cyril said quickly. *He's still there,* he thought. *Sebastian. Hovering between us like some ghostly galleon keeping the weary travelers from the safe shore they seek.*

Keeping her arm through his, Cyril led her to the door of their grass shack, looking toward the beach where Noah and Kekoa were splashing one another in the clear warm water. "Emily, does Kekoa still go and see that Chinese boy he befriended?"

"Why, yes. He often goes over to the settlement. Why?"

"We must try to explain to him that he shouldn't eat and drink from their bowls . . . or sleep in the same bed as his friend."

"*Mai Pake?* The Chinese disease?" Emily could not bring herself to say that other dreaded word.

"I didn't want to upset you, but that's what is in the newspaper. The lepers are to be isolated. The prevalence of the disease is causing great alarm throughout the islands. The legislature has passed an Act to Prevent the Spread of Leprosy. The health board is empowered to enforce segregation of known lepers."

"But where will they send them? They will need doctors . . . people to care for them. Who would volunteer to go with them, knowing they were condemning themselves to death along with their patients?" Emily's

401

dark eyes were wide with concern, already seeing sick people trying to care for themselves. In her imagination she could hear the pathetic ringing of the biblical St. Lazarus rattle; the cry "Unclean!"

"Do you remember the first time we went to Maui with Josiah, and we were blown off course in the squall? We passed a remote peninsula on the island of Molokai—a flat promontory of land called Kaupapa?"

Emily shivered in the warm air. "A desperately lonely place—lashed by stormy seas . . . and sheer mountains walling it off from the rest of the island."

"The islanders call it the place of no sunset. The health board has purchased the land, and the first group of lepers—about one hundred and forty, I believe—who are in the advanced stages of the disease are to be sent there."

"Do they understand? The islanders . . . that their loved ones will be taken away and they will never see them again?" Emily whispered, tears brimming over and glistening on her cheeks.

"I'm very much afraid when they do, many of them will resist the order. They will hide their lepers from the health board." Cyril turned and looked at her, his brow creased with worry. "We must speak with Kekoa. I heard today that a member of his Chinese friend's family shows the mutilation of the disease, and will be one of the first to go."

Emily watched Cyril walk down the palm-lined path to the beach. Her heart was beating rapidly, as though she had been running. When she brushed back her hair from her brow, she was startled by the icy touch of her own fingers. It was as though some terrible avenging god were making his presence felt.

The government's planning was poor and the reaction of the islanders to the seizing of beloved family members was exactly as Cyril had predicted. Obviously, no one had any real concept of the problem . . . or the numbers of lepers in their midst.

Word soon spread around the island that the first group to be sent to Molokai were advanced cases, yet no doctors or able-bodied people were sent to care for them. There were a few existing huts left behind by the former inhabitants who had been evacuated by the health board, and the new settlers were expected to share the meager accommodations and care for themselves.

Several weeks later Emily returned from their garden one morning visibly shaken. Cyril was seated at the desk one of their friends had made for him, scribbling notes on a sheet of music. He put it aside and went to gather her into his arms. "What is it, Emily? You're pale as a ghost."

Her lip was trembling and her shoulders shook as she looked at him with frightened eyes. "I went to get some taro . . . I knew Kekoa was there because he was going to do some hoeing . . ." Tears were swimming to the surface of deep brown eyes.

A cold hand closed over Cyril's heart. He already knew what she was about to say; he had suspected it himself for some time.

"Kekoa . . . he was talking to me, laughing and teasing the way he always does . . . and he swung the hoe—and h-h-hit his leg. Oh, Cyril, the steel blade buried itself in his flesh—"

Cyril closed his eyes briefly. "And he didn't know he had done it. He felt no pain." They were statements, not questions.

"Oh, dear God in heaven! Hold me close, dearest, I can't bear it."

Stroking her hair, Cyril held her tightly in his arms, but his eyes were fixed on the unseen horror. "Emily, he has the disease. I've suspected it for several weeks. I haven't spoken to Kekoa, but I warned Noah about sharing Kekoa's bowls. I've given the matter much thought and decided if Kekoa is afflicted, then we must separate him from Noah. But Emily, I can't let him go to Molokai. I must take him away and hide him from the authorities. I shall go with him and take care of him."

"No, no, no," Emily sobbed. "You can't leave us. Oh, Cyril, I love Kekoa, too . . . but you must send him away to Molokai."

"Emily—listen to me," Cyril said patiently. "You don't know . . . I've shielded you from hearing what it is really like on Molokai. There is a superintendent who climbs down the steep cliff path *once a month* . . . that is all the supervision they have. The departures for the colony now are more like funerals—everyone knows they are going to a lingering and horrible death. And the lepers themselves—once they get to that forbidding place, they are running wild. The isolation and the disease seem to affect their minds, as well as rotting their bodies. They are reverting back to the ancient ways, because Western medicine men have failed them . . . calling on the old gods . . . it's only a matter of time until they start making sacrifices again. Corpses are simply thrown in the lake, because it's the easiest way to dispose of them. But, worst of all . . . some of the most depraved have formed a village—they call it the Village of Fools—and they say . . ." Cyril's voice broke with anguish.

Emily was staring at him, her face a mask of horror and disbelief as the words tumbled from his lips.

"They say . . . some of the men steal children—little boys and girls—for the worst depravities you can imagine. Emily . . . many of the children are there without the protection of parents—as Kekoa would be!"

Emily's knuckles were between her teeth, her body trembling violently. Cyril held her face between his hands. "Remember the fugitive Koolau . . . the one we heard had taken refuge in a valley on Kauai after he killed the sheriff who tried to take him in? I heard in town that he has also killed two militiamen who went after him. Such is their horror of being sent to Molokai."

"But how can anyone know all of these things are true?" Emily whispered. "Surely the stories are exaggerated, as they are spread by frightened people."

"The missionaries refuse to get off the boats there now. They sail to the peninsula to give comfort to those going into exile. Emily, these stories are true, and many more so horrible I cannot relate them to you. I have a duty to Kekoa; I must hide him. You must be brave, dearest."

Emily sank to the ground and wept.

Cyril and Kekoa left that day and did not tell anyone where they were going. Emily filled the long lonely hours with Noah, teaching him all he would need to know when he went to study music in Europe, making sure he practiced the difficult pieces of other composers as well as creating his own music. They missed Cyril and Kekoa desperately. Luana had chosen a husband and they saw little of her.

Emily no longer found joy in the fragrant beauty of their island. Even the sun seemed to have lost its brilliance since Cyril's departure. He had become her whole life. Every moment with him was like a rare polished gem.

Everywhere it was strangely silent without their animated conversation. They had always had something to tell each other, a new thought to share. Gone, too, was the laughter, stilled by the dread disease Kekoa had contracted.

She thought of Sebastian sometimes, always with sadness. Their marriage had been a mistake they both stumbled into without giving any real thought to what they were doing, she realized now. Yet she had loved him. It was odd that now she realized she had loved Sebastian like a brother, despite her determination to give him the son he wanted so much. But Cyril . . . her love for him was all-consuming. Her cheeks had burned with shame when she fought to suppress the wild beating of her heart and longings she had never expected to come to torment her.

Emily wept now that their love had never been consummated. Perhaps by the time Cyril returned to her she would be an old lady. He would never know how completely and absolutely she had loved him.

He was so darkly beautiful—so pure of mind and spirit and body that he would never be the one to approach her. He had suffered in silence from the same exquisite pain that she endured; she knew it as surely as she knew the sun would descend each evening into the sea.

The minutes dragged interminably by. Then, one morning, Emily looked up and saw the familiar loose-jointed loping step of the man coming up the path from the beach. She was on her feet, running to him, Noah racing along at her side. They both flung themselves into Cyril's embrace. It was several minutes before Emily's bubbling joy slowed to a mere simmer and she saw the haunted sadness in Cyril's eyes.

"Kekoa?" she asked.

"The disease had taken his fingers and toes. . . . Oh, Emily, he was so brave. He never complained. He spent hours carving this. . . ." Cyril held up a crudely carved wooden tiki figure. "One of their gods—to protect me from the affliction. Toward the end he worried constantly that I would catch the disease from him." Cyril gazed at her in anguish, fighting to control his emotions.

"It must have run its course more swiftly than . . ." Emily began.

"He didn't die from it, Emily." Cyril's voice echoed the pain that shone liquidly from his eyes. "He went for a swim early one evening . . . he just swam out to sea and didn't return. . . ."

Emily enfolded him in her arms and held him as though she would never let him go.

The discordant notes on the piano shattered the warm stillness of the air. Ugly sounds, like an unthinking child beating on the keys. Emily raised her head, puzzled. She was picking flowers for the *luau* to celebrate Noah's fifteenth birthday.

Afterward, she remembered the moment in all its poignant detail. The waterfall cascading down dark lava rocks into the topaz pool. A pair of tiny white birds fluttering about the pink and yellow blossoms. Deep green foliage turning polished leaves to a sky so brightly blue that it seemed the heavens had opened their portals and smiled on the fairest islands in the universe.

From beyond the reef came the slow rhythmic breaking of white-capped waves. A girl laughed somewhere and it was the sound of innocence. Over the scent of the flowers came a faint hint of spices, borne on tradewinds that caressed her body and murmured through her hair.

It was as though in that one moment all of the joy and happiness of their years together was bound in her memory for all eternity, so that in moments of darkest despair she would be able to reflect on it all, know how beautiful it had been and how worth the price they must pay.

She did not hurry to Cyril. She walked slowly, tasting the fragrant air, feeling the silken texture of the flowers in her hands, the softness of the earth beneath her feet. In the sound of the falling water and whispering wind, she heard the echoes of a thousand shared words and thoughts.

How happy they had been! And Noah . . . he was strong and beautiful, never striken with the miseries of wheezing chest and abscessed tonsils such as she and Cyril had endured in their bleak childhoods. Noah had grown tall like Sebastian, but was of much leaner build. He was nothing like his father in either body or temperament. Poor Sebastian, she thought, how much more difficult life had been for him. He had never known the beauty of the world that she and Cyril—yes, and Noah, too, despite his youth—had discovered and savored.

Cyril was walking toward her. He moved stiffly, puppet-like. She stopped, gasping, as she saw him lurching directly toward the underground oven where the pig had been roasting since dawn in readiness for the *luau*. Cyril moved like a sleepwalker, unseeingly, oblivious to everything in his path.

She screamed his name at the same instant he tripped on the boards placed over the oven. One leg went down into the hot coals and it was an agonizingly long moment before he withdrew it, his eyes fixed on Emily as she ran toward him.

Cyril was on one knee, trying to stand up. The

blank expression on his face tore Emily's composure to shreds. By the time she reached his side and slipped her shoulder under his arm to help him to his feet, she was sobbing hysterically.

As though coming to his senses, Cyril began to speak, reassuringly. "It's nothing. It probably means nothing. I have no feeling in my fingers, Emily. It's odd, but even after all this time, sometimes just before it rains my missing fingers seem to ache . . . I didn't mean to frighten you . . . I became impatient when my hands refused to find the notes . . . why I . . . "

His glance followed her stricken stare to his feet and he saw why he was having trouble standing up. One foot had slipped into the hot lava rocks of the underground oven and his foot was burned black. Huge blisters had formed and broken, exposing the weeping flesh beneath. He stared disbelievingly at the oozing flesh, blinking and shaking his head. *He felt no pain.*

Cyril sat on the beach, staring out to sea, watching the eternal waves form translucent green tunnels, roll toward the white sand and shatter into plumes of sparkling spray. A small pink crab scurried over his bandaged foot and he picked it up carefully and placed it on a sun-warmed rock.

The surf-riders were getting into position, sitting astride their boards. They waited for the exact moment the curling wave would pick up the heavy wooden boards and send them hurtling toward the beach, bronzed invaders riding magic chariots faster than the fleetest ships. Noah was one of the darkly tanned bodies out there, but from this distance Cyril was unsure which one. There! They were up, the wave curving over their heads like a glass temple, making a sound like the whistling breath of all the creatures of the deep sighing in unison.

Noah had brought him almost as much happiness over the years as Emily had. Cyril had always thought of Noah and Kekoa as being his sons and had wept tears of pride and anguish over both of them.

Cyril's thoughts turned to Emily and he was overwhelmed by a mixture of joy and pain. That she would even consider such a sacrifice . . .

Surely no two people had ever been blessed with such a love, for all its bittersweet poignancy. It seemed he had been born loving her. He loved her in new ways every day. Each hour with her made his soul more complete. It was as though the wondrous unfolding of their love for each other began afresh each time their eyes met. Cyril sighed. If only . . . if only . . . the physical expression of their love were not denied them. For he wanted her, he had wanted her for a very long time with a desperate yearning.

In Emily's arms he knew he would find fulfillment. All the wraiths of past disappointment and fear would be banished in her tender embrace. He would be the man she believed him to be. He knew this as surely as he knew he could never tell her how he had wanted her all this time. He loved her more than he loved himself and, knowing the depth of his own love, understood her love for him. He knew she would put his desire above her own feelings if he were to ask her. Had she not clearly demonstrated that he meant more to her than her own deepest terrors?

Cyril groaned aloud. *He could not let her do what she insisted she must do. . . .*

He glanced at the sun. So little time left. . . . This time tomorrow—He pulled himself to his feet, picking up the walking stick Noah had made to help him move about. He limped toward the house.

Emily had packed their belongings and was standing in the middle of the empty room, head on one side, fingers absently twirling a strand of hair. As soon as she saw him she went to him and, when he drew away from her, seized his arm and held on tightly.

"Emily, Emily . . . my beloved. No, no, and a thousand times no. You cannot go with me. We've been over it so many times. My darling, I could not bear to see you disfigured. . . . Have mercy on me."

"You can't stop me from accompanying you to Molokai, Cyril," she said gently. "You know you can't. If you won't allow me to go with you, then I shall
409

simply follow on the next boat. After they put me ashore, you know I shan't be allowed to come back."

"Please, Emily, in the name of God . . . don't do this. I love you more than I love life. Our time together has been the only happy time I have known. I want you to live . . . I shall die happy knowing you will go on living . . . oh, dear God, help me!" His stricken eyes and tormented face did not deter her. She placed her fingers on his cheeks and kissed his mouth to stop his pleas.

When she released his lips, he said in a strangled voice, "Noah . . . you will never see him again."

Emily helped him to sit down and sat close beside him, her arms tight around his body. "Cyril, we have enjoyed all of Noah's childhood. He will soon be a man who will want a life of his own. He has been looking forward to studying music in the European cities. . . . We would have lost him to the world then. Your . . . sickness . . . has just hastened that time. No, dear, please listen to me. I told him everything. I felt it only fair."

"He knows I am not his father?" Cyril was silent for a moment. "I suppose he wants to go to San Francisco and find Sebastian?"

"Perhaps sometime he will. . . . He tells me you will always be his true father. He wants to study music now. He wants to take his music to the world so that we can be proud of him before we . . . before . . . He knows I must go with you to Molokai, that I would die if we were parted. He understands. Oh, Cyril, he loves you. . . . The love we three have will go on forever. But dearest, I don't want him to come to the boat when we leave and hear the mournful funeral chants of those who come to bid us good-bye. Could we go today—while he is swimming—instead of tomorrow? If we could leave before he comes back from the beach . . . see, I've written him a letter and placed it with all of your music."

Cyril's lean frame was shaking with sobs and he buried his face in his hands.

Emily spoke softly, her voice and gentle touch antidotes to his agony. "Darling . . . don't, please. Oh, my dearest, all these years we've been so happy together, we shared so much—yet we suffered, too. How many times did we touch accidentally and draw away from each other in fear that our caresses would lead us to what we feared as much as we desired it? How many kisses for joy would have turned into kisses of passion, had it not been forbidden? I know your lonely walks on the beach at night did not grow less as the years went by. Did you not know that I lay awake, too, tormented as you were . . . feeling your pain and need along with my own?"

Cyril raised his head. His hollow cheeks were filled with tears, his eyes burning so intensely with emotion that his lips moved soundlessly, the words lost in the terrible anguish that was bearable because within the terror was one small seed of hope.

Emily's pale fingers smoothed back his straight dark hair. She was smiling, her eyes luminous with love. "Even that forbidding peninsula can be a paradise if we are together. Don't the same warm winds caress Molokai that send the petals fluttering on the other islands? Doesn't the same brilliant sun shine there? Even if we cannot see the sun set because of the mountain, we shall see it rise. And isn't that better—to see the beginning, instead of the end? Because, my dearest, Molokai is going to be a beginning for us. Not an end."

Cyril caught his breath, his arms going about her in sudden awareness of what she was really telling him.

"Darling . . . don't you see?" Emily said shyly, "There we shall have to answer to no one. Be bound by no taboos. Cyril, my beloved husband, on Molokai, waiting to die together . . . we can be really free at last."

--⟨ CHAPTER 38 ⟩--

Reconstruction laid a punishing fist on the Southern
states, and nowhere more heavily than in South Carolina. Carpetbaggers, wives and families of Yankee gar-
risons, freed slaves wandering aimlessly, returning Confederate veterans—all thronged country roads and
devastated cities.

Cerise and the other women watched in helpless rage
as the Gentry plantation house was put to the torch by
a group of Yankee stragglers only hours after Rual and
Sebastian called to bring food and announce they must
leave for the North. Mark had been sent with his
regiment to round up Confederate troops who were still
fighting isolated skirmishes. There had been no word
from him.

The house in Columbia had also been destroyed by
fire. The women, accompanied by the faithful Moses,
who had found his way back to them, managed to get
on a train for Charleston, where Austin and Dahlia's
parents' home stood, badly damaged by shelling, but
offering more shelter than any other Gentry residence.

Cerise was weak and did not yet have full use of
her right shoulder and arm. Dahlia and Rose Gentry
grew pale when they had to change the dressing on the
fearful wound, but Cerise was merely impatient to
regain her strength. She was unconcerned that the
terrible scar would mar her previously flawless body for
life. It was enough to be alive. She was needed. Aunt
Rose's mind sometimes took her back to happier days,
while Dahlia's gentleness and easily bruised sensitivity
could not cope with the harsh realities of the new
order in the South.

There was also Moses, Tannie, and two other black house servants to care for. Sebastian and Rual had seen to it that they had food, but the house needed repairs, there were taxes to be paid, and everyone was desperately in need of clothes.

Accompanied by Moses, Cerise went out to sell their few hoarded valuables—most of which had been concealed in the pockets Tannie had sewn into their hoop skirts before they evacuated Columbia. Cerise haggled and bullied her way about town, standing her ground before swaggering Yankee soldiers and tolerating no interference from freed slaves. She went home with the money she raised, gave it to Dahlia for safekeeping, then went to her room and fainted dead away from exhaustion.

Shortly after setting up housekeeping in Charleston, Aunt Rose presided over a family conference one evening. They had dined royally on fresh meat and vegetables which had been delivered from a local source, paid for by Sebastian.

"There is a delicate matter we must discuss, Cerise," Aunt Rose said. Her fingers plucked at her threadbare skirt in obvious discomfort.

Cerise bristled in readiness for the expected criticism. She had already accurately guessed that Aunt Rose's occasional flights of fancy were her way of dealing with situations over which she had no control, but could not accept. Aunt Rose was very much in charge of her faculties in regard to situations she could control.

"We cannot receive Yankees in our home," she continued. "Charleston society is very close-knit—the plantation was more isolated. What we could hide from view there will be very much on everyone's tongue here. We should all be ostracized if we allow any Yankee into our home."

Cerise refrained from pointing out that they had just eaten a large dinner provided by Yankee money. She believed the food had come from Rual and did not, therefore, consider it charity. She would have been as outraged as Aunt Rose had she known Sebastian was responsible.

413

"Since Rual and his father have gone north to obtain their discharges from the navy, you need have no fear they will call on us—at least not wearing Yankee uniforms. You may instruct Moses to slam the door in Mark McKnight's face if he comes calling—which I very much doubt."

"Oh, dear . . ." Dahlia said. "He has been so kind to us. Why, what in the world would have happened to us if he hadn't come and evacuated us from Columbia before the town burned to the ground? Surely now that the war is over we can put bitterness and regret behind us." Her cheeks were pink. She had never disagreed with either Aunt Rose or the strong-willed Cerise before. Ignoring their hostile stares, Dahlia plunged on: "Austin wouldn't want you to hate all Yankees, Cerise. I know he wouldn't. He'd want you to rebuild your life—go on living. Wasn't he always so full of life himself? He was so high-spirited, full of fun. . . ." Her lip trembled slightly, and she finished in a whisper: "Mark loves you so." She turned and fled from the room.

Dahlia went to her room, her cheeks burning. She was terrified that Aunt Rose would notice that letters bearing northern postmarks arrived more frequently for her niece than for Cerise, who had a brother in the North. Dahlia had explained to Rual why he could not call on her, but the letters arrived regularly, nevertheless.

She had been convinced she could never love again when her fiancé died at Gettysburg. She was even more confounded when she found herself responding to the shy giant who was Cerise's half-brother. Rual was huge, clumsy, rugged-looking rather than handsome. Beneath the brawn and muscle, however, lurked a gentle and sensitive soul that had reached out comfortingly to Dahlia in her loss and despair and brought the promise of restored order to the chaos of her shattered young life.

Rual and Sebastian had visited the plantation almost daily, despite Aunt Rose's protests and vapors, until Cerise was back on her feet. Several times bands of

Union soldiers, bent on laying waste, had been stopped by the presence of the two sailors. Father and son had departed for the North when they believed there would be no further burning and looting. They were too optimistic.

Had it not been for Dahlia's frantic plea that Rual not come to Charleston, he would have returned in a white heat of rage when she wrote they were living there because the plantation house had been razed to the ground.

Rual was touchingly solicitous and engagingly open in his admiration. From her own sensitive nature Dahlia recognized a kindred spirit. Yet she was torn by divided loyalties. Rual was a hated Yankee and represented all the misery that had descended upon her in these past years. She had lost her lover, her brother, her mother, and her home. She did not know whether her father was alive in a Yankee prison or buried in some unmarked grave.

Sometimes she felt it simply wasn't fair that Rual should come into her life with his shy smile and gentle words. A Yankee was not supposed to look at his father and sister with devotion and pride shining in his clear blue eyes for all the world to see, nor treat a shy, frail girl like herself with such deference. A Yankee was a widow-making, baby-killing monster with a burning brand in his hand and death in his eyes.

She and Cerise had kept from Aunt Rose the fact that all of the food magically appearing on the table came from "those hateful Yankees—I'm sorry, my dear Cerise, but he's only your *half*-brother, isn't he?"

Cerise had obstinately refused to see Mark when he called. After trying several times, Mark disappeared. Dahlia fretted that her sister-in-law was perhaps more patriotic, in a way, than she. For while Cerise denied Mark, Dahlia secretly replied to Rual's love letters with timid little notes that were hardly protests at all.

A tap on her bedroom door interrupted her thoughts. Cerise came into the room, closing the door carefully behind her. She took in Dahlia's tear-stained cheeks and the letter she was hurriedly pushing under her pillow.

"Let's talk," Cerise said, sitting down on the bed beside her and giving her hand a reassuring squeeze of sympathy. "You are right about Mark and me. I do love him. I've never loved another man—I'm sorry, Dahlia, not even your brother, Austin. Austin and I were children, in love with the idea of being in love. Real love is caring more about the other person than yourself. But it's a fragile blossom, Dahlia. So many outside forces can destroy it. And perhaps most devastating of all is when love clashes with one's own sense of integrity. Mark and I met at the wrong time. Just as you and Rual met at the wrong time. Oh, yes, I know he's been writing to you."

Dahlia withdrew the crumpled letter from beneath the pillow and smoothed it out with tender fingers. "Oh, Cerise, what's to become of us all? Will things ever be put in order?" she said disconsolately.

"Yes, I think so. In time. In time I shall get over loving Mark. And you'll get over Rual. Didn't you love the boy who was killed at Gettysburg? We'll get over it—maybe even love again." Cerise sounded far from certain, and there was a furrow of tension between her eyes.

"But . . . why do we *want* to get over loving them? Cerise, it hurts so much—"

"Because we have to love ourselves, first. And we went through too much. Mark is my love and Rual is my brother . . . but I can't forgive them for what they did to this beautiful state, nor for snuffing out so many useful lives. We have to live with ourselves, too, Dahlia. We have to be true to our own ideals."

Dahlia sighed. "It would be comforting to spend my life with Rual. I'm afraid I'm not as strong as you. I'm ready to forgive all Yankees and forget all the horrors of war because I care so much for Rual. The only reason I hide my feelings for him is because of Aunt Rose. She was always more of a mother to me than my real mother . . . and with Uncle Will dead, she has no one else. I can't desert her and go to live in the

North with Rual, so I guess my love is hopeless. But you and Mark . . . why won't you at least see him?"

Cerise bit her lip. "I'm afraid if I see him again I'll weaken."

"Feeling like that," Dahlia said slowly, "surely he must be more important to you than your ideals. Forgive me, honey, but do you really mean 'ideals,' or do you mean you feel guilty because you loved Mark when you were married to Austin? Perhaps if you could answer that question, truthfully, in your own heart, you would be able to accept your love for Mark. No one should have to do penance for the rest of her life for a sin that didn't really hurt another person—"

Cerise gazed into Dahlia's earnest eyes and marveled at the insight of her shy sister-in-law. It was no wonder that Rual had been so bowled over by her. Dahlia's delicate beauty of face and soul had been eclipsed by the flamboyant handsomeness and *joi de vivre* of her brother, Austin. But, Cerise suspected, there was a great deal more to Dahlia's sensitive and intuitive mind than anyone realized. Dahlia's words haunted her for the rest of the day.

That night Cerise lay awake, as she had every night since her last meeting with Mark. She reflected wryly that so far her life had been far from the "orderly progression of events" she had once blithely asserted it would be.

She loved Mark with an all-consuming passion. She had ached to feel his arms about her even as she told him she never wanted to see him again. Yet she sent him away believing she hated him. She had been filled with guilt and remorse . . . for her dead husband, for the lost Cause . . . and anger because Mark had chosen to fight on the other side. Still, she did not understand why she was punishing them both by denying their love.

Nothing made any sense. The Confederacy was dead, Austin was dead . . . President Lincoln was dead by an assassin's bullet. . . . Was that the final solution to everything—death? She herself had cheated death only to condemn herself to a sadder fate.

She got out of bed and walked through the moonlit
417

house, standing amid the rubble of the ruined piazza. *I wanted to be right . . . I wanted to be in control. I didn't want to be tossed about on the sea of life like a piece of flotsam, as my mother was. Nothing was to take place that was not pre-planned.*

"Oh, God," she murmured aloud. "I'm going through hell wanting Mark, needing him, loving him . . . and I sent him away simply because it wasn't pre-planned. . . ."

"Miz Cerise," a soft voice said behind her. Moses stood in the dark hall, a frown of concern creasing his kindly face. "You all right, Miz Cerise? Somethin' I kin get for you?"

Cerise went to him slowly and wrapped her arms about his frail old shoulders, hugging him fiercely. "Moses, Moses . . . you're no longer a slave. You're free . . . *free.*"

He patted her arm anxiously, soothingly. "I knows that, Miz Cerise. Miz Cerise, you is goin' to get your death of cold, wanderin' 'round like this."

Cerise stared at him, comprehension dawning. "Why, Moses—you've always taken care of Aunt Rose and Dahlia, haven't you? And you'll probably go on taking care of them, sharing God only knows what hardships with them . . . not because you have to, or anyone expects you to . . . but because that's what you want to do. Moses, you know what I really want to do? I want to find out where Captain McKnight is stationed. First thing in the morning I want you to go down to Yankee headquarters."

"The Yankee ahmy told me," Moses said, late the following day, "there was still some skirmishes. Some of our gentlemens was still fightin' the bluecoats. . . ." Moses was choosing his words carefully, his eyes not meeting hers. Cerise felt fear and panic begin to swell in her breast.

"Skirmishes—fighting . . . Moses, not Captain McKnight—please, he's all right? Where is he?" Her voice rose to a scream. *No, not Mark, too! Oh, God, this is*

418

my punishment for sending him away. For denying our love.

Moses rolled his eyes toward the heavens, seeking some way to break the news gently. "Cap'n McKnight done got shot, Miz Cerise. They say pretty bad—"

All the way to the field hospital Cerise prepared herself for the worst. Would he be crippled, as Austin had been? Would he live? Did he still love her?

She no longer saw the devastation left in the wake of Sherman's march to the sea. Mark was no longer a hated bluecoat. He was her dear, dear love and he was hurt—wounded, perhaps, mortally. Was he dying even now, while remembering the hateful words of anger she had flung at him? What if she arrived too late to see him? "I can't bear it!" She had spoken the words aloud.

Seated opposite her on the crowded train was a young man whose empty left sleeve flapped against a barely recognizable Confederate coat. "Ma'am?" he asked politely. "You all right, ma'am?"

Cerise nodded, embarrassed.

The young man's eyes surveyed the ruins of a plantation house moving across the window of the train. "It's hard to bear, and that's a fact," he agreed bitterly. "You lose your home, ma'am?"

She nodded again.

"My folks had a farm. . . ." He sighed. "Reckon there ain't much left of it except fields either blackened by fire, or gone wild. I've been making my way home from a Yankee prison hospital. . . ."

Hospital . . . Mark. Will your sleeve be empty, too? Will you clump about on a wooden stump instead of a leg? What shall I say to you? How can I explain? What she actually said when she looked at his bandage-swathed head was, "But you said it was all over! Why did you go and get yourself shot when it was all over?" Then she put her face down on his chest and wept.

His hand came up slowly to touch the riot of red-gold curls bursting from the restraining pins. "I was careless, my love . . . and my left flank was always vulnerable. . . . You see, I don't hear very well out of that

419

ear. There—I've told you something I've never admitted to another soul."

She raised a tear-stained face and her golden eyes were sparkling with mischief as well as relief. "I knew that—did you think I believed you to be perfect? My darling, having one small part of you not working properly just makes you human. But your wound. . . ?" Only half of his face was visible, the right eye and cheek thickly padded with bandage. Her heart beat uncomfortably as she waited for him to speak.

"I probably won't be as handsome as you remember. . . ." He smiled weakly, adoring her with one bright blue eye. "But they don't believe I shall lose the eye. . . . I dare say they'd discharge me and send me home if I had a loving wife to take care of me. . . ."

Cerise bent to kiss his lips, feeling his heart beat next to her own.

They were married by the army chaplain, Mark still lying in his hospital bed and Cerise standing beside him in a faded and patched dress. The simple ceremony was the most beautiful moment of her life, and she wished her mother could have been there. Only Dahlia was present. Aunt Rose pleaded illness and worried herself sick wondering how she would explain the wedding of Austin's widow to a Yankee, with Austin's sister in attendance. Cerise did not attempt to reach Rual by wire, since on the same day she visited the field hospital a letter arrived from him. The letter proved to be the only disconsolate blot on the happy day.

Cerise,

    I planned to come back to see you, soon as I was officially separated from the service, but there's a ship leaving today for the California coast and I shall be on it.

    You said in your last letter there hadn't been any improvement in conditions in South Carolina, but that the Gentrys were keeping their heads above water. I know how proud they are. They'd probably rather starve than accept "Yankee" help. But, Cerise, the shipping company is making

420

money, and half of it is yours. So please get in touch with Ned and tell him where to make some deposits to your account.

Funny how we all think that passing through great danger unscathed should mean we are rewarded by gaining our most desired goals. . . . You know I hoped Father and I could work together after the war. He's not interested in me or the shipping company, I'm afraid. He's sailing for Burma to resurrect the Monarch Butterfly from her hibernation place. He didn't invite me to go with him.

Cerise, I don't know why you acted so cold to Mark McKnight, because he loves you in a way Austin never loved you. Of course, it's none of my business. But Father and I both like Mark very much and hope you won't hurt him. Once you get through all that limey reserve of Mark's, there's a man of great courage and integrity underneath.

Take care of yourself, Cerise, and please look out for Dahlia.

Your brother, Rual

A letter had come for Dahlia also, and after reading it, she retired to her room and did not emerge again that day.

Cerise was so busy preparing to bring Mark home from the hospital that it was several days before she became aware of the fact that Dahlia had withdrawn into herself completely. She moved about the house wraith-like, barely speaking, not eating.

"Good Lord, Dahlia, what is it? Are you ill?" Cerise asked when she came upon her sister-in-law staring unseeingly out of the window one afternoon.

In her own happiness, Cerise had not given much thought to Rual's departure for California and how it might be affecting Dahlia. Now she recalled the letter that had arrived for Dahlia at the same time as her own. "Dahlia, dear—he'll come back. He's a sailor. He's just gone on a long voyage, that's all. You know he won't be able to write until he reaches port, and that could take weeks."

Dahlia turned red-rimmed eyes in her direction. "I'll never see him again. Oh, it's all my fault. I pretended I didn't care, when I love him more than I ever loved anyone before—more than anything in the world."

"Of course you'll see him again," Cerise said briskly. "Where did you ever get the notion he wouldn't come back?"

Dahlia's fingers slid into her apron pocket. Rual's letter, dog-eared from many readings, was withdrawn.

Cerise took it and scanned it impatiently, then slowly reread it, her eyes brimming with tears as she did so.

My Dearest Dahlia,

This will be my last letter to you, so please be patient and read what I have to tell you.

In your letters you have begged me not to come and see you, because of the effect you felt my appearance would have on your Aunt Rose. Your last letter explained the obligation you feel toward her and made it very clear that you felt it your duty to care for her as long as she needed you. Dahlia, I guess when I read that, all my hopes fell, but more than that, I realized how insensitive I've been in persisting to send you letters that you were too polite to return unopened. I guess I kept hoping that while you read my letters and replied to them—formal notes though they were, with no hint you felt for me what I feel for you—that someday you would come to care for me as I care for you.

I understand now the impossibility of the position I have placed you in and do truly want to beg your forgiveness. How very unfeeling you must believe me to be.

I'm going away on a long voyage—how long I can't tell. I won't embarrass you by writing until I have either succeeded in the quest I am setting for myself, or realized that I must fail despite my best efforts. Perhaps when I write to you again you will have had time to grieve over all you have lost and open your heart again to all that might be.

There is not another person on this earth I could tell what it is I am going to try to do. But, Dahlia, I feel you alone will understand and wish me well. You see, I am going to attempt to find the two men who stand between me and my father.

One is his old enemy—the man who marooned him, taking him away from my mother and me forever. While Erik Gunnar still walks the earth and sails the seas, my father can never know peace of mind. Dahlia, revenge is an ugly human passion, and I'll confess to you that I find its pursuit against everything I believe in. Yet I know my father's hatred of that man is a passion stronger than any other in his life. He must rid himself of it by knowing the old score is settled before he can accept the love of his sons.

And that brings me to my second quest. I told you of my half-brother, Noah. I'm going to try to find him and bring him and Father together.

If I can accomplish these goals, then at last perhaps I will learn if my father can love me. I fear he sees me only through the barrier of his hatred for Gunnar and the anguish of losing Noah.

I am filled with dread, Dahlia—dread that I will not succeed . . . and dread that I will. Erik Gunnar is Cerise's father. But will my own father be satisfied with anything less than Gunnar's death?

And Noah—if he takes what I feel to be my rightful place at my father's side, will I be able to bear it?

Despite my doubts and fears, I cannot go back.

My dearest Dahlia, for better or worse, I'm a man who gives his love without reservation, once and for always. I will always love you . . . but I love you enough to want to put your happiness before my own. I won't write again unless it is to inform you I have succeeded in my quests. My darling, after that it will be up to you. If you want *me to come to you, one word from you and I will move heaven and earth to be at your side.*

Cerise looked up at Dahlia's stricken face through a blurring of her own tears. "Write and tell him to come to you," she urged. "Send the letter to Ned in New York. He'll know where Rual's ship will call en route."

Dahlia wiped her eyes. "I can't. For one thing, Rual needs to do this. If I prevented him from attempting to do these things, it would always be between us. Besides, I haven't the right to even try. I can never leave Aunt Rose. You know how . . . forgetful . . . she is at times. She cared for me when my own poor dear mother was unable to. Now I must care for her."

"I believe Rual will wait for you forever, if need be," Cerise said gently. "He's always been steadfast in his loyalties. You can see that from what he writes about Sebastian."

Dahlia's eyes brimmed with tears. "I shouldn't have let you see Rual's letter. . . . How thoughtless of me. Now you know that your brother is seeking out your father, possibly with murder in his heart. Oh, my poor Rual, how torn by his love for his father he is that he must try to avenge a debt against your father."

"Rual won't harm my father," Cerise said confidently. "I know him too well. He wouldn't knowingly hurt anyone. Not outside of combat, anyway. He's so soft-hearted he couldn't kill a fly. . . ." Her voice trailed off as an awful possibility crossed her mind. "Oh, God!" She was thinking of the crafty-eyed and self-pitying bully who waylaid her in San Francisco. A man of no feeling at all, who coldly threatened her mother. "Oh, God," Cerise said again. "What will happen if Rual really does find Erik Gunnar?"

Cerise wrapped her arms about Dahlia, understanding at last the other girl's terror and foreboding that she would never see Rual again.

424

--◂{ **CHAPTER 39** }▸--

The rouge had settled into Cassie Madigan's wrinkles, creating a network of red paths across the heavy layer of face powder. Her eyes twinkled merrily, however, and her golden curls were more luxurious than ever. "Sebastian's son," she said. "You look more like him than he does himself!" Her laughter rang out as she picked up a tiny bell on the table beside her and rang for her maid.

Rual grinned at her and ran his hand through his hair. "I'm sorry we all gave you such a hard time when I was a boy. I didn't know—about you and Mother being partners."

"Who told you?"

"Cerise."

Cassie smiled fondly. "Such a pretty girl—so like Garnet. How is she? That red-haired husband of hers get through the war in one piece?"

"He died in a prison hospital. Cerise is fine, though. She stayed in the South with Austin's family, helping them hang on to at least some of their possessions through Reconstruction. Mark McKnight has been trying to get her to marry him."

Cassie settled back more comfortably in her chair. "Mark McKnight. That would be Sebastian's half-brother? I'll get some of my best whiskey in here and you must tell me all about him . . . and yourself . . . and Cerise, and, oh, everything. What about Sebastian?" She turned as the maid came into the room and instructed her to bring a bottle of the best.

Cassie noted immediately the cloud that appeared in Rual's bright blue eyes at the mention of his father's name. Just like his old man, Cassie thought, anyone can read him like a book.

Sebastian's illegitimate son was uncannily like his father, she noted as they conversed. There was the same fearless honesty in his eyes, revealing vulnerability when it came to his own deepest emotions. He was a young man who could easily be hurt, for all his fearsome physical strength. "You're a sailor, like your father?" Cassie asked gently.

Rual smiled. "Yes."

"But didn't Garnet—I mean, she invested a lot of money in the Balmain Shipping Company."

"Oh, yes. I'm a director of the company, and so is my father, though neither of us spends much time in New York. Ned runs things for us. We lost a couple of ships to Confederate raiders during the war, but we made tremendous profits on our cargoes, in spite of the wartime marine insurance rates." Rual looked down at the glass in his hand and the pause lengthened.

"If you just got into port, maybe you'd prefer the company of one of the girls, instead of talking to an old lady—" Cassie began.

"No. Thank you. There's a girl back in South Carolina. Dahlia, Austin's sister." Rual fumbled in his mind for words to explain that his love for a girl in far away South Carolina was hopeless. She had turned him down. Yet he could not bring himself to be unfaithful to her. Would a woman in Cassie's line of business understand such feelings? Would anyone?

Sometimes he wondered despairingly if it was always to be his fate to love someone who could not love him in return. His father . . . Dahlia.

Looking into Cassie's wise and pitying eyes, Rual grinned sheepishly, trying to hide his pain.

"She's waiting for you?" Cassie asked, knowing from his expression she was not. Cassie saw in his eyes the same torment she had seen in Garnet's all the years she waited for Sebastian to return to her. "She's a lucky girl," Cassie added. "You managed to inherit all of the best traits of Garnet and Sebastian, Rual. I can tell just by looking at you."

426

"She's not exactly waiting," Rual admitted defensively. "But she can't go on mourning forever, can she? One day she'll forgive and forget. The war, I mean. They lost so many of their men, the Gentry family. And her Aunt Rose is an elderly lady—Dahlia couldn't leave her." He looked around helplessly, then added with a touch of defiance, "I'll go back for her one day. But I can't be tied down to a wife until I do what I have to do."

"And what's that?"

"Find Noah Balmain." Rual twisted the glass in his hand and added, as though to himself, "My half-brother. We're a family of half-brothers and -sisters, Cassie. I reckon that's been our whole problem from the start. All the halves that couldn't get together and make wholes."

"And you think I can help you?" Cassie's glance was suddenly guarded.

"No. But I think you can help me with my other quest. I heard Erik Gunnar came to San Francisco. I thought you could help me find him, because I'm going to settle my father's debt with him, once and for all."

"He did come here—years ago. I believe he was part-owner of a whaler and lived in Lahaina, in the Sandwich Isles. What do you plan to do?"

"Kill him." Rual distantly heard himself say the words. He told Cassie how Sebastian had been marooned by Gunnar. In the back of Rual's mind there was another voice, trying insistently to be heard. *It won't make any difference. . . . If you succeed where he failed—find Gunnar, kill him. . . . It won't change anything. You're still just his bastard. . . .*

Sebastian and Rual had parted company at war's end on a sour note. Rual had hesitantly asked his father to return to New York, so that together they could rebuild the Balmain Shipping Company. Sebastian looked away uncomfortably.

"I think not, Rual. You and Ned can handle things. . . . I wouldn't feel right, knowing it was your mother's money. I'll sign my share of the company over to you."

"Where will you go?" Rual asked dully, the pain of

427

rejection constricting his throat and anger starting a slow ascent from the pit of his stomach.

"I've got the *Monarch Butterfly* in a yard in Burma. Soon as she's seaworthy again, I'll pick up a cargo and sail her."

Rual's anger exploded. "In search of your long-lost wife and son," he said bitterly. "Your true son. What do you care about your bastard?" *You could at least ask me to sail with you.*

"Rual, that's not the way it is. I told you, it's Garnet's money—" *A man who lives off a woman—even a dead woman—isn't a man.*

"Tainted money? Is that it? She was only your mistress, and her way of making money wasn't genteel enough. Damn you, you can go to hell. I don't need you—" His voice broke and he turned away, blinded by a misting of his eyes he refused to believe was tears.

"I want to pay off my debts," Sebastian said stiffly. "And among them is finding Erik Gunnar, who marooned me. Can you understand, Rual? After that year all alone on that tiny bit of land, I was never the same again. I reckon I forgot how to put other people before my own needs—it's something you can't understand unless you've had to survive it. Rual . . . please. Don't let's part like this. I didn't mean to hurt you. God, boy—"

"Even my name," Rual said. "You called me after the king's faithful servant. Is that what you wanted me to be—King Noah's faithful vassal?"

"Your mother chose your name, not me . . ." Sebastian began, but Rual was already walking away from him.

Cassie was speaking to him and it was some minutes before her words registered. The whiskey was going to his head; he was not used to it.

". . . I should have gone to Sebastian that night," Cassie was saying, "told him that Garnet and I owned the Red Garter—instead of letting him think she was just a whore here. I guess I was afraid of losing her— but I lost her, anyway. If only we could all be more honest with one another, Rual. If only we could accept people for what they are and not what we want them to be."

Rual stood up, blinking his eyes rapidly. "I'll try to call on you again before I sail, Cassie."

He had no difficulty in finding Erik Gunnar in Lahaina. The first islander Rual asked quickly pointed out the shop whose diamond-paned window faced the waterfront. It was filled with scrimshaw, coral necklaces, shells, and tiny full-rigged ships in narrow-necked bottles. Rual stepped into the cool, dim interior and saw the man sitting at the worktable.

He was smaller than Rual expected, but then, of course, he was seated. His hair and beard were streaked with gray. Gnarled fingers moved slowly as he etched the leaping dolphin on the whale's tooth. Then the red stare rose to meet Rual's eyes.

"I am Sebastian Balmain's son," Rual said.

Erik Gunnar's hand moved with surprising speed. The ancient whaling lance hanging on the wall behind him was clasped in that knotted fist and he sent it crashing through the air with startling accuracy. Rual had barely begun to move aside when the rusty metal sliced through the flesh of his upper arm.

Rual spun around, dazed by the blow. Dimly he saw Gunnar reaching up for a second lance. Rual flung himself forward, diving toward the reaching arm. He seized the hand about to close over the lance. Gunnar swung his leg then, knocking Rual's feet out from under him. Rual's knees felt as though they had broken under the impact. He looked up to see Gunnar, still seated on the chair, about to kick him again. Rual grabbed the faded bell-bottom trousers leg as it came toward him, and pulled with all his might. To his horror, the leg came away in his hands. Gunnar toppled from the chair and crashed to the floor, cursing and clutching at his thigh.

Slowly Rual climbed to his feet. He still held the wooden leg, looking at it uncomprehendingly. Blood was seeping through the cotton material of his shirt sleeve. He looked at the man on the floor, then handed him the leg silently. He looked away, pressing his hand

429

to his own bleeding wound, as Erik Gunnar pulled up his trousers leg to reattach the wooden limb.

"I was going to kill you for what you did to my father," Rual said, feeling a wave of pity wash away his hatred for what this man had done to Sebastian.

"Don't feel sorry for me," Gunnar growled.

"I don't. But I couldn't respect myself if I fought a one-legged man." Despite his words, there was compassion in his eyes.

Gunnar glared malevolently as he dragged himself back onto his chair. "So Balmain got off the island?"

"A ship picked him up—a year after you marooned him. When I see him again I'll tell him he can forget about you. You're just an old woman with a gift shop. At least he's still living like the man he always was. Reckon there's some justice, somewhere."

The frown lines between the red eyes deepened in anger. "That's true. I tell myself that every time I see your brother."

Rual felt a wave of dizziness and was not sure if it was caused by the throbbing of his torn flesh or by the crafty grin that twisted Gunnar's face.

"He's home from school, young Noah. His mother took good care of me, after I lost the leg. What she did for me balanced the books a bit. So, your old man spent only a year on the island. Did he tell you how long he put me away for?"

Gunnar was still muttering into his unkempt beard when Rual stepped out into the street. He turned to look back at his father's enemy and saw only a pathetic old man hunched over a table of whales' teeth, his wooden leg hidden by the bell-bottom trousers that were the only reminder of the man he had once been.

The young doctor who stitched up Rual's wound told him proudly of the island's most celebrated son.

"Noah Balmain is a genius," he said. "He will rank with the great composers of the century. He is still studying—in Paris, I believe. He's home for the summer, however. You'll find him surfing, I'm sure, or else playing for the children in one of the mission halls.

They say he has turned down concert offers from all over the world. He's waiting, they say, until he finishes his first symphony. By the way, since you're new to the islands, I should warn you to stay out of brawls. There's a curfew for sailors, and the new laws are strongly enforced. I won't report this wound, as you say it was accidental . . . but—"

Several days later Rual sat on the hot white sand and watched the bronzed and brawny islanders swimming in the gentle summer breakers. His half-brother, Noah, looked more like Mark McKnight than Sebastian, Rual reflected. Leanly built, handsome, with smooth dark hair. Except Noah's eyes were dark, whereas Mark's were Balmain blue.

Rual's secret appraisal of his brother gave him a sense both of awe and dismay. Despite the fact that Noah rode the waves with the islanders and had spent the previous evening playing the piano in a waterfront bar, he was not really one of them. There was a dark and enigmatic aloofness about Noah, as though he were enclosed by an invisible wall. Watching him play the piano and suddenly raise his head, as though becoming fleetingly aware of the audiencce that listened in silent rapture, was to see a man well aware of his place in the universe. Rual ached with envy at the thought of how proud Sebastian would be to discover this son he had fathered.

Sitting on the beach as Noah came through the shallows toward him, Rual considered keeping his mouth shut—sailing away and never telling either of them the whereabouts of the other. Eventually, however, the whole world would know of Noah. Besides, Rual had to live with his own conscience.

Noah's black eyes registered little surprise when Rual approached him and, with typical abruptness, announced his identity.

"Your father still searches for you and your mother," Rual said.

"My father is on the island of Molokai," Noah said quietly. "He is dying of leprosy."

"Sebastian Balmain is your father." Rual tried to suppress the rising wave of anger. "And he's sailing the seas somewhere."

"Biologically, perhaps, the man you speak of is my father. But the man who made me what I am is Cyril La Flair. I don't know Sebastian Balmain, despite the fact I bear his name."

"I reckon he'll be hard put to recognize you, too," Rual said after a moment. "What about your mother? Where is she?"

For an instant there was naked pain in the mysterious dark eyes, quickly hidden again. "My mother is where she wants to be."

"If we could talk about our father—" Rual's anger was fading. There was much more to the story of Emily and Cyril and Noah than anyone had suspected. Rual felt it acutely in Noah's stark reference to his mother, when the anguish in his eyes was worse than anything Rual felt about his own estrangement from his father.

Noah turned his attention to his surfboard, hoisting it to his shoulder and beginning to walk back up the beach. Rual followed, biting back an oath as the hot sand scorched his bare feet. Noah seemed oblivious to it.

The presence of the brawny sailor at his side forced Noah to remember the empty time after his mother and Cyril left for Molokai. Noah's moods had ranged from grief over their loss to anger at them for deserting him. Yet never once did he question his mother's decision to accompany Cyril into his bleak exile. Or to choose to die of a horrible disease with the man she loved more than herself, more than her son, or even glorious life itself.

Eventually Noah had done as they wished. He sailed for Europe to study music. He filled his life with this to the exclusion of all else. Slowly he began to see triumph in tragedy, beauty in ugliness. The enduring legacies left to him by his mother and Cyril were not his alone; they were to be shared with the world. He would express the delicate and fleeting wonder of life and death by the means he had been gifted with above all others—his music.

He turned to his half-brother, walking at his side, and wondered if he loved Sebastian in the way Noah had loved Cyril. He supposed Sebastian and Rual must have some reason for seeking him out. He said, "I must confess I have little curiosity about the man who fathered me."

"Then at least have the compassion to satisfy his longing to see you." Rual's own love for his father blazed in his eyes. "He is a good man, a man you'll be proud to call 'Father' when you know him. His only crime was loving two women . . . and God knows, plenty of men are guilty of that. Only Sebastian had an old-fashioned sense of honor, and he couldn't cope with it, so he went back to sea, because he didn't know what else to do."

It was true, Rual thought. Funny, how, in defending his father, Rual himself at last understood him. *How wrong I was,* Rual thought, *to believe Sebastian left my mother and me with never another thought. . . .*

"Perhaps I shall meet him one day," Noah was saying indifferently.

"Yes. By God, you will," Rual agreed. "And he's going to see you in all your glory. They tell me you've been invited to give concerts all over Europe. You'll give one for your father."

Rual was no longer wondering how he would compare to Noah in their father's eyes. He thought only of the joy and pride Sebastian would feel in his legitimate son. A man could die happy knowing he had given the world a son like Noah. Rual did not even recognize how selfless his love for his father truly was.

--⋇{ CHAPTER 40 }⋇--

The spring of 1871 saw the opening of the Royal Albert Hall in London, and, shortly thereafter, Cerise and Mark arrived to attend a concert and a family reunion.

"He must be a Balmain, after all," Mark said, "to bring the family together at the Royal Albert Hall. It's the sort of flamboyant gesture Sebastian would have made in his heyday."

Cerise gave her husband a sidelong glance from beneath a flutter of gold-tipped eyelashes. "I really shouldn't go to the concert with you—in my delicate condition."

Mark moved behind her and slipped his arms about her, resting his hand on the squirming passenger in her womb. "Ah! He kicked me!"

"Not 'he'—a daughter. I shall have a daughter, whom I shall name Garnet, for my mother. And she'll be a holy terror."

Mark laughed and turned her around to face him, leaning across her distended abdomen to kiss her lips tenderly. "Have mercy on me, woman! One holy terror in my life is all I can handle. But as far as you missing Noah's concert is concerned . . . I'd have bought every seat in the house if I'd known you were even considering it, although that might have stolen some of Noah's thunder."

"I'm not staying away. When did I ever worry about convention?" Her eyes teased him and her dimples showed mischievously. "Do you think Sebastian will arrive in time?"

"I expect he'll sprout wings and fly here if necessary."

"I do hope Rual . . . I hope he won't be hurt again."

434

"Rual obviously worships the ground Sebastian walks on—or perhaps the sea he sails on would be a better statement," Mark said thoughtfully. "It's a pity Sebastian hasn't been able to see it. The ghosts of Emily and Cyril . . . perhaps they'll be laid to rest when we meet Noah."

Mark slipped his arm about her as they went downstairs. "Have I told you recently that I adore you?"

Cerise smiled. "Not for an hour or so. Oh, Mark, I'm so happy. I can't believe anything will happen to spoil it."

Rual's train steamed into Euston Station and he watched the white cloud of steam diminish as they came to a halt. Mark had persuaded Ned to buy their first steamer and Ned had commented, "Good thing Sebastian sailed away. Silly old fool would never accept the fact that the brief glory of the clippers has passed. Wouldn't he roar with rage at having a steam kettle under the Balmain flag!"

Rual had been angry. He understood how a real sailor would be reluctant to give up the glory days of sail. He knew that steamers would eventually replace sail ships as surely as the train replaced the carriage. It was inevitable, but he hated for Mark and Ned to be right and his father to be wrong.

He wondered if his father would arrive in time for Noah's concert. He had sent a letter to the Moulmein shipyard where Sebastian had left his clipper while he enlisted in the navy. If the Burmese manager forwarded it, and if it reached Sebastian, and if there was time . . .

Rual reached out to assist an older man as he struggled to remove his baggage from the overhead rack. Then he swung his own bag down and stepped out onto the platform. *No matter what,* he thought, *I'll be able to bear it . . . knowing that she's waiting for me.*

The letter had been waiting for him when he returned from Lahaina to San Francisco. It was several months old and had been forwarded by Ned.

Dahlia wrote:

*I pray for your safe return, and forgiveness for
my own foolishness. I should have told you how
much I love you. You had a right to know.*

*Rual, we heard yesterday that my father is dead.
Aunt Rose and I are the only ones left now. I cannot marry you . . . not while Aunt Rose lives. She
cannot accept you because you are a Yankee—no
other reason—and, alas, she believes the war continues and that someday all of our menfolk will
return to us. Her mind wanders, Rual, and I
haven't the heart to force her to accept the truth.*

*Nor can I deceive her by seeing you in secret.
But perhaps we can write to each other from time
to time? My love is strong enough to endure
through all eternity, and I believe yours is, too.*

It was not in Rual's nature to wish the old lady dead.
He held no grudge about Aunt Rose's hold on Dahlia,
but, rather, admired and accepted the girl's devotion.
It reinforced his knowledge that someday he and Dahlia
would be together. There were lonely years to be dealt
with, but a sailor was used to lonely years. He would
survive. Hadn't Mark waited years for Cerise? And
how happy they were now. It lifted one's spirits just to
be in the same room with them. Rual was looking forward to seeing his sister and her husband at the concert. Watching them together, he knew that the family
curse of hopeless love had ended and that one day he
and Dahlia would know the same happiness.

Rual had bullied Noah into giving this concert. His
half-brother had protested he was not ready.

"You've been ready ever since your mother and Cyril
left for Molokai," Rual said. "You told me yourself
you've been writing music ever since you can remember. What are you waiting for—Emily and Cyril to
die? For God's sake, man, give your music to the
world while they're still alive, so they can know your
accomplishment and share your triumph. I've a feeling
news of your success—aye, 'fame' is the word I want—
will reach even that godforsaken spot."

Noah closed his eyes briefly. "It's been some time

since they were able to send messages back with the boat. They are both in the advanced stages of the disease and can't live much longer. Perhaps you're right . . . but Rual, if I agree, you must give me your word you will not let Sebastian know that my mother is still alive. I believe it would be indescribably cruel to both of them."

"You have my word," Rual said.

Rual arrived at the concert hall early the following evening. Seats had been reserved in the orchestra stalls, and, as the lights were dimmed, only he, Mark, and Cerise were in their places. Mollie Flanagan had not traveled from Liverpool because, as Mark put it, she was "a little under the weather." Rual left a seat between his own and the aisle, though there remained little hope that his father would arrive in time to use it.

The orchestra leader and the soloist, Noah Balmain, were on stage and the concert was beginning. The capacity crowd leaned forward as he raised long, flexible fingers over the piano keyboard. Noah Balmain made an arresting picture. Smooth dark hair, bronzed skin, black eyes that flashed briefly over the audience as he took his bow. Intense eyes, soulful and mysterious. He was a trifle thin, and, had it not been for the tanned skin, he would have been almost too delicately handsome.

Not understanding classical music, Rual was not at first aware of the gathering momentum of the orchestra and the sudden hush as the piano solo began. He marveled only that Noah's fingers could execute the complicated chords with such apparent ease. Rual wondered how long it had taken to develop such expertise. Noah played with a curious, loose-jointed grace, and this music was very different from the island music Rual had heard him play at their first meeting. Gradually Rual became aware of the images the music was conjuring in his mind.

The hushed auditorium had vanished, as had the musicians and their instruments. Gentle seas were caressing a sun-drenched beach; Rual recognized the sound.

437

He blinked. Beckoning palms, and, beneath them, dancing figures. Canoes skimming over sparkling water, cascading waterfalls. Blossoms drifting on sensual lagoons. Rual leaned back, closing his eyes, feeling himself borne away on a wave of peace and tranquility.

Abruptly, the music changed. Ominous notes crept into the gentle melody, portending approaching discord. First the rumble and roar of a volcano, and then the gathering momentum of an approaching tidal wave. The volcano erupted; the tidal wave dashed the revelers away with its fury. The music was angry now. The disharmony ceased to be nature's wrath, and became the blundering cruelties of humanity itself.

Rual thought of the conversation he had had with Noah in the Sandwich Isles. His music was telling the world of the infamy done to those gentle islanders in the name of God, religion, and progress.

But there was much more in the music. Against the sweeping panorama of the islands and the sea, the raging elements, the clash of old and new ideas, was a story so heartbreakingly beautiful it could only be the story of a single man and woman. A man and woman whose love was eternal and could not be touched by evil men, disease, slaughter. Yet the composer was not sparing his audience. He made them feel the pain of those two. Rual squirmed in his seat.

Hushed, tragic accents now . . . silence except for the piano. Rual felt a lump form in his throat and a hand close coldly over his heart. He half-rose from his seat, wanting to escape the torment that was too great to be borne. Someone restrained him. Vise-like fingers closed about his arm and he looked down to see Sebastian sitting beside him.

Rual opened his mouth to speak, but his father shook his head.

Having brought his listeners to the brink of despair, the composer suddenly gave them hope. Life went on. The tradewinds murmured new promises, the cleansing tides brought renewed dreams. The finale was soaring, glorious.

Everyone was on his feet smiling, crying, and cheering. The maestro laid down his baton and leaped from the podium to embrace the young pianist whose composition had filled the hall with magic.

When the shouting and curtain calls were at last over and it was possible to be heard over the din of acclaim, Rual turned to his father and said, "You made it."

Sebastian nodded, trying to compose himself. His face was streaked with tears.

Mark leaned forward. "As soon as the crowd thins out, we can go join him. Cerise and I met him briefly before the concert and he's expecting us."

Sebastian brushed clumsily at his eyes, staring at the slim young man departing from view. He looked so like Emily . . . played the piano like Cyril. The program said his composition was called *Dreams in Paradise,* but Sebastian knew that Noah had told the story of Emily and Cyril with his music. Oh, God, what could have happened to them to cause him to write music that tore out your heart that way? Yet it must have turned out well for them, in the end. Just when you thought you couldn't stand it, all at once there was hope.

Sebastian was glad Rual was at his side. It was comforting to have him there when he faced the stranger who was Noah. To think that he had fondly imagined that that gentleman in evening dress with his intense, dark eyes and delicate, mobile fingers would one day go swinging up the shrouds with him to reef sail! Sebastian wanted to laugh aloud at his foolishness but dared not because he knew the sound would be a sob.

"Come on, Father, we can get through now," Rual said, steadying him as he stumbled into the aisle. Sebastian felt the comfort of Rual's touch, his work-roughened hands, the sailor's roll to his walk as they found their way backstage.

The dressing room was crowded with well-wishers, but, seeing them, Noah rose, his dark eyes fixed on Sebastian. In a voice that sent memories whispering along his father's senses, he said, "I'm glad you were able to come, sir, and happy to meet you at last." Emily's voice . . . but deeper.

Sebastian stepped forward and took his son in an awkward embrace, released him, and said, "Noah . . . your mother?"

The dark eyes were impenetrable. "She died."

"Cyril?"

"He is also dead."

Mark stepped forward to cover the silence. "Your music is magnificent. Your future and probably your immortality are assured tonight. May I offer my congratulations? I've arranged for a private dining room for all of us. . . ."

The scene blurred for Sebastian. The conversation, introductions, and explanations were muffled. They spoke of the music and the terms were meaningless to him. Allegro, andante, subtle shading, infinite mellowness, form, and fluidity.

They went to dinner and the evening passed. Polite questions about Sebastian's seafaring days were made bearable only when Rual spoke emphatically of the vanishing breed of men who drove tall ships down the thundering wind. What did a pampered passenger steaming placidly across the ocean know of real sailors? Like himself, Rual was obviously ill at ease with the erudite conversation that flowed between Noah and Mark.

Sebastian absently ate the Dover sole and watched Cerise. She was tranquilly beautiful with that madonna-like loveliness that comes to women in the last part of pregnancy, but the fire and passion still lurked in the golden eyes. She and Mark were obviously totally enraptured with one another.

Dawn was breaking when Sebastian wished Noah good luck with the tour that would take him to all the European capitals.

"Maybe we can meet again?" Sebastian asked awkwardly.

Noah's dark eyes regarded the stranger who was his father. "Yes, of course. After my tour—that is, if you are not at sea." He appeared to be as ill at ease as his father.

Sebastian looked at his feet. "We don't live in the

440

same world, do we? We're not even ships that pass in the night. Concert halls, music—I don't know anything about them." He shook his head.

"I'm glad we met," Noah said, offering his hand.

Sebastian took it, being careful not to crush the delicate, long fingers in his calloused palm. "So am I."

"And we will meet again."

"Yes. We will, by God."

Silently, Sebastian and Rual walked through the misty and deserted streets.

"Let's go down to the river," Sebastian said. "There's something I want you to see." Neither of them spoke of Noah. He might have been a creature from another world.

Daybreak came surging up the Thames, silvering the dark water and sending shadows floating across the decks of silent ships as masts and riggings stirred in a westerly breeze.

Rual saw her at once. He stopped. His breath caught in his throat. Surely there had never been such a sight . . . nor would there be again. Dipping gently with the waves that lapped at her side was a Yankee clipper, the most beautiful ship ever to grace the seas. Proud and tall, her furled sails were like the wings of swift sea birds, poised for flight. The *Monarch Butterfly*, strained at her moorings, yearning to be free.

Sebastian smiled and thumped Rual's back affectionately. "Ned's little schooners . . . Mark's smelly steamboats," he said gruffly. "How can they compare to my proud lady?"

"They can't, Father," Rual answered, feeling the lump form in his throat again. "She's the most elegant ship I've ever seen." All at once Rual knew the time would pass swiftly until he and Dahlia were reunited.

"Come on, then," Sebastian said, throwing his arm about his son's shoulders. "There'll be a flood tide in an hour and a fair wind to the southern seas."

Escape to the World of ROMANCE and PASSION

Romantic novels take you far away—deep into a past that is glittering and magical, to distant shores and exotic capitals. Rapturous love lives forever in the pages of these bestselling historical romances from Pocket Books.